OldEarth

MELCHIOR Encounter

A. K. Frailey

Hardcover Edition

Cover Design: A. K. Frailey and James Hrkach

ISBN of Hardcover: 979-8-9874047-0-6

The Writings of A. K. Frailey

Books for the Mind and Spirit

https://akfrailey.com/

Contact

akfrailey@yahoo.com

Historical Science Fiction Novels

OldEarth ARAM Encounter

OldEarth Ishtar Encounter

OldEarth Neb Encounter

OldEarth Georgios Encounter

OldEarth Melchior Encounter

Science Fiction Novels

Homestead

Last of Her Kind

Newearth Justine Awakens

Newearth A Hero's Crime

Short Stories

It Might Have Been—

And Other Short Stories 2nd Edition

One Day at a Time and Other Stories

Encounter Science Fiction

Short Stories & Novella 2nd Edition

Inspirational Non-Fiction

My Road Goes Ever On—

Spiritual Being, Human Journey 2nd Edition

My Road Goes Ever On—A Timeless Journey

The Road Goes Ever On—A Christian Journey Through The Lord of the Rings

Children's Book

The Adventures of Tally-Ho

Poetry

Hope's Embrace & Other Poems 2nd Edition

Audible Versions Now Available.
Check book details on Amazon
for current listings.

Dedication

To loving husbands, faithful wives,
and their unpredictable families.

Their roaring like that of a lion,
They shall roar like young lions.
Yea they shall roar, and take hold of the prey,
And they shall keep fast hold of it,
And there shall be none to deliver it.
And they shall make a noise against them that day,
Like the roaring of the sea;
We shall look towards the land,
And behold darkness of tribulation,
And the light is darkened with mist thereof.
~ ISAIAH 5:29-30

And the redeemed of the Lord shall return,
And shall come into Sion with praise,
And everlasting joy shall be upon their heads:
They shall obtain joy and gladness,
And sorrow and mourning shall flee away.
~ISAIAH 35:10

Prologue

Landscape of Their Days

—Planet Helm—

Song, in her petite elven form and dressed in a dark green tunic over grey leggings, strolled along the wooded glen, soft brown soil cushioning each step while pink blossoms waved in a gentle breeze. She stopped and breathed in the deliciously sweet scent of spring.

Birds twittered from the branches: bluebirds, redhearts, and goldenhues. Even a pair of orangefires insisted on wishing her a good morning.

She smiled and bowed in the customary greeting of Bhuac and nature's citizens.

A fierce greenhawk swooped in and, with its bulky body, bristled, sending the gentler folk into a frightened frenzy. The joy-filled chirping turned to cawing and sharp screams of distress.

Her heart twisting, Song watched, helpless to alter the scene, for though she ruled the planet, her influence in the wild only reached so far. As the spiritual leader of the Bhuac world, she joined compassionate understanding with honest realism. Though leadership was not her chosen role, she accepted what fate and her mother's last plaintive request—save her people—demanded. Today, she must be brave as well as wise.

Pounding steps along the wooded path turned her attention. A figure jogged forward, long black hair flowing over thin shoulders, clear eyes narrowed in concentration. A strong woman suffering from unaccustomed weakness.

Kelesta? A Bhuac who had chosen to marry an Ingot, even such a noble one as Zuri, bears a unique burden.

Slapping her hand against her chest, the woman came to a skidding halt before Song and heaved deeply to catch her breath. "They're going back!"

Song's heart clenched; she froze. As if understanding the gravity of the moment, the feathered feud ceased, and silence descended. Only the sun continued to shine unabated. With a start, Song realized that she could not sense a thing. She could never foretell the future, but she could usually see through deception. There was no lie in Kelesta, only fear and confusion in the face of an unknown future. The solid ground of tradition and experience had fallen away.

"Did you hear me?" The woman drew closer, her hand reaching, either to awaken her mentor or to grasp needed strength.

Song nodded. "I heard. The Luxonians and Crestas are returning to Earth." She forced a calm smile. "It is good to see you again, Kelesta. Where are your husband and daughter now?"

A darted glance at the sky and a facial spasm spoke louder than words. "They've gone too." Kelesta's gaze fell. "Ark passed on, and his son Tarragon is taking his place." She straightened her shoulders. "Teal is sick, and Sterling is…preoccupied. A Luxonian named Mauve has stolen his heart." She sucked in a fresh breath, like one readying herself for painful truth-telling. "Zuri wants to teach Nova about humanity's true nature. Perhaps to make room in her for"—Kelesta flapped her arms like a bird perched on the edge of flight—"something." She shrugged. "She certainly isn't interested in me."

Freeing herself from the snare of professional distance that had held her for much too long, Song wrapped her arm around the young Bhuaci woman. "She loves you—

she just doesn't know it yet."

With a muffled sob against the older woman's shoulder, Kelesta gave way to tears. "She can't love someone she doesn't know. She refuses to even consider what Zuri and I offer."

The sun, still on its ascent, shone brightly from the golden sky. "Let's return and have a morning cup with biscuits and honey-jam. You've come home just in time to help me face the coming storm. Like the daughter I never had, we can help each other through these hard times." She braced herself. "Suffering is the price we all pay—for our families and our world." She glanced at the sky. "Humanity measures time in such small increments; they do not see the landscape of their days. They are about to undergo a momentous change, and they have no idea of the long-range repercussions."

"But what about Zuri, Nova—and all the rest?"

Song clasped Kelesta's hand and started down the path, her feet padding on the soft, springing soil. "They must learn too. It is what all the living must do, or they die in stagnation."

Kelesta brushed a low hanging branch out of her way, pink blossoms falling on the path as she kept in step with Song. "But what if she learns the wrong lesson and refuses her father and me? What if we lose our daughter?"

Tears aching behind her eyes, Song admired the trees' glory and silently beckoned the spirit that gave life to the birds. *Give me strength.* "Freedom is the highest praise our Creator can offer us." She squeezed her friend's hand as the birds burst into fresh song. "It's our trial to endure what our loved ones choose."

Chapter One

Hairy Hedgehogs

—Britain, Fifth Century—

Melchior felt the sneeze pulsing through his head like liquid fire. Squeezed under his bed, arms lodged tightly against his body, he had no opportunity to stem the rushing tide. "Agh! If-only, Chloe-dusted, more-thoroughly! Slovenly house-maaaaaid! Achoo!"

The smarting pain to his head when he smacked his skull against the wooden frame definitely checked the relief of the explosion. Melchior grimaced. The real object of his interest lay just out of reach. He stretched as far as his short stature would allow, but the vellum roll merely sat there, completely indifferent to his struggle.

"Aw! Hairy hedgehogs! Why can't I do this *one* thing? Why does everything have to be so damnably difficult?"

"Father! Faaaather!"

Melchior's head smashed against the underside of his bed once again as he struggled to extricate himself before his daughter entered the room and found her noble father's backside peeking out from under the bedstead. He had his reputation to protect...among other things. But Melchior's respectability could hardly cloak his body at this crucial moment. Although he wiggled backwards as fast as he could, the sneezes grew in proportion to his anxiety. "Oh, Mother Most Holy, I'll say my devotions more regularly if only—"

"Father...? Father! What in Wodin's name are you doing down there?"

Melchior's whole body slumped against the dusty

floor. "One more incident like this,"—his eldest daughter had warned him just yesterday in her most despairing tone—"and I'll have to send for Aunt Martha."

Yes, yes! Roaring rabbits! He was getting old, and perhaps a tad bit forgetful, but that wasn't what led him to squiggle under the bedstead. He had a perfectly good reason for getting down on all fours and lodging almost his entire body between his hard bed and the dusty floorboards. It was all because of that treacherous roll of vellum. He needed it. He must have it! Who cared for dignity when the whole world waited on the brink of despair for this one piece of momentous news?

Angels above be praised! He had discovered the most amazing thing. He, Melchior, son of Jeremiah and Freda, simple thane, wordsmith, and inventor had discovered—well, it had been revealed to him in a dream—the one *unifying principle of reality*! He knew it, and he *knew* he knew it. Or at least he had known it last night when he woke up in the pitch black with the vision still clear in his mind.

He had done what any intelligent, honest, decent man would do. He struck a flame to his candle, retrieved his quill, and, snatching his precious roll that contained all his inspirations, wrote down this most amazing bit of universal truth. Why, the world would never be the same once he shared what he had learned!

After having scribbled down the vision in its entirety, exhaustion overwhelmed him. He carefully rolled the vellum and placed it beside his bed. When he awoke this morning, he remembered his great good luck, but to his horror, he saw no sign of his treasure. He searched frantically all over the room, tearing it to pieces. Not that there was much to tear apart; his personal possessions consisted only of a bed, a desk with one leg slightly shorter than the others, and a single straight-backed chair.

He had tossed his clothes upon the floor in his desperate search...or had they been there already? Never mind that!

Perhaps the roll had merely fallen and rolled under the bed? When he'd gotten down on all fours, which was no easy feat, he could see the edge of what looked very much like his precious document. Without premeditated thought, he began to squiggle...and thus...here he lay...bare legs sticking out from under his bed. What else might be laid bare, he shuddered to think.

"Father, are you ill? Having a fit of some kind

Melchior sighed.

"Oliver! Come here! I think Father has had a fit and died half under his bed! Hurry!"

"Hurry, Oliver!" mimicked Melchior under his breath. "Hurry and save your already dead father! Bah!"

Before either Oliver or his eldest daughter, Adele, could rescue him, Melchior managed to squiggle backwards the last bit and fully extricated himself from the humiliation into which he had plunged himself.

He sat there, his head propped on his arm, which was propped rather casually upon his knee. He stared at his two children, rather surprised that the whole brood hadn't followed them up the stairs into his little sanctuary. After all, their house only had a few rooms, and every squirrel and bird knew exactly what went on inside each. He blinked like a cat as he waited for the inevitable.

"Father, what *were* you doing? You scared me half to death! I thought...well...I don't know what I thought, but—"

Melchior raised his hand wearily. "Don't say another word. I know what you imagined, and I must say, you've a deplorable lack of faith in your father. Do you think I'd die in such an unceremonious way? When I'm ready to depart for the next world, I'll let you know."

He looked at his son, whose mouth hung slightly open.

Although Oliver possessed a kind and gentle soul, he was not the brightest candle on the lampstand. But he was strong, and that was worth something. "Help your father to his feet, Oliver."

Oliver obliged.

Melchior surveyed his eldest daughter and then his son. His shoulders slumped. They were truly the kindest people he knew, but times were hard, and there was so much decency being lost from their everyday world that his heart nearly broke when he thought of it. He remembered the stories his father and grandfather used to tell of the Roman days and how things used to be. But now, all was rot and ruin. There was little of the old grandeur left.

If only his wife, Edwina, had not passed away, leaving him to manage everything. He still owned a small portion of his lands. As a full-fledged thane, he maintained five hides as the law demanded. And he possessed a name and reputation as an educated man. He was considered wise in a land of ignorant, inarticulate.... Oh, never mind! He must not think of it. If only Edwina had been able to pass along more of her own noble strength. But she had been so busy raising the babies and maintaining the household that she'd had little time to speak about the past and what they had known—their honorable name and inheritance stolen.

Melchior forced himself into the present. "Where are the others?"

Oliver stared, but Adele spoke up in her usual brisk fashion. "They've gone to the festival. Don't you remember, Father? You gave permission last week. Lord Gerard is holding a feast in honor of his daughter's betrothal to Lord Marlow, with games and races and food and drink. You promised everyone might attend."

"At this hour? Why, the sun has just risen!"

Adele studied her father, one eyebrow raised. "You've been up half the night again, haven't you? Oh, Father!"

Melchior grimaced at the reproach for he *had* been up half the night; undoubtedly the morning had flown by while he slumbered, but still... Melchior fell to his knees again.

Adele shrieked. "What now, Father?"

"My roll! My parchment fell on the floor—that's why I was half-buried under the bed when you found me." Melchior struggled to his feet and carefully appraised his two children, eyeing not only their size but also their agility and mental acuity. He pointed to his daughter. "Adele, get under there and retrieve my roll. It's very important, and I must have it!"

Adele shook her head in silent reproach before she dropped to her knees, wiggled under the bed, and returned with the roll pinched daintily between two fingers. She held the dusty vellum out to her father. "What's it this time?"

Melchior pursed his lips, although his eyebrows furrowed anxiously. What if he had imagined the whole thing? What if he had dreamed that he had discovered the *one great unifying principle of the universe*? Honesty battled with prudence. Prudence won. "I've discovered something very important, but I'm not ready to reveal it yet. The world, as it stands today, isn't ready for what I have to offer. We live in a land of fools ruled by barbarians."

"Father! Don't speak so loudly! King Radburn is very powerful and has many spies. Besides, we owe him our allegiance." Adele's gaze dropped; her cheeks flushed.

Practically hissing, Melchior wagged a finger in admonishment. "Yes, they are rather treasonous words, but they have meaning—at least they should." He'd had more intelligent conversations with merchants than with lords, and the Saxon king was the most loutish man he had ever met. King? Melchior could name three hunting dogs with more sense. But that was none of his business. All he had to do was manage his own estate, keep his children alive, and stay out of trouble.

He snatched the roll from his daughter's outstretched hand. "Yes, well, this will help to keep my mind on better things." A sudden frown crushed his heavy brows over his eyes. "Why, then, aren't you two at the celebration?"

Adele ran her fingers through her hair, a sheepish grin spreading over her face. "We're going, but I had things to attend to. You want something to eat? Some bread and meat?"

Melchior rubbed his lean belly. Yes, food would definitely help. Hot food and a mug of warm ale would go a long way toward improving his mood. Then he could read over his work in the quiet of an empty house. Peace and quiet? This would be a prize! A worrisome thought stopped him cold. "Is *everyone* going?"

"Not Selby. I'm leaving him behind to watch over things. In case you need something."

Melchior put on his most benevolent face, a wide smile to match his wide, innocent eyes. "Ah, let the poor man go. Even if he can't partake, he can watch, and you might slip him a little something."

Adele pursed her lips, her scowl disagreeing. "I don't know if Lord Gerard would like that. Slaves aren't invited to such things. Father, what can you be thinking?"

Melchior could feel his opportunity slipping away. Selby had an uncanny ability of finding him alone when he least desired company. The old fool would sidle forward with a ridiculous complaint or some "momentous" news: the cow had calved, the oats were up, it looked like a storm was coming, and then the garrulous codger would start to chatter. He could chatter a man's two good ears right off his head.

Melchior aimed his gaze and spoke so clearly that no one could mistake his meaning. “Adele, I order you to take Selby and the rest with you. Say that they’re to help with the children, the cooking, or the cleanup. Say whatever you wish but take them and stay a good long time!”

Adele sniffed. Clearly, she understood all too well. “Please, Father, don’t let your eccentricities cause trouble. Lord Gerard’s nephew Robert will be there today, and he might—”

Oliver cleared his throat, his gaze shifting from his father to his sister.

Adele took the hint. “As you say, Father. We’ll leave in a few moments. I just need to get my cloak.” Adele glanced at her brother. “Get Father’s food, will you, Oliver? See that Selby carries in the tray and a flask of ale.”

Obedient as always, Oliver turned away.

Melchior watched his son go with an ache of regret. There was so little to praise. Suddenly his heart smote him, and Melchior called out to his son’s retreating figure. “Have a good time, Oliver! Dance with one of the pretty maidens for me.”

Oliver turned and considered his father. His eyes mournful. Without a word, he continued on his way.

As soon as everyone was gone, Melchior picked up his scroll and carefully unrolled it by the window. He stared wide-eyed, anxious to uncover its marvelous contents. First, there was the part about the stars’ alignment, which he had begun to chart five years ago after he had seen a propitious sign leading him to believe that his future was exceedingly bright. After a bit, he had become frustrated with the clouds forever covering the night stars, so he began to record his family tree, and, although it wasn’t particularly detailed, it pleased him to have the whole family in one place. Then, of course, there was that bit about animal husbandry...but his interest had faded after a disease nearly carried off all the cows. In the margins, he printed quotes of learned men that he soon memorized. He used to recite them at gatherings to amaze his family and impress his friends.

Finally, here it was. Why? What's happened? The first few words were clear, for he'd still had some ink on his pen; he must have wet it with his tongue as was his usual habit but... *Oh, flummoxed foxes!* He had forgotten to dip his pen in ink. All that remained of his vision were some scratches and stray marks where his fingers had smudged the material. Just a few faint words were all that bore testimony to his vision, his wonderful knowledge that would save the world from disgrace and utter ruin!

Melchior stepped away from the light and fell heavily onto his bed, his hands hanging at his sides. How could this have happened? How could he have both been given such a gift and then had it snatched away all in one pitiless day? Did God not care for him? Did the Heavenly Host laugh at his attempts to understand his mighty world? Or was this the work of the devil to send him straight into the arms of the mistress of despair? If so, Beelzebub almost won.

Sighing, Melchior rose from the bed and returned to the light streaming through the window. He noticed a few readable traces upon the parchment. Melchior considered throwing the whole document into the fire, but then he remembered the cost of vellum, and he would have nothing to write upon if he threw this away.

Bah! What does it matter? The greatest knowledge in the universe has just slipped through my fingers. I am not likely to have that vision twice! And I can't even remember the first thing about it other than it was lovely, and I was happier thinking about it than I had ever been in my life. But it's gone now. The treasure has been stolen not only from my grasp, but from my mind as well. Oh, Lovely Mother, have you no pity for your servant?

Melchior heard the song of a bird just outside his window. It was a perky sparrow bouncing about from branch to branch as if it had nothing better to do than dance away the day. But as Melchior stared, the light fell on the vellum in such a way that the first scratches were discernible, and Melchior bent in closer. "What's this?"

"And he showed me a river of water of life, clear as crystal..."

Clenching the vellum in frustration, Melchior shouted, "What in eternity does that *mean*?" Yet his heart was lightened, for although his entire vision did not come back to him, he did sense the unspeakable joy he had known when he had first sat upon his chair in the blackness of night and wrote the message he was sure had come from God. Well, if God did not want him to know the whole message now, so be it. God was a mystery. He still had hidden within him this marvelous secret, and when God wished him to remember, he would recall the vision in full. And next time, he would dip his quill in ink!

Chapter Two

No Rest for the Weary

Melchior leaned back on his chair with the vellum limp in his hand and considered his people's long, distinguished history. *Why am I here, Lord? At least I have a few moments to think sensibly—and perhaps carve and write a bit, the work of a man of spirit, not a beast of burden.*

His gaze strayed out the window to the tree line in the distance.

The forests marched up the hills and over the horizon unto the sea where they threw up their arms in amazement at the sight of so much water, which none of them could drink. The land barely remembered the Roman roads that traversed the hills and valleys. Flowers with their slight green stems conquered the stone and mortar that had once been the pride of Rome. Roads to castle ruins whispered of kingdoms now burned and abandoned. The Anglos and Saxons were hardy conquerors. They knew how to destroy that which they could neither understand nor control. Reading and writing were not for them. You could neither eat nor wear words upon a page. Thoughts were but phantoms while deeds left their mark.

Melchior's family tree, sketched upon his vellum, was incomplete, but he knew his ancestors had prospered for some time on the Celtic island to the west. His earliest remembered ancestor had been a strong, valiant man by the name of Georgios, but where he had come from and what had led him to the edge of the world, no one knew save God alone. From Georgios had sprung a mighty line of goodly men who eventually settled in the Roman-

Celtic lands. They, too, thrived until barbarians arrived.

The cry rose from despairing lips, *"Invaders are driving us toward the sea, but the sea offers us no home!"* Famine and destitution settled in, and only the strong and the fortunate survived. Many sold their children just so that the little ones might, at least, have the scraps from their master's table. It was said, *"It's better to live like a dog than die like one."*

Three generations passed since Melchior's grandfather ruled his holdings with proud dignity. His own father, Jeremiah, had been a strong but shrewd man who knew better than to deny their defeat. Yet he would not despair of the last hope of a valiant heart—that one day his people would see prosperity again. Using ancient names passed down through oral tradition, Jeremiah had named his sons after the wise men who came seeking Christ. He assured them that, though they may not see the hope of salvation with their earthly eyes, they should keep the flame of hope kindled, for one day they would be well rewarded. *"God does not abandon His own."*

Melchior's brothers, Balthazar and Caspar, died in one of the many famines that nearly destroyed the remnant of their culture, but as the lands recovered so did Melchior. He had inherited his father's intelligence and embraced the memories of his brothers' gentleness. He learned to work the plow, handle a scythe, and organize the servants and slaves into a useful mob. Now that his daughter was grown, he left the care of the estate to her.

Melchior could barely suppress the ironic grin that twisted his lips out of countenance whenever he thought of his estates. What estates they were! He owned an unruly forest, which hid uncountable deer and a multitude of small game and a little more than a handful of thatched houses, although six of them were rented out to servants who worked their meager farms. Every family had at least one small garden, though several had two or three. Some families had a talent for raising more weeds than vegetables, but the wheat crop had done well for several seasons now, and Melchior had hopes they would not starve this winter. They also grew oats, rye, and barley. The barley was used as a cereal and the base for beer. He made sure that plenty of land was set aside for the barley crop. If one had to starve, it was always better to do so in a cheerful frame of mind. There were also two pigsties and one hill that had enough grass for the grazing of a small herd of cattle.

Melchior never liked to roam there after he had seen a man gored to death by an angry bull. His slaves cared for the cattle and, though he winced at the idea of someone getting injured, it would be nothing compared to the trouble he would have if one of his animals maimed a freeman. Then he would have to pay the wergild, and that could add up to more than a poor man could pay. Though holding lands made him a thane, he was by no means rich. He'd known churls who, with their craft and invention, had managed to hoard up greater sums than he had ever seen in his life.

Despite his misfortunes, Melchior knew he was a lucky man, for he still had his eldest daughter, Adele, living under his roof, managing his household. She nearly despaired of ever marrying, but secretly Melchior was relieved when every suitor had turned out to be unsuitable. One was too old, and as he was the first to ask, Adele, at fourteen, had felt that she had time and luck in her future and so turned him down. She could not have known that a series of battles would take a great many eligible men off to the northern coasts, where they promptly fell, never to offer marriage to anyone. After that, she'd had only one other suitor, but he had a glib tongue and over-merry wit that set Melchior's teeth on edge. He swore he would not have a fool for a son-in-law and wouldn't allow the man on his property. The next news Melchior had heard of the young fop was that he had died trying to jump his horse over a gully. Melchior had merely remarked, "It was a fitting end."

Weary of his reminiscences, Melchior supped on venison, bread, and ale. He then clumped down the stairs and sat on a bench near the dwindling fire. He began carving the intricate edging of a fish on a signboard he had prepared. He loved the project, for he found his muscles relaxed, and he could let his mind wander into invigorating territory.

After a bit, he decided to go outside and survey his estates, evaluate the crops, notice which tools needed mending, and pay close attention to the stables, for horses were as valuable as slaves. After a long, meandering stroll, Melchior considered the descending sun. It was late, and the dusk was rising, but he still had time to compose something before the throng returned.

He glanced toward the path that led to Lord Gerard's estate, which was blocked from his sight by the gentle curve of a green hill. His second son, Wilfred, would have taken the best horse, leaving the second and third best for Adele and Oliver. The other children, Gilda, Martha, and Thomas had been taken ahead by the servants. Undoubtedly, they'd be content to eat and be entertained for some time longer.

Melchior scratched his grey beard. The idea of translating ancient scripture into a language any churl could understand sparked his interest, but he wondered if it was worth the effort. There were some worthy churls who still thought like men, but they were few and far between. Still, it would keep his writing skills sharp and stand as a worthy topic the next time he was forced to meet with the landowners. No one would understand what he was talking about, of course, but if he said that he knew a good story, everyone might quiet down and listen. Melchior grinned as the image clarified itself in his mind. There was enough material in Genesis alone to last him through years of forced gatherings.

He was about to step inside when he stopped, perplexed. The distant thundering of hooves pounded nearer. Melchior closed his eyes. Sucking in a deep breath to manage his disappointment, he turned and considered his two-storied estate.

It wasn't imposing by any standards. He did not gild his house with carvings on every post and beam. He preferred a solid structure, wood-framed with a steeply peaked thatch roof. Gazing fondly at the top floor where he slept and worked, he sighed. His gaze slid to the large rectangular first floor with stone fireplaces at each end. The front doors were thrown open, and he could see all the way to the kitchen with the sitting room off to the side. The ample storage rooms and well-fitted bedrooms connecting to the main hall were discretely concealed. Heavy oak beams ran down the center while lesser beams crisscrossed at angles. The extra boards used for large gatherings leaned against the walls, and thick straw covered the floor. Wide enclosed benches made extra beds when they had guests.

Melchior's heart swelled with pride.

A cow mooed in the darkness.

Past her milking time, no doubt.

The thunderous hooves shook Melchior out of his reverie. *By Heaven, isn't a man allowed one peaceful evening?*

Bent low over his horse, Wilfred came into view. His horse ran as if a pack of wolves chewed its tail.

Melchior scowled.

Wilfred was often foolish, but he was never known for

cruelty.

As impatience warred with anxiety, Melchior waited for Wilfred to jump down and explain himself.

But the boy did nothing of the sort. He flew past his father at an alarming speed.

"How now, Wilfred? Explain yourself! Where are you going?"

The youth spoke not a word but kept his head down as his beast spurred forward.

Dust kicked high and made a swirling haze, cloaking the departing figure.

Melchior stared, perplexed, and waited for the dust to settle before he turned once again, this time to a larger number of thundering hooves pounding near. Foreboding chilled Melchior's bones.

Five horsemen charged into view. Each man bent low and rode as if the devil himself drove them on.

Melchior considered stepping onto the path, forcing the cavalcade to stop, but he hesitated. *They'd just run me over.* Instead, he stepped onto his wide porch and called out, "What's happened? Why the haste?"

Dust enveloping his figure, the last man flung back only a single word. "Murder!"

Chapter Three

Love and Jealousy

—Hours Earlier—

Adele dressed in her finest—though not very fancy—blue dress, rested her heavy head against a post in the noisy, bustling hall and considered the scene before her.

In a bedazzling embroidered gown, Corliss, Lord Gerard's daughter, wound a long, dark strand of hair about her index finger. She stared adoringly at her betrothed, and when his gaze encountered hers, she turned shyly away. Her next move involved leaning in tantalizingly close to Lord Marlow's chest but not quite touching him.

Adele sniffed. She could learn a lot from Corliss, if only she was willing to smile when she didn't mean it and marry a brute she didn't love.

Despite her proximity to her betrothed, Corliss still canvassed the room for appreciative attention.

In his clean breeches and white tunic top, Wilfred stood by the kitchen door and stared unabashedly at the woman.

Corliss winked at him and grinned.

What foolish daring!

The ruckus of loud conversations mixed with dense smoke rising from the central fire gave Adele a headache. The smoke was supposed to swirl up the chimney, but with all the stewing and roasting and the considerable number of people eating, drinking, talking, laughing, and stirring the air, the confused smoke could not find its natural escape. If not for Lord Gerard's handsome nephew Robert—who leaned casually against a post on the opposite side of the room, his blue eyes occasionally turning her way—Adele would have joined the children playing outside.

Commotion caught her attention.

Lord Gerard abruptly broke free from a group of drunken companions and stomped to the high table perched upon a dais. He lifted his cup, sloshing the dark ale, stared like a happy hound, and shouted for all to hear, "Hear me! Momentous news! As you know, I've been blessed with the loveliest daughter this side of Hadrian's Wall, and Lord Marlow has asked for her hand." He pointed at his daughter, sloshing more of his drink.

Acclaims and yells greeted this common knowledge as if it were a revelation from the gods.

Lord Gerard waved impatiently. "Listen to me! I've accepted his offer, and I want you all to know and remember that I am offering him possession of half my lands, upon my death, to keep for all posterity."

Loud exclamations shook the rafters.

Lord Gerard held out his hand. "But know this too! Listen! You're my witnesses! He's promised me a bride price of twenty head of cattle, fifteen beehives, and ten sheep. And he says he will double that when he sends the morning gift!"

Feet stomping, spear butts pounding the wooden floor, and loud yells both praising and swearing by the gods at the immensity of the gift drowned out all further revelations. Apparently satisfied with this uproar, Lord Gerard clumped down unsteadily from his perch and strode to his daughter. He gave her an extravagant kiss on the cheek and then a swat on the backside, as if he could not decide whether she was a grown woman to be congratulated or a small child to be teased.

Adele's lip curled. The spectacle could have been worse, but it didn't seem fair that a maiden a full five years her junior should get married with so much good fortune while she, so capable and hardworking, still went unnoticed by any male worth considering.

At least Corliss was marrying one of the few men Adele could never, under any circumstances, desire. She shuddered.

Lord Marlow stood at the head table with bronze skin and thick, black hair that fell over his eyes and in heavy waves down his shoulders. How much of his ample middle was muscle, fat, or padding from his heavy clothing? Three rings and several metal armbands decorated his person. Forever speaking in guttural tones, his expression, when he wasn't looking at his beloved, tended toward dark and brooding.

Adele had heard rumors about a cruel streak in the man, but she hated to give credence to the servants' gossip. They always imagined horrible things.

Selby had once warned her that he had seen Lord Marlow whip a man nearly to death for taking his best horse without permission. Later, it turned out that the man had needed the horse to get help for his badly injured son, but Lord Marlow did not care for that excuse and so had the beaten man and his family moved off his lands.

Adele had insisted that Selby exaggerated. But the old slave only nodded gravely and said that men who live on another man's ancestral estate tend to bear secret grudges. "They'll never rest easy."

Adele watched Lord Marlow closely and wondered if *he* would rest easy with his bride.

~~~

Oliver roamed about the room, watching but never
~~~

engaging any man in conversation. He noticed Wilfred's pointed stares at Corliss but merely shook his head, ignoring the implications. The room was large but not large enough for all the smoke and noise. He edged his way toward the door and, as the sun neared the horizon, decided to check on the horses.

As he crossed the courtyard, he noticed a commotion, and he edged up closer. Young children gathered in play, his younger sisters Martha and Gilda among them, and sure enough, his youngest sibling Thomas gripped Lady Nadine's hand for all his worth. Oliver smiled. Thomas had the uncanny ability to find the highest-class person in a setting and attach himself like a barnacle to a ship. Unfortunately, that led to uncomfortable situations, for few lords liked small children and none liked to have their feasting and drinking interrupted. Oliver watched the scene from a distance. He could tell, without adding up the details, that Lady Nadine was a disappointed woman. She bore a smile the same way that Romans bore a standard in battle.

"Catch, my Lady!" A small child called to the noblewoman, who was doing her best to attend to several calls at once.

Thomas yanked Lady Nadine's hand, intent on engaging her full attention.

Alarmed, Oliver stepped forward.

But Gilda, preternaturally mature at twelve, raced up and grabbed Thomas' hand. "Leave her be, you pest!"

Thomas howled, but Oliver rushed forward and scooped Thomas into his arms. "You want to go to the stables? I bet the Lord's horses are the grandest in the land!"

Thomas' eyes darted from Lady Nadine to his big brother who, it was clear, had full possession of his body. He screamed louder.

Lady Nadine squeezed her eyes shut as she pressed her hand to her temple. Trembling, she sank down on a bench.

Oliver grimaced.

Gilda shook her head and pointed, directing Oliver to take Thomas away.

In accustomed obedience, Oliver nodded and toted Thomas toward the stables, the little boy's legs swinging and his screams growing hoarse as they went.

~~~

Gilda drew a sigh of relief and then looked to the assembled group: children of various churls and servants.

Standing in the middle of the green courtyard, Lady Nadine should not have been spending her time this way. Her husband would think it beneath her dignity. But she sought out children, and they enjoyed her kindness and welcome. Pressing her hand over her heart, her breath grew as ragged as a ripped sheet. Illness was common enough, and Lady Nadine never rested easy.

Gilda's throat constricted at the sight. She glanced around. *If I was married to a man like Lord Gerard, I'd be uneasy too.*

It was true that Lord Gerard had important things on his mind, what with the upcoming council concerning the borderlands. Heated arguments had broken out over who owned the fine woods leading into the forest.

Her father had stayed determinedly out of the dispute. The last time he delved into a border question he had discovered five of his sheep with their throats cut.

Gilda stepped nearer. "Would you like some refreshment, my Lady?"

"It's strange that you, daughter of Melchior, should care what happens to me." The woman stared fixedly at
~~~

Gilda. "At least we can sit in peace awhile. Call the servants to take the children away." She dropped onto a solid wood bench.

Gilda ran to the servants' kitchen. "The Lady is worn with care! Come, take the children."

A few servants exchanged looks, but they slowly budged themselves from their comfortable stools.

As the women shuffled forward, gathering the aimless and discontented ragamuffins, Gilda propped her hands on her hips, silently urging them to hurry.

Selby slouched toward the stable.

"Selby, take Martha and Thomas home. They're being troublesome.

Selby retreated into the stable and just as quickly returned with Thomas on his shoulders. He took Martha by the hand. "We best hurry. The cows need milking."

As soon as the crowd thinned, Gilda ran back to Lady Nadine, imagining herself taking the lady's hand and leading her toward the hall for a nourishing meal. But the bench was empty, the courtyard nearly barren of inhabitants.

Gilda ran in a wide circle, wondering where a weary woman could have gone in such a short time.

Wilfred pelted past her.

"Wilfred, come here! I lost Lady Nadine..." But her brother rushed into the stable, oblivious to her pleas. A grumble rose inside. "Well, I'd think you'd care!"

Gilda stood undecided, but then the smell of roasted pork made inroads into her mind, and her stomach rumbled. She turned toward the feasting hall.

A hand gripped her shoulder.

Oliver, out of breath and scowling, stopped her. "Don't go in, Gilda!"

Gilda stared at her brother. "I'm looking for Lady Nadine. Did you see her pass this way?"

Oliver glanced over his shoulder, then bent in low and whispered, "She didn't pass this way, and she won't be passing this way again."

His solemn tone, wide eyes, and the bright pink spots coloring his otherwise pale cheeks sent chills down Gilda's spine. "Why? What's happened?"

Oliver clasped her hand in his own. "It's time we're home. Selby is gathering the servants."

"But Father won't expect us so soon. Feasts usually last into the night."

"This one won't."

The two walked forward in silence. Just before they entered the stables, they were thrust to the side as Wilfred, astride his horse, broke forth at a full gallop.

As she tried to yank free of Oliver's grasp, Gilda screamed, "Wilfred!"

But Oliver clutched Gilda's hand tighter.

Wilfred's horse pounded furiously down the road.

The two could only stare at the vanishing shadow, the thumping hooves quickly growing faint.

Suddenly, a shriek tore through the air.

Her heart clenched, Gilda jerked free of Oliver's grip and ran into the deepening gloom toward the hall.

She halted in shock as Adele, normally so calm and controlled, skittered forward with wide, alarmed eyes.

Adele screamed at the top of her lungs, "Run, Wilfred! Run!"

Several men dashed up from behind. One grabbed Adele's arm, held her in place, and slapped her across the face.

Adele fell to the ground in a heap.

Too shocked to move, Gilda cried out, "No!"

Oliver sped ahead. Before the man could strike again, Oliver tumbled him to the ground and pummeled his head against the earth.

Adele staggered to her feet, her hand over the blazing mark on her face. “Stop, Oliver! Don’t kill him! Oh, Lord, it’ll only make things worse!”

Other men dashed to the stables and mounted horses, ready to give chase. Those who stayed behind grabbed Oliver by the shoulders and pulled him off Robert.

Oliver climbed to his feet, shaking the restraining arms away.

In blind loyalty, Gilda ran to her brother and wrapped her arms around him protectively.

Adele heaved deeps breaths, and her voice trembled, “Lady Nadine has been stabbed!” Tears formed in her eyes as she glanced at her little sister. “The poor woman’s been murdered, and Lord Gerard thinks Wilfred did it!”

Gilda, wretched with horror, could only whisper, “Stabbed? I just left—” Bile burned her throat. “But why does Lord Gerard think—”

“The last thing she said was, ‘Wilfred.’ Lord Gerard swears that he saw Wilfred running away when he found his wife.”

Gilda’s knees buckled, but Oliver caught her and lifted her into his arms.

Lord Gerard barged forward, his pale face taut with strain. He raised a shaking hand to his men. “Don’t bother with them. Undoubtedly, they didn’t know about their brother’s deed. Surely, the man is insane.” He pointed at his nephew. “You’ve better things to do than strike a worthless woman.”

Lord Gerard turned his gaze and glared at Oliver. “Go! And take your ragged servants with you. Don’t think I didn’t notice that you foisted them upon my tables, leeches that you are!” He shook his bejeweled finger. “And tell your father that we’ll not wait to hang his son. It’s our right and duty to see justice done!”

Oliver turned his back on the outraged fool.

Gilda could only cry in silence.

~~~

Adele turned once more toward Robert. This time, instead of warm admiration, she felt cold, stinging nausea rise in her throat. She marched faster to keep pace with her brother, and they entered the stables alone.
~~~

Chapter Four

Nikolas

Nikolas never felt that all was right with the world, but as a merchant, he knew that a pleasant disposition did much to charm customers into returning a second and a third time. As a tall man with dark hair and blue eyes who took after his father, a man who had made his living from the sea, he had natural benefits. Though his mother had died when he was young, his father, Osborn, had taken him fishing every day, and they had grown to understand each other as few sons and fathers ever could.

His younger sister had not fared so well. She had been fostered out to a wealthy landowner who, after a few years, had adopted her and raised her as his own. Osborn often regaled his son with magnificent stories of great men and women who had started out as fosterlings, though at the mention of his daughter, he'd grow silent and thoughtful.

She had grown up in the southwest, where vast trade opportunities made for high living. Growing strong and beautiful, she married a wealthy man and, by all accounts, lived a charmed life. Still, Nikolas could never be jealous of her handsome situation, for he had the enduring love of his father, which he'd not trade for any fortune—land or coin.

Not that coins had much value these days. Nikolas jingled the few bits he had been given in exchange for his fine goods: a sharp blade with a beautiful bone handle, a set of horn drinking cups engraved with ornate runes to keep evil spirits at bay, and a half-pound of salt.

Like the boy who traded his cow for a king's promise

only to discover that the king was a fool in disguise, he stood in his shop's drab interior, appraising the oddly shaped coins. Their rough edges and lack of imprint brought a flush to his face. These were homemade coins passed along as a remembrance of better days! Every Saxon would laugh at his stupidity, while any visiting Roman would sniff in superiority.

The Britons were already suspicious of commerce, and they would be more judicious than he. Besides, the natives preferred to hold up in what fortresses they still owned or could wrestle back from the invaders. As a full-blooded Saxon, Nikolas was fully aware of the resentment many Britons felt toward him and his kind. But he also knew that he, as his father before him, had little to do with the momentous changes in this country.

Skirmishes still broke out, and the episodic battles would probably never end, but Nikolas enjoyed life as a churl. As a hard-working man, why shouldn't he build a home on these lands as well as anyone else? Should the bloodthirsty warriors who came destroying and ravaging get everything?

With these thoughts muddying his concentration, Nikolas didn't notice the arrival of two men who were as different from him as an oak tree is from a mulberry bush. Both husky and laden with vast muscles, rounded stomachs, and broad chests, their sleeveless, fur-lined tunics tied with twine-knotted belts revealed more about their physiques than Nikolas cared to know.

The first man's intense glare, tousled brown hair, and deep guttural speech reminded Nikolas of a kettle about to boil. The other man stood nearly as tall, though his hair glowed red, and his eyes reflected the blue sky.

Nikolas' heart pounded. He forced a smile. It was never wise to show fear to any man, much less to men like these. Just like with wolves, they wouldn't bother anyone but for the fun of the chase. Killing a person and eating the carcass would be a mere formality.

Nikolas started out bravely enough. “Hello, warriors! If you are looking for food, you’ve come to the wrong place. I sell only simple tools.”

The first man’s twisted grin dropped Nikolas’ stomach to his knees. He clenched his few worthless coins and wondered why he had bothered to get out of bed this morning. *I’d have done better to pull the covers over my head and hide from the light of day.*

He widened his own smile and pointed toward a row of helmets, shields, spears, and battle axes that he had gleaned off fields before the victors had claimed everything. Nothing but the dregs of battle, but for a poor man they’d be better than nothing. Nikolas’ worse-for-wear-weaponry often did brisk business.

This particular warrior did not seem impressed. His grin turned into a snarl. “We didn’t come to banter with you, trader. My name’s Harold, son of Harold, and this is Terrill. We’ve come from the south on important business. If we wanted some of your wares, we’d have let you know, like this, you see!” Harold peered at Terrill significantly.

With this slight encouragement, Terrill proceeded to do a fairly good imitation of a troll having a temper tantrum. He ripped one of the battle-axes off the wall and threw it to the ground, where it landed with a heavy thud. Terrill’s gloved hand, embedded with iron spikes, glinted in the light.

Trying not to imagine what those metal pieces could do to flesh and bone, Nikolas nodded in sober understanding, but his face grew hot. He may be nothing more than a fisherman turned trader, but he still had the same blood as these two, and he was taller by almost an inch. Still, his eyes darted toward the gloved hand. “What, exactly, can

I do for you?"

Terrill thrust his chin out. "You can keep your eyes open, that's what! You have eyes, don't you?"

Nikolas chewed his lip. *Harold is definitely the brighter of the two.*

Harold placed his hand on Terrill's shoulder and spoke more to the point. "There's been a murder in the south, and the scoundrel got away. He was last seen heading north. We think his father did some conjuring trick using the powers of his god, but we know the guilty party can't have gotten far. So, you're to use those eyes of yours and tell us if you see the son of Melchior come this way."

Nikolas' throat went dry, for he knew Melchior well. In truth, his tiny shop was just north of Melchior's home. His father had often spent time with him, exchanging stories and talking nonsense. When Osborn had died, Melchior had helped to lay him at rest.

A choking sensation gripped his throat. "Which son committed murder?" He knew the kind of men these two represented. Justice and truth meant little to them. If they could brag that they had brought a murderer to justice, they'd sleep well—even if they had hung the wrong man.

Harold leaned in with a conspiratorial whisper. "The second, the cocky one, so full of wild ideas. Had eyes for Lord Gerard's daughter, he did. Everyone knew it. Bound to come to no good end."

Nikolas heaved a sigh of relief. At least it wasn't Oliver. He picked up the fallen battle-ax. "I'll keep my eyes open, but I doubt he'll pass this way."

Terrill pursed his lips and jabbed his finger into Nikolas' shoulder. "Just see that you do your part! Lord Gerard is grievously upset. He wants this matter taken care of quickly. You understand?"

Even though Nikolas would have liked nothing more than to end the conversation, he couldn't help asking one more question. “Why? What’s Lord Gerard’s concern in the matter?”

“You fool! It’s his wife that was murdered!”

Nikolas stiffened with horror. He snatched his cloak from a peg and hurried toward the stable, repeating an agonized refrain, “God, no!”

~~~

Harold watched the lanky merchant scurry away, astonished at the young man’s daring.

Terrill was not one to handle the unexpected with grace. “Hey, fool, where’re you going? We told you to stay here and keep your eyes open!”

Harold ran up behind Nikolas, grabbed him by the shoulder, and spun him around. “We didn’t give you leave to go!”

Nikolas reached back and, with an ungloved but tightly clenched fist, hit Harold hard on the chin.

Unprepared for the assault, Harold staggered and fell, his hand shooting to the pain in his jaw.

Using his weight effectively, Nikolas pressed his dirty, leather-clad knee hard upon Harold’s throat. “Tell your troll to stand back, or I’ll break your neck!”

Harold didn’t need to gesture much to explain the situation, though he guessed Terrill would be inclined to risk anything to get his hands on Nikolas.

Nikolas, however, continued to put enough pressure on Harold’s throat so that just a few frantic gestures stopped Terrill in his tracks.

Nikolas’ voice dropped to a ragged whisper. “Lord Gerard’s noble wife was my honorable sister, and I’ll know how she died. No rest will comfort my eyes nor will
~~~

food nourish my insides until I know who did this and see justice done to the fullest measure!" He pressed his knee a final time against Harold's throat for good measure and then stood.

Without a backward look, Nikolas strode away.

More annoyed than pained, Harold rose to his feet unaided.

Terrill stood frozen, his mouth hanging open.

As Harold rubbed his neck, trying not to look too grateful for still being alive, he spoke hoarsely. "We'll have to watch that one. He's not what he appears."

"I think we should beat him to death."

Harold smacked his foster brother on the ear. "You oaf! Didn't you hear him? His sister is Lord Gerard's wife...his dead wife, I mean. He'll have the ear of the Lord all right. And his words were not spoken in idleness. I know when a man makes a vow, and that man made a vow he'll live by."

Terrill followed the retreating figure with hooded eyes. "Or a vow he will die by."

Harold nodded, but his eyes shifted from Terrill to the swiftly departing figure on the horizon.

Chapter Five

Hope So

—Lux—

Teal, dressed in a peasant's brown tunic with a long hood, stood beside a fountain carved to resemble a woman pouring water from her jug into a child's basin. The water sprayed in a glorious arc, creating rainbows in every direction. Beyond the first note of surprise, Teal refused to care. His fingers flew over his datapad, ideas flowing so fast he could hardly keep up. Despite achy shoulders and a throbbing neck, he wouldn't slow down.

"There you are! We've been looking for you everywhere." In a white shirt and matching, loose trousers, Sterling flounced forward, a cat-like grin stretching across his face.

His thoughts tumbling to a halt, Teal frowned. "Who's we?"

Sterling boomed a hearty laugh.

Alarm spread over Teal. He slipped his datapad into a deep pocket and faced his old friend, the newest Supreme Judge.

Drops landed on Sterling's black hair. He glanced aside and pointed to an outdoor shop and off-world cafe. "Let's practice eating, shall we? I haven't tried anything human in ages. What are they concocting these days? Better than that swill you brought me last time, I hope."

"If I remember correctly, you enjoyed their wine."

Teal kept pace as Sterling jogged across the quiet street and bounded to the colorful seating arrangement. "Their fruits and vegetables have something to offer—especially when fermented." As Sterling eyed the menu scrawled in neat script on a mounted board, he waved at a Bhuaci server in petite Elven form.

Dressed in a bright yellow brassiere with a long flowing skirt, the server hustled up smiling. "What would you like? We have drinks and dishes from all parts of the universe. If we don't know it, we're quick to learn. Just try us and see."

Teal plunked down on a chair under a blue awning and rubbed his neck. The throb had grown to a painful ache. "We'll take a small order of lake fish, carrots, barley bread, and weak beer, Earth-style." He scrunched his nose at Sterling. "Unless you'd rather try venison?"

Sterling lifted his hands. "I'll trust your culinary advice." He glanced around, his gaze searching. "I just hope that you're ready for what you'll find when you return."

Irritation flashed through Teal. "You mean *we*. *We're* returning together, remember? We have a lot to accomplish in a very short time. The Supreme Council wants a report by the end of the cycle, and I have yet to make contact with everyone." He narrowed his eyes. "What did you mean earlier when you said, *we've* been looking for you?"

Like an Ingot with a short circuit, Sterling's gaze froze. "I thought I told you. About Mauve. She's extraordinary. The youngest Luxonian to reach first level in history. A real beauty with a Bhuac's sensitivity and an Ingot's calculating sense."

Teal searched his mind. *Mauve?*

The server drew near with a large tray balanced in her arms. She carefully laid the table with cutlery, placed golden mugs at each place, then slid plates with fish, carrots, and bread rolls before each Luxonian. "Here you go. The chef seasoned accordingly." She grinned. "If there's anything else I can help you with, let me know." She trotted off.

Peering at the plate, Sterling winced. "There's no getting out of it?"

Teal took a sip of beer and wiped his lips. "Of eating or returning to Earth?"

"This isn't a good time for me to head off-planet. Someone else, a more experienced Supreme Guardian, should go."

Teal chewed the savory fish thoughtfully. "Of all the Supreme Guardians, you are the newest to ascend and the most experienced in Earth matters. You're perfect for the job." An uncomfortable thought wiggled into his mind. "Is this about Mauve?"

"Of course not. I simply hate traveling. Always have. You know that."

"If it makes you feel better, she can come."

Sterling's eyes widened, hope kindling. "You'd be all right with that?"

"I'm bringing Cerulean, and Zuri has Nova with him." He tore a roll in half and shrugged. "Why not?"

Blinking, as if fending off tears, Sterling stared at the fish. He picked up his fork and cut a modest portion. Like a swimmer jumping into the deep end, he plunged the morsel into his mouth, chewed, and nodded. "Not bad." He guzzled the beer and grinned. "This I could get used to."

Teal savored a mouthful of carrots and sighed. "So long as we stick to schedule and set the proper example for Cerulean, I don't care who you bring."

A buzzer sounded.

Teal pulled out his datapad and scrolled through the message. He looked up and met Sterling's inquiring gaze. "It's Zuri. Says he has great news." He pointed to the food. "Let's finish up. He's waiting."

Sterling bounded to his feet and waved his hand over his apparel. Instantly he appeared dressed in a blue cloak, green tunic, and yellow stockings with black slip-on shoes. "Think I'll fit in?"

Teal choked and tried not to roll his eyes.

—OldEarth—

Zuri, wearing a coarse tunic over the simplest remnant of his armor, paced along a worn path, the sun setting behind a distant, emerald-green hill.

With a flash, Teal appeared before him in a peasant's outfit.

"There you are. I was afraid you'd have to wait till morning to see."

Smirking, Teal bowed low. "Hello, Zuri. So glad we meet again."

"None of that now. We haven't time. I want you to see this family! They're magnificent and, to top it off, there's been a murder. Some folks are running about insisting that Melchior's son did it, but I hardly think so. Not the warrior type, if you know what I mean. I'm thinking it was the husband—though I have no—"

Teal faltered, his shape growing hazy. "By the Divide, I don't know what you're talking about."

Zuri grabbed Teal's arm and tugged him down the path. When they rounded a bend, a cottage stood before them, resplendent in evening hues.

"That's Melchior's place. He has a bunch of children, servants, and even a slave or two, yet he manages to keep his property intact and his head attached. In these parts, that's something to be proud of." He squinted in the failing light. "You all right? You look a bit…fuzzy."

Teal lifted his hand and nodded. "Just been over-busy."

Zuri glanced around. "Where's Cerulean?"

"He's taking care of Sterling. With strict orders to hurry him along, with or without Mauve."

"Who's Mauve?"

Teal rolled his shoulders. "His newest obsession."

"Uh, oh."

"You can say—"

A chime sounded.

Zuri tapped his chest, and a holographic image of a Cresta with stringy yellow cilia drizzling from his head and dressed in a dark green bio-suit with matching boots appeared before them.

"Tarragon reporting for duty."

Teal frowned.

Leaning toward Teal, Zuri dropped his voice low. "Ark's son. Remember the pod…"

Teal nodded. He focused his gaze on the Cresta. "Thank you for being so prompt. But I thought we were going to meet here at—" He glanced at Zuri.

"Melchior's cottage."

Tarragon waved a tentacle. "I wanted assurance that someone would be there to greet me. I am still on board my ship, but I'll shuttle down shortly." He eyed Zuri. "If you'll confirm the coordinates?"

Suppressing annoyance, Zuri pulled a datapad from his sleeve and tapped in the information. "Just be sure to stay out of sight. Your aircraft had better be native sensitive."

"Of course. The Cresta are experts of disguise."

Zuri chuckled. "Ark was anything but!" Realizing his mistake, a flush warmed his cheeks. "Sorry. No disrespect. I greatly valued Ark."

Tarragon shrugged. "I hardly knew him." With a smart salute, he signed off, and the hologram evaporated.

Zuri slapped his face. "Oh, that went well. Don't you

think?"

Looking haggard, Teal sighed. "He's a hard one to figure. I've introduced myself through the years, but he never responded, and Ark had little information to offer. I thought he'd be at Ark's passing-on ceremony, but he never showed. His mother did, though. Gave me an earful. More than I really wanted to know about Cresta mating—"

The pounding of horses' hooves sent Zuri scurrying to a hedge row.

Teal blinked away and then reappeared at his side. "We'd better move further off. We don't want Tarragon showing up in the middle of a family dispute."

"Going to be a blinking challenge to train someone new. And now we have Sterling and Mauve to deal with."

Teal shrugged. "It could be worse. We could have the Mystery Race on our heels. At least we're safe there."

Zuri glanced at the starry sky, a sinking sensation enveloping him.

Chapter Six

King Radburn's Proposal

Melchior slumped in an oversized armchair, his chin buried deep in his hands. His children, arranged around the fire-lit room, slouched in mournful silence. Even Thomas drooped in weariness, a half-built block castle perched precariously between his chubby legs.

Dark tapestries drooped from the high walls, catching slivers of the flickering light, while the beams overhead glowed like beaten bronze. Though a large fireplace stood at each end of the hall, only one blazed. The other fireplace sat cold, heaped with dead ashes.

Oliver sat on the left of the large central table, his hands folded, while Adele sat on the right, bent over her sewing. Gilda perched close to the fire, examining the flames as if she could read them, while Martha knelt near Thomas, helping him with his towering construction.

Melchior closed his eyes, but he could not rest. Images of Wilfred's face and form growing up under his tutelage mixed into a cacophony of blurred pictures. Wilfred had a foolish disposition, it was true, but the boy was still his son. Melchior felt that *he* was the one being chased across the fens and mires. It had been over a day now since Wilfred had run away.

Oh, Mother of God, have mercy on me and protect my son. I don't have friends to take up my cause, and few will care for the outcome. There's already been so much bloodshed. Who cares if a few more drops are spilt? Yet shouldn't we care? Shouldn't each drop weigh the same? Oh, God!

At that moment, the sound of hooves pounded near, and

Melchior jumped to his feet, only to sway with dizziness.

Adele and Oliver rushed to his aid, reaching out to support him.

Selby trotted from the kitchen to the front door and threw it wide open.

Heavy, jingling weaponry filled the crisp night air.

Melchior squeezed his eyes shut and tried to regain his composure.

A massive intake of breath, the sound of swishing cloaks, and the distinctive thud as everyone knelt abruptly on the ground.

Melchior opened his weak, red-rimmed eyes. In the doorway stood a man he had hated all his life.

They were nearly the same age, though Melchior appeared older. *And for good reason. This devil has been coddled beyond compare. Born to a warrior who wanted a rich and powerful son and so grabbed at everything, including my family home and lands....*

Melchior trembled at the memory of being held fast by bigger, stronger men, watching his father beaten into submission. It had been only through clever reasoning, a demonstration of his son's remarkable reading abilities, and energetic pleading that Jeremiah had been able to keep the few outbuildings and small parcels of land.

Yet, once again, this man appeared on his doorstep. *Why? To tell me he has killed my—* Melchior began to sway.

King Radburn put up his hand in a conciliatory gesture. "I know what you're thinking. But in truth, I come here for justice's sake. I, like many others, want to discover who killed Lady Nadine. I do not believe it was your son, and for that cause and purpose, I have arrived here now to look into the matter, to stave off that which would only add to mutual misery."

Melchior looked into King Radburn's eyes. *Is it*

possible? Can snakes grow into men? Can the inheritor of so much dirty villainy bring forth the clean scent of righteousness? Melchior swallowed hard and tried to shake off the supporting embrace of his well-meaning children.

"If this be truly so, then we welcome you with a good will. We're distressed beyond all measure by the news that my son is blamed for the murder of so good a lady, and I, too, only wish to see justice done. If my son did indeed commit this grievous crime, then I would want justice for his soul's sake. Though I'm his father, I am not blind to his faults, yet I don't think him capable of the murder of anyone, much less of a lady he so loved and esteemed. Lady Nadine was ever kind to him."

"For this very reason, I also have doubts. I have seen the two together, and it was clear that this son of yours was loved...by many. I see no reason for his murdering Lady Nadine. And though I've killed a fair number of men, at least I always had a reason—most men do. Besides, your son's interest seemed in another direction of late."

Melchior straightened, his eyes narrowing. These were not the words he expected, but he could not deny his relief. Still, it was clear that King Radburn knew of some private matter concerning Wilfred. His blood ran hot.

Stepping forward, Adele brought forth a tray with hot-spiced drinks and thick bread heavily smeared with butter and honey.

Oliver arranged the two best chairs by the fire so that Melchior and King Radburn could sit while they ate and drank. He even dragged over the wooden footstool that Melchior liked to use on cold winter nights when he sat warming himself by the fire.

Without a word of thanks, King Radburn allowed the footstool to be placed under his mud-caked boots.

Oliver stood guard while Adele took the younger children to bed.

In little time, King Radburn washed down the warm bread with a long drink. He wiped his mouth with the back of his hand and grinned. "I remember when I first came here. Just a boy at the time, and you were standing next to your father much as I was sitting next to my father astride my horse. Father and son facing father and son. We had the better hand. More worthy men. Neither your father nor your father's father had a warrior's instinct. Christians—or some such thing. Am I right?" King Radburn cocked his head and grinned.

Cradling his hot drink in his hands, Melchior nodded, a flush working up his cheeks.

"That's what I thought. Useless thing, Christianity. Never heard of it till I came here. My father laughed loud and long when he'd heard the story—your God crucified by the Romans! Gods can do as they like, of course, but I don't love them. Once the Romans left—"

Melchior rose and stood as tall as his short frame would allow. "We Britons held our own against the Pics and you Anglos and the Saxons, and all the vicious barbarians who assembled their might against us. We're still free...many of us. We may not own the lands we once did, and we may not enjoy the prosperity of old, but we're still men with minds, and that is more than I can say—"

Someone squeezed his hand.

Adele stood at his side. "Father, please, the King is our guest."

Staring ahead as if seeing into another world, Melchior shook his hand free and dropped heavily onto his chair. "Yes, forgive me, *King* Radburn. It's said, 'The anger of man works not the justice of God.'" He paused as his gaze dropped to the floor. "I'm very worried about my son."

King Radburn nodded in benevolence, yet his eyes had

narrowed considerably. He turned and stared at Adele before shifting his gaze back to Melchior. He gestured with his chin. “This one, she’s not married yet?”

Melchior peered into his daughter’s anxious eyes. He took her hand and gently rubbed her fingers as if to smooth away her fears. “She’s too beautiful for a common man and too good to leave me.”

King Radburn stroked his chin. “It’s not wise for a maiden to wait so long; she’s almost past her prime. Especially considering that her father is old, and her brothers are...well, it’s not wise.” He stared hard at Melchior. “Let me do you this one additional service. I’ll find her a husband, as well as attempt to save your son.”

Melchior’s gaze swept across the floor. His mind frantically circled a single word. *Why?* But he could say nothing.

Pounding feet echoed in the entryway.

He looked up, glad for the interruption, and saw a young, bearded warrior enter the room. The man whispered in the king’s ear.

King Radburn grinned, dropped his caked boots heavily to the floor, and straightened. “Seems you have another guest.” He stood. “I’ve other matters to attend to, but remember my offer. I’m a man of my word, for good or for ill. I’ve set my mind on finding a husband for your daughter there.” He appraised Adele’s face and form. “It’ll be a noble challenge.”

Adele blushed.

“Not because you are not beautiful, my dear, but rather to discover a man truly worthy of you.” King Radburn stepped forward and stroked her face with his broad thumb. Abruptly, he turned away and gestured for his man to let the newcomer pass before he departed.

Nikolas entered the hall, bowed formally to the king, and then turned his gaze to Melchior.

King Radburn peered narrowly. "Are you of my lands? I don't recognize you."

"Nikolas, Osborn's son. I inherited nothing but my body, the air, and the smell of the sea, but now I own a small shop north of here. I'm a merchant of various wares, my King."

The narrowed gaze did not waver. "You didn't answer my question. Are you of my lands?"

"The small patch I live on is mine by right, and I have never been called into your service, though I'm willing if ever you should need me."

One of the men leaned in and whispered in the king's ear.

King Radburn's eyes widened. "Oh, yes. Osborn's son. You live on the ancient hill." He smiled grimly. "Tell me, do you sleep well at night?"

Nikolas glanced at Melchior.

King Radburn didn't wait for an answer but merely waved. "Never mind. I leave you now to discuss matters at your leisure, but please do nothing in haste. I assure you, I'll do everything I can. Then we shall see, won't we?"

He turned toward Adele offering his most charming smile. "Thank you for the hot drink and the excellent bread. I will remember your kindness." King Radburn swooshed away as unceremoniously as he had entered.

The room stilled, except for relieved sighs.

Adele staggered to a chair, her face draining of all color.

Oliver stirred the dying embers to life as if to animate the room again.

Nikolas strode toward the hearth and rubbed his chapped hands together. "If I'd realized, I'd have waited some distance away, but I mistook them for mercenaries. I was afraid of what they might be doing in here."

Selby shuffled into the room to retrieve the dishes and sniffed. "If you can't tell that there be the king's horses and the king's men, and the king himself, why, it's blind you are!"

Adele swung around in fury. "Shush, old man! He's not a *king*; he's a monster!" Without another word, Adele fled from the room.

Oliver stood wide-eyed.

Melchior only shrugged. "It's been a difficult day. Let her be, Oliver. She is overwrought. Her future has just been thrown into murky waters."

Nikolas frowned as he propped his foot on the chair King Radburn had vacated. "Tell me how this happened, Melchior. You know well that Lady Nadine was my sister. Why in Heaven do they think Wilfred murdered her?"

Melchior snorted and pointed toward Oliver. "He was there. You tell him, Oliver. Everything you told me, exactly as it happened."

Oliver stepped closer, his face contorted with the memory, rubbing the back of his neck. "I was outside, trying to keep Thomas from trouble. We were walking toward the stables when Wilfred rushed by all out of breath, clearly upset. I didn't know what troubled him, but I could guess—"

"Why do you say that?" Nikolas observed Oliver intently, like a cat staring down at its prey.

Oliver looked up, one eyebrow raised. "It was obvious he was going to have words with Lord Gerard, or rather, Lord Gerard would have words with him. Not personally, of course. He'd send one of his men for that, I suppose. He wouldn't want to get into a brawl on his daughter's betrothal day." Oliver looked around at the stricken faces in front of him, and his brow furrowed.

Melchior sat up, his eyes brighter than they had been.

He wagged his finger at his son. "What's this? You didn't tell me he'd been in a brawl!"

Oliver shook his head. "And I don't say so now. I didn't see any struggle; I just supposed that Lord Gerard would have his revenge. Wilfred was making eyes at his daughter. The two were quite bold. Selby told me that Wilfred would pay a heavy toll for letting his eyes travel so."

His body trembling, Melchior bellowed, "Selby! Selby, you fool, come here this moment!"

Both Selby and Adele bustled into the room.

Adele spoke while Selby tucked his hands under his armpits and stared at Oliver. "What's the matter, Father? What's happened now?"

Melchior waved his daughter away and beckoned the old slave.

Selby shuffled closer. "Yes, sir, what'll you have, sir?"

"I'll have your loyalty! Haven't I been a good master? Haven't I always taken care of you?"

Selby's eyes watered as he knelt down in submission. "Yes, sir. Course you have. What do you want me to say?"

Melchior studied the old man, shivering as he realized what Selby had said was all too true. Was Selby capable of telling the truth for truth's sake, or was everything a matter of getting what he wanted, staying out of trouble, or being spiteful when he felt in the mood?

He gestured for Selby to stand, but Selby remained kneeling. Melchior would have none of it. "Get up, I command you! You were there when Wilfred was in the great hall with Lord Gerard, and you saw things. I know you did. Don't deny it! What was Wilfred doing that upset Lord Gerard?"

Selby hunched his shoulders, his eyes glancing off everyone in the room. His tone dropped to a whine. "Lord

Gerard and his men had been doing a lot of hard drinking, and you know how men get in such cases. Why, they take an honest man and perceive evil when he's done no real harm."

Nikolas interrupted. "Selby, where did Wilfred spend most of his time?"

Selby's black eyes flared. "He was with the other men, of course, as I was trying to tell—"

"Who did he talk to? What held his attention?" Melchior tugged the old man's ragged sleeve.

Selby's eyes shifted.

Melchior rose from his chair, fury beyond reason boiling inside him. "Selby, if you value your life, you'll tell me exactly what happened inside that hall! You know why Lord Gerard was angry, and you know why Wilfred was running away. Now tell us, or I'll have you whipped like Lord Gerard does his own, but I won't be so kind as to let you die in peace!"

"Father!" Adele rushed to Selby's side and put her hand protectively on his shoulder.

Tears slipped down the old man's cheeks and onto his stained tunic. All pretenses died in an instant.

Oliver, standing in the background, blinked and swallowed hard.

Selby stared for a moment before he shrugged; his voice dropped low and husky. "I'm an old man, and my life has been meaningless from start to finish. I thought to protect you, but I've never been very good at that, try as I might. I'm a slave, after all. I've no will of my own. I don't even own my own soul, they say. So, I'll tell you what my eyes recorded, and you can learn what you didn't want to know. Then you can whip me or beat me to death...it'll matter little to me. Death would only be a comfort now."

The old man stood hunched and told exactly what he

saw, how Wilfred had flirted openly with Corliss, and how Corliss made good use of every opportunity to expose Wilfred to her father's glare so that Lord Gerard could not mistake the meaning and the insult. How after getting sufficiently drunk to muster his courage, Lord Gerard had made a bold speech to seal the arrangement with Lord Marlow, and then he sent men to apprehend Wilfred on the sly. He told how he, Selby, had seen Wilfred approach Lady Nadine and then had run away, fleeing for his life.

"And that's all I know from that moment to this. I never saw young Wilfred again, and I'm sorely afraid I never will. I've heard it said that friends never see each other in hell. It isn't allowed, at least not close up."

Adele patted the old man's shoulder, like one might stroke a special pet. "You aren't going to hell, Selby. Why'd you say such—"

"But yes, certainly I must. All slaves do. For if it is true that we live and die without a will of our own, then we cannot become holy souls. Don't tell me that they've slaves in heaven?" Selby's gaze fell to the ground. "And Wilfred, he's as unrepentant a young man as ever I did see."

"Shut your mouth and go!" Melchior wrapped his arms around his middle; his stomach gripped in painful knots.

Selby shuffled off, leaving the room in aching silence.

Melchior gestured to Oliver. "See that the old fool gets to bed; he needs rest, or he'll be no use to anyone."

Oliver turned, but Nikolas stopped him in the doorway. "Oliver, you said that Wilfred was out of breath; perhaps he had been in an argument. Do you think he spoke to Lord Gerard?"

Oliver scratched his head. "I don't think so, for Lord Gerard's voice carries, and he'd been calling for his wife shortly before. I heard no other shout of any kind."

Nikolas nodded slowly. His eyes darted toward Melchior. "Thank you, Oliver. Why don't you get some rest as well? I'll stay and take care of your father." He glanced at Adele. "See that everyone is set for the night, and I'll get Melchior to his bed. Tomorrow is another day, and we best be ready."

Adele's eyes warmed to this unexpected kindness.

Nikolas stepped forward, speaking in an undertone to Adele. "Get some rest yourself. I'm not blind to the fact that it is you, more than anyone, who keeps this house in order. If there were a man in the kingdom fit to claim you, he'd be the lucky one. Pity that we live in times where worth is measured in power, not decency."

Adele blushed, but as she crossed the threshold, she hesitated and whispered, "Thank you."

Nikolas smiled.

Melchior noted the warm exchange but was too weary to care.

Chapter Seven

Wilfred's Surprise

Wilfred hunched over his Mooreland horse as it pounded over the turf in the wind-swept highland. If he ever thought to ask himself where he was going on his wild run, he would have said, "To the shore, to the sea, toward the rising sun," or some other glorious expression, for he had imbibed a variety of romantic notions along with his thick, brown bread and warm mead during his youth. He had sampled morality from a variety of tables. His eldest sister modeled the ever dutiful and industrious child, while his older brother was much the same—when given proper instruction.

He saw little use in following their examples, for Wilfred was convinced that his father couldn't possibly need him. While he saw Gilda as preternaturally able, Martha so innocent, and Thomas so adorable, he didn't see himself playing any useful role. He had admired old Osborn and his son Nikolas, though he never desired to become like them. Independence was a fine thing, as long as it led to a life of comfort and substance.

The model of his ambition was most clearly defined in the person of King Radburn. Wilfred warred within himself for admiring the very man who had caused his family so much misery.

Yet there were few men alive who embodied the spirit of romance so well as the seafaring pirates and mercenary warriors who came and went with the season's tide.

King Radburn tamed wild hearts and trained them to serve him. Those he found not to his liking, he sent to Lord Gerard. Wilfred had spent a great deal of time ingratiating himself with his neighbors, eating the crumbs that fell from the master's table and not hating him for it. It was an indisputable fact that if the new lords of the land had not gained from the spoils of war, someone else would have. At least, Lord Gerard tolerated Wilfred enough to allow him to wander about his lands freely; a freedom, he realized, he would pay for dearly.

The fear-induced sweat that had broken across his skin during the long night ride had disappeared in the chilly air, and as the haze of a hidden sun rose over the riotous sea, he looked at the shore's rugged beauty, and his spirit filled once again with romantic visions. Though, as his horse slowed to an exhausted plod, he remembered why he had been running in the first place. His spirits dropped from their heights and landed ignobly in the light snow, which was just beginning to fall around him.

He took a deep breath to cleanse himself of all anxiety and tried, for the first time since his long run, to think of a plan. Where would he go, exactly? Biting his lip, his gaze swept the shore. This was unfamiliar country. He had to go where he had never gone before, or he would be easy to find. After all, he reasoned, if he didn't know where he was going, how could anyone else?

He scanned the landscape. A few boats rested upon the shore, but there were no ships anchored at the docks. A fine situation! There was usually at least *one* ship waiting to be loaded at any port. Wilfred's eyes swept across the expanse once more, from the rocky crag from which his horse plucked a meager breakfast to the sandy shore. The horse whinnied in equal disappointment. He would find no easy future here.

But where could he go now? He must go somewhere fast. Men hounded his steps, ready to accuse him of the unthinkable. A shiver of horror slithered down Wilfred's spine. As he sucked in a deep breath, he spied the outline of a small cottage. He nudged his horse in that direction, and with a low whistle of pleasure noticed smoke rising from the chimney.

Wilfred tied his horse to a post and trudged his way through the fierce wind that froze his ears and stung his eyes, toward the door of the low thatched cottage.

Before he made it up the pathway, the door burst open. A man stood with his hands on his hips and a large knife sticking out of his leather belt.

Wilfred doubted that this was the kind of man who would show all his weaponry at once. He tried to make his wind-blown voice sound cheerful. "Hello, can you help me? I was going to take a ship out—"

"You'll not go today!" The man's bellowing voice cut through the high wind and sounded as ominous as the roar of the sea. "There's a storm a-brewing, and every seaman knows it. Any man with eyes can see that!"

Wilfred's gaze swept up the incline, and though he could no longer look down upon the swirling sea, he recognized the iron-gray clouds and shivered as biting cold swept into every fold of his garments. The gale grew in ferocity with every breath. He could not deny the man's point. "Ay, I agree, yet my predicament doesn't get any better with this news. Is there some place I can stay the night, or a few days, until the storm abates?"

A thickset woman appeared behind the man's shoulder, speaking in a foreign tongue.

The burly man shook his head at the woman and then shook his fist at Wilfred. "We want no boarders here. I've kindred to look after, and with winter coming on, I barely have enough to feed those under my care. Besides, who'd look after your horse? There's little enough for the sheep."

Wilfred felt the full force of the cold, damp wind as it began to seep into his bones. For the first time since he had fled Lord Gerard's estate, terror struck home. He had imagined that he would simply ride to the seacoast, catch a departing ship, and realize his dream to become a pirate or a mercenary, but he had forgotten about winter, food, and provisions for his horse. *His* horse, why, the animal wasn't even his own! The wind bit his nose and ears; he tried not to tremble. "Is there no place I could find a bit of shelter?" Humiliated and afraid, Wilfred begged his next word. "Please."

The hefty woman spoke from behind the man's back, and he scowled, throwing rough words over his shoulder. The woman only reacted in kind, throwing out more words. The man turned, and for a moment, they shouted back and forth so rapidly that Wilfred wondered if they were even speaking of him or if in the ruckus some new trouble had sprung up between them.

Finally, the woman shoved herself through the doorway. Drawing her woolen shawl tightly over her shoulders, she shouted while pointing north, "The widda will help ya! The Widda Brunswick." She thrust her waving hand into the cold air and gestured to indicate a winding road up a steep incline. "Top of the mountain she is. Get now, before ya freeze!"

Wilfred watched as she gestured for her husband to shut the door against the wind, and he did so in surly agreement.

Without another word, Wilfred found himself alone in the approaching darkness, which was not the cloak of night but rather of storm clouds wending their way across the island. The snow swirled heavily, and thick layers covered the ground.

Turning his forlorn horse away, Wilfred mounted and began the ride up the mountainside, switch-backing as he lost the path. He began to fear falling off the edge, but just as his horse was on the point of exhaustion and his nerves nearly spent with anxiety, he saw not the humble abode of some poor widow but the outline of a great walled fortress and the parapets of an imposing castle. With a determination born of desperation, he made his way to the tightly barred wooden doors.

He took the hanging wooden mallet and began to pound throbbing blows against it. In the howling wind, it seemed as if he made no noise at all, and his spirit, faint with hunger and cold, began to fall again. But just as he turned to look for a sheltered wall to lean against, the sound of wood and metal grated against his ears.

A man shouted, "Who's there?"

Wilfred yelled over the howling wind, "A lost traveler! Please allow me shelter for just one night."

The massive doors swung open.

Wilfred found himself out of the wind's reach. He fell forward as the weight of the storm suddenly lifted.

The ruddy face of a middle-aged man appeared in the doorway. The man, nearly the same age as his father, carried himself with the bulky force of a body well used to heavy labor.

Wilfred stared in shock. *He could snap a tree trunk in half.*

The man stared back with an appraising gaze. "So, what are ya doing out in the middle of a storm?"

"I'm lost. Heading out to sea, but the ships weren't—"

The man shook his head. "You're poor and hungry that's for certain. Aye, the Widow will see to your needs, though why she does is more than I can tell. You're the fifth one today. Perhaps she's building up an account of good deeds. Hah!" He grinned, revealing a set of crooked teeth. "I don't know my religion well, but if the master's fate is still in doubt despite all her efforts, well, it's not her fault, is it? If he doesn't arrive in paradise, I'm a thinking she'll make it, and to own the truth, that'll be the better for the rest of us." He turned and gestured abruptly, ordering Wilfred to follow along smartly.

Snow fell in the inner courtyard, but the wind was not so fierce. Wilfred appraised the imposing structure towering before him. He had never seen the likes of it in his life. He had imagined that every seaport was a busy, colorful place, as men described it, but he quickly understood that, in truth, ports were very much like people: each one a bit different. He led his horse forward, and soon a youth came to take the reins and direct the animal to a large, warm stable. Wilfred hesitated, wondering if he should follow the horse or stay with the porter.

The burly man shouted back, "Hurry now or miss your supper!"

Relieved beyond measure, Wilfred hustled along. He soon found himself inside the shelter of a warm, well-lit kitchen with a great fire and a large wooden table with several other wayfarers already drinking to their hearts' content. Wilfred's romantic heart sprang back to life, and he flushed with the warmth of fresh excitement. A hot cup was placed within his reach, and he was told to sit down; there'd be food in a bit. The smell of roasting meat and bread baking in the oven tantalized his nose as well as his stomach.

Wilfred slouched down and sipped the strong ale, wiped his face of all wet, and let his hood and cloak fall off his shoulders. Rubbing his hands together, he stared at the warm fire, which spat and hissed to the tune of fat joints sizzling on the enormous spit. All the horrible cold and fear melted with the bits of snow off his clothing, and he smiled warmly, looking around the room, wondering but not really caring why everyone else sat idly by. There were shouts from the main hall, and he could hear rough voices bantering and challenging each other during the long, stormy evening.

Wilfred half considered looking into the next room, but he remembered the woman's determined look when she spoke of the "widda," and the fierce argument between her and the man. Could there be any danger here? Certainly not. The cold and the wind were much worse. Wilfred leaned back against the solid wall and slid into a comfortable repose.

Suddenly, a shout jolted him to attention, and all the kitchen folk bestirred, rising to their feet.

The lady of the manor had come to offer the blessing before the meal. Wilfred roused himself and rubbed his eyes, attempting to stand, but his cloak caught on the edge of the table, and he was trapped in a half-standing position.

The lady strolled into the room with several men on either side. She looked about and offered her welcome. "I wish you all a good meal and better fortune in your travels. May the God of heaven bless you and this food you are about to consume. But please, before you eat, remember my husband in your prayers and ask God to keep his soul safe."

All bowed their heads in hasty attempts to please their benefactress.

Wilfred tried once more to free his cloak, but his awkward efforts caught the lady's eye. Wilfred gazed at her, embarrassed at first, then astonished, for there in front of him stood the very likeness of Lady Nadine.

~~~

Widow Brunswick eyed the youth in front of her. He looked like no one in particular, though there was
~~~

something familiar about his eyes. She also noted his red-faced embarrassment. *Oh, but youth are always so strange.*

She'd never had any children. Her husband would probably have liked to have had a son, but she hated the thought of pregnancy, and the idea of a wet nurse made her shudder. It was hard enough when her serving women were so afflicted. They had to be sent away and a replacement found, and it was always challenging to break in a new servant. She did her duty in making sure that everyone who came under her care had food and warm clothing. *That* was quite enough. But she noticed the stare the young man gave her, and she was determined to find out what it meant.

As soon as the evening meal ended, she sent her man, Demetrius, to see if the boy was still in her home, although considering the weather, she was fairly certain he could be no place else.

She paced across her lavish bedroom and met her servant at the door. "Bring the boy here. But clean him up, will you? I hate the smell of unwashed boy; you know I do. It makes me ill."

Demetrius, a well-trained Greek servant, acknowledged this truth stoically and turned to his duty.

"Oh, one other thing…."

Demetrius lifted one eyebrow, a smile of understanding in his eyes.

"Stay near in case I need you."

Demetrius nodded and bowed gracefully out of the room.

It was ridiculous to ask; he always stayed close by. In truth, he was nearer to her than anyone.

After the boy had received a proper scrubbing, Demetrius showed Wilfred to the anteroom. Even through the doorway, his voice was clear and determined as he instructed the youth, "Widow Brunswick will attend to you in a moment. She's a busy woman."

After a moment, with a loud and pointed, "Ahem, you may come in," he announced her readiness to receive guests.

Wilfred stepped into her room and met her gaze. His eyes widened.

Her mind racing, the Widow Brunswick knew too much to let any secret pass unchecked. "So, young man, tell me about yourself. You were caught in a storm and waylaid here by accident?"

Wilfred bowed, recited his name, his father's name, and little else.

Pieces of the puzzle fell into place the moment Wilfred mentioned Melchior's name. Now that she had a close look, she could see that the resemblance started at the eyes but didn't end there.

The Widow Brunswick had not been born wealthy, but she had been born beautiful, and that was worth as much as gold. She had been lucky enough to catch the eye of a powerful man and, like many young girls, she was married off. Already pretty and demure, she gave herself an air of respectability by acquiring the practices of Christianity, though her husband never became a believer.

After a great deal of suffering, she found that prayers offered more than pretense, they offered hope. Her husband had laughed at her strange habits, but that did not matter. She had fared well with her barbarian husband because while she found solace in faith, he discovered her unexpected strength.

The Widow Brunswick was Osborn's wife's sister, Nikolas and Lady Nadine's aunt. She knew her niece well, for they traveled in the same circles, and they both suffered from similar fates. At one time, they lived near enough that Lady Nadine had confided her darkest secrets to her.

Sixteen years ago, Lady Nadine had become pregnant, and she was horrified by the prospect of having another child. She already had a daughter, Corliss, and she had seen how her husband adored her. She feared this child would be a boy, and she hated the idea of her husband warping a son.

She turned to her neighbor, Melchior's wife, Edwina, and poured out her despair. Edwina told her that God would send a solution in His own good time. Neither of them suspected what that solution would be.

Months later, both women went into labor and brought sons into the world. Against Lady Nadine's wishes, her son lived, and against Edwina's dearest desire, her son died. When Lady Nadine was told of Edwina's tragedy, she carried her babe to Edwina and convinced her neighbor to switch the living for the dead. She advised Edwina to tell Melchior that the baby had only appeared dead but then rose again as a blessing from God. In her blind grief at losing her son and at Lady Nadine's insistence that she would kill her son otherwise, Edwina accepted the living babe. And the switch was made.

The child grew, and Melchior never knew that Wilfred was not of his flesh and bone. Lord Gerard grieved, never suspecting that the well-tended grave of his son really contained the remains of another man's child.

Upon hearing whispers and rumors, Widow Brunswick suspected the truth, and she confronted her niece. The young mother denied it. Some months later, Widow Brunswick's husband was awarded a large piece of land with a castle up north. They dutifully took possession.

Now many years later, that very same baby, grown to manhood, stood before her. But what was he doing here in the middle of a snowstorm?

Widow Brunswick refused to be in the dark for long.

Chapter Eight

Rest in Peace

Lord Gerard's shoulder twitched as he marched at the head of his wife's funeral procession. He brushed his shoulder, unnerved but trying not to show it as he wiped away what felt like the touch of his deceased wife's bony hand. He did not care for anyone else to know, but he could not abide gravesites; thus, he could not, with any level of comfort, attend his wife's funeral. But attend it he must. It was mostly ceremonial, involving a bevy of women who wailed wonderfully or woefully in accordance with their pay; skilled chanters, also paid, who sang well-versed chants that could stir the heart to incredible heights or depths, and the high priests, with their various incantations beseeching the spirits of the dead to rest in peace—and to never come among the living again.

The problem was not that Lord Gerard didn't believe in these ceremonies, but rather that he believed in them too much to be comfortable anywhere near a corpse. He saw no problem with dispatching a man or even an occasional woman, but he certainly didn't want to be around when the spirits rose to ascend to their new abode, wherever that might be.

When this supernatural event was supposed to occur, Lord Gerard was never certain. His wife used to say that it happened at the moment of death, but his old father had cheerfully reported that it was not for a full three days after the body had ceased to breathe. Because of all the delays—the investigation by King Radburn, the arrangements for the funeral procession, and the wait for his hideous brother, Richard, to show up—the dreaded event had been delayed for three full days. Despite the drop in temperature, the body was no longer safe to leave unburied.

By the time the procession began, Lord Gerard's nerves were pitched to the breaking point. He had not slept well the whole time she lay in the room nearest his chambers, where everyone imagined he would want the body, though that was the last place in the world he would want it. In fact, if he had been able to toss her body into a swamp the first night, he would have done so. Fear of being caught in the act kept him from actually attempting it. That his wife's spirit was hovering somewhere near, he was ghastly certain. He tried once again to brush the grizzle fingers away in as inconspicuous a manner possible.

His brother, Richard, only a few feet away, gave him a startled look, their eyes meeting only for an instant.

Freezing drizzle fell from a gray sky, and the crowd mourned at a brisk pace. This, Lord Gerard encouraged with a right good will. He had made sure that the procession started at noon, for he felt certain that when the sun was at its highest and brightest, the disembodied spirits were forced to hide in regions lowest and farthest. He kept his head tilted as far away from his wife's brier as he could without actually appearing to disdain the remains of his beloved. Six men carried her remains, though one could have done it easily; she had always been a thin, light, little thing.

Strange, I've never been intimidated by her before, but now that her body is a mere shell of decaying flesh, she's more terrifying than a host of blood-lusting Celtic raiders. He shook his head at the incongruity and raised his hand to brush her bony fingers off his shoulder.

Blast the stars out of the sky, Richard is watching!

His brother stepped next to him and peered with concerned eyes. "All right?"

Lord Gerard rubbed his shoulder. "Just a bit stiff."

Richard's gaze swept to the professional mourners.

Lord Gerard strode across the snow-blown moor toward the family gravesite that, new as it was, still had a fair number of cairns. Maintaining a steady pace, his mind went back to the day of the festival and how immensely proud he had felt. He had played a good hand with the "Master of Arrogance," as he liked to refer to his soon-to-be son-in-law.

He had never liked Lord Marlow, but he did love his daughter, and in return, Corliss appeared to love him. She had readily agreed to marry Lord Marlow. Since he was the richest man around, save the king, the whole arrangement had seemed ideal, although deep inside, he harbored a few gnawing doubts.

Lord Gerard blushed with chagrin as the image of Wilfred's face filled his mind. Corliss had not only tricked Lord Marlow into believing that she was in love with him, but she had also tricked her father into believing that she was not in love with anyone else.

Thrusting aside all other concerns, Lord Gerard focused on the funeral. Lady Nadine was laid to rest under an impressive cairn of white stones. He insisted that the stack of stones be twice as high as any other, so that no animal would bother her slumber, and so that *he* could finally get some sleep.

As the funeral concluded, Lord Gerard turned homeward for a large drink of the strongest ale ever brewed.

When bony fingers clutched his shoulder, he nearly jumped out of his skin.

"Hello, Gerard. It's been a long time. Sorry about your wife. If you need...anything."

Lord Gerard clenched his teeth and glanced around as the assembled mourners broke into small groups and headed for home in much the same way as attendants at a festival, after the last course has been served and the last game played, shuffle homeward. He rolled his arm, releasing his overwrought shoulder from his brother's embrace.

"Thank you, Richard. I appreciate your offer, though I mean to hang the murderer if it's the last thing I do."

As a tall, muscled man given to long silences and deep pondering, Richard peered at his brother with a penetrating expression.

Lord Gerard shrank from the attempt to plumb his depths. Their father, Gordon the Gifted, was given to loud curses and sly winks. As he could outdrink and outswear any man alive, he was considered blessed by the gods—hence the appellation "gifted." Now that his father was dead, his uncles had moved on to other lands, and his wife had been murdered, Lord Gerard preferred to focus on matters at hand. He sighed and turned away.

Again gripping his brother's arm, Richard held his brother back. "Tell me, Gerard, do you know why the young man wanted to kill your wife?"

Lord Gerard rolled his eyes and started away. "The boy was making eyes at my daughter. Lady Nadine probably scolded him. He grew angry and killed her."

Richard's long legs kept pace with his brother. He stroked his chin. "But I heard that the boy is the son of Melchior, you know, the father—"

Lord Gerard halted and glared. "I know the boy and his father! I let Wilfred roam my lands freely. He followed my men about like a puppy, and I was willing to help him on his way in the world—preferably out to sea—but I wasn't blind to his faults. His boldness toward my daughter was inexcusable. She may have encouraged him, but still, he had no right—no right at all!"

"But if he loved your daughter, all the more reason *not* to kill your wife."

Lord Gerard tromped across the courtyard. "Who says a man in the heat of passion makes sense? Besides, I was there, wasn't I? I saw my wife stagger; she fell into my arms—" Suddenly, Lord Gerard stopped. He looked hard into his brother's face. "Let it be! My men will find the boy and take care of the matter. She's in the ground now, and as far as I'm concerned, the faster we settle with the murderer, the faster this will be over and done." Lord Gerard charged through the manor entrance and stomped up the stone steps.

With pounding steps, Richard followed him inside the manor. "Don't you even want to see the boy before your men hang him?"

Lord Gerard hurled back a single word as he hurried to his room. "No!"

~~~

Richard shook his head. *Strange. Why would Wilfred kill the mother of the woman he loved, the daughter of a man who was generous with him?* He meandered up the steps leading to his guest room. *Stranger still that my brother says that his wife fell into his arms...a man she hated.*
~~~

Chapter Nine

Corliss

Corliss paced her room in a frenzy of uncontrolled fury. "I'll never sleep again, I'll never eat again, and I'll never marry that horrible man!"

She had refused to walk with her father in the funeral procession, refused to see her soon-to-be husband, and had slapped every servant who had come within arm's reach.

Her mother's murder horrified her, and though she knew that Wilfred could not have done the deed, she was certain that he would pay the ultimate price. He was a handsome man who loved her, and that was enough to make him pleasant to be around. She did not care much for Lord Marlow, but his wealth and position made him simply too good to refuse.

A jealous man, Lord Marlow was fully capable of arranging matters so that Wilfred would be blamed for murder and killed without question. Her mother's life would be a small price to pay for revenge.

Corliss wrung her hands and threw herself on her bed as an ache throbbed in her chest and nausea boiled. "Poor boy! To be hung must be an awful thing! Men chasing you—grabbing you, flinging you to the ground, beating you, and then wrapping a thick rope about your neck!" She put her hand to her throat and imagined a rope squeezing the life out of her. She screamed.

Heavy pounding on her door silenced Corliss.

"Let me in, or I'll bash this door to the ground!" Lord Marlow was rarely in a jesting mood.

Corliss considered her options. If he were capable of

killing her mother, then would he not be capable of killing *her* if she displeased him? Was marrying for position and wealth really worth the risk? She stared at the closed door, grateful for the thick wood between them. "I don't feel well. Go away!"

"I will not! I'll be hanged if you tell me what to do!"

Panic shot through Corliss. He had never used that expression before. Did the image of hanging dangle as heavily in his imagination as it did in hers? She scurried to the door and released the bolt.

Flinging the door open, Lord Marlow stomped into the room, his expression black as thunder. "We know where the murderer is hidden."

Backing up, Corliss could feel the thick, prickly rope about her neck. Her legs trembled. "Yes?"

"He was heading toward the Widow Brunswick's castle!"

Her back against the wall, Corliss frowned, perplexed. "What does that mean? Is he safe then?"

"Safe from justice?" Lord Marlow seethed with fury.

Corliss stared at her betrothed, terror seeping through her limbs.

Scratching his bushy chin, Lord Marlow softened his voice. "Tell me, woman, what do you mean?"

When a man asks a question in a softened voice, he wants to discover something he already suspects. *Was he using me as much as I was using him?* She cringed. "I merely meant that Wilfred should have a chance to explain himself. Perhaps he didn't kill my mother."

Leaning in, Lord Marlow towered over Corliss. "Keep your mind on what you know best, the arrangements for our wedding." He glanced away. "We shouldn't wait. I'll speak to your father, but I think he'll agree. The sooner we wed the better."

Corliss stifled a scream.

Lord Marlow grabbed her, his fingers digging into her arm.

She jerked away, flinging off his touch. She scurried to the other side of the room, near the door. "I'm upset about losing my mother, and I don't want to get married now." She lifted her head high, and though her courage faltered, she heard her words as if they came from another person. "I won't marry you, after all. I've changed my mind."

"You don't mean that. Your mother was just murdered. Someone might come after *you* next."

Corliss peered into his eyes and saw not slavish devotion but a brutish fury. Had she never looked into his eyes the whole time they had known each other? Or had she never looked far enough to see into his heart?

As a small child, her parents had taken her for a winter walk near a frozen pond. Her mother warned her not to go onto the thin ice, but she didn't care. She stomped up and down in defiance of the good advice. The ice held—at first. But when she brought her foot down the third time, it cracked beneath her. Regardless of her fear, she braced her nerves against every natural impulse and sauntered up to her mother and smiled at her.

Now, as she looked into the eyes of the man she had to marry, she shivered.

Chapter Ten

Prove Entertaining

—OldEarth—

Cerulean stood with a gray cape about his peasant tunic in the Widow Brunswick's outer courtyard, rubbing his frozen hands together. He couldn't believe his luck. Good or bad, the concept of chances bewildered him. Though as he stared at Sterling blatantly snuggling against Mauve in broad daylight, he suspected that he had the worst luck possible. *A Supreme Guardian should know better! We're here to make a formal inter-alien report concerning humanity's development, and Sterling doesn't even seem to care.*

Dramatic throat-clearing turned Cerulean's attention.

Despite Sterling's wealthy merchant attire, a thickset guard glared at the Sterling and Mauve's open-air romance. "You two better watch yourselves, or there'll be hell to pay." As he studied Mauve's full-figured beauty wrapped in a richly embroidered dress, his brows lowered and bunched. "There's not a man inside who wouldn't take to you, darlin', but your gent there will get the worst end of—"

A heavy bell bonged, scattering his dire concern.

Cerulean glanced at the castle tower.

Every man, woman, and child came to a halt and bowed their heads. A general murmur rose as voices joined in prayer.

After the final amen, heads lifted, and the throng progressed through the gated entry.

Cerulean jogged up to the guard. "What was that?"

Jerking his head back as if struck, the middle-aged man stared. “You’re barbarians, then?” He nodded at Sterling who strolled away with Mauve’s hand encased in his own. “Noticed you didn’t pray the Angelus either. Best stay in the shadows before someone decides to interrogate your purpose in these parts.” He waved them on, gusting air between his lips.

Once inside the inner courtyard, women with bundles flung over drooping shoulders and children leading stubborn goats poured down avenues abutted against merchants’ shops.

The scent of baking bread tickled Cerulean’s nose. “Let’s get something to eat before we meet Teal and Zuri.”

Three chattering women occupied a rustic bench outside a bakery shop. An artistic sign in green and red, Bakewell’s Bread & Ale House, hung above the front door.

Mauve sidled up and peered down her nose at the comfortable women.

They paid no mind until the youngest of the three tipped back her head and considered the buxom beauty tapping her foot impatiently.

Mauve swelled in size, her face darkening.

The young woman’s eyes widened in alarm, and she shot to her feet.

Sterling stood back, smiling.

Assessing Mauve’s luxurious dress, intimidating stare, and disturbing abilities, the three women arrived at a silent agreement and hurried off.

Happy as a conquering cat, Mauve released her breath and pounced on the bench. She patted the space next to her.

Sterling strolled over and perched on the edge.

Having not the least desire to squeeze into the small

space left, Cerulean dug coins from a deep pocket. "I'll get us something to eat." He tromped inside the dark shop and ordered bread, cheese, and cider.

A girl with extraordinarily broad shoulders stepped up next to him, eyeing his every move.

Annoyed, Cerulean ignored her.

A servant paced forward, inspected his coins, and then waved him to the door. "I'll bring a tray out."

Uncertain about the money he had offered, Cerulean swallowed his question and turned to go.

The broad-shouldered girl grabbed his arm. "You paid too much."

Cerulean glanced from her gloved hand to her face. "Nova?"

She furrowed her brows. "How'd you guess?"

Pursing his lips, Cerulean smacked her clutching fingers off his arm and started forward. "Gloves like that haven't been invented yet." He stepped into the bright sunshine and searched for Sterling and Mauve. "You must be more careful." The empty bench sent alarm bells racing through him. "Where'd they go?"

Nova tugged off her gloves and pointed to a large tree. "Over there."

Mauve chatted with three long-haired, hulking men while Sterling stood by glowering, his arms crossed high over his chest.

Cerulean bit his lip. He peered at Nova. "You were supposed to meet your father at Melchior's house, weren't you?"

Nova shrugged. "Yes. But I wanted to look around first. Mom always wants to know what I'm doing. It takes forever to get it through her primitive brain that I'm fine. When I meet Zuri, he can explain it to her." With a dramatic eye-roll, Nova snorted. "You'd think I'd never been off-planet before. I can't wait till I'm fully autonomous."

Cerulean blinked in the noon-day light, confusion blurring his thoughts. *As in alone? Why would any sane person want that?*

Nova nudged him. "Looks like Mauve might be in for more than she can handle."

One of the three men had sidled in close and wrapped his arm around Mauve's shoulder, while another played with the hem of her dress, lifting it in a daring tease. The other man chuckled, clearly waiting his chance.

Sterling flushed, glowing red around the edges.

Oh, no. Not good. Cerulean jogged forward with Nova at his side.

Sterling glared from Cerulean to Nova and mouthed the words, "Do something!"

Like a determined bather crashing through ocean waves, Nova muscled her way into the midst of the three flirting men and grabbed Mauve's arm. "Come now, the apothecary awaits. Your treatment isn't finished."

The three men jumped back, disgust curling their lips.

Cerulean had to clamp his lips together to maintain a sober demeanor.

Without a backward glance, the three men hustled away.

A pout formed on Mauve's face. "I was just starting to have fun." She shrugged and pointed to a servant carrying a tray laden with bread and cheese in one arm and a jug in the other. "Is that our food?"

Cerulean huffed. "Yes, but now that Nova is here, we can meet up with—"

Mauve waved him off. "After we eat. I'm dying to try everything!" She licked her lips as she accepted the tray.

Sterling stood back, uncertain.

Nova plucked the jug from the startled servant, yanked off the cork, and lifted it to her lips. After a hearty swig, she wiped her chin. "Not bad. Though not quite acidic enough."

The servant stared at Nova, his mouth gaping.

Cerulean peered at his three fellow travelers, squeezed his eyes shut, and wondered why he had ever left home. *I want to become a guardian but not with these idiots.*

~~~

Tarragon, a wide cape around his portly body and a scarf covering his modified breathing helm, plodded toward a large wood pile and nodded at the man wielding the ax. "Ingot Zuri, I presume?"

Dressed in a stained peasant tunic, Zuri wiped sweat from his brow and swept his gaze up and down Tarragon's form. "You think that's native sensitive? Humans will know something is amiss the second they see you." He peered across the field to Melchior's manor home as servants bustled in and out the kitchen doorway.

A vulture soared silently overhead, and a cow mooed from a distant field. Two black cats raced across the grass.

A small child toddled through the garden gate and entered the field. Its wonder-filled eyes fixed on Tarragon.

As if brushing a fly away, Tarragon tapped his arm three times.

The child fell to the ground.

Zuri's eyes bulged, and his jaw clenched. "What'd you do that for?" He sprinted forward.

"Move another step, and I'll stun you, too."

Zuri froze. Slowly, he turned and met Tarragon's gaze.

"I hated to demonstrate, but you didn't leave me much choice." Tarragon shrugged. "Being a Cresta is usually an advantage, but when dealing with such limited terrestrial beings, I have to make necessary adaptations. I may not fit in exactly, but my stunner makes up for small
~~~

deficiencies."

Arriving from around a thatch shed, Teal strolled toward them. He lifted his hand in salute. "You surprise me, Tarragon. Most Cresta can't get past their superiority to see their deficiencies."

Teal patted Zuri's arm. "Don't be so horrified, my friend. Ark was one of a kind." He narrowed his gaze at Tarragon. "If I ever see you stun another human being, I'll report you to the Ingal. They won't take nicely to breaches in diplomatic relations with the Luxonian Supreme Council."

Though cold by nature, Tarragon felt a chill spread over his body. Not an unpleasant sensation. "I sent a spy-rodent into their feasting hall last night to get a feel for the place. Most interesting. Haven't risen much above the mammal population, have they?"

"Your personal assessments do not give you leave to stun them because you've failed to take proper precautions." Zuri hefted his ax over his shoulder. "I'm going to check on the child."

Jogging forward, Teal intercepted him. "No, let me. You've still got too much Ingot around the eyes to fool anyone—no matter what story you make up." Perfecting his humanoid figure, Teal trotted forward, glancing over his shoulder. "Stay put. I'll be right back."

Tarragon tilted his head and considered the two specimens before him. *If humanity fails to interest me, at least these two should prove entertaining.*

Chapter Eleven

Martha

Melchior placed a letter aside and peered out the window of his room, waiting for what fate inevitably held in store for him. He hated to acknowledge it, but he did have an older sister, Martha. Their mother, Freda, had wanted to name her Mary in honor of Jesus' good friend, but Melchior's father, Jeremiah, insisted that while Our Lord needed a faithful woman, *he* also needed a good cook, and of the two sisters Martha seemed the better choice.

Martha, true to her namesake, *was* a good cook. By all accounts, she was an excellent cook and proficient at running a household. When Melchior's brothers died and their mother passed on, she took care of all the household details. But then she married and moved away just before invaders made off with much of their family lands and fortunes.

If she had stayed, the invaders wouldn't have walked all over her as they did her father and brother. She may not have been a man, but she was almost as strong and certainly as bull-headed.

When his wife, Edwina, had died, Martha had bustled home with all due speed to manage everything. She trained the girls to take over where their mother had left off. With the household settled, she returned home, and the subsequent years passed with nary a word.

Managing her own affairs was an all-consuming task—but when gossip reached her ear that Wilfred had been accused of the murder of Lady Nadine, she wrote that she must come to assist him once again.

When Melchior learned of her imminent arrival, he

swallowed hard, then called for Adele and Oliver. "*Do* something!" But the two merely ginned, obviously relieved at the thought of Martha's energetic return.

Early on the fifth day after Wilfred's disappearance, Melchior's spirits sank as he peered out his window and perceived his sister's portly figure astride a stout horse riding into his yard. Everyone else, except a few servants, still slumbered in peaceful repose.

Martha, unable to abide laziness, bustled into the main hall, her arms flying as if she couldn't wait to hug all her nieces and nephews at once, and perhaps shake out a few floor mats at the same time.

"Melchior! Meeelchior! Where are you, Brother?" She looked around at the faces of the few servants who rushed into the room. Her voice carried and strands of gray hair flew almost as freely as her hands. In the early morning light, with her bright red cheeks, disheveled hair, flailing gestures, and bellowing voice, she appeared more like an apparition from the nether world than a close relative.

Before she had a chance to ask the servants what they were staring at, Melchior bestirred himself from where he watched on the upper landing and clumped down the steps. His soft leather slippers flapped, his cap drooped, and his temper flared. "What in Heaven are you screaming about? I heard you before you crossed the threshold! Why, the Earth shook with every footfall! Don't you know how to approach a Christian household?" He then muttered a Bible quote under his breath, "'Better to sit in a corner of the house than with a bawling woman.'"

That was enough of an introduction for Martha. She flung her desperately-in-need-of-something-to-do arms around her brother and laughed and cried at the same time. "Oh, Melchior! I'm so glad to see you. You can't imagine the terrors I imagined on the way here."

Melchior broke from her formidable grip and rubbed his hand across his just-kissed cheek. "I've imagined a few things myself!" But when he saw her sincere expression, he repented of his impatience. "Welcome, Sister. We're glad you've come. I don't know what you'll do with yourself, for my daughters have become as competent as their dear mother in managing—"

"Don't be silly, Brother. When a tragedy like this happens, it's not the household that needs attention but the heart and the mind. We must do all we can to save the boy. He's not guilty—we all know it—but we must find the real murderer!"

As if the sun had exploded, Melchior froze. Nikolas had said as much the night he visited. His legs growing shaky, Melchior needed to sit down.

Martha took charge. "First, you must get dressed and break your fast."

Adele and Oliver stopped on the threshold, while Gilda and Martha squeezed past and ran forward, open-mouthed and grinning at this magnificent stranger.

Her gaze flowing over the children, Martha smiled. "My dear, Adele! You've grown as lovely as your mother. And Oliver, what a fine strapping lad you be! I bet you are good at—everything!"

Oliver blushed.

Martha shook her finger at the little girls. "Baby Gilda! And my darling Martha, my namesake, you must be a good cook!" More hearty laughter. "Where is Thomas—the tiny wee thing—"

Selby plodded forward carrying a screaming Thomas in his arms. "He just woke up and is not happy, as you see."

Martha, with unerring instinct, scooped the child in her arms and peered down at him. "No breakfast unless you stop squalling!"

Thomas craned his neck, his gaze searching the room. He reached out for Oliver.

Oliver stepped out of reach, his hands lifting in surrender.

Martha marched past, directing everyone to the kitchen. “Someone is readying breakfast; I can smell the fire.” She halted and wrinkled her nose. “What, are they burning the pot?”

Without so much as a by-your-leave, she marched to the kitchen, calling over her shoulder, “Melchior, get your body properly covered before we eat!” With that, she could have plowed her way through the Red Sea.

Melchior prayed he wouldn’t sink into the mire.

~~~

Martha slumped on a wooden bench under an old oak tree with a hot mug of mint tea steaming between her entwined fingers. The delicious meal of fried bacon, boiled eggs, and bread slathered with honey had comfortably filled the empty places of her stomach. She felt better for the food, though her heart still ached with dread.

Gilda pranced in the garden, sniffing the very last of the season’s flowers.

Melchior stepped into the doorway.

Before he could dart back inside, Martha patted the bench at her side. “Come, Brother, sit with me awhile! Breakfast should hold you for a few moments, at least.”

Melchior shook his head, his eyes bloodshot and red-rimmed. Reluctance in every feature, he slowly worked his way outside.

Martha scrutinized his slouched shoulders and weary
~~~

face. She gestured to Gilda. "Little one, come here. You were born to run a vast estate! Show me your skills and get your father a good strong brew of the finest strengthening herbs for his blood."

Gilda smiled shyly, nodded, and scurried to the kitchen where all the servants were assembled, eating their own repast.

Martha patted the bench again, daring him to refuse.

Melchior plopped down heavily on the bench. "Go on, then, tell me all the things I've done wrong since you left. How you'd have managed affairs better, never losing the bulk of our family estates, and how Wilfred wouldn't be running for his life at this very moment." He sighed.

Grief as palpable as a lead weight pressed on both their hearts.

For a diversion, Martha stared at a flock of blackbirds. "You know, every year when winter comes, I worry about them." She waved to the birds to clarify her point. "I think to myself, how are they going to manage in the next months when it gets cold and the snow comes? There'll be no fruit or flowers, and they surely don't have any storehouses the way we have...so how will they survive? And when they come to my yard, I always go out and throw them whatever crumbs I may have, and they eat them greedily enough. Yet, I never have enough to feed them all. And I think, ah, but I'll be seeing their poor, pathetic corpses lying about the place before long, it being such a harsh winter, so cold and all."

Martha turned and gazed upon her brother's worn and despairing face. "But, don't you know, I never do. Every year the long winter ends, and the sun and the warmth return. I look around and, yes, here or there, a dead bird or two but nothing like I imagined. Nothing like I thought there ought to be, considering." She sipped her now-cooled tea.

The birds twittered away in the treetops, singing a dozen different songs, and the sky shone in radiant blue hues, which made the heart glad because it was—what it was.

Martha smiled a secret smile. "I love their songs. They're so glad to be alive, and I can't help but be happy for them."

Slumped forward, Melchior glanced at the sky. "I can't hear their song, not now. Not really."

Pressing the cup to her chest, Martha peered at her brother. "You're worn out, Melchior, worn to a mere shred of your former self." She straightened and lifted her voice in authority. "It's true, you've known dire times, but your daughters have turned out wonderfully well, and you ought to be proud of them. I know you've suffered much, but you've also been blessed. Things could have been worse." Martha squeezed his hand gently.

A tear meandered down Melchior's cheek.

"Dear Brother, do not be despondent. Wilfred is under the Widow Brunswick's protection, and if I know anything about that lady, she'll let no harm come to him."

"It is not just Wilfred that upsets me, though that is surely cause enough for alarm, no matter what the Widow Brunswick says or does. It's...how do I explain? I'm a wineskin with no wine left. I am all drained out."

Martha shook her head, bewildered. "What else has happened?"

"I lost the mystery of the universe. I woke up one morning, and I was sure I'd discovered the meaning of my existence, the purpose of all life, but I couldn't remember what it was. Then I remembered I had written it down, but..."

Incredulity struck Martha like a slap in the face.

Melchior shut his mouth, pursing his lips tight.

"Go on, Brother, tell me. What happened? I must hear."

"You shall hear no such thing! Good heavens, I saw your look. I ought to keep my silliness to myself."

Setting the empty cup aside, Martha clasped her brother's hands and rubbed his fingers. She looked him in the eye. "You feel these fingers, Brother? These are the fingers that cared for you as a boy. Like the birds, I find myself confronted with mysteries all the time. I don't know why I was born into this family, yet I was, and I accept the authority of the One who made it so. I yearn to understand better. Maybe I should accept my fate—I am not a great woman made to achieve great things—but Melchior, *you* always had the mark of holiness about you. God protected you, and He did so for a reason. If He gave you some insight, some understanding...do not be afraid. Accept it."

Melchior groaned. Taking back his hands, he covered his face. "But that's just what I can't do, for I've lost it. The vellum I wrote the secret on was blank. I forgot to dip the pen in ink. There were only a few stray marks."

"What did they say?"

"Nothing but nonsense. 'And he showed me a river of water of life, clear as crystal...' At first, I felt joy at the words, the thrill of a secret that I alone knew, but as time unfolded, I find I can't remember my joy. I can barely remember the words. All hopes are barren. Why did I dare think that God had passed such a gift to me? It was an arrogant thought, and I'm justly punished for it. Now all is defeat and utter ruin."

Martha threw her hands up, beseeching heaven. "Ruin? Melchior, let's start with your family—"

Melchior broke in roughly, almost brutally. "My family! Certainly, I have a most capable daughter in Adele. King Radburn has deemed it necessary that *he* look for a husband for *my* daughter. Do you know what he said to my daughter's face in my hearing? 'It will be a challenge!' The King, our wonderful lord and master, jested that it would be a *challenge* to find someone worthy of her, but we all understood his real meaning—that she is not worthy of the best husband and too proud for the worst!"

Melchior slapped his hands together and wrung them, fury obviously building. "And then, look to my eldest son if you will! All the men from coast to coast call him not Oliver, but 'Harried' because he is ruled by others. Then, of course, there's Wilfred, the fool who made love to Lord Gerard's daughter under his very eyes! He may not have killed Lady Nadine, but he'll be lucky if he lives to return home! Poor Gilda is a competent child, but she will fare the same as her sister. While bred for better things, no man but a brute will have her. Martha, your namesake, you ought to take her and raise her as your own. At least then, she might have a chance. And young Thomas is the worst of the lot, raised to be a tyrant in a world of tyrants. He will fight hard in a cutthroat world, and he might just end up with his throat cut."

Martha clenched her hands, no longer attempting to comfort her brother for her mind reeled with the forbidding pictures he had so eloquently drawn.

Melchior sniffed, rubbed his face vigorously, and straightened. His voice softened. "I shouldn't speak to you so. After all, you came here in good faith, and a good help you've always been. You fixed a marvelous meal, and if I had even an ounce of decency, I'd be grateful. I'm in a black mood. Pay me no mind." He stood and sniffed the air. "It smells like snow." He gazed down at his sister. "It is unmanly to give in to despair."

Martha stood also and swung the last drops of her tea upon the ground in a low arc. "Yes, I suppose that's true. Unwomanly as well." She stared up.

The birds sang from a hundred different trees.

She grinned. "You know, I like that saying you remembered...the one about 'the river of life, clear as crystal.' It's beautiful. Not like the kind of beautiful we see with our eyes, but the untouched beauty of the soul—like a newborn baby or a spring day or a bird's song. It's more than what it is—if you know what I mean."

Martha tucked the cup under her arm as she picked up a mat drying in the sun. "Maybe God only gave you that much, not because He wanted to taunt you, but because He knows it's all you really need to know right now. As for the children, I wish yours were mine, but *you* were gifted with them, not me. He has faith in you."

Taking in a deep breath of air, Martha smiled exultantly. "You're right; it is going to snow." She strode back toward the doorway. "And everyone will be hungry as bears before it comes. I'd better get Oliver to bring in extra wood. If you see Adele, tell her to have the men hunt up fresh game. Your stores aren't fit for a long winter, and who knows, but this might be the longest yet. We'd best prepare!" With a renewed song in her heart, Martha bustled into the house.

~~~

Melchior stood alone, brooding through a blank stare where his sister had left him. A tug on his sleeve caught his attention.

Gilda stood before him, bearing a large steaming cup of tea. "Sorry it took me so long. I couldn't find Selby, and Adele was busy, so I asked Chloe, and she took so long getting everything just right. You know how she is." Her eyes brightened. "It should be good. I added plenty of honey, and Chloe swears by the saints above that it'll perk you right up."

Melchior gingerly accepted the hot cup and took a
~~~

tentative sip. He tried not to grimace. His daughter didn't need to see his misery laid bare. "It tastes good. I'm sure I'll be outrunning Thomas soon." He forced a disarming smile, but as she remained by his side, he scrambled for something to say. "When did Chloe get back? I thought she was tending to her mother?"

"Her mother died, and then she had to manage her brothers."

Melchior's grip slipped, and the hot liquid burned his fingertips. "Manage them—how?"

Gilda skipped toward the faded flowers again. She bent low and sniffed a flower whose scent had long since departed. "Put them into service. One went to a blacksmith, one to the butcher, and the last to Lord Gerard's men."

A shiver rose over Melchior. "She sent her brother into the service of that—"

"He was willing to train him properly."

Melchior closed his eyes as the hot cup burned his fingers. He could hardly imagine one of his own sons raised by that vicious man. He swallowed hard. In Wilfred's case, he had done worse. He had let him be raised, not by the lord himself, but by the lord's lesser men. Bile rose, nearly choking him.

He glanced at his daughter and appraised her beautiful body bending to each flower in turn, getting her fill of their faded loveliness before the snow covered them.

"Go in and assist your aunt. We must help her so she can help us."

Gilda faced her father. "Finished your tea, then?"

Melchior swallowed the last drops and offered the empty cup.

With it in hand, she strolled lazily into the dark interior.

Melchior stopped on the threshold and looked over his shoulder.

A bird sang with joyful abandon, and the scent of snow filled the air. Wearily, he stepped inside.

Chapter Twelve

Neighbors

Nikolas sat on a fallen log on the outer edge of a ravine in the valley between Melchior's home and Lord Gerard's manor, eating the last of his midday meal: a thick piece of chewy bread and a thin piece of dried meat.

Despite the bright sun, a cold wind raised goosebumps on his arms. If he had known what dark secrets his investigation would bring to light, he might have stayed safely and ignorantly at home.

After hearing all that Melchior and his family had to tell him, he had interviewed the servants, asking questions and trying to imagine in his mind's eye what happened from various points of view. Now, he had a pretty accurate idea of where everyone had been, except for the most critical moments when Lady Nadine had disappeared from Gilda's sight.

He could not be sure where Lord Gerard had been during those last moments of his wife's life. Those who saw him said that he had spoken to several of his men and then ran outside. *They* said, *he* said, he'd heard someone call his name, but where he went and what he did, no one knew.

Any hope of justice for his sister and any possible future for Wilfred depended on him now. He must be bold enough to do the unthinkable: to go to Lord Gerard's manor, ask for admittance, and interview the great and ruthless lord himself about that terrible day in the hopes of ferreting out the truth. He realized with harsh clarity that his status as Lady Nadine's brother would carry no weight at all, for Lord Gerard would see him for what he was—a poor merchant who had not visited his sister for many years.

Nikolas rubbed his chin. He could go to Lord Gerard's kitchen servants and ask what they knew. Possibly, he could offer some of his wares in return for information.

The image of his deserted shop rose in his mind. Leaving it idle all week was certainly a good way to get plundered. *Lord, I need help.*

With a deep sigh, Nikolas stood. There were no cowards in his family, and he didn't want to disgrace his father's memory by refusing to try every means available to discover his sister's murderer and save a friend from an untimely death. Instead of continuing west, Nikolas turned north.

In the northlands, a fierce black-haired and brown-eyed middle-aged Celt named Nolan managed not only to keep ahold of all of his land, despite invasions, but he even expanded his territory by kidnapping, one by one, nearly all of his neighbors. He kept them well entertained in as charming a manner as he could muster, but without granting them the pleasure of freedom for the necessary number of days needed to arrange a transaction. He always managed to wring out an agreeable concession and pay some meager token in coin or cattle, though no one ever said the trade was worth the uncomfortable process. "Rather like having your tooth extracted," said one landowner.

Nikolas shared a small sliver of earth with Nolan, but the Celt never tried to get any concessions from him. He always said that Nikolas' land was too small to carve up, and besides, if he needed something from him, he had other things worth bargaining for.

Still, Nolan held a certain charm. One bitter day in the dead of winter three years ago, Nikolas had become deathly ill, and had no one to care for him. When apprised of the situation, Nolan ordered Nikolas brought to his home, made sure he was well cared for, and prevented plunderers for decimating his shop during his confinement. Dumbfounded by this kindness, Nikolas wondered if the Celt was a secret Christian, but the man protested, claiming that he merely hated to see an innocent man suffer without any decent profit.

The evening shadows had lengthened considerably by the time Nikolas appeared at Nolan's door. The servant bowed low and invited him inside with a wave. "The master is interviewing a man."

Stopping on the threshold of the main hall, Nikolas blinked at the scene before him.

Clearly having the advantage, Nolan pressed his foot on the chest of a medium-sized, yellow-haired man. Both men dripped with sweat.

Deciding he'd do better to arrive at another time, Nikolas took a step backward.

Nolan glanced up. "My friend! You're just the man I wished to see!"

Nikolas hesitated.

"It's not what it looks like! I'm questioning this fellow. Just want to see if he has what it takes to become one of my men." He considered the man and sighed. "He said he was a mercenary from Rome." Nolan grinned. "No wonder they ran!"

Nikolas wondered if madness ran in Nolan's family.

The Celt lifted his foot and waved the fool away. He shouted after the retreating figure, "If you mean to plunder or slaughter me, you'd best learn how to stay on your feet first."

After charging across the hall and flinging his arm around Nikolas—who couldn't help casting one pitying look at the departing figure—Nolan muttered, "Things aren't always what they seem, are they now?"

Considering that he had come here with the express purpose of becoming *less* baffled, Nikolas decided to solve one mystery at least. "Why was he here? Was it really to—?"

Nolan grinned, showing the gap where one of his teeth used to live. "He was caught wandering my lands. *Said* he'd heard I was in need of a strong guard." Nolan shook his head, the picture of an honest man weary of lies. "But he was sent by someone to do mischief—not to rob, of course, for what I have can't be carried off, but to gather some proof of my supposed wrong-doing so they can bring charges against me and accuse me of nefarious crimes."

Nikolas stopped before the kindled hearth, as if that might help him think clearly. "But why accuse you? Wouldn't it be easier just to kill you?"

Nolan squared his shoulders. "Not so easy as you imagine! Besides, even these marauding villains like to feel good about themselves. What these fools want is my reputation. They want to make me look guilty so that they can be free to hunt me down like an animal. Nasty, they are!"

With his large hand placed on Nikolas' back, Nolan turned Nikolas toward his large, well-appointed tables. "When was the last time you ate, my lad?" Without waiting for an answer, Nolan sucked in a deep breath and stretched his arms wide. "My, but a good thrashing always makes me hungry!"

After a large dinner, followed by a long and rambling walk with Nolan charging through the bracken as if enemies lurked behind every leaf, and then the better part of three cups of ale back at the hall, Nikolas finally found the courage to tell Nolan about his present predicament.

Nolan took the information in stride. "I know Lord Gerard well enough. We are almost neighbors, you know, but not quite. Lucky for him." Nolan gulped his drink as they sat before a roaring fire, the wind whipping over the thatched roof and under the eaves.

Nikolas appraised his surroundings in the comfort of a gentle haze and the cheerful glow of the firelight.

Nolan could have had a much grander house, but he believed his wealth was in his land, not his house. He did not have a wife yet, though he was looking. He had considered a fair number of women, but he always changed his mind at the last moment. He had earned a fine reputation as an eccentric, and few maidens rose to the challenge. Even fewer fathers wanted him as a son-in-law, though some were willing to make a deal if they could get their lands back. Nolan only laughed at those offers.

His home was a humble affair, four ample rooms with a large garden in back, a small garden out front, and acres upon acres of rambling woods, lush green hills, verdant valleys, and a couple of meandering streams. Nolan also kept a large number of slaves and a few servants to manage his various trades; this included farmhands, goat herders, house servants, a quality head cook, a notable metalsmith, and several skilled weapons makers. He treated everyone in the same brusque manner, and though the servants were supposedly freer than the slaves, neither group felt they had much choice as to their future. Yet, because Nolan loved to eat, and he knew it took a healthy body to do a good day's work, he always fed his servants and slaves well. He was generous to those he took a liking to. Those slaves, servants, churls, or thanes he found irritating, he sent away.

Nolan tapped Nikolas on the knee. "Now, as to this matter with Lord Gerard, don't you worry; I know just what to do. In the morning, we'll meet with him. Leave me to handle everything. I'm as interested as you to see the murderer brought to justice, but these things must be handled with care." He winked at Nikolas as he leaned back expansively. "We'll pay a visit to his lordship tomorrow, and then we shall see."

Nikolas' tired eyes closed as his chin fell to his chest. Knowing it was too late to disentangle himself, he stifled a low groan and hoped that Melchior would forgive him.

Chapter Thirteen

Wisdom

"'*Neither shall king, nor tyrant in thy sight inquire about them whom thou hast destroyed.*

For so much then as thou art just, thou orderest all things justly: thinking it not agreeable to thy power, to condemn him who deserveth not to be punished.

For thy power is the beginning of justice: and because thou art Lord of all, thou makest thyself gracious to all.'"

Widow Brunswick's heart fluttered as she sat on a hard chair in her cold room.

"From *The Book of Wisdom*, my Lady." The priest peered at her, his lopsided smile hovering like a bird about to take flight. "I hope you see its significance?"

The Widow Brunswick nodded in a stately manner. She did see, but she had not yet decided if she wanted her priest to know that. She liked to keep others in the dark concerning deep matters. Still, she liked this man, this Father Caedmon. Though he was old, he stood straight and took his priestly vows seriously—more seriously than some, anyway. He was no humorist, except for the occasional knowing smile. He was a monk by choice but a priest by proclamation.

When she had first come upon him in his woodland hut, he had insisted that he was just a poor servant of God, dedicated to a life to prayer and quiet service and unworthy of any higher calling, but she had thought otherwise. Her husband had been good enough to agree. Besides, an honest man was too valuable to live as a hermit out in the woods, eating only roots and berries.

She saw to his training, bringing in the best tutors available—which was not much in these barbaric lands—but was better than being instructed by deer and squirrels.

"You may go now, Father, and please get some rest. I know you've been up half the night with your prayers again. And I do wish you would eat more. I fear you'll faint away at some inopportune moment."

A smile flittered over the priest's face. How bowed and backed away.

Widow Brunswick stopped him. "Oh, Father, remember to come to dinner *on time*. We are having a guest, and I want you to meet him."

The priest nodded and turned again.

The Widow Brunswick, unable to comprehend his total lack of curiosity, stopped him once more. "Father, don't you want to know who is coming?"

Patience incarnate, Father Caedmon shrugged. "You will tell me, my lady?"

"Since you ask, it is the king himself, King Radburn. Apparently, he is very interested in young Wilfred and wants to see an end to this investigation. Without bloodshed. Which should make you glad."

Father Caedmon's gaze turned inward, grief shadowing his eyes. "Bloodshed is very painful, my lady, but sometimes, it's necessary." He turned to go.

This time, the Widow Brunswick did not stop him.

~~~

Wilfred liked to imagine what it would be like to eat his meals at the high board, dining on dainty slices of meat, chewing luxuriously on various soft breads baked into exotic shapes, biting into deep layers of spice cake with
~~~

sweetened fillings, and sipping exotic wines out of an ornate golden cup. But when it came to the actual process of biting, chewing, and swallowing in the presence of the more elegant members of society, he found that it wasn't as wonderful as he had imagined.

At Lord Gerard's table, he had always felt at home since he was usually seated with the men-at-arms or beside the sailors who had come in from the sea. Pirates and bandits, half of them. Yet, it was all the more fun for that. They were men who knew how to work hard and play hard. They ate and drank as if there were no tomorrow, which made for sporting evenings to be sure. The very idea of table manners was scorned. Everyone talked and ate at the same time, spitting and swallowing, laughing uproariously, slapping others on the arms or backs. If a serving woman came within reach, all considered her fair game.

But now, he found himself in the presence of people who set their table very differently, sat very straight, and ate slowly—very slowly—chewing methodically, as if every bite were meant to last. And perhaps that was no wonder, for they ate the strangest fare, things Wilfred could only guess at. The dishes were so dressed up and smothered in sauce that he had to bend low and sniff to ascertain the ingredients.

The Widow Brunswick's frown informed him that his sniffing was not appreciated, so he sat up straighter and closed his eyes on the first bite, hoping to decipher the food elements from taste alone. But even this trick had deceived him on more than one occasion. He had thanked his hostess for wonderful roast pork when it had been grilled beef, and an excellent boiled hen when it had been sauced fish. He dared not say anything now, for he had been at the Widow Brunswick's home for almost a fortnight, and he was running out of entertaining ways to cover his blunders, hardly surprising, as his stock of charming commentaries had been low to begin with.

Tonight, his skin prickled with anxiety. Not only was Widow Brunswick watching him like a hawk, but also the priest with his wry smile glanced at him out of the corners of his eyes. But worst of all, the king stifled everyone.

His face burned with anxiety. Wilfred knew why King Radburn was here, but did everyone else know? He had never mentioned that he had been accused of Lady Nadine's death, but Widow Brunswick had made no secret of the fact that she had learned of the affair. She explained her connection to the Lady, so Wilfred was dreadfully aware that he was sleeping under the roof of the aunt of the woman he supposedly murdered. He had tried to make an escape by saying that he must be off to sea, but Widow Brunswick had retorted that as long as he was a guest in her house, she would see to his needs and make all the arrangements at the proper time. He had little say in the matter.

A spoon clattered to the floor, and Wilfred looked up.

Demetrius stood stiffly behind Widow Brunswick's chair, glaring at King Radburn.

When Wilfred thought he could not stand one more moment of chewing, chewing, chewing, he nearly jumped out of his skin at the sound of King Radburn's voice.

"So, my young scoundrel, I see you found a place to hide away while Lord Gerard nearly bites his fingers to the bone wanting to get his hands on you."

All chewing stopped.

Wilfred froze, but his instincts told him to make a run for it. He stood and appraised his situation. Demetrius watched his every move. He swept his gaze over the multitude of guards and men-at-arms—the presence of a King demanded as much—and realized that he wouldn't make it to the door. Wilfred glanced at his hostess and blinked in confusion. He had been too comfortable. The impetus to run seemed unnecessary, as if Lady Nadine's murder was some kind of nightmare that belonged to the world he had left behind. Now, it was too late.

The Widow Brunswick waved her hand. "Sit down, boy! You know how I hate drama." She glared at King Radburn. "That was not kind of you, throwing out such an accusation like a clap of thunder from a clear sky. You're a king now, and you must learn to—"

"Madam, with all due respect to your age and your dead husband's name, I *am* the king, and as such, *no one* lectures me!" King Radburn rose and motioned for two of his men to stand on either side of Wilfred. "As I was saying, you have found a most fortunate friend, my boy, but I wonder, do you realize just how fortunate you are?"

With Demetrius' helping hand, Widow Brunswick stood. "That is not for you to say, *King* Radburn. For you do not know all; if you knew, you would not be speaking so publicly now!" The widow shoved her chair vigorously aside and swept across the room toward the ornate doorway. Just before she crossed the threshold, she turned. "I'll be in my rooms. I expect to see you, Wilfred, and the king may follow in your wake!"

Nausea bubbled the scant dinner in Wilfred's stomach. Slowly, he rose to his feet again. He nodded to the guard on his right. He needed to pass, but he could hardly make the man move.

King Radburn signaled that Wilfred could go.

Wilfred shuffled to the doorway. Then he looked back at the king, who still stood in the center of the room.

"Are you coming then?" The words slipped out, a child's plea.

"I'll come when I'm ready." He motioned to the food on the table. "I've not yet finished my meal. You may tell the Widow Brunswick that I have a few things to attend to. Then *she* will be summoned into my presence." King Radburn motioned for his guards to seat themselves at the vacant places.

The priest, still seated, quietly sipped his soup.

Wilfred's gut ached as if he had been kicked. The image of him flying over the moor on his horse ran through his mind. *No. The king's men are everywhere.* Wilfred turned and walked out the doorway and up the winding, stone steps to the Widow Brunswick's room.

He knocked lightly.

Demetrius opened the door.

Wilfred stepped in.

His face an impenetrable mask, Demetrius stared at Wilfred. "Wait here. The widow is indisposed."

Wilfred perched on a window seat, an assortment of embroidered pillows cushioning the hard stone. His shoulders slumped as he clasped his hands in front of him. Melchior's face rose before him. Melchior was probably worrying about him. *I wish I'd said goodbye.* He had gone out seeking adventure, but adventure had snuck up behind him and pummeled him in the back.

The Widow Brunswick swept into the room. "You shouldn't worry too much about what that pompous fool says." Her eyes softened. "We both knew the truth, but we pretended it wasn't there, didn't we?"

The heroes in the old stories his mother told as bedtime stories filled his heart. If he was to have any merit in this tale, he must tell the truth. He did not know *why* this was true, but he knew it *was* true. "No, I didn't realize you knew the truth about me."

Widow Brunswick's gaze hardened. "And what is the truth?"

Wilfred stared through a veil of tears. "I was in the wrong place at the wrong time. I went to Lord Gerard's festival, the one he held to announce the betrothal of his daughter, Corliss, to Lord Marlow and...and...his wife was murdered. She spoke my name before she died; everyone thinks I did it."

The tears burst their dam. He was sorry that she had been murdered and even sorrier that everyone imagined he could do such a terrible deed. Wilfred dropped his head to his chest and clenched his hands. "She was a kind woman, gentle and sweet. I always liked her, though I rarely ever spoke to her. I would never have hurt her."

The widow's voice softened. "So, you cared then? At least you did that; few others did as much."

Wilfred frowned. *There's more to this sorry tale?* A tap on the door cut off his question.

Demetrius flung open the door, and the priest stood on the threshold.

The Widow Brunswick removed herself to the other side of the room and, contrary to custom, sat down. Her eyebrows rose, and she rekindled her authoritative voice. "I didn't send for you."

Father Caedmon shook his head. "No, *you* did not ask for me, but that does not mean I was not called."

"No more riddles! Don't we have enough confusion? Who sent you, then?" Suddenly, her eyes blazed. "If the king asked you here to bargain—"

Father Caedmon lifted his hand. "Not the king. Let's just say that common sense sent me here this night. What I have to tell you,"—he turned and faced Wilfred—"and *you* is important enough to keep me from my evening prayers, for charity demands justice. If I do not speak, there will be little justice here tonight."

Baffled, Wilfred and plunked down on the nearest chair.

Demetrius frowned.

The widow waved her hand wearily. "Speak then, for charity's sake, and get it over with. For once, I'll be glad to send you off to your prayers."

The old priest gestured for them to come closer as he spoke softly. "What I have to tell is not for all ears, so listen well. It will not be repeated twice."

Demetrius moved the widow's chair closer and took a position at her side.

Wilfred leaned in, his heart racing.

The old priest began his tale. "Many years ago, a young woman came to me and told me a terrible secret."

Widow Brunswick pursed her lips. "Are you sure this is *your* tale to tell?"

Father Caedmon's eyes glistened in the dim light. "It's a tale that must be told if truth is to be served. I'm not the only one who knows, but it'd be best if Wilfred hears it from me."

Widow Brunswick sat bolt upright. "What do you mean? Has the tale been told abroad?"

"You're not the only one who hears whispers. Now, if you please, I'll go on." He gazed at Wilfred. "This part of the story you will find hard to believe but, trust me, you will not be the only one surprised this night."

Wilfred nodded in stoic acceptance as if he must allow a surgeon to do his duty.

The priest folded his hands and began again. "Some years ago, a young woman conceived a child, but she was afraid of what might happen if her son were raised by her husband. She delivered the child on the same night as her neighbor, a less fortunate woman whose baby did not live. The babies were switched and the secret kept for many years."

"But as her son grew under her eyes and she could not call him hers, she regretted her decision, for it is never wise to deny the truth, especially when it runs as deep as blood."

"Oh, stop playing with words and tell the boy everything!" The Widow Brunswick's eyes filled with tears as she gently stroked his head. “She shouldn’t have done it, though I understood why she did—still it was wrong. Even with all the fostering that goes on by necessity, it was wrong to deny you your rightful heritage.”

Confusion swirled through Wilfred.

“Boy, don’t you understand? You are that baby that was switched at birth. You were Lady Nadine’s son!”

Wilfred jerked upright, astonishment tearing his thoughts to shreds. Fear slithered over him.

A heavy knock rapped on the door.

With swift steps, Demetrius strode across the room and swung the door open.

Unable to speak, Wilfred stared open-mouthed at Father Caedmon.

The Widow Brunswick rose to her feet.

One of the king’s men stood in the doorway. “Wilfred, son of Melchior, you have been summoned to the king’s presence on the charge of murder. Lord Gerard has arrived, and witnesses await you for questioning.”

The fury that broke forth from the widow was unlike anything Wilfred had ever heard from a lady before.

She stomped forward, her right hand waving like a banner. “The insolence of that man! He may call himself a king, but he’s nothing more than a raging—”

The king’s man cut the Widow’s speech short. “This boy is not the only one being charged. You are charged with treason for hiding a known suspect and trying to intercept the king’s justice, for it has been reported that you sent your own man to misdirect the king.”

Widow Brunswick’s fury dwindled and passed like a summer storm. Her face paled; she staggered a step. “He says what? That I sent....” Her gaze fell to the floor as if she did not dare look anywhere else.

Putting a hand under her elbow, Demetrius steadied

her. He led her to her chair, but his gaze met Father Caedmon's. "Would you take Wilfred down while I help the widow make herself ready?"

The priest nodded.

Wilfred trembled with so many emotions he could hardly name them all. Blindly, he followed the robed man down the winding stone steps and into the main room. The murmur of voices rose as he approached, but all sound ceased the moment he entered the hall. Several men stood together, mostly men-at-arms, whom he recognized from the king's retinue, but there were also several new warriors, heavily armed, their clothes stained and mud-splattered. As Wilfred glanced around, the man he had dreaded seeing since that awful day when Lady Nadine had died stood glaring at him.

Her pallid and contorted face rose up in his mind. Oh, if only he had not promised to meet Corliss behind the blacksmith shop. If only he had not been there to see Lady Nadine stumbling toward him, a dead woman walking. She'd called his name in the most plaintive tone imaginable. Wilfred's heart had broken at the sound, and fear had frozen him to the spot.

He saw Lord Gerard rush to his wife's aid, but even as she fell into his arms, she seemed to gain some supernatural strength. She struggled to her feet, waving feebly at her husband as if to brush his touch away. Lord Gerard stayed on his knees, watching his wife weave into the distance as if watching a corpse depart from its cairn.

Wilfred had stared at Lord Gerard's appalled face, and Lord Gerard had glared at Wilfred. The two men had locked onto each other's eyes while Lady Nadine, seeing nothing, had stumbled forward and, by some unnatural strength, made it to the entrance of the great hall, where she fell. A trail of blood led across the ground, and Lord Gerard had called out, "Murderer!"

Now as he looked into those same eyes, he trembled harder than ever. At the time, he had felt certain that Lord Gerard was as horrified as himself, but as time had passed and he reviewed the matter, he had decided that Lord Gerard must have been the murderer. Now, as they stood face-to-face, confusion overwhelmed him.

The priest's words came rushing back...babies had been switched…he was Lady Nadine's son. He was *this man's* son? Impossible! Wilfred had never seen a man faint except in drunkenness, but he wished for that insensibility now.

Father Caedmon strode to his side and gripped his arm. "Do not be afraid. I was only half done telling you the news, but this is not the place. Do not despair, and don't say too much."

Though he felt that the world had tipped upside down, and he was sliding into an abyss, the priest's calm presence and reassuring words did much to stiffen his spine. He remembered his earlier resolve to hold fast to the truth. If it was true that he had been switched as a baby and that Lady

Nadine was his mother, then *his mother had been murdered.* His interest was no longer simply to clear his name but to find the murderer and bring justice to her departed spirit.

"Stop daydreaming, boy!" Lord Gerard stepped forward and peered at Wilfred, his face flushing. "No one can protect you from due justice. I'll see to that!"

The widow's voice cracked the air. "What do you know of justice? You've been a murderer yourself more times than I can count, you and your father before you. Don't imagine that just because you triumphed on the field of battle that the scales of justice have been balanced."

Demetrius whispered in her ear, but she waved him off.

"Do not counsel me now. I'm old. Look there, Father

Caedmon doesn't mind that I speak the truth. They can do with me as they will, but I'll no longer be silent. I know who killed Lady Nadine, and it most certainly was not her only son!"

Chapter Fourteen

To Have a Heart

Nikolas and Nolan rode hard to Lord Gerard's estate and discovered that he had left, the Widow Brunswick's manor his destination. After a brief consultation, they rode on to Melchior's cottage to apprise him of the situation.

As they entered the yard, disorder met their eyes; everyone bustled about in anxious duty.

Nikolas ran inside, his heart pounding.

Adele stood in the front room, directing the melee. As she folded a heavy blanket, she grinned at Nikolas. "Oh, my father's sister, Martha, has come, and she's decided that before winter arrives in full force, the house must be cleaned from top to bottom! My poor father is near despair with distraction."

Striding in after Nikolas, Nolan shook his head and growled, "What's this? A woman who disturbs a man's domain? Is she out of her mind? Melchior's son is about to be hanged, and she buzzes about like a queen bee? Where is the wench that I may stare stupidity in her face?"

Adele's eyes widened in outrage.

Nikolas winced. "Adele, listen, Nolan doesn't believe that Wilfred had anything to do with the murder. Can I leave him here peacefully"—he glared at his friend—"while you take me to your father?"

Adele dropped the woolen blanket onto a neat stack and nodded. She shot Nolan a severe look as she headed to the steps, murmuring to Nikolas, "Rude, insufferable man! An ox in the fowl pen could do as much."

"That's as good a description as ever I've heard—and

you don't know the half of it. He's a thief and a mercenary, but he doesn't seem to know it. He thinks he is an honest man who steals from those who deserve to get pillaged."

Adele stared. "How can you bear to be friends with him?"

"Friendship is perhaps too strong a word. Let's just say that he likes me for some reason, and I haven't discouraged him."

Her fingers trailing against the stone wall, Adele climbed the steps. "Father is in his room. He's been hiding for two days and must be getting tired of being stuck up there. He hardly eats, but he insists that he won't come down until we are all done with the mess-making, as he calls it."

"Doesn't your aunt have any sense? Can't she see that he is already deranged, what with the charges against his son?"

"That's why she's done it. He feels helpless, so she's trying to get his blood stirring. She wants him to yell and stomp his feet—bring him to life."

"That might get someone killed! I don't know your aunt but—"

"Her name is Martha, and she is a good woman."

"Certainly. But I have a solution that might save Melchior's sanity, as well as your brother's life. Nolan and I are following Lord Gerard and King Radburn to the Widow Brunswick's manor. If we hurry, perhaps we can intercede before any decisions are made."

Adele quickened her pace. "Oh, in that case, you'd better hurry. Go up and speak to father. I'll see to his horse and arrange provisions for the ride."

In retreat, she brushed by Nikolas, who flattened himself against the wall. Hesitating, she bowed her head. "I had wanted to ask but—"

Nikolas gazed at Adele, her dark hair falling across her face, dust mingling with her dignity. Nearly overcome, he cleared his throat, “Ask me anything, Adele.”

Her voice dropped low. “I heard that Lady Nadine was your relation. Is it true? Was she your sister?”

Nikolas swallowed back an ache in his throat. “She was fostered out very young, but she married well, or so I thought. I kept my ears open for news of her. Though far or near, always, she remained my sister.”

Tears filled Adele’s eyes. “I’m sorry. Your sister was murdered, and everyone says it was my brother who did it, and yet you’re helping us, even now?”

Nikolas pressed Adele’s hand. “I would help anyone who needed me. I know what it is to need—”

Suddenly, Melchior’s voice boomed from the top of the steps. “Who’s there? Adele? You know I don’t want to see anyone.”

“Don’t worry, Father. It’s Nikolas. He is going to see Wilfred, and he wants you to come along. I am going to make the arrangements.” Adele’s gaze glanced off Nikolas as she turned and fled down the steps.

Melchior’s voice boomed. “Nikolas? I thought you’d be tending that shop of yours.”

Nikolas bounded up the steps two at a time. Reaching the landing, he pounded his friend on the back. “I have someone watching over business for a few days.”

Melchior cocked his head, stared at Nikolas a moment, then led the way to his bedchamber. “Come and sit while I get myself properly arranged. My house is all disarranged! My sister came upon me and decided that mixing up my things and airing out every bit of cloth and stick of furniture would do us good.”

Melchior stripped off his outer garments and stood, large-bellied, with his long undergarments sagging on his body. He grabbed a shirt and a pair of trousers and tugged them on.

Nikolas stared intently out the window.

Punctuated bursts intertwined with grunts and sighs. "Where is that sleeve? What have they done with it? Oh, there it is. Fools! Who turned it inside out? Let me see...this belongs to the legging, doesn't it? Confound it and confiscate it! They went and washed it and now look!"

Nikolas forced himself to turn his gaze.

Melchior stood oddly attired. Either the garments had shrunk, or he had grown alarmingly.

Nikolas rubbed his stubbly chin thoughtfully. "You look like a lion wearing the skin of a mouse."

Melchior snorted. "Thank you much! This will do nicely when I go before the king." Melchior stomped to the head of the stairs. "Adele! Get up here and save your father's life, or I'll never forgive you!"

Nikolas fought the grin breaking over his face.

Adele clambered up the stairs, mumbling, "What now, Father? I'm trying to get things ready, but Aunt Martha and Nolan have met and—"

At the top of the stairs, Adele appraised her father with a long stare, her lips pursed. Then she smiled, struggled briefly, then burst into laughter.

Fearing that the rest of the household might bound up the stairs, Nikolas jumped to his feet. "Adele, could you manage this? I hardly think he'll impress the king—"

Bustling footsteps pounded up the stairs. Martha called, "What is going on, brother? First, mad shouting then mad laughter. Have you all lost your wits?" At the top of the steps, she took in Melchior's unhappy visage and staggered forward. "Brother, what are you doing in those clothes? I washed Wilfred's garments, and now you put them on?"

Nolan shoved past Martha and stopped before

Melchior. "What in the fires of Hades is happening in this house?" He stared at Melchior. "I say now, that *is* a look! What do you think you're going to do, strike pity into the king's heart? I'll tell you; it won't work—the man hasn't a heart to strike pity into!"

Martha muttered as she opened a cabinet and pulled out a stack of clean clothes. "No truer words were ever said!" She bustled her brother further into the room. "Now, put on your proper clothes, and I'll set the others where Wilfred can find them. Come downstairs when you're ready. The provisions are set, and the boys are saddling the horse."

As she swept to the steps, Martha nodded politely at Nolan. "It's a good thing you are doing for this family. I don't think I could air another blanket!"

Nolan pursed his lips and nodded significantly at Nikolas. "A woman of sense and charm. A widow by any chance?"

Nikolas nudged Nolan toward the steps. "We'll wait downstairs."

Tugging off the ill-fitting garments, Melchior grumbled. "Don't go without me! Oh and, Nikolas, when you see Adele, be sure to tell her that you'll be back soon."

Nikolas blinked. "You mean I should tell her that *you'll* be back soon."

"No, just tell her what I said, and it'll be about right."

Nikolas blushed all the way down the stairs.

Chapter Fifteen

Bear Our Burdens

—OldEarth—

Song dangled from a web, watching and waiting. When Melchior's last footfall sounded on the bottom step, she let out a dragline, caught a breeze, and swung to the windowsill. There she morphed into a sparrow and flew across the yard onto a garden post.

Teal stood talking with his son on the edge of the woodlands, every motion sharp and emphatic.

Cerulean stared at the ground, his shoulders stooped low for one so young. He carried a heavy weight. One she could not see but imagined well.

Sitting on a high branch of an enormous oak, Zuri leaned against the trunk, his legs dangling, his gaze searching.

What is he looking for?

The jangling of harnesses caught her attention.

Nolan and Nikolas left the stable with three horses ready for travel, hefty saddle bags draping over the animals' broad backs. The two men chatted. Then Nolan laughed.

A strange light flashed at the tree line, and Song flew toward it.

Teal lay unconscious on the ground.

Cerulean stood hovering over him. "Father? What's wrong—"

Morphing into an elderly woman dressed in widow's clothes, Song hustled in close, beating Zuri to Teal's side.

With eyes closed and his shape indistinct, Teal's pale

body lay still as death.

Zuri crouched beside Cerulean. "What happened?"

Cerulean shook his head, his voice strained. "I don't know. He was lecturing me about showing proper respect to Sterling, when suddenly he went limp."

Placing her hand on Teal's chest, Song listened carefully. His human heart had ceased to beat, but his Luxonian vibrance still flowed—too slowly. "He needs deep healing." She glanced at Zuri. "My ship is on the coast. We must get there quickly."

Cerulean blinked. "We're Luxonian. He should return—"

"He's too weak to make it to Lux. I have powers you know little about. I'll see to his needs while you carry on in his stead."

Shading his eyes, Zuri searched the landscape. "Where the hell have they gotten to?"

Focusing on Teal, Song didn't look up. "Who?"

"Sterling and—"

With Sterling trailing behind, Mauve hustled from the woods. "What's going on?" She pointed to the distance as Melchior stumped out of his front door and traipsed across the yard. His horse stood waiting. "They're setting out to the Widow Brunswick's. We must hurry! Sparks will fly when—"

Cerulean's eyes flashed. "Can't you see? My father has collapsed."

Sterling crouched opposite of Song and pressed his hand to Teal's forehead. "How long has he been like this?" He glared at Cerulean. "You didn't tell me he was sick!"

Tears filled Cerulean's eyes as he stared at Sterling. "He said he was fine. I told him that he didn't look very well, but he only said I was being rude."

Mauve's face puckered. "Sterling, they can take care of

it. Let's go before we miss everything. I bet Nolan has—"

Flicking a geo-location map before his face, Zuri hefted Teal into his arms. "I see your ship. Take whatever shape you like; just keep up with me."

Song stood and faced Sterling. "You're in charge now and must lead the others." With a flicker of distaste, she swept her gaze over Mauve and zeroed in on Cerulean. "I'll take care of your father and let you know as soon as I can." She turned to Zuri. "I'm faster than an Ingot. When I'm ready, lay him on my back then jump on behind to keep him steady.

With a deep breath, Song morphed into a sleek black horse.

With Cerulean's help, Zuri thrust Teal over her broad back and leapt on behind, clasping Teal's limp body in his arms.

Song reared and took off at a run.

Cerulean's gasp rang in her ears as she raced like the wind.

~~~

Abbas led his son to the stone hearth at the south end of the Widow Brunswick's great hall, where a fire crackled and warmed the chilly air. "Rub your hands together, Omega. Like this." He demonstrated, chaffing and wringing his hands in perfect imitation of a human in need of warmth and comfort.

Dressed in matching minstrels' outfits, with yellow stockings, green tunics, and blue cloaks, the two figures added significant color to the drab room.

Omega grinned as he leaned close to the fire. He stuck his fingers directly into the flames.
~~~

An elderly servant stopped wiping down the hefty wooden table and gasped.

Abbas slapped Omega's hand away, grinning stupidly at the woman. "Just a foolish prank. No harm done."

Grumbling, the matron frowned. "Do the like before the widow, and you'll find yourselves out in the cold." She pointed to a wide doorway. "There's food set aside in the kitchen there. If you sing well enough, you might be allowed to eat it. But there's goings-on here that puts entertainment out of every head these days."

Omega spun around. "You think he's guilty—the boy?" Not waiting for an answer from the blustering woman, Omega turned to his father. "If he is guilty, will he be hanged? I'd love to see a hanging!"

"Tut, tut, young fool. You'd love a hanging until it be your own! Or that of someone you love. Arrogant child." The old servant glared at Abbas. "You teach him nothing but idle songs, then?"

Surprised by the heat rising to his face, Abbas bowed low. "Guilty as charged, I'm afraid. His life has been nothing but traveling and seeing the univ—world." Confusion made him more honest than usual. "His mother spoiled him at home, and I'm doing little better on the open road."

Wiping her hands on a dingy rag, the woman snorted. "You're storing up trouble for yourselves. A spoiled child is a plague to us all." Stumping toward the kitchen, she flung a parting glance over her shoulder. "Watch what happens to Melchior and young Wilfred. Maybe you'll learn a thing or two. A father has as many hearts as he has children—and they can all be broken."

Omega chuckled as he watched the servant stump out of the room. "She's got spirit, Father. Most humans are so dull, but she's—" He shrugged. "I don't know, alive." He stared at his father. "You think the Luxonians will find out that we're here and try to stop us?"

An aged priest in a gray tunic stepped into the room, stopped short, and stared. His eyes widened, alarmed.

Abbas nudged his son toward the doorway. "We should leave." He dropped his voice low. "Luxonians only know us as The Mystery Race, but perceptive humans"—he peered at the priest—"well, they could be much more dangerous to our purpose."

Omega stared at the old cleric as he passed by. "What purpose"

Dread filled Abbas. He didn't have a clue.

—Private Transmission from Kelesta to Nova—

My dear girl,

Before you get too involved with your human studies, I want to make sure that you understand our place in the greater scheme of things. We Bhuaci do not wield the kind of power needed to influence the direction of universal events. Our role is a humble one.

Your father and I have learned to seek power within. Despite your father's Ingoti advantages, he rose to unparalleled heights when he freed himself from his synthetic coils. Together he and I set a direction toward something greater than productivity, even better than happiness.

I cannot presume to tell *you*, one of the rarest of jewels, a product of love between Bhuaci and Ingoti, but I must warn you, that though you bear our gifts, so you bear our burdens too.

My kind have much to offer, yet Bhuaci are also famously duplicitous. And Ingots can be callous brutes.

Look well before you follow in another's footsteps.
I will love you always, but you must judge for yourself.

~Your mother, Kelesta

Chapter Sixteen

Lies Tucked Away

Harold didn't particularly mind standing guard, but he was getting mortally sick of Terrill's running commentary about how the king would see the boy hang before morning.

"You can see it in the king's eyes. He means to do it tonight. Mark my words, that boy's going to—"

"Shut up!"

"Why? What's the matter with you?"

"Nothing's the matter with me, but this castle has ears, and it's never wise to make predictions, that's all. Besides, the boy is right behind us. He can probably hear every word you say."

Terrill wagged his head, widening his eyes and shrugging his shoulders to show his complete disdain for that consideration.

Harold darted a quick look behind.

Wilfred sat on the cold stone floor, probably wishing that he had never directed his horse to the top of this hill and knocked on the gate. He should have stayed in the snow and the cold, where he would have died a relatively peaceful death. The king had listened only briefly when the widow tried explaining Wilfred's birth, but neither the king nor Lord Gerard had believed a word of it.

The widow had looked for Father Caedmon to bear witness, but he was nowhere to be seen. Must've slipped away during her short recitation as the bells were tolling time for mid-day prayer.

Slime oozed from the walls, forming irregular pools, and Harold smelled the musty moss growing in cracks and crevices. Rats scratched about.

Behind the locked door, Wilfred smacked his hand upon the wet stone, rattling his chains.

Harold imagined the pain that defiant act caused, though he didn't dare imagine much more.

Wilfred sat slumped in the dark corner, his arms wrapped around his knees.

Harold looked away.

Father Caedmon hobbled forward, a small bundle in his hand. "Good evening. I have orders to see the prisoner. Will you let me in?"

Terrill blurted his words before Harold could stop him. "Orders from who?"

Uneasy, Harold stepped between the two. It was said that the spirits of the dark fled from the priest, and he could command sinners to repent with his piercing gaze. Harold jerked a collection of ancient keys from a hook and quickly unbolted the heavy door. He whispered to Terrill, "You want to get us killed? If the king is in the mood for a hanging, a couple more necks won't make much difference. Besides, this good priest is known for his, well, his *goodness*. Step out of the way. You're throwing a shadow, and I need to get this open."

Terrill complied without a smidgen of grace, rolling his eyes.

Harold diligently ignored him.

Father Caedmon entered the dim room, making the sign of the cross.

Wilfred sat up, clearly bewildered, but he did little else.

Father shuffled over. "Stay, my son. You must be exhausted. Here, I'll sit next to you. I saved a bite of bread from supper."

Wilfred accepted the bundle silently and unwrapped the bread.

Terrill watched from the doorway.

Harold tugged his sleeve. “Let them be.”

“What’s wrong with you? We should stay and listen. What if they plan to escape?”

Harold jerked Terrill aside. “They’re about as likely to escape as you are to turn dust to gold! Now mind your own business.”

Terrill slouched to a corner.

Harold crossed his arms and prayed he wouldn’t hear too much.

~~~

Father Caedmon eased himself to the floor and crossed his legs. “You know, Wilfred, not every man makes a discovery like you did today, learning that you were Lady Nadine’s son.”

Wilfred snorted. “And Lord Gerard’s too, don’t forget.”

“Yes, a son with more than one father. Many would be content with less.”

“I would be content with less! I was happy with Melchior as my father. But now, I’m about to be hanged, and I see no one trying to save me.”

“There is one Father that you have yet to recognize.”

Wilfred slumped. “Please, Father Caedmon, I know you mean well, but if you have come to preach to me, you’re wasting your breath. Melchior often spoke of the Christ, but I want a God who can outwit his enemies, not be crucified by them.”

Father Caedmon accepted this with stoic composure. “So, who did you used to wish to emulate?”

“You’ll laugh now, but I spent my youth dreaming that I was like Lord Gerard or the king. I’d have been content
~~~

to be one of their men-at-arms. I just wanted to be free and have adventures."

Father Caedmon shifted his weight. "How do you like your adventures so far?"

Wilfred threw his head back, banging it against the hard wall. "No more than I like my new father. I don't understand how he could have—and then to turn on me all of a sudden. I never did any harm, except..."

"Except?"

"There was the matter with his daughter."

Father Caedmon remained silent.

After a brief struggle, Wilfred explained everything that had happened between himself and Corliss, how he had seen Lady Nadine before she died, and how he was convinced that Lord Gerard had done the deed.

Father Caedmon gestured for Wilfred to stand. "I don't know what will happen next, but I assure you, I will stay with you. And we'll not be alone. Our Father above cares for you. Tell the truth and keep your head high. If you are truly sorry for your sins, God will forgive you, and you can start afresh."

"But what if Lord Gerard and the king don't believe me? What if I am hanged?"

Father Caedmon limped forward, pushing the door open. He offered his hand to Wilfred. "Come, and we shall see. Better men than you have died for other men's sins. It wouldn't be the first time. Or the last."

"That's not very comforting, Father."

Father Caedmon swallowed a lump in his throat. "No, it's not."

~~~
~~~

Harold nodded as the two men passed.

Terrill glared and spat to the side. "Why'd you let them go? We should've interrogated them. We could've softened the boy up and Lord Gerard would—"

"You're a fool. Didn't you hear them? The boy didn't do it."

"He just said that so the priest would help him."

Weary beyond words, Harold started for the steps. "If being told that innocent men hang as likely as the guilty, well, then his idea of being helped is quite different than mine."

"They'll both hang unless they confess."

"Just be quiet until I see the king. I'll take the blame for letting them out. Don't worry. At least this way, we know the truth." Harold climbed the steep steps, huffing as he went.

"When did you start caring about the truth?"

Harold kept climbing. "I've always cared—you just never noticed."

~~~

The Widow Brunswick had little spirit to fight the menace now in her home. Lord Gerard frequently offered his men in service to the king, so the two would not break ranks easily. *But I have one more secret to reveal…*

King Radburn had a son out of wedlock and had managed to hide the truth from nearly everyone. The mother, a high-ranking lady from a foreign land, could have been killed for her indiscretion. She found a foster mother, who raised and loved the boy, but in a fit of drunken melancholy one night, she told the young man the truth. Intelligent and ambitious, he ran away to seek
~~~

his father but was captured at sea and sold into brutal hands until the Widow Brunswick accepted him as a personal servant, a gift from her husband.

After several years in her service, the youth grew into a worthy man, changed his name to Demetrius, and entrusted his secret into her care.

In him, Widow Brunswick found a friend with whom she could share her deepest thoughts.

She alone held the knowledge that would bring both the king and Lord Gerard to their knees. The two men were always at each other's side, though she doubted they knew each other's secrets. There were lies tucked into the folds of every family's fabric.

As she sat in her room, mulling over her options, Demetrius stood at her side.

She caressed his hand. "It was you who tried to turn the king away, wasn't it? When I think of all you have done—your faithful service, your kindness...even a son could not have been more loyal. I always meant to make things better for you."

Demetrius murmured softly.

The widow released Demetrius' hand. "When I first heard about Lady Nadine's death, I thought, now I can do something! But neither the king nor Lord Gerard care for the truth. They just want to hang someone, preferably not each other."

Footsteps shuffled outside her door, a thump, and then the door was flung open.

King Radburn stepped in, fully arrayed in riding clothes. "I'm leaving, and in my absence, I expect you to treat Lord Gerard as an honored guest. Now that he has found his wife's murderer, he will see justice done. My part is accomplished."

The Widow Brunswick trembled with rage. "I'm surprised you have lowered yourself to come to my room." Desire for revenge burned hot. "You wanted to appear masterful before your men, yet you sneak away into the night." The widow strolled to the window. "If you leave now, you'll miss the best part. I will not let this evening pass without making known the *full* truth."

The king crossed the room and pushed his face close to hers. "You *know* nothing! You're only breeding lies so that you can cover your part in hiding a murderer."

"My lies? How about yours? I know about your son!"

The king drew his sword and rushed forward.

With his face contorted in horror, Demetrius thrust himself between the two and took the full force of King Radburn's deadly blow.

The widow screamed, "My boy!"

Demetrius fell, gasping, his gaze locked on the widow.

Blood dripped from the king's sword as he backed to the door.

The widow cradled Demetrius' head, his eyes half-open, in her arms, sobbing.

Lord Gerard rushed into the room, his sword drawn. He stared first at the widow, then down at the dying man, and then finally to the king.

King Radburn wiped his blade on a hanging tapestry.

Lord Gerard stepped close and dropped his voice low. "I don't need to know. Just tell me what to do."

King Radburn considered his blade. "Let him be for the moment. When he is dead, call the priest. After all ceremony is done, bury the body in the woods." He slipped his sword into his scabbard and started for the door. "I never want to hear this incident referred to again."

Lord Gerard bowed.

Hooves pounded in the outer courtyard.

The widow cringed. "Not now!"

Lord Gerard ran to the window and called down, "Who

goes there? It's late, and the Widow Brunswick does not wish to be disturbed."

A voice called back, "The father of the accused is here to see that proper justice is done. Open the gate so that we may enter."

King Radburn swore under his breath and motioned to Lord Gerard. "Tell them that I am here to see that justice is done, and they can wait in the next town for word of my report."

Lord Gerard relayed this message, but a new, determined voice called up, "Nolan here. I own a bit of land close by, and I'm a friend of young Nikolas, the brother of the late Lady Nadine. He has as much right as anyone to see to this matter. Let us in, or we'll have a merry time battering down the door."

The king cursed again. He shook his finger at Lord Gerard. "Tell them we'll meet below." He marched to the door. "Have one of your men bring up the accused and get rid of that body!"

The widow wailed. "Don't touch him!" She called her serving woman. "Magdalena, get Father Caedmon. Tell him he must come at once. Demetrius is dying!"

As the young woman ran off, the gates creaked open.

The widow clutched Demetrius' hand until the spark of life faded from his eyes. Then her heart fell into an abyss.

~~~

Lord Gerard met Melchior, Nikolas, and Nolan in the great hall. "The king has already taken this matter into his own hands. You do not need to be here."

Melchior slid from his horse and sighed as he pulled off his hood. "I'm glad to hear you say that. King Radburn assured me of Wilfred's innocence. He was determined to look into the matter and see that justice is done." Melchior
~~~

glanced back at Nikolas and Nolan. "Lord Gerard, I believe you know these men: Nikolas, your late wife's brother, and Nolan, your neighbor."

After tipping his head in mock civility, Lord Gerard turned away. "Make your own introductions to the king. I don't care who you brought. The devil himself cannot save your son now!"

Chapter Seventeen

To Cling so Hard

Gilda sat on a tree stump and watched Martha hang a beautiful tapestry on the line to dry. The servants could have managed this chore, like many others, but Martha was not one to sit idle.

Selby shuffled across the yard, a fierce scowl etched across his forehead.

Gilda turned and watched him. "Martha?"

"Yes, dear?"

"What's wrong with Selby?"

Martha pulled the fabric to hang exactly square. "Wrong? Nothing's wrong. He's just being Selby is all."

"But he's different."

"How do you mean?"

"Since Wilfred ran away, he's been angry. He never talks or laughs at all. Don't you think that's strange?"

"He's an old man and a slave at that. What does he have to laugh about?"

Gilda tilted her head, perplexed. "That night when Nikolas came and asked what had happened, Father ordered Selby to tell everything that he knew. He even threatened to whip Selby if he held anything back."

"So?"

"You think that hurt his feelings?"

"Likely as not, the old man just has a stomach ache." Martha finished her adjustments and stepped back, satisfied. She looked at her niece. "It's no use trying to figure them out. Slaves are different from us. I can't say how it happens, but it's true. Once a man is made a slave, he doesn't have the rights of other men. He doesn't even have the thoughts of other men. He's just a slave.

"When Selby's wife and children had to be sold during the hard times, we felt bad, especially considering how useful she had always been to Edwina. Her name was Dota or Dora or some such thing." She pondered the matter. "Yes, Dora. Anyway, she was a bright little thing with a gift for bringing babies into the world, best midwife in the country. She helped Edwina survive that dreadful pregnancy with Wilfred. A miracle of God, no doubt, but Dora was at the center of it.

"When Edwina announced that Dora had been sold off, their crying was enough to break your heart. But broken hearts won't pay dues, so the task was done.

"Selby knew well the ways of things, so after a time, he got used to his loss. Perhaps Melchior was a little hard, not allowing anyone, not even Selby, to mention Dora's name again. Eventually, Selby calmed down and took Wilfred and you other children to his heart as much as he had taken his own. Maybe he remembers them at times. If that's the case, and I say *if* for it might be nothing more than a stomach ache, he'll get over it just as he did last time."

Martha braced her hand against her forehead and peered at the sky. "About time for a fitting meal—the men have been hauling timber today; they'll be hungry."

Gilda bounded off the log.

Selby passed again, sour-faced and slump-shouldered.

"I wonder how I'd feel if I were a slave."

Martha jerked back. "Perish the thought! You're too beautiful to become a slave."

"But I'll become a wife, and a wife's life is much the same."

"Goodness, child, you think the strangest things! A wife is a part of her husband. Two become one. The husband has an obligation to love his wife. No one is obliged to love his slave."

Gilda's eyes followed Selby's form through the slanting rays of light. *But I wonder how I'd feel.*

~~~

Oliver laid crossbeams on the floor of the storage shed in anticipation of a new shipment of lumber that would shortly arrive. He hummed as he worked, inhaling the sweet smell of sawdust and the last cutting of straw as his skin warmed against the pleasant chill of the oncoming winter.

"Ahem."

A mixture of excitement and foreboding sizzled through Oliver.

Corliss stood at the entrance, her thick hair waving in the breeze and her eyes downcast in humility. Her long dress clung to her shapely body.

Mastering himself, Oliver met her gaze. "Anything I can do for you, Corliss?"

"I just slipped away for a bit. Father is gone, and I wanted to ask if you have heard anything about Wilfred."

"I've heard nothing, though you can ask Martha. She'd be the first to hear anything worth knowing."

Corliss stepped back and hesitated. She eyed Oliver. "You were there and saw everything. You think that... What do you think happened?"

Oliver shrugged. "I was there, but I didn't see everything that happened."

Corliss entered the darkened storage shed. "But you saw some things. You saw how Wilfred looked at me?"

Oliver clenched his hands into fists. "Most everyone saw that."
~~~

Corliss' cheeks flamed. "You must understand that I really liked him. I think... Did my father do anything or Lord Marlow?" Corliss darted forward, her hands raised as if to forestall any interruption. "I only ask because I thought I saw my father talking to his men, sending them to capture Wilfred."

"Yes, I saw that too. After Lady Nadine was found dead. Only then did the chase begin."

Corliss wrung her hands together. "You don't think that my father went to kill Wilfred but killed my mother by mistake?"

Oliver's eyes widened. "You think that she died defending Wilfred from your father?"

Corliss stared at the ground, wrapping her arms around her middle. "Or Lord Marlow."

Oliver shook his head and repositioned a piece of timber. "Your father likes to plan ahead, not lose his temper and make a public mistake. Lord Marlow, perhaps, but he was inside with the others when your mother was killed; many have said so. Besides, both men are excellent warriors. Neither would've missed their target. If they intended to kill Wilfred, he'd be dead already.

Selby appeared from around the corner and halted in his tracks. The old man wagged his finger. "Woman, you've caused enough trouble. Oliver needs nothing you have to offer. Isn't one son enough? Or must you have them all? You'll be trying to catch little Thomas before long!"

Flushing with fury, Oliver struck the old servant a blow to the face that would have sent a less-hardened man to his knees. "What gives you cause to be so cruel, Selby? You'll not add to her suffering while I'm around."

With a gasp, Corliss fled.

Oliver watched her go, his heart pounding. After she

was out of sight, he turned back to Selby.

Selby wiped his bloodied lip, peering at Oliver through resentful eyes. "You're a strange one to defend the likes of her. Honest and decent where the rest of the world is corrupt, you'll defend her honor?" Selby blinked like a disturbed owl. "Daughter of the devil. She just feels guilty about sending an innocent fool to his death. Likely as not, she'd send others if it pleased her. She's had no hold with the truth."

"Selby, you're the one keeping secrets. I don't understand what you're about, but I'm certain of it."

An ugly grin marred Selby's face. "Didn't you wonder why Lord Gerard said that his wife died in his arms, yet we all saw her stagger and fall in the hall?"

Oliver's eyes narrowed. "Yes, I wondered."

"Well, let's just say that there was another person there—someone even Lady Nadine feared. When she cried out, Lord Gerard heard and he called, but it was too late. By the time he arrived, she was nearly dead. But then Lord Gerard saw the truth, and he grew afraid. He's terrified of the dead, and rightly so. Many souls have a claim of vengeance on him. So, when she climbed to her feet, he fled, bold Lord that he is."

"Selby, how do you know all this? Who was Lady Nadine afraid of?"

Selby smiled and shook his head knowingly. "Someone we should all be afraid of—justice."

His skin prickling, Oliver didn't want to further this conversation. *Is the old man mad?* He turned away and stared out the window.

Riding forward, two men motioned toward their wagon loaded with lumber.

Oliver shook off a prickly feeling and motioned to Selby. "We need to get this job done before winter descends, so make yourself useful and call all hands."

Selby turned.

Oliver called after him, "Sorry I hit you. By all that's holy, I'll never do it again, but I just couldn't help myself."

Selby shrugged. "You don't have to explain. I'm not a man; I'm a slave. Did me a favor. I'd thought there was one decent man left on earth, so I clung to this life. But now, it's the same horror here as there, so no reason to cling so hard. It's a relief, really." He shuffled away.

As Oliver watched the old man retreat, a lump swelled in his throat and nearly choked him.

Chapter Eighteen

A Season for Everything

Adele sat on her favorite chair by the window in the main hall off the kitchen, hunched in a small pool of light. With painstaking care, she sewed up rips, stains, and burns in their best embroidered tablecloth.

The dinner bell rang long and loud.

Dirty, sweaty day laborers paced by the window and into the kitchen, their shuffling feet and mild conversation catching her ear. A halting shadow passed, and she looked up.

Oliver limped wearily to the kitchen. His angry scowl matched his disheveled appearance.

She sighed, grateful once again that Martha had taken over much of the meal preparation, for dealing with the men, their extensive appetites, and unpredictable moods exasperated her overwrought nerves.

Few men possessed the qualities she wanted her future husband to have. She had imagined her particular hero for so long that the picture had become as old and frayed as the worn tapestry in her lap. After the king's promise to find her a husband, she refused to revisit her once-favored dreams. Men in the real world repulsed her. Layers of dirt tanned the laborers. Merchants smelled bad. They all laughed too loudly, winked at each other when she passed, and then laughed again, as if she was on the outside of a joke that she was too stupid to understand.

She harrumphed. How many of them could manage her duties? They were good at doing the chores set before them—lifting, toting, cutting, building, planting, harvesting, tending shop or sheep, whatever the case might be—but she had to oversee the running of the whole household and the management of the estate.

She had seen to the meals of twenty to thirty people for years. She oversaw the management of shops, animal care, butchering and the storing of meat, planting of the crops and the harvest storage, house laundry, and even the care of the ill and infirm. She also arranged the funeral ceremonies and took care that cairns were built properly, and families buried together. She oversaw the spinning and weaving rooms and the making of clothes, trying hard to keep up with the styles of the day.

Though Oliver was a great help, and Gilda was a responsible child, she alone carried the heavy load of keeping everything running. It was taken as an accepted fact that the farmhands would know what to do, carpenters would know what repairs to make, and disputes would be settled without too much ill-will. When her father's sister had come, anxiety played on her exhausted nerves. Would Martha be displeased? But Martha reveled in mighty responsibility.

Adele had relaxed in relief. Now she sat and listened as deep voices bellowed and teased in the kitchen,

Suddenly, everything went quiet.

Adele's hands fell onto her lap, the needle half-pulled through. *Oliver must have just stepped in.* This was strange, for Oliver never excited comment, except an occasional snicker.

She laid her sewing aside and paced into the large kitchen.

The men sat at the table as usual, everyone eating in silence. That is, they were chewing and swallowing, but the whole place seemed stretched like a thread ready to break.

Oliver perched on the edge of a bench, tearing a piece of bread from a large golden loaf with the vehemence of a man wringing the life out of a chicken.

Adele stepped back and turned away. A stab of foreboding sank deep into the fabric of her being.

She marched into the private dining area.

Martha sat on a rocking chair in front of a lively fire, chatting amiably with Gilda. They sipped drinks and ate thick stew from wooden bowls. Normally, the women ate after the men, but Martha had made a new custom: whoever worked with her was allowed to eat ahead of the rest. It was both a privilege and an incentive.

Adele marveled at the simplicity of Martha's arrangement, even as her own stomach grumbled.

Gilda looked up. "Hello, Adele. Are you hungry? We've plenty."

Distracted from her earlier concerns, Adele nodded. "Yes, thank you. Where are little Martha and Thomas?"

Martha smiled knowingly. "They said they would faint away, so I gave them a little meat and cheese and sent them out to chase butterflies."

Gilda frowned as she scooped gravy with her bread. "But there are no butterflies this time of the year." She peered at Martha. "You know that as well as anyone."

"So I do, but *they* don't."

Gilda's lips pursed. "You tricked them?"

Laughing, Martha stood and pulled a loaf of warm bread from a shelf above the hearth and placed it on the table. "How you talk, child!" Then she filled a wooden bowl with meat and vegetables. "First, you imagine yourself a slave, and now you think I'm tricking the babies! No, they'll look for butterflies and find none, and then they'll know a little more about life. There is a season for everything, even butterflies." Martha set the dish of hot stew on the table and motioned for Adele to sit.

Adele slid onto the bench.

Martha frowned at her. "What's wrong with you, I'd like to know. First, I hear Oliver shouting and now you come in here looking like you've seen a ghost. What's the matter?"

Adele stirred the stew and blew on the rising steam. "Oliver was shouting? That's not like him. Did you hear what he said?"

Martha tapped her fingers together. "Not really. But that doesn't matter. Things have been strange since your father went away. I suppose everyone is worried about Wilfred, but some might be just as worried about what might happen to your *father*."

Her bowl empty, Gilda rose to her feet, a scowl etched on her forehead. "Why? What do you mean?"

With a "tut-tut" expression, Martha waved all worries away. "Oh, I shouldn't be saying anything. After all, I might be imagining things or...well, there are some mysteries still left in this world." She grinned. "I'm talking nonsense." She ushered Gilda to the door. "Keep an eye on the little ones, all right? I'll see that Adele eats, and then I'll take a long nap. Call me when the sun crosses over the oaks and the shadow reaches the shed."

Gilda sighed and ambled to the doorway. On the threshold, she looked back and then stepped away.

Martha sat down and closed her eyes, exhaling a long breath.

Adele sipped the soup, the hot savory liquid warming her insides. She ate until her mind calmed. "Is father in danger, then?"

Leaning back in her chair, Martha opened her eyes. "He might be but not for the reasons you suspect. I happen to know that the king has matters he would like to keep private, and Widow Brunswick knows things about the king's past. The king heartily dislikes the widow and anyone the widow tries to defend. If she gets out of temper, which is not unlikely, she might say something everyone will regret, and the king might do something in revenge. You see, the king's father wronged our family mightily, and there is nothing like inherited guilt to make you hate a man. Even an innocent man like Melchior."

Adele twisted the bread into fragments. "But the king said he wanted to know the truth. He said he didn't believe that Wilfred did it. He acted like he cared for us and wanted to do us a favor...he even said...he would..." Adele's breathing rose in heavy, uneven breaths, dizziness enveloping her.

Martha leaned forward, watching her niece's expression. "What did the king say he would do?"

Adele blinked back hot tears. "Find a husband for me. He rubbed my cheek." Adele jerked her hand to wipe the memory from her skin, and her bowl clattered to the floor, splattering stew and scattering breadcrumbs. She jumped to her feet.

Martha snatched a rag tucked under her belt and began cleaning up the mess. "Think nothing of it. I'll throw this out to the birds."

After Martha arranged the disordered spill into a neat circle, she stood and appraised her niece. "Listen to me, child. I understand your disgust; you are not the only maid revolted by the touch of that man, though there are some who don't have the same sense. But what I said was true; he bears his father's guilt towards us, and that makes a man angry, not kind. What King Radburn says and what he does are often far distant. I would not count on his assistance for anything. Besides, any man of his choice would be too much like himself and loyal to him alone." Martha wiped her hands on her apron and took a step nearer. "In addition to that, I have heard strange sounds at night, which leave a bitter feeling in my heart. I fear that Lady Nadine does not rest easy, and her spirit is abroad."

Adele swayed. Clenching her hands together, she looked her aunt in the eye. "What do you mean?"

Martha smiled sheepishly as she returned to her chair. "I know, I'm acting like one of the children, but it's true. I swear by all that I hold dear that I heard a voice the other night...and it sounded like Lady Nadine.

Adele sucked in a deep breath, her eyes straying to a picture etched into the doorframe. Her mother had requested that an angel or a martyr be carved onto every door and window frame. This winged creature, probably an angel, held a spear aloft in triumph. Her mother had always said that God understood the need for protection. *Surely God uses his servants to protect the innocent.* Though crude, the carved image calmed Adele's pounding heart. "When did you hear this...this...sound?"

"More like a conversation—a one-sided conversation. A lady was talking to someone and asking questions...accusing. I couldn't hear much, and I can't remember everything, but the voice said, 'I loved you. I would've kept your secret...' Something like that. Anyway, my hair just about stood on end, and my heart nearly leapt from my chest."

Adele stared into the dwindling fire. "When did this happen?"

"The night your father left."

"Father wasn't here?"

"No, poor dear, he had enough to worry about. The last thing he needs now is a ghost roaming about."

Adele closed her eyes, insane laughter bubbling up inside. She bit her lip. Without a word, she rose and tiptoed to the kitchen.

All the men had left, except for Oliver. He sat alone, methodically chewing a piece of bread and staring at the air.

Adele returned to her aunt. "If you heard it, could Oliver have heard it?"

Martha shook her head. "You would've, more like, for your room is next to mine while his is across the way. No, I don't think he heard a thing. If he had, he would have gone to investigate, thinking it was a thief."

Adele looked around the weathered room, weariness pressing like a smothering blanket. "If you hear the sound again, please wake me, and we will look into the matter."

"I probably just let my imagination run wild. It may have been a servant with a belly ache for all I know."

Adele bowed her head in goodbye and walked to the kitchen, coming up behind Oliver. She placed her hand softly on his shoulder. "Did you get enough to eat, Oliver?"

Though his shoulder flinched at her touch, his expression upon seeing her, changed from irritation to sadness. "Yes, I'm well enough."

"You seem out of sorts. Has anyone been bothering you?"

Oliver smiled a crooked smile. "No. Just tired."

Her mind moving onto practical matters, Adele peered around the kitchen, surveying which jobs needed to be attended to next.

Oliver faced her. "Adele, do you know anything about Father? I mean, about what's happening?"

"Nothing more than you. Father went to speak with the king at the Widow Brunswick's, and Nikolas and Nolan have gone along to assist. We have to trust to fate and friendship, for we don't have much else."

As Adele turned to the door, Oliver stopped her. "Do you think that our sins follow us?"

Adele's fingers dug into the doorpost, pressing the indentation of a mystical carving. She stared out the doorway upon a peaceful rural scene: Gilda playing with the little ones in the autumn garden. "What do you mean?"

Oliver rose, his chair scraping over the flagstones. He lumbered up behind his sister and stood there. “I just wonder if perhaps we make mistakes, we do wrong, and then we forget about it. Then later, when things are going along smoothly, something comes along to remind us of our past. We suddenly realize that others may have been living in hurt all that time. Maybe even God has been living in hurt—and maybe—He hasn’t forgotten.”

Unbidden tears burned in Adele’s eyes. She turned and clung to her brother, resting her forehead against his broad chest, saying only, “Oh, Oliver.”

Chapter Nineteen

Son of Sorrow

Melchior stood silently in the main hall as Father Caedmon prayed to God, the Holy Virgin Mary, and a long list of saints for the soul of Widow Brunswick's servant Demetrius, so recently departed, whose body now lay on a pallet on the stone-cold floor.

"Amen," intoned the assembly.

Father made the sign of the cross over the body.

The priest's protégés, newly professed monks Stephen and Mark, stood to his side, clearly trying to concentrate on their own prayers, but that was a hard task considering the situation. Prickly sweat beaded their foreheads and stained the armpits of their gray robes. It was rather awful being caught between heavenly saints and earthly villains.

King Radburn paced before the hearth, grimacing. The way he cut the air with his hand and his grumbling undertone dispelled any doubts about his participation in the upcoming funeral rites. Everyone knew that he had murdered the man and that he planned to leave as soon as possible. And he would have, but Widow Brunswick, after gaining some measure of self-control and descending the steps with her chin held high, had insisted that he meet with her and Father Caedmon privately.

Father Caedmon's head had jerked up at the announcement.

Melchior, Nikolas, and Nolan were told to wait, but the widow insisted that Father's two helpers assist her now that she had been deprived of her faithful servant.

Before she left the main room for a more private setting in the library, she stopped before Melchior. "Despite my personal loss, I have not forgotten my duty as hostess. Take your friends before the fire and rest yourselves. We have much to discuss. The king and I must settle an important matter first. If all goes well, he will leave my home having cleared your son's name. If not, well, we will see."

She turned and marched into the next room.

The king followed stiffly. Behind him padded the priest and his two obedient but hesitant young monks.

After a short time, the five reappeared.

The widow's eyes shot flames as she strode into the great hall, while the king's gaze darted in all directions. He did not protest when Father Caedmon ordered that Demetrius' body be laid out in the small chapel to the right of the main hall.

Melchior watched with hawk-like eyes, but he could not discover the mystery inside the mystery. *Where is my son?* He met the widow in the middle of the room and cleared his throat.

She nodded slowly. "Yes, of course, to the matter that brought us all here this night. Your son, Melchior, is cleared of all charges. He did not kill Lady Nadine."

A great intake of breath met this news, especially from Lord Gerard, who protested vehemently. "What in the devil's name are you saying? There has been no investigation, no trial! Why, I haven't even been able to question the boy yet."

Widow Brunswick snarled, "You haven't been allowed to torture a confession out of him, that's true. But the king and I"—she glanced sideways at the king—"have decided that there is not enough evidence to warrant further questioning. The boy merely went outside for a breath of fresh air and was found guilty of murder. Rather unlucky of him, wasn't it?"

Lord Gerard clapped his hands together in fury. "That's

not how it happened, and you know it! The king knows it!" Lord Gerard turned on the king, his eyes red with rage. "I told you everything that happened, and you admitted that most likely the boy went to meet Corliss and accidentally met up with Lady Nadine, who tried to stop him, and he killed her in a fit of passion."

Father Caedmon raised his hand and said with authority, "Lady Nadine was indeed murdered, and we do need to discover who did *that* terrible deed, but I think we are forgetting something a little closer to our immediate interest. There was a murder here recently, and we know exactly who did it."

All eyes turned to the king.

King Radburn stared at the widow. "We just settled that. We decided to drop *all* charges."

Nolan spoke up. "It seems to me that we have a lot to discuss, too much in fact, to hurry the matter. It's late now, and I, for one, am tired and hungry. I'm sure that Melchior and my young friend are famished and exhausted as well. Can we call a truce for the night? No one is to leave. When we assemble in the morning, let us bring forth everyone involved, including young Wilfred. We can lay the matters before an impartial judge—perhaps Father Caedmon could suggest a trusted, impartial man. Could we all agree to accept his honest decision and leave it at that?"

Nolan surveyed the assembly and smiled broadly. "Unless someone here is afraid of the truth? We can always go back to our homes and let battle strategies plan out other options."

The king glared at Nolan.

Nolan stared at Lord Gerard.

Lord Gerard pursed his lips in disgust.

Father Caedmon smiled.

Melchior glanced at the widow.

She, poor woman, stared at the floor as if she did not care if it swallowed her whole.

King Radburn cleared his throat. “I will accept this *kind* offer only because I wish to serve on the side of justice. I know the Widow Brunswick thinks I murdered her slave without provocation, but tomorrow I will prove to all that I am an innocent man and that *my* honor, at least, is still intact. In the meantime, keep the boy under lock and key. No one knows what a desperate youth may attempt. Certainly, he knows more than he is telling. He was right there when the woman died, and he must know who did it. In that case, he should be thoroughly interviewed.”

Alarm sped through Melchior. “But not tortured!”

The king smiled coldly. “I had hoped to be off on an urgent matter in the west tonight, but that will have to wait.” Without another word, he turned and marched from the room.

Nikolas exhaled a long breath and stepped nearer to Nolan. “Brilliant! How did you ever think of it?”

Nolan grinned. “My grandmother could tell a tale that would stand your hair up on end. I just imagined I was in one of those.” He frowned. “There are more secrets in this manor than murderers, and when we understand the secrets, we will solve the murders.”

“But why did the king murder the widow’s servant?”

Father Caedmon interrupted. “If you are wise, you’ll not ask another question tonight. Wilfred is resting safely; he’ll be sharing a room with my young assistants. Now go to bed and get some sleep. After what you hear tomorrow, you may not rest so easy.” The priest turned and ushered his young assistants out the door.

Nolan nudged Nikolas. “Let’s find some food. Afterwards, I’m so tired, I’ll sleep like a stone.”

Nikolas yawned and followed his friend to the kitchen.

The widow and Melchior stood alone in the great hall.

Melchior stepped forward with his hands clasped. "I've not had a chance to thank you properly, Widow Brunswick, for all you've done to preserve the life of my son."

The widow waved feebly. "Little enough, I assure you. I always try to shelter the homeless or travelers caught in a storm. He was just one among many, or so I thought, but I've learned much since then."

Thoughts of what might happen to his son tied Melchior's stomach into knots. *Oh, God, help me.* With forced composure, Melchior nodded toward the chapel. "Would you like to pray?"

Tears formed in the widow's eyes. She clasped his hand and led the way.

A clammy chill pervaded the dim circular room. Thick tapestries hung from the curved walls, while chairs stood empty before the body of her faithful servant, still dressed in his tunic, stretched out on a pine board.

The Widow Brunswick stifled a sob.

Not sure what to say but realizing that he must understand the situation better, or his son's life might fall forfeit to his ignorance, Melchior broke the silence. "My dear lady, I know you have just lost a trusted and valued servant, and we feel these things deeply, but I was wondering if you would tell me something about my son. Can you shed light on the mystery of Lady Nadine's death?"

The widow stared at the prone figure. Bloodstains had turned dark brown, almost black. She did not appear to have heard Melchior. "I'll have my women ready him for burial in the morning. Normally, we would have attended to the matter right away, but..." Her voice faded.

Melchior bowed his head.

Her tremulous voice rose again. "He was more than just a servant; he was like a son. Never knew his mother and father. They abandoned him for all the usual reasons. Strange how if a man and a woman break the laws of God and then have a child, they think the solution is to break another of God's laws. What strange minds people have! I shouldn't tell you, but I'm in the mood to reveal secrets. Or perhaps I am sick of lies." The widow turned her glistening eyes on Melchior. "Can you accept the truth?"

As if a knife pressed against his throat, terror rippled over Melchior. He could think of only one honorable answer, however. "With the grace of God, I can accept anything."

"*Anything?* How easily we say those words! And of course, since we invoke the name of The Most High God, we think we are assured of a good outcome, but God is not so easy, no. He's not tame." The widow leaned forward. "Many years ago, a powerful man enjoyed a tryst with a beautiful woman, but they were from different lands, and she was married to a dangerous but well-respected ruler. She found she was with child, and I can only imagine how she pleaded with her lover to accept the babe when it was born, but he would not.

"She gave the baby to another woman and died in grief and bitterness. The poor boy ended up a slave and, in time, was brought into my household. He was intelligent and well educated. We had many fine discussions together, and my heart came alive in his company as it had never done with my husband. If he had been older or had I been younger, who knows...but, no, it was never like that between us. We were faithful and looked after each other. He was my best protector, and I made sure he had everything he could ever want. Except his family. I never could give him his father or his mother, and though it may not seem like much to those who have never done without, the intimacy of blood relations means everything to someone who never knew them.

"I did not know his secret until I told him mine: my sister married a good man and had two children, but they were a poor family, and she died too soon. The son lived with the father and made a living on the sea, but the daughter was fostered to a wealthy family and married well, for she was beautiful. Her name was Nadine, and she became Lady Nadine, wife of Lord Gerard."

A slow hiss escaped Melchior's lips.

The Widow Brunswick lifted her hand in warning. "Wait now; there is more. When Lady Nadine gave birth to a daughter, she was glad, but after seeing how her husband raised the girl, she hated her husband and feared for a son who would grow up under his hand. But the fates conspired against her, for a year later, she gave birth to a healthy boy. On the same day, a neighbor's baby died during childbirth. Upon hearing of it, Lady Nadine made a bold plan and begged her neighbor to raise her son, while she took the dead child and gave it a good burial. And so the switch was made, and her son grew up as her neighbor's child, their husbands being none the wiser."

As if his body had turned to stone, Melchior sat rigid. Foreboding filled him.

The Widow Brunswick tapped her fingers together.

Melchior's voice was husky when he managed to force his out words. "Whose wife…changed babies…?"

The widow's lips trembled. "Yours."

Melchior jumped to his feet and marched to the slit of a window, which carved a black rectangle in the night air. "My Edwina did this? She gave me another man's son?"

The widow wrung her hands together, her voice pleading. "Demetrius was like a son to me, though he never knew his parents. His father would not claim him from the first, and he would not claim him today—even after he murdered him. I ask you, who is the parent, the one who loved him or the one who rejected him?"

Melchior turned slowly around and stared, shock washing over him like a cold rain. "The king was *Demetrius' father*? Oh, Heaven, help us! Are we all punished then?"

"Yes, I see what you mean. Does the king, in his unrepentant guilt, hate *all* sons?"

Melchior dropped onto the chair. "How did the king react? I am supposing *that* was the conversation you had behind locked doors when we first arrived?"

"I told him that he had killed his own son, and he looked quite amazed, completely at a loss for words. I had expected to surprise him; truly, I had hoped to horrify him, but that man is beyond horror. He did agree to drop all charges against your son if I would never tell anyone about this—shall we say—*indelicacy* of murdering his own son."

"Does the king know that Wilfred is Lady Nadine's son?"

"I suspect he has already heard a rumor, for walls have ears and this story, though kept close, has been told more than once."

"Am I the last to know that my son is not my own?"

The widow dropped her gaze.

"Does Wilfred know?"

She looked at him with despairing eyes.

Melchior's shoulders slumped. *Dear God, give me strength.* He sucked in a deep breath. "Does the king know who murdered Lady Nadine?"

"No more than you or I. He just shifts his words to fit the climate. If he wants the support of Lord Gerard, he promises to find and punish the murderer, even if he has to kill an innocent man to get the job done. When he speaks with you, it seems he has another goal. What that would be, I don't know." The widow's body shuddered through a yawn. "Demetrius always reminded me of my rest time, so good about watching over... Oh, I must let him go." She rose feebly to her feet.

Melchior took her arm and led her gently to the stone steps. "Please, do rest. Tomorrow will be difficult, and I, among others, will need your strength."

The widow shuffled forward, her back bending under heavy grief. After she climbed the first step, she looked over her shoulder at Melchior. "You do forgive Edwina, don't you?"

Melchior swallowed and rubbed his hand across his brow. "'If we say that we have no sin, we deceive ourselves, and the truth is not in us...' I'll need to forgive myself first." Melchior looked away. "I once told her in a heat of fury that if Lord Gerard ever had a son, I would gladly kill him just to rid the world of his kind. My hate is turned against me now. But a son is a gift, whether given through blood or sorrow. I care no less for the boy, if that comforts you."

Widow Brunswick nodded and climbed the steep steps. "You're a better man than most, Melchior."

Melchior sighed. Turning away, he shuffled back to the chapel, where he crept in and sat down, tears burning his cheeks.

Chapter Twenty

One Lifetime

—Planet Helm—

Song sat in a padded chair at Teal's bedside, her hands clasped and her head bowed. It was an old room, the remnant of the first prayer-house ever built on Helm. The teak wood window frames, baseboards, rafters, and furniture had ripened to a rich sheen, giving the space a comforting, ever-lasting feel.

Steepling her pale fingers under her chin, her gaze traveled over Teal. After cleansing his body and making proper infusions with hypo-static thoughts, words, and actions in order to restore balance to his spirit, her attendants had left her to guard him in quiet prayer.

He lay still and quite naked on the bed.

You won't like that when you wake up.

After inhaling a bracing breath, she climbed to her feet and padded to a shelf loaded with neatly folded blankets on the fat wall. Though the temperature huddled close to the Bhuaci comfort zone during the day, it often dropped below freezing at night. She selected a forest-green blanket from a colorful selection and carried it to the bed, where she lay it gently over Teal.

With a groan, Teal opened his eyes to mere slits. "Song?"

She patted his hand and forced a smile. "Yes. I'm here."

Teal grimaced and licked his lips. "What—happened?"

"You collapsed." Song perched on the edge of the padded chair and leaned forward. "Don't worry. Cerulean is safe. He's with Sterling and the others on Earth, continuing their mission."

Teal's eyes widened, alarm filling them. "Where am *I*?"

"On Helm. Zuri helped me get you to my ship and we—"

"I must go back!" His voice wavering, he struggled to rise. "Now!"

Song laid her hand on his chest. She didn't need to press. He had no strength to resist. "You'll go back. In time. But not today. For now, you must rest."

His jaw clenching, Teal's eyes narrowed. "And if I refuse?"

Unbidden tears filled Song's eyes. "You will die."

Teal stared at her, comprehension in his twitching expression. "But Cerulean…"

"He will learn. Just as you did. As your father did before you. We are allotted one lifetime. You can only live yours. Not your son's."

Teal's gaze traveled to the ceiling and stopped, frozen.

Song glanced up. A spider dangled by a web from the beam above. Was it anyone she knew? Probably not. Likely just an honest spider looking for the day's meal.

A tear trickled down Teal's cheek, his face as still as carven stone.

Song stood, her long gray-blue dress barely touching the flagstone floor. "Sterling must lead, and Cerulean will follow. They have much to teach each other."

With an almost imperceptible shake of his head, Teal continued to focus on the ceiling.

"Though I have never given birth to flesh and blood, I have mothered many. The hardest part of love is not holding a dear one close, it's letting them go."

Song reached the doorway when she heard his raspy response.

"I will see him again."

She padded through the arched hallway. *I pray so.*

—OldEarth—

Zuri paced before his daughter, clenching his hands as he struggled to keep his anger from bursting to the surface.

In the background, Melchior's home stood silent in the glow of late evening. A vigorous autumn storm had passed, and wet grass clung to his boots, leaving snags of broken stems and splashes of mud in his wake.

"I don't understand why you can't follow a few simple rules. It's not as if I am asking you to do anything outside of ordinary protocol. Every representative has to stay with the group unless he or she has been given express direction to go alone. Everything must be recorded, and the details are sent in a formal report at the end of the cycle. You know this. I've complained about the bureaucracy often enough."

Nova scowled. "It's not because you and mom are being hypersensitive? Parents primeval?"

Zuri raked his fingers through his short blond hair. "By God in Heaven! Your mother is tending to Teal on Helm. I'm here as an Ingoti representative. We just want you to do your job. Correctly. No more running off, you understand?"

"Mauve didn't think it was a big deal."

Owls hooted in the distance, and a rough cough sounded from the house.

A stooped, old man shuffled from a barn doorway and labored to a ramshackle house set near the woods. He mumbled under his breath.

Zuri grabbed his daughter's hand and yanked her

further down the dark path. "Mauve is hardly a proper role model. Neither is Sterling, at the moment. But that hardly matters. You know better. Cerulean is a child, but even he knows!"

With a snort, Nova kicked a stone in the path. "All you can see is a child—not a young man or a young woman. Is there nothing between babyhood and old age?" She stomped her foot. "You don't trust me."

Fury flooding his mind, Zuri could hardly think. He threw back his head and stared at the faint stars. *God, help me.*

A throat clearing jolted Zuri. He spun around and peered into the gathering darkness.

Sterling, dressed in a grey cloak and red leggings, stepped forward. "I hate to interrupt a private moment, but I'm having trust issues of my own."

A smothered laugh from Nova earned a hard glare from Zuri.

Sterling gathered them closer with a beckoning motion. "Mauve has taken to the minstrel life—and all that entails—leaving me to wonder why I worked so hard to become a member of the Supreme Council."

Zuri winced. "You'd be happier playing the fool?"

The twisted grin that played over Sterling's face sent a shiver over Zuri.

"There lies my dilemma. I don't mind playing a fool. I just don't like being played for a fool." Straightening, Sterling pointed to the house. "She can play to her heart's content while I investigate the Mystery Race. Someone has been leaving traces of their presence all over Earth without any formal introduction to the Inter-Alien Alliance."

Zuri rubbed his forehead. "They can't be left unchecked. But I must stay and keep an eye on Melchior's family. Something very strange is developing. The powers which ruled Neb may have returned, leading another family into open treachery." He glanced at Nova, anxiety tying his stomach into knots.

"I'm taking Cerulean with me." Sterling glanced aside. "Perhaps Nova would like to accompany us?"

Surprised but pleased, Zuri nodded in what he feared might to be too eager an assent. "That'll work. I have to check on Tarragon. He's been following the events at the Widow Brunswick's, but I can't let him wander around freely. If only he would blend in better. But he doesn't seem to care. Not an ounce of natural sensitivity."

Nova scoffed. "He's a Cresta. What do you expect?" She faced Sterling. "Cerulean is in the kitchen playing the dutiful servant. But I'm sure he'd approve of a change of plans." She shrugged. "I'd like to see what these mystery beings look like. Though I suppose they're good at disguises. Still, actions reveal the inner person, right?"

In farewell, Sterling clapped Zuri on the shoulder. "She's got Kelesta's insightful nature. If she doesn't go into a flirting frenzy every few moments, we'll get along fine."

Nova grimaced. "I never flirt. No point. Being mixed-race—I'm as sterile as a Cresta laboratory. Investigation will be my life. So, let's go investigate."

Sterling held out his hand.

Grinning, Nova accepted it.

Zuri watched the two colorfully dressed figures stroll toward the kitchen entrance, his heart relaxing. Then he remembered Teal. *If only you were here.*

Chapter Twenty-One

The Great Unknown

Corliss tried to rub away the shivers running down her arms. When Oliver struck Selby, she scurried inside the house and hid in one of the storerooms just off the kitchen. She wasn't sure if this was to any advantage, but she couldn't stand being cooped up in her own house while Lord Marlow demanded she go about preparing for their wedding. Sick dread filled her.

When Martha revealed to Adele her fears, describing the strange conversation she had heard the night before and her suspicion that Lady Nadine's ghost walked the earth, Corliss' heart began to pound in her ears. Was her mother wandering abroad, no longer ensconced in her cairn? Suddenly, Corliss had not the slightest interest in discovering the truth; she just wanted to be free of mounting terrors.

Adele stepped into the main kitchen, heading toward Oliver.

Corliss crouched low and clutched the storeroom door, trying not to give way to dizziness.

Suddenly, Martha yanked the door open and glared down, a stout-handled broom firmly grasped in her hand. "What on the saints' good earth are you doing, girl?"

Blackness taking her sight, Corliss swayed.

Martha caught her by her shoulders. "Don't faint here, for heaven's sake. The servants will be back at any moment. Adele went to speak with Oliver. Want me to fetch her for you?"

Corliss struggled to her feet and straightened. "No. She wouldn't understand. She's probably mad enough for what I've done."

Martha leaned her broom comfortably against the wall and propped one hand on her hip. "Well now, you might want to explain that. What have you done?"

A flash of understanding clarified Corliss' thoughts. "Oh, I mean what I've done in the past—for getting Oliver angry. Though it wasn't really my fault. Your servant was quite rude."

Martha scowled. "Rude? You must be mistaken. We have no rude servants." She narrowed her eyes, her gaze appraising Corliss. "You must be Lord Gerard's daughter—all grown up, I see."

"Yes. I'm Corliss. It was my mother who was killed, and—" She stopped herself. She had no idea why she was about to blurt out her fears to a stranger, but she felt an uncontrollable need to confide in someone, and this stout woman seemed strong enough to handle any amount of dreadful knowledge.

Martha's gaze softened. "Come here and rest awhile. We can chat a bit before duty calls or the servants begin preparations for the next meal." Martha dropped heavily onto her chair.

Corliss bit her lip. She was torn. On the one hand, she wished very much to crawl home to bed and cry her fears away. On the other hand— "Can I trust you?"

Martha laughed. "Trust me with your life if you will; I'm no villain. But beware, walls have ears."

Corliss closed her eyes and swallowed hard.

Martha took the girl by the arm and led her to the bench. "Here, sit. I was only trying to make a point not scare you to death."

“But you said—I heard you say—you think my mother rises from her gave and walks the earth, talking to herself.”

Martha flushed. “Now, if I had realized that walls really did have ears, I’d have kept my mouth shut.” She pushed Corliss onto the bench and sat next to her, leaning close to speak privately. “It’s true; I heard a disturbing voice. I plan on staying up tonight to find out who it is.”

“How can you? I mean, won’t you be terrified? It might be an angry spirit and she, or whoever it is, might do some mischief.”

Martha studied the ceiling and seemed to consider the girl’s words. “Yes, it might be, but I am not afraid. Well, not so terrified that I’d back down from my duty. I’m not alone either. I have friends, and I’ll bring them with me.”

Incredulity filled Corliss. “Friends? Who?”

“Saint Mary, the mother of God, to begin with. She’s always good to bring to terrifying places. I’m sure she understands. Then—”

“You mean *spirits*? Are you out of your mind? The spirits are all in league against the living. Th-they can drive a man mad.”

“Oh, no, that is where you’re wrong. I’ve heard countless stories of spirits giving aid to those in need.”

Corliss shook her head. “Demons frighten me. My father is terrified of them. He can hardly set eyes on a dead body or a cairn.”

“Considering your father, that’s only sensible.” Martha stood up and retrieved a bowl. She scooped out the last of the stew and handed it over. “You’d better eat. There’s no saying how things will go tonight, and I suspect that you have as much interest in this matter as anyone.”

Shock running through her, Corliss accepted the bowl.

"You mean the two of us—alone?"

Martha sighed. "I thought I just explained that. We won't be alone, but if you insist, we'll ask Oliver and Adele to sit with us."

"You think they would? A night without sleep is a high price to pay when there's so much work to be done."

Amusement glinted in Martha's eyes. "They're not so overworked as all that. Besides, it'll just turn out to be someone with a stomachache." She marched to the door then glanced over her shoulder. "What'll everyone at the manor house think if you don't return tonight?"

As a combination of relief and excitement coursed through her, Corliss chewed the tender stew meat. "I snuck away. Lord Marlow and Richard are out hunting."

Martha pursed her lips. "In that case, I'll send Oliver over to explain that I've asked you to stay as my guest. If Lord Marlow arrives demanding to know why, I'll give him an earful. But I doubt he will. Men are usually content after a hunt, as long as they're well-fed and given plenty of drink."

Corliss wiped a bit of gravy from her chin. "My father's storehouses are full to bursting. I'm sure they will lack for nothing."

Martha nodded. "Now eat your stew, and don't play any tricks. I've enough worries. I'll find Oliver and speak to Adele, and we'll make it a quiet evening."

A fresh shiver ran up Corliss' arms at the thought of spending time with Oliver, but this time, she was neither cold nor uncomfortable.

~~~
~~~

Martha, wrapped in a thick nightdress and a grey shawl, leaned against the wall with her legs stretched out on her bed. At the slightest move, a loud creak emanated from the bed frame. She shrugged it off.

Looking pale and weary, Adele perched on a small chair in the corner. With each crack, her gaze flicked from the bed to Oliver.

Martha shuffled into a comfortable position. "My little noises will make everything appear normal. I always move about a bit before I finally get to sleep."

Hidden in the shadows, Oliver stood still as a statue with his arms folded over his chest.

Corliss crouched in the opposite dim corner, shivering on a thick mat with pillows that Adele had laid out for her. Her eyes were wide open and trained on Oliver, who appeared to be doing everything in his power to ignore her.

The early hours passed in silence, the slow passage of time weighing heavily.

Corliss began to nod.

Adele rested her chin on her hands, her eyelids drooping.

Martha's head relaxed into the folds of her pillow, and she closed her eyes.

A low moan jerked everyone wide awake.

Martha stared through the darkness at Oliver. With an intake of breath, she shook the vestiges of sleepiness away.

Again! A strange and horrible moan, as if a man were near his end after a long and terrible torture.

Oliver stepped forward, the floor creaking.

The moaning stopped.

A moment of absolute silence.

Then again, a grievous moan, as if from someone in torment.

Oliver dashed through the doorway.

Martha scuttled up behind and stared after his darting form.

A hunched shadow loped across the main hall.

Oliver turned and started after it.

Suddenly, it fled, jerking and limping across the grounds.

Oliver gave chase.

With a cry, Adele scurried after Oliver.

Smashing down her fear, Martha hurried behind.

Oliver captured the shrouded figure, groans and choked sobs punctuating the air.

Recognizing the figure, Martha reached out, an unspoken question on her lips.

Selby hung limp in Oliver's grip, clearly demented. Selby's twisted expression sent tremors through Martha's body. The evil in the old man's eyes sneered at her.

It had been Selby all along.

Chapter Twenty-Two

An Enraged Dragon

—Several Hours Earlier—

Richard sat in front of a roaring fire with a board loaded with sumptuous food and drink set between him and Lord Marlow. He wanted to snarl, though he was far too sensitive and dignified to allow anything to disfigure his finely sculpted features. But a headache pounded right behind his eyes, where a snarl would have liked to start—if he had allowed it.

At the present moment, he did everything in his power to keep his temper intact and his exhaustion from snapping his frayed nerves. He had spent a long, tedious day in the woods with Lord Marlow, and even though he was an expert with a bow and arrow, as well as a spear, a sword, and any number of finely wrought knives, *and* he knew perfectly well how to handle a horse, he had been pulled up short by Lord Marlow, as if he were nothing more than a farm boy out on his first hunting expedition.

"Here, here, keep your head about you! We have the fiercest stags in the world in these woods. Stay behind me and follow my lead. I know where I'm going."

You know where you're going? Richard had seriously doubted that, barely controlling the snort which would give vent to his utter contempt for his companion and self-declared guide.

Richard liked to think of himself as something of a stoic by nature. He loved good literature, and he read everything he could get his hands on. His natural inclination was to read the way most men drank. As he watched Lord Marlow gulp down large swallows of ale and chew noisily on a dripping chunk of meat, he again stifled his sneer. He loathed this man, and he could hardly understand his own violent reaction. Lord Marlow was not an exception but an accurate example of most men he knew. Richard blew a long breath between his lips.

Lord Marlow, mistaking the sound for one of pleased comfort, leaned back heavily in his chair, sloshing a bit of the brew he held in one hand, while with the other, he gripped a slab of roasted pork. "Didn't get our stag, did we? What's the difference? Lord Gerard has enough to feed ten villages."

Lord Marlow swallowed the hunk he had been noisily chewing, took another swig, then reached for a piece of bread. "It's good to let the stags know you're about. I could've had that last one, but you sniffed and scared him off! You probably have your meat provided by your slaves, but I like to keep the manly arts. The feel of blood on a man's hands gives him a sense of rightness, keeps him close to the gods of Earth and sky."

Richard snorted.

Lord Marlow refilled his mug of ale, eyeing Richard narrowly. "I don't know how you do it, living so near the king—probably swarming with Romans and barbarians. I'd be wanting to cut everyone's head off. Ha! That'd be a hunt, wouldn't it? Kill all the—"

A servant stepped in and bowed low. "A man would like to see you, sir."

Lord Marlow rose unsteadily.

Annoyed, Richard jumped to his feet. Why would his brother's soon-to-be son-in-law presume that he was master of the manor when he, as *brother* to the absent lord, naturally stood in that place? Curbing the desire to make a scene, he let Lord Marlow play his role, no matter how undeservedly he possessed it.

The servant retreated and reappeared leading Oliver.

Lord Marlow pointed with a shaky finger. "By the gods! What are you doing here? You're the brother of that scoundrel. Or are you a servant?"

Richard advanced with his arm outstretched in polite welcome. "Pay no attention. He's been on the hunt and is now drinking himself into a merry stupor." He waved him aside. "Let's go into the other room, and we shall discuss your purpose."

Lord Marlow spluttered, "Stop! I'm soon to be wed to the lord's daughter and that makes me the lord's son, which outranks you—you..." Lord Marlow swayed and lost his balance but then righted himself, puzzlement replacing anger. "Where's Corliss?"

Oliver stepped forward.

Distracted, Lord Marlow lurched toward Richard. "That's what you need—a woman. Corliss is mine. I mean to keep her!"

Oliver squared his shoulders. "That's why I've come, my lord. Aunt Martha invited Corliss to spend the night with us. They are supping together and will sleep early. She will return tomorrow."

Richard grinned.

Melting into scowling petulance, Lord Marlow boomed, "What? Without my permission? Who said she could leave this house or stray beyond these borders? Who does your aunt think she is, inviting her without asking me first?"

Oliver stood his ground. "No one thought to ask you. She is safe and happy, and my aunt and sister are glad for her company."

Relief mixing with spiteful joy, Richard offered a formal bow. "Thank you, Oliver. She's had a bad time, what with her mother's death. I couldn't be more grateful to your aunt. Please tell her so for me." He led Oliver toward the entryway. "And tell us if there is anything we can do for you."

Oliver tipped his head respectfully and left the room.

Lord Marlow swayed, his mouth open, a bit of bread and spittle caught on his beard. "What are you doing, sending him away like that?! I'm the lord, and I want Corliss back now!"

In the bright glare of insight, Richard's head cleared of all confusion. "No one told *me* that you are master here, and as long as my brother *is my brother,* then my niece is under my protection." He leaned in. "You are not married yet and may never be."

Lord Marlow blew air like an enraged dragon. "How dare you!" His face flushed, his eyes unnaturally wide, he gripped the knife tucked at his side.

Richard shook his head. "You can't get away with another murder."

Lord Marlow stumbled backwards. "I never murdered anyone. I'm an honest man."

Richard clenched his jaw. He had been plagued by nightmares where Lord Gerard argued with Lady Nadine, and then Lord Marlow handed him a knife. An ache tightened his throat. Lady Nadine had loved his brother—in the beginning. But love had turned to hate all too soon. Now, here was another beast planning to replay the nightmare. Except Corliss would fight—once she saw the man for the monster he really was. He shook his head decisively. "I doubt that very much." He appraised the drunken lord. "I'm going to my room now. You can try to stop me, and I'll beat you for the fool you are, or you can go back to your meal. You'll see Corliss when she returns tomorrow."

Richard knew that the real battle he needed to fight was between himself and his brother. With utter contempt warming his face, he turned and marched to the winding staircase.

The words, “Me, a murderer? We’ll see about that!” rang in his ears just as he was knocked to the cold, stone floor.

Chapter Twenty-Three

Our Natures That Deceive

Harold kicked his foster brother's foot as the young man slumped against the stone wall, snoring in the shelter of the cool barn, his chin on his chest.

He rubbed his own sweaty, stiff neck. *Lordy, I smell like old straw.* When Terrill didn't respond to the first summons, Harold kicked him again, harder.

Terrill awoke with a start. "Hey!"

"Time to rise, fool. The sun is up, and the king wants the boy." Harold glanced around the stable, scratching his rough beard.

Three rays of sunlight streaming from a bank of high slit windows fell on the straw-covered floor, blanketing the ground in golden threads.

Harold blinked back an ache behind his eyes.

Terrill yawned, stretching and muttering a few curses. His dusty tunic, stained with last night's porridge, hung askew on his body.

The glorious moment shattered, Harold marched across the courtyard.

Dew on the lawn glinted like earth-born stars. Some fool in a colorful getup scampered across the way. The sturdy shelter sat caddy-corner of the courtyard, humble yet definitive, seeming to say, "Though my timber is freshly cut, I belong here as much as any of you ancient frames."

Knocking sharply on the heavy oak door of the priests' abode, Harold stood with his shoulders squared.

Terrill slouched against the wall.

The door creaked open, and they were admitted into a

dark hallway, which soon transitioned into a large, bright space where the sunlight streamed in through round windows. The beams converged above an altar at the end of the room. A carved figure with a thoughtful expression stood against the wall. Harold stared at it transfixed while Terrill merely glanced aside and yawned again.

Father Caedmon knelt before the altar, intent on his prayers. At the sound of the yawn, he looked over his shoulder and then rose to his feet.

Terrill and Harold waited in silence.

Father Caedmon called aside, "Wilfred."

Wilfred stepped from an enclave on the right, his clothing cleaner but no less disheveled than Terrill's. With hunched shoulders and downcast eyes, he appeared resigned to the mysteries of fate.

The four men met in the middle of the room.

With a harrumph, Terrill led the way back to the front door.

Coming in line with the statue, Harold pointed and turned to the priest. "Who did that carving?"

Father Caedmon smiled. "A man condemned to death. He finished it just two days before he died."

Harold blinked, astonished. He had imagined it was the work of a highly paid artisan from some foreign court. "A condemned criminal, you say? What had he done?"

"Not a criminal but condemned to an early death nonetheless with an illness no one could cure."

"The man should've been in bed, saving his strength. Then he could've made other beautiful things."

Father Caedmon's eyebrows rose, his gaze gently searching. "Who cares about beautiful things?"

Terrill snorted.

Flustered, Harold would not give up his point. "Some of us do. If nothing else, he could've lived longer."

Father Caedmon's eyes danced. "Why live longer?"

"No one wants to shorten their days, given a choice."

Father Caedmon's smile broadened as he strode toward the dark hallway. "He didn't shorten his days. If anything, he lengthened them right into eternity."

When Wilfred stopped and stared at the statue, Terrill reached back and plucked his sleeve, pulling him from his reverie.

Wilfred sighed and attempted to arrange his clothes into a more presentable appearance.

Terrill opened the broad front door and snorted. "Hurry up! The day is young, but it won't get much older for you. The king is in a foul mood, and he'll see you hang before it's over."

Once outside in the glaring light of day, Wilfred wrapped his cloak tighter, shivering despite the warm sun.

Father Caedmon shook his finger at Terrill. "Foul mood or no, I'll see that this boy gets justice, and mercy, too, if he needs it. Another priest will be in attendance. He will listen to all sides, and he'll see to it that no question is left unanswered in the matter of Lady Nadine's death."

The four men marched across the compound and into the main hall.

Staking a place to see events clearly, Harold took his post guarding the doorway. He looked around the stark space. For such a wealthy woman, the Widow Brunswick didn't spend much on folderol, entertainments, or festive decorations. Monstrous black beams cross overhead, while massive fireplaces at each end stood dead quiet. Five tables pushed together at the head of the room made a gathering place for family and close friends at mealtime, while twenty other tables and benches filled the remaining space.

Terrill nudged him and rubbed his stomach meaningfully.

Harold shook his head and crossed his arms. He ignored his own empty stomach as anxiety coursed through him. *Let's see what fair justice God offers the lad. Then maybe...*

King Radburn sat in an ornate chair at the head table, the Widow Brunswick ensconced in her own chair at the opposite end. Lord Gerard sat closest to the king at a table perpendicular to them, while Melchior, Nikolas, and Nolan were spread further down. Father Caedmon and Wilfred took up the humblest position at the foot.

Wilfred met Melchior's eyes briefly in a painful exchange; no words were said.

A man wearing a black robe over a simple tunic paced off to the side. The slanting morning light from high slit windows fell across him as he gestured dismissively to the king. "No, thank you. I prefer to remain standing. It helps me think." He surveyed the solemn crowd. His short-cropped, gray hair belied his vigorous physique. Though he stopped near the Widow Brunswick, his open arms embraced the wider audience.

"My name is Father Neumann, and I want to thank the Widow Brunswick for calling me here today as arbitrator of this case. Father Caedmon explained the situation last night. He did not share the details, however, for he'd rather I decide this matter without any prejudice." The priest bowed his head. "Though I must be honest and say that no man is without his prejudice, even myself. But after listening to all sides, I'll do my best to come to an honest conclusion, and may the Lord, God of Hosts, enlighten my understanding."

Still wearing his expensive fur cloak over his gold-embroidered tunic and fancy leggings, Lord Gerard appeared as grand as ever.

Except for his scraggly hair. Harold ran his hand over his head, grateful for his thick locks.

Like a petulant child, Lord Gerard snorted. "Just get on with it! We don't have all day."

King Radburn waved Lord Gerard's comment away. "I accept your offer, good Father. I know that once you hear all the facts, you will see fit to punish the guilty and free the innocent. I have no other interest in *my* mind." The king smiled benignly.

The widow snorted this time.

Harold smiled and settled his stance into a comfortable position. *This ought to prove interesting, if nothing else.*

It took the better part of the morning for everyone to have his say, recalling events as they knew them. Father Neumann listened carefully and interrupted several times to ask detailed questions.

Though he had not been near the actual scene, Harold could soon imagine the series of events in vivid detail.

Servants slipped in twice, offering food and drink. No one ate, though many accepted drinks.

In the dwindling afternoon heat, Wilfred was finally allowed a chance to give his account of what happened. His summary sounded like the desperate pleas of an already condemned man. "Everyone was screaming and shouting. I didn't know what to do, so I ran!"

Harold furrowed his brow, perplexed. Though it seemed clear to him that Wilfred did not kill Lady Nadine, it was equally obvious that no one else in the room had either. Too many witnesses testified that everyone in the room had been somewhere else when the deed was done. Still, something about Lord Gerard's testimony did not add up, and Father Neumann's frequent glances at his brother priest hinted at his doubts.

In red-faced passion, Lord Gerard stood up, pointing his finger at the boy and shouting, "You little liar! You arranged to meet my daughter outside the hall, and when Lady Nadine found you, she tried to stop you, and you—

like the coward you are—stabbed her!"

Grasping the edge of the table for support, Wilfred's face drained of all color. "I didn't! I swear it! I was going to meet your daughter, that's true, but we never saw each other. I heard someone calling, and I became frightened, so I hid. I saw Lady Nadine come forward, a-a-and-I saw her fall into *your* arms."

Everyone stared at Lord Gerard, who had grown pale in turn. "How dare you accuse me? I'm not the one on trial!"

Nolan climbed to his feet. "You, as well as anyone, had a good reason to kill the lady." He leaned over the table and looked meaningfully at Lord Gerard. "Melchior told me about Wilfred."

Widow Brunswick wavered to her feet, strands of hair flailing like naughty children from the crooked bun on her head, and pointed a shaky finger accusingly. "Yes, he certainly did have good reason to wish his wife dead and this boy to take the blame! His wife hid the fact that she had switched her living son for a dead one, and Wilfred was really her own. How long have you known the truth, Lord Gerard?"

Lord Gerard fell heavily back onto his chair. "By the gods, I *didn't* know. Not until the king told me yesterday."

All eyes swiveled toward the king.

Widow Brunswick let out a cackling, half-mad laugh. "He has his own secrets to keep, so he thought to cover them with other men's tales. He killed his own son yesterday, though he professes he knew nothing of the matter."

Father Neumann gasped.

The widow wagged her head. "We are not among angels, Father."

Striding across the room, the priest waved Wilfred to

his chair, though his face had grown ashen. "There are many secrets inside each man, but not *all* secrets need to be told here. I fear that we have a tangled web that goes back a fearfully long time." He gazed searchingly and landed on Melchior. "You've an honest face. Tell me how this boy, Wilfred, came to be *your* son?"

Melchior blinked in the strong light and sucked in a bracing breath. He stood, his knuckles pressing the tabletop. "Yes, I can explain much— perhaps *too* much—but considering that my son's life hangs in the balance, I do not think circumspection wise."

King Radburn scrambled to his feet, spittle flying with his words. "No, this is unjust! I must tell my part first, for the matter with the slave will be brought forward, though what that has to do with Lady Nadine's death, I cannot see. Still, for justice's sake, I demand the right to defend myself."

Heads nodded and shoulders shrugged, so the king strode to the center of the room. He paused and folded his hands.

A bad taste filled Harold's mouth. His king appeared more like a deceiving dramatist than an honest leader.

"Many years ago—a lifetime now, I was a youth who knew that fate had something wonderful in store for him. I was sent on a long voyage, for reasons we will not go into now, and on that voyage, I met a beautiful woman. We fell in love." A playful twinkle sparked in his eyes. "You cannot understand, Father, but when real passion takes a man, there is little he won't do for the woman he loves. In this case, I gave her a son. I didn't know that until much later. We had to separate—her husband was a powerful man with an evil temper.

"Fearing her husband's fury, my beloved passed the child along to a trusted friend, who proved not so trustworthy. By evil fate, the boy ran away and was caught and sold. Unbeknownst to me, he became the Widow Brunswick's slave."

The widow murmured under her breath. "More son than slave."

Harold shook his head. *But a slave, nonetheless.*

The king's face flushed. "Yesterday, when the widow attempted to use her knowledge against me, I pointed my sword in a gesture of defiance, and her slave got in the way! Through no fault of my own, he took the sharp end. I never knew the boy. You'd hardly expect me to wear the mask of grief now, do you?"

Harold's stomach twisted.

Melchior dropped his head onto his hands.

Gasps and murmurs arose from the assembly

Father Neumann's groan of sorrow trumped King Radburn's dramatic ending.

"It was not my fault! The old hag could've told me! Hang her for keeping secrets!"

Father Caedmon stood and turned his attention from the king to Melchior. "We can offer no further justice for that poor man now. Please explain about Wilfred, for this is more to the point of our meeting."

Melchior nodded his assent. "I recently learned that I was not the father I thought I was"—he grimaced as he looked at the king—"while you learned you were a father you never planned to be." His forced smile contrasted with tears brimming in his eyes. "God knows that I felt like Wilfred's father." Melchior's gaze shifted to the young man sitting across the table.

"'A diligent woman is a crown to her husband...' And Edwina was the most diligent wife a man could ever hope for, but she did have her stubborn moments. I learned to leave her be or risk making a difficult situation worse. When our third child was born, she suffered terribly, and we both feared that the child would not live. She grieved, as any woman would. When she came to me after what I thought was the death of our son, she announced that the baby had not died but was alive, and I feared that she'd gone mad. Truly, I feared for her sanity, but when the servant brought the baby to me, and I saw a living child, I fell to my knees in amazed wonder. I believed that God had wrought a miracle for the sake of my wife.

"Thinking back last night after the widow told me the truth, I realized that likely there were many moments when my wife had wished to tell me what she'd done. But I'm sure I made that impossible. She knew I'd not be happy to learn that Wilfred was not mine but planted rather like the cuckoo who places her egg in another's nest."

Lord Gerard glared at Melchior. "I never gave my son to you, and if I had known of my wife's treachery, I would've killed her—gladly. But I didn't know. And when I looked at the boy, though I have always been kind to him, I did not see myself in his countenance." He snorted. "I gain nothing at your loss! I have been betrayed thrice over—by my wife, my son, and my neighbor."

Father Caedmon lifted his arms. "We've all been betrayed in some measure or another. It is a disease of human inheritance, but more often than not, it is our natures that deceive, not our conscious will. Lady Nadine *thought* she was protecting her son, and Melchior's wife chose to serve by loving a helpless baby. Did they do wrong? Yes, by all that is sacred and right, they did a grievous wrong, and for this we are now all assembled in suffering. But do not blame the wrong on those who knew nothing of it. They surely have enough guilt to bear in their own wrongs than to be burdened with those they had no hand in."

Lord Gerard shoved his chair back as he rose. He marched across the room and stared out the window.

"Where is *my* justice? How do I demand amends from those most guilty when they are both dead?"

Father Neumann spoke quietly. "Leave justice to God. He will see it done more perfectly than any man."

Staring at the blue sky, Lord Gerard sniffed derisively.

Wilfred paced to Lord Gerard. With his hands clasped behind him like a supplicant, he stood behind the tall man. "I have always admired you and been grateful for your kindness." He looked over his shoulder. "I owe my greatest allegiance to the man who raised me, but no matter where I was raised, I loved your wife, who was my real mother, and I would never have harmed her, for she was always gracious and kind. Without knowing the truth, I loved her."

Slowly, with barely controlled emotion, Lord Gerard turned and faced his son. "As you loved my daughter—your sister?"

Harold cringed for all of them.

Chapter Twenty-Four

My Blood

Oliver, ignorant of all events at the Widow Brunswick's castle, focused his attention on the dark forces rising at home. After nearly nodding off in Aunt Martha's room with Adele and Corliss in attendance, he jerked awake at the sound of hurried footsteps and a prolonged groan out the window. He raced into the chilly night, and then stealthily crossed the dark ground.

A disheveled, hunched creature gamboled about as if in mad play.

In pantomime, Selby acted multiple roles until a violent scene ended with the words, "It's all you deserve for what you've cost me!"

Oliver crept nearer, his stomach churning at the old man's over-bright, craze-filled eyes. Gathering his courage as a bulwark against growing terror, he held out his hand. "It's alright, Selby. Just me. Oliver."

Selby offered no resistance when Oliver took him by the arm and led him home.

Whimpering like a child, his voice rising and falling incoherently, Selby suddenly slipped into a new role. He twisted out of Oliver's grip and pulled a sharp knife from a hidden fold.

The sight of Lady Gerard bleeding to death from multiple stab wounds flashed through Oliver's mind. His heart clenched. *You blamed her—for what?*

Selby stabbed the air. "I am a MAN!" Then, with equal suddenness, he fell to his knees and started rocking and groaning. "Don't you have eyes? My flesh and blood... It's your fault! Ohhhhhh, Gooooddd!" He panted. His breaths rose in a staccato rhythm that tore through the silent night.

"They were *mine*! M*y* flesh, *my* blood. You took them! My girl's gentle smile..." Selby choked and spat. "Damned hard heart. No God for me!" Sprawling in the dust Selby's voice dropped to a whisper. "My helpless Dora. Oh, God, why?"

Oliver clamped his hand over his mouth, nausea rising at scattered memories—His wife and daughters being dragged to wagon, screaming. A sobbing Selby held back by three strong men. *Oh, God. He's been suffering through hell all these years.*

Scampering to his feet, Selby stabbed the air again, staring into the moon-glazed night. "It's all you deserve!" Exhaustion took over, and Selby dropped the knife.

With utmost caution, Oliver bent down, retrieved the knife, and stood transfixed. Pain throbbed in his chest. He stood uncertain until he felt a hand on his shoulder.

Martha shook her head, her gaze fixed on Shelby, and pressed Oliver's arm in gentle commiseration.

Adele and Corliss scurried up behind. The house, glowing with candlelight, loomed in the background. With a gasp, Adele clasped Corliss' hand in a tight grip.

After wiping away her tears, Martha strode to the shivering old man and gripped him by the arm. He spoke over her shoulder to Oliver, "We'll have him watched day and night. He's likely to do himself some harm."

Bile rose into Oliver's throat. "He already has." He lifted Selby's limp form and carried him unprotestingly to his quarters, a little hut set back in the field. A single room with a small, enclosed garden and odds and ends lined up along the outside wall.

Oliver entered the hut, kicked a broken pot out of his way, and strode to the bed. He flipped a gray blanket aside and lay Selby on a shabby cot.

With closed eyes, Selby groaned, rolled to his side, and slipped into a childlike slumber.

A thickset dog ambled in, wagging its tail. It jumped onto the bed and curled up close to its master.

Oliver patted the animal and arraigned the blanket over Selby. An urgent thought tugged at his mind: *I must tell Father.*

He strode outside and faced his aunt. "Martha, I'll get Richard and bring him here to keep watch. Then I'll find Father and tell him, so the case against Wilfred can be dropped before any further harm is done."

Martha's eyes gleamed in the moonlight. "We don't know for sure. He may not have done it. He may just be a mad man."

Oliver sighed as he bent lower, whispering, "He stabbed the air, saying, 'It's all you deserve for what you've done!'"

Martha shook her head. "But it wasn't Lady Nadine; it was Edwina who sent Selby's family away. Surely, the old man knows that. It was a matter of economy."

Light from the half-moon silhouetted Adele's and Corliss' shivering forms.

Oliver groaned, "Economy makes a poor soulmate." He glanced over his shoulder. "He's sleeping now. I'd better go."

Martha folded her arms, her chin up. "I'll keep watch. There are few who can best me, least of all a demented old man who has lost his strength."

"I'll call for help, nonetheless. If he did kill Lady Nadine, he is mad beyond all reason, and I wouldn't want you in a struggle with a killer who cares nothing for life. Richard or his men will surely come to keep the peace till I return with father—and Wilfred, God willing."

Shivering in her nightdress and robe, Corliss whimpered.

Oliver motioned to Adele. "Take Corliss home." He glanced at Corliss. "If you've a mind to keep out of trouble, let my sister stay with you."

Martha snorted. "What if Lord Marlow wants to help?"

Grief morphed into fury, heating Oliver's face. "No! I don't trust the man."

Martha pressed his arm. "You've learned a hard lesson. Trust is a dear gift, too often undeserved."

Oliver led the women home, aching to see his father's face.

Chapter Twenty-Five

Everyone Has Questions

Tarragon plodded across the wet sand, enjoying the scent of saltwater infiltrating his breather helm. The sun, still white but dropping low in the sky, lit the cave entrance, turning the black stone into shiny pillars.

His ship was situated far enough back to be out of sight but not too far for his exhausted legs and aching feet. He shuffled forward.

The rhythmic sound of the seashore mellowed his soul, rolling the irritations of the day off his heavily burdened shoulders. *Why I thought that there'd be anything of interest here is beyond reason. I must've been out of my mind.*

With a verbal command, the ship's bay door opened, spreading a sheet of yellow light at his feet.

He plodded onto the incline and let it lift him inside.

How glorious! Home at last.

After a refreshing swim in the pool, he changed into a clean bio-suit, poured an extra-large Nutrient Green into his breathing helm, and plopped down on the plush sofa arranged before his favorite console.

He draped two tentacles—one right, one left—setting the ship's system into active mode and regulating the spy alarms to high alert. He hardly wanted a surprise visit from the Mystery Race.

He wrapped his two most used, thus most stretched and weary, tentacles on the top of his head for a much-needed rest. A snug fit, they probably appeared like a fleshy crown. But appearances never concerned him, so he concentrated on his active tenacles, dexterously tapping the console, scrolling through significant data.

Ingots hardly interested him normally, but the female, Nova, had caught his attention. Her bestial attitude—contradicting her betters and challenging authority—dropped her beneath his notice at first. But then, in a sarcastic exchange while on the road, Sterling related her history to Mauve, whereby the ridiculous Luxonian female took the child's part in everything.

Blowing bubbles at the memory, indignation rose fresh in his mind. Mauve should not exist. She was completely useless! Sterling was only worthwhile as a figurehead. Clearly, Teal stood as the real force behind their Inter-Alien Committee. But as his health waned, so the young Luxonian Cerulean waxed. *That should prove interesting.*

He shook his head. He must know more about the mixed-being—the Ingot-Bhuaci. *How was her existence even possible?*

He scrolled through reports, medical journals, and even a couple of dramatic fiction tales before he found what he was looking for: the marriage certificate. Yes, the two had been allowed to marry on the basis of her ability to maintain her humanoid form nearly indefinitely and his complete rejection of all techno-armor.

Tarragon rubbed two of his tentacles together. He really must speak to someone about all of this. Yet who to trust?

Leaning back on his chair, Tarragon closed his eyes and remembered his mother's oft-repeated dictum: "Trust a fool, if you're going to trust anyone. That way, you know what you're getting."

Slapping his chair into the upright position, he swiped the datapad on his chest.

A holographic image of Mauve appeared before his eyes. A brilliant blue sky framed her face.

She scowled. "What're you doing? It's late, and I'm hot on the heels of the Mystery Race." She glanced over her shoulder. "There's an important meeting, a trial of sorts, planned here in the main hall. I'm going to use my alluring skills on Mystery Man and Son. Though, they're not really all that mysterious."

Tarragon's disbelief spread as a snarl over his face. He could feel it, and he didn't care. "*You* found them?"

"Yes, I did!" The boastful triumph in her voice did nothing to soften the covetous gleam in her eyes. "The older one plays a minstrel-fool. His son is also a fool." She shrugged. "Hidden in plain sight."

Instantly, Tarragon felt his brain sizzle with daring thoughts. He put on his most innocuous expression. "I'd hate to upset Sterling since I know how much he values you. Stay safe and return to my ship." He dangled an offer that he knew perfectly well would repulse her no end. "We can enjoy some Crestonian cuisine."

The disgust that rippled over Mauve's face tickled Tarragon to the core. "I'm going to become this mysterious alien's new best friend and find out why he's here."

"Can you do that?" His voice trilled with a perfect balance of challenge and disbelief.

"Watch me!"

"I will, most certainly. But, if you happen to get into trouble, offer up the mixed-breed. I'm sure that even the Mystery Race has never seen the like. You might be able to make a deal, and we'll all profit from the exchange." He smiled, showing his ruddy gums, but that couldn't be helped.

Mauve laughed. "I like the way you think!"

Voices rose behind her, and bright patches of clothing swirled in the background.

"I must go. But don't think for a moment that I'd risk that girl's life. She's as dear to me as—"

The screen went blank.

Tarragon blinked. Had she exited? Or did someone—He shrugged and checked his monitor. It faithfully reported Mauve's exact location up until the moment the screen blanked. He knew where to look—the kitchen in the Widow's castle on the hill.

He sighed. "Though, I'll definitely have to get new boots."

~~~

Abbas didn't like to do it, but he could not allow her to continue her transmission to the Cresta. *Interfering wretch.*

Mauve fell to a floor in a heap in the dim corner of the main hall.

Omega ran ahead and nudged her still form with his foot. "Is she dead?"

Abbas shook his head. "I never extinguish a life unless there is no other alternative."

With a furrowed brow, Omega stared at his father. "Why not?"

A shiver ran through Abbas. Did he really have to explain? He didn't remember anyone explaining the precept of the sacredness of life to him, but then, maybe he had learned it from his parents' example. "Life is sacred. We live by that understanding. Or we die by its absence."

Straightening, Omega nodded slowly and glanced around.
~~~

Exasperated by this new complication, Abbas waved at the prone figure.

Mauve disappeared.

A kitchen maid, a little thing with a babyface, sauntered through, spied their presence and stopped. A hesitant smile quivered on her lips.

Meeting her gaze, Abbas clapped Omega on the shoulder. His fool's costume slick against his hand. "We're lost. Can you tell us where to settle for the night? With all the awful commotion, we don't want to get in the way."

The child skittered forward, her shoulders hunched and her eyes searching the empty room. "Oh, be that the truth. Awful, it's been. The poor widda. Never imagined such goings on, her being so good and faithful. And her best servant too!" Tears filled the girl's eyes. "Wicked men. I hate 'em all."

Omega ginned, his face flowering with the thrill of excitement. "Are all men wicked?"

The child gasped. "Oh, not so! There's a woman around about that's wickeder than the devil himself, I'd say. Drawing men like bees to honey. Only so she—"

A voice called from the kitchen doorway. "Edda!"

Flushing, the child curtsied and ran off without another word.

Omega nudged his father. "Where's Mauve now?"

"I put her where she could do the least amount of harm."

Omega waited.

"On the Cresta ship."

"But they'll wonder how she got there."

Abbas pressed his son's shoulder. "No matter. Everyone has questions. It's finding the answers to the ones that interest us that really matter."

"I'd like to see her face when she comes to. That would be fun."

Laughing and chattering filled the air, and men stomped into the room, followed by servants carrying platters of bread and meat.

Abbas jumped onto the low dais and shoved the remark from his mind as he faced the incoming assembly. It was time to play the fool. He only hoped that his son wouldn't take his role too seriously.

Chapter Twenty-Six

Just the Man I Need

Oliver pounded on the heavy wooden door, then leaned against the doorpost, expecting it would take some time for someone to answer. To his surprise, the door flew open almost immediately.

Richard, his shirt smeared with blood, his face haggard, and his eyes red-rimmed but glaring with determination, grinned crookedly. He grabbed Oliver by his shirt and pulled him close. "You're just the man I need."

Oliver's stomach clenched in a tight knot. "What's happened, my lord, that you're so bloody? Has there been an attack?"

Richard spluttered a strangled laugh. "Oh, yes, someone attacked. It was not a force of arms, however, but rather madness itself. Lord Marlow tried to kill me, but I beat him off. His corpse is lying there"—he pointed with a blood-stained finger—"in the hall. He should be burned like the pagans of old."

Stupefied wonder overwhelming him, Oliver stumbled into the house. *Two cases of madness in one night?* "Why would Lord Marlow do such a thing? He was going to marry Corliss! What would he gain from attacking you?"

Richard waved wildly, directing Oliver to follow him inside the entry, skirting the main hall, and headed to a flight of steps along the wall. "Do not look to the right. Just follow me. We'll retire to my room. The servants slept through it all! Two men fight to the death with no one to watch. One might think the worst of me, but when I tell my brother, there will be no questions. I did *him* a favor. Marlow would've treated Corliss like a— I saved her a life of humiliation."

Oliver's mind went numb. Despite the warning, he could not help catching a glimpse of the irregularly shaped dark stain meandering across the stone floor. A now-familiar drop in his insides warned him to take several deep breaths.

When they reached the top floor and crossed to his room, Richard pointed to two chairs carved with vines intertwining frightful heads.

Oliver's stomach churned as he tried to shake off dizziness.

Richard fell heavily into a chair. Slapping his thigh, he smiled grimly. "If I were a proper host, I'd offer you food and drink, but I don't feel like a proper host. I feel like a murderer, and I must say, it does nothing for the appetite."

Fighting nausea, Oliver leaned in. "Are you a murderer, sir?"

Richard rose and strode toward the window. He stared blankly ahead, speaking to the darkness. "When will the sun rise?"

Oliver spoke softly, feeling the need of the sun's comfort himself. "It's nearly time now."

Richard turned and faced Oliver. "After he jumped me, I only had to wrestle his knife out of his drunken grip. Then I stabbed him in the chest." His voice dropped to a whisper. "As he lay bleeding and groaning, I watched his life leak away." He blinked back tears. "The sun will rise, though I do not know if I want to meet it."

Oliver closed his eyes and imagined Martha's calm, intelligent face. "Tell me how it happened."

With his head lowered, Richard detailed the events leading up to Lord Marlow's death.

Oliver listened patiently, picturing each step in his mind.

When Richard stopped, the rising sun brightened the

horizon.

Oliver stood up. "He attacked you, so you had little option." The urgency of the situation with Selby rushed back into his mind. Then Wilfred's fate swung before him. He straightened his shoulders. "You may have saved Corliss from a terrible marriage, but she still needs you. I need you. I know who killed Lady Nadine, and it was not Wilfred."

Richard's head snapped up. "Who, then?"

"Selby, our slave. He blamed Lady Nadine for sending his wife and children away. I must go and tell my father at once."

Richard shook his head. "Lady Nadine had nothing to do with other men's slaves. She was little more than a slave herself. Why would the man think such a thing?"

Oliver paced toward the steps. "I don't know. But tragic events often stay hidden for a ponderous long time. Only later generations learn the true history of their elders."

Richard followed Oliver. "Can we learn from madness?"

The two stopped at the bottom of the steps.

Richard tromped into the hall where Lord Marlow lay sprawled on the floor. "I'll have him buried on his own lands, and I'll notify those who need to know. The servants will clean up this mess before Corliss returns."

Oliver gripped his arm. "Selby sleeps like a child in his own bed for now, with my aunt as guard, but I don't like leaving. He may remember what he revealed in the night, and no one knows when a fit will take him again. Corliss is Lady Nadine's daughter, and though she can in no way bear any guilt from the old man, he may not judge it so. Madness knows no reason."

Richard straightened up. "It has been a night of death, but I'll do what I can to begin a better day. You go to your father and brother. I'll send men to bring Corliss home and leave a guard to keep watch over your servant, if need be."

Oliver nodded. "We have men enough to watch over Selby, but if you keep Corliss under your protection and allow Adele to return with her, then my heart will rest easy. I have a long ride ahead."

Richard gripped Oliver's hand. "Go with God."

Oliver nodded and trotted toward home. *I pray so—for all our sakes.*

Chapter Twenty-Seven

Glad Tidings

Melchior stood in the open square before the castle door and held the Widow Brunswick's hand for longer than strictly necessary for a proper leave-taking. Then he bowed low.

The widow, covered from head to foot with a long dark wrap, peered out from the folds, her eyes pinched with strain.

"When I first came," Melchior said, "I thanked you for preserving the life of my son, yet now I know that you have done much more for many years. Edwina was wrong to keep her secret from me, but truth is not safe in a world ruled by pride. Yet, you have known such evil and loved us anyway."

The folds of Widow Brunswick's garment closed around her as drops of rain splattered on her black gown. "I merely decided whom I would love and whom I would hate. There is little honor in that."

Father Caedmon stood unobtrusively aside, no hint of his own opinion.

Melchior wiped rain from his eyes. "God will judge us better than we do."

"I fear He will not be as lenient as we are toward our wayward selves."

"Surely, if He died for our sins, He will forgive our transgressions."

"If on Judgement Day, He shows us what we have done in light of His forgiveness, I don't know if I could bear it."

After mounting his horse, Nolan signaled that the

king's guards, Lord Gerard's retinue, and Nolan's men were saddled and ready to leave.

The widow nodded her goodbye and took Father Neumann's assisting arm. The two returned to the castle.

A stableboy led Melchior's horse to his side. Using the last of his weary strength, he managed to mount it.

Standing just off to the right, Father Caedmon patted Wilfred's leg as the youth sat astride his horse. "I will pray for you. You have a difficult road ahead—being a son to two such different men."

Wilfred smiled, even though the drops of rain looked like tears on his face. "Truly, I have three fathers, for I know that God has preserved my life through your care."

A grin spread across Father Caedmon's stern features. "Then you have learned more than most, my son."

Grimacing and glaring in turn, Lord Gerard and the king started through the gates, their men in tow, without so much as a goodbye or a murmur of gratitude.

Melchior followed Nolan, while Nikolas, ever slump-shouldered, rode behind Wilfred.

The long ride was broken up twice for rest and refreshment. The Widow Brunswick had sent them on their way with their bags well stocked with provisions. These they ate in silence the first day.

After a mild rain, they stopped in a grove of trees for the night. The drizzle had quit, and stars sparkled clear and bright in a cold black sky.

Sulky, the king ordered his men to prepare his bed close to a blazing fire, "Make it good and hot!" with a tent of fir tree branches to keep drips off.

Nolan, bundled in a thick cloak, sidled up to Nikolas, his voice breaking through the dreary quiet. "Why are you so morose? I thought you'd be happy the boy is free from the noose, but you seem as grieved as ever."

Shivering in his thin wraps, Nikolas hissed as he

gathered twigs, "You seem to forget that it was my sister who was murdered, and though none of these men are guilty of the act, I have learned things that make my blood run cold. How is it that my sister so feared her husband that she would give away her own son to be raised by another? That tells a grievous tale, and I am guilty of not knowing it. I might've done something to save her had I known how hard her life was—how desperate her condition."

Ordering the men in general, Lord Gerard slapped his hands together and shoved one of his men toward the woods. "Get wood now and hurry. I want a hot stew before I die from this damp!"

Focused only on the conversation at hand, Nolan spluttered as he leaned in to Nikolas. "Bah! Are you one of the gods that you can see all? No man can keep watch over every innocent girl. She was married to a brute, which is more often the case than not."

Tossing his few sticks aside, Nikolas spat his words. "There are many good men who love their wives, and if I had known, I would have done something! If only she had told someone—someone other than the woman who conspired to replace a dead baby with a living one!"

Melchior climbed wearily to his feet. He pulled his damp hood off his grizzled head and strode over to the young man he had always considered his friend.

Leaving his flint near a smoldering pile of leaves, Wilfred stepped between the two. "Please, don't argue about it now. What's long since done cannot be undone."

From across the flickering light of the campfire his men had kindled, Lord Gerard cleared his throat. "I suppose you blame me for her unhappiness. That I am the *brute* you speak of so glibly?"

Nolan laughed abruptly and sat on a jagged log. "He knows his name, he does!"

Nikolas kicked Nolan's foot, stepped around the growing fire, and glared at Lord Gerard. "I ought to kill you for destroying her happiness. It seems to me that a man who kills the soul is just as guilty as one who kills the body. Father Neumann said that Wilfred was clearly not the murderer and that it was obvious that none of us did the deed, but he merely meant that none of us stabbed her with a knife. But you, you stabbed her in the heart when—"

Lord Gerard leaped to his feet and grabbed Nikolas by the collar. "When what? When I acted like a man and demanded that she obey me and not fret about matters beyond her wit? When I went about the business of making a home and gaining lands and wealth so that she would have food and comfort enough? I made her more than the poor maiden she was born to be, daughter of some luckless fisherman!" He pushed Nikolas off with a hard shove. "I will take no scolding from a churl who is little more than a slave himself!"

All humor gone, Nolan pounded over to Lord Gerard, his fists clenched and ready for a fight.

Standing before a hastily assembled lean-to, the king's voice rang out sharply against the night. Two fires, King Radburn's and Lord Gerard's, now illuminated the makeshift camp. "Sit down, fools, before I take matters into my own hands. I have men here at my side, and I can call for others easily enough. As your king, I should order you all hanged on the nearest tree. I have more men than you, Nolan, despite your boasting, more than enough to have you swing before you could call for assistance. And who would question me? None."

Jerking his shoulders back, Nikolas retreated to a place before the king's fire.

Nolan paced a few more steps under a large oak tree and then turned and watched

The king threw a stick into the fire and stood facing Lord Gerard. "It seems to me that this matter of Lady Nadine has gone on long enough. Frankly, I am bored with this intrigue, and I wish it were forgotten. If the mystery could be solved, I would see it done, but enough time and effort have been wasted. Your wife cannot be raised from the dead. Accept your loss and find some other woman to comfort you."

With a strangled gasp, Lord Gerard stepped forward, but the king's glare kept him at a distance. "Someone came onto my lands and murdered my wife, and you want me to *forget* it?"

"Yes, exactly. Forget it. I have other matters to think about."

"What else matters?"

"There are many matters of importance that you know little of, but for your information—I have decided to get married."

Melchior's throat closed, and he could not speak, though a general murmur of surprise among Lord Gerard's men and a few glad chuckles from the king's retinue rose from the darkness. Nolan and his men seemed only to study the situation, offering no opinion. Nikolas stared with wide, frightened eyes.

The king's smile glimmered as he stared at the firelight. "I've been considering the matter for some time." He looked up, his gaze landing on Melchior. "Now that I know that your son is not a murderer, your family is cleared of doubt. I am quite awake to the danger of marrying a woman I cannot trust. In all my adventures, I have met only two women I could trust. One is long dead, but the other is the daughter of the only honest man I know."

Melchior's stomach drew into a painful knot.

Nikolas jumped to his feet and Nolan gasped.

The king raised his hand toward Melchior. "I wish to congratulate you, my friend. Your daughter, Adele, will be my queen. Instead of carrying home dreadful news, you'll bring glad tidings to all."

Caught between rage and terror, Melchior did not move a muscle, though his heart fell further than it had ever fallen before.

Chapter Twenty-Eight

Jealousy Burned Deep

Martha had never envied a mouse before, but the task of keeping guard over a deranged slave stretched every nerve near the breaking point. When a gray mouse skittered past, keeping close to the wall before darting into his hole, Martha almost wished she could trade places with him.

Soon after the sun had risen, Gilda peeked into the room. "Why are you in here, aunt? The others told me you'd come to watch over Selby, but it isn't your job to watch over sick slaves."

Martha's overextended nerves snapped like a thread. "Why on Earth are *you* here? You should be in the house, breaking your fast with the others. I told—oh, never mind. Nobody ever listens to me anyway."

Gilda stared wide-eyed. "You're angry? You sound like father." The girl's discontent was palpable. "Where's Oliver? Is Selby very sick?"

Martha turned in her seat, fury building inside like thunderclouds on a hot summer day. "What? Only *three* questions? Are you sure you don't have others just waiting to trip off your tongue?"

Selby stirred uneasily, though his eyes remained closed.

Martha rose stiffly and grabbed Gilda's arm roughly, directing her to turn around. "Listen to me now,"—she said in a quieter tone—"and be a good little lady. March right back to the main house and stay inside until I return. Keep all the children inside too." She looked warily behind her, but Selby slept on. “I’ll come along in a bit. There’s been some…unpleasantness...and I don’t want you getting into trouble. You understand?”

Gilda tilted her head, her gaze shifted, and she grinned. “Well, at least, Selby is all right.”

Martha whirled around so fast that she nearly bumped into the man she had spent half the night being terrified of. “Selby?” She stepped back, considering his blank expression cautiously. “You are all right, then? We’ve been worried sick about you.” She gestured frantically behind her back for Gilda to move off.

Gilda frowned and stayed put.

Selby stared at Martha, his eyes growing wide with wonder. “Why are you here? Have I been walking in my sleep?”

Martha knew a good opportunity when she saw it. “Do you often do that, Selby? No one warned me.”

Selby turned back to his bed and snatched up the blanket, shaking it roughly. He spoke over his shoulder. “Yes, I’ve been known to walk in my sleep a time or two. My Dora used to tell me it was a most annoying habit, for she never knew where I went, till one night she found me in the garden digging up turnips.” Selby turned again, a dark look in his eyes that did not match the smile on his lips.

Fear shivered over Martha. “Oliver heard you calling out in the night. He found you in the yard and led you home. You were overexcited, so I’ve been watching over you.”

A slow chuckle rose from Selby. “Oliver always was a good boy, the kind who’d feel bad—even for a slave. But boys grow up and change.” Selby clamped his mouth shut, his face growing rigid. “I’ll go to the house now. I’ve a wonderful appetite, so rest your mind. I’m not sick."

Martha stepped aside and let Selby pass, her mind whirling. "Selby? How has Oliver changed?"

Selby stopped and shrugged, staring over his shoulder at her. "Don't mind me. My words don't matter. You shouldn't have let me sleep so late, sick or no. I'm only a slave. When I wear out, you can always get another."

Selby's tone rang with far too much authority for Martha's

comfort. *In truth, he thinks he's my equal.* With a shake, she gathered her courage and trailed after the man.

~~~

Adele watched the slumbering girl lying next to her in the large and comfortable bed and sighed. She wanted to hate Corliss, but she was completely exhausted, and she wasn't sure it was worth the effort. Even though she had slept the balance of the night and well into the morning, still her whole body felt heavy and listless. The whole experience with Selby had left her drained. *Is the curse of some terrible sin haunting my family?* As she understood it, each person was allotted a certain time on Earth for a specific purpose—something that had a great deal to do with learning to love and forgive. *Why do those things have to be learned? Perhaps our lives are a quest of learning not to learn—not to hate or clutch bitterness.*

Corliss shifted in her sleep, and her arm flailed in the air before it fell soundlessly onto Adele's lap.

Adele shoved the thick covers aside, moving the arm with them, then tiptoed across the floor, cringing over the icy stones. She stepped to the long window and sucked in the fresh air of a sunny new day. The folk below bustled with various duties.

Last night, Richard had met her and Corliss at the door
~~~

and escorted them to their room. He had never been a very talkative man, but he seemed especially taciturn, offering only a few pleasantries before retiring to his room. The servants had been hard at work, even at that unnatural hour, for several of them scurried past lugging heavy buckets as they passed. Adele frowned at the memory, but every bit of her speculative nature had been drained away by worry.

She glanced back at Corliss, whom she should now consider a friend. Could a woman as unpredictable and uncontrollable as Corliss ever be a friend? She really ought to pity Corliss. After all, a slave had killed her mother, and if Lord Marlow had been demanding to see *her*—Adele shuddered—*she* would not be sleeping so serenely.

The whispered sound of her name being called caught her ear.

"Miss Adele?"

She crept to the door and opened it a crack.

A servant girl with a ragged shawl thrown over her thin shoulders peered through pale blue eyes. "Sir Richard asked me to see if you was awake yet, and if you was, I was to tell you he has food ready and that you shouldn't wait for Corliss, for she's been known to sleep until the sun reaches its peak."

Adele smiled. "I'll be down directly. Thank Sir Richard for his kindness and—well—just tell him, I'll be there soon."

The young girl curtsied as she backed away. "Follow the steps to the landing. I'll be there waiting. The main hall is in the back."

"I know where to go. Don't wait for me." Adele had never dressed so quickly in her life. Though she felt self-conscious about appearing before so lordly a man in so bedraggled a fashion, she could hardly wait to tell Richard about Selby. She prayed that Lord Marlow was still away hunting.

The hall looked quite different from the last time she had seen it. At that time, it had been bursting with lavishly dressed guests, loud voices ringing in boisterous conversations, and servants hurrying about. Fires had burned from hearths at each end of the room, and the smell of roasting meat had filled the air. Heady scents from platters of meat, bread, and desserts arranged on long boards had nearly overwhelmed her.

Now, the room stood quiet and empty. The walls were bare except for the usual tapestries, which seemed dark and shabby in the morning air. Only one fire burned, a pitiful attempt to bring cheer to such a large space, and a few dishes lay forlornly on one table.

Richard stood at the head of the table, his chair pushed back, staring at her. He waved her forward. "Sorry if I woke you, but I thought you might be hungry after last night's—adventures. You're used to much nicer company at meals, but we must make do. Here, sit. Some roast venison perhaps? Or a bit of quail? There is bread and cheese and more than I could ever eat."

Adele walked to the table, her stomach twisted in knots. It was absurd that Lord Gerard's brother would treat her like a fine lady. Did he not know his father had been the one to force her family out of this very house?

Richard's face flushed. "Excuse me. I'm upsetting you, but I'm at a loss…"

A blush heating her cheeks, Adele dropped her gaze. "It's just that this is strange, indeed. You see—" She glanced at the open doorway. "Will Lord Marlow be joining us?"

Snapping, Richard glanced away. "No, Lord Marlow will not be joining us."

His sharp tone startled her. "Has he returned home,

then?"

Richard clamped his hands together. "Lord Marlow is dead."

"Dead?"

As if ceremony could ease her tension, Richard politely pointed to the food though his hands shook. "Here, please, eat something. I doubt you'll have much appetite after I explain what's happened."

Had death become a stalking beast that snatched at her heels? Her heart pounding, Adele nearly fell onto the chair. "What happened?"

Richard slipped into his own chair and leaned back. He stared at the ceiling. "I killed him."

Adele gasped.

Richard sat up and leaned in. "I didn't want to! He jumped me like a ruffian. I had to fend for my life."

Bewildered with sick dread seeping through her body, Adele pictured Selby's face. "Had he gone mad?"

"I believe so. Or rather—as I had the whole night to think it over—I believe he was always mad. Just no one noticed."

"How?" Adele shook her head. "I just can't imagine..."

His face slack, eyes emotionless, Richard's voice dropped to a whisper, drained of all animation. "He jumped me. I knocked him down, grabbed his knife, and when he came at me again, I stabbed him in the chest."

Desperately in need of fresh air, Adele rose shakily and paced away. After calming herself to a modicum of stability, she returned to her chair. "But why would he attack you? He was to marry Corliss. Killing you would not serve that end."

"I planned to speak to my brother about his marriage. He was not the right man for Corliss."

A snort turned Adele's attention.

Richard started from his chair.

Arrayed in a simple red dress, Corliss stood on the threshold. With her head held high, she surveyed them through proud eyes. "I owe you a debt of gratitude, uncle. I was thinking of killing him myself or killing myself. Instead, like the gallant man you are, you solved my dilemma."

Striding up to Adele, Corliss reached out, concern in her half-glazed eyes. "Don't fret, Adele, it makes you look awful. Suitable men are not so few that I need to worry. I'll find a better one. In the meantime,"—Corliss turned to Richard—"how does one thank an uncle for murdering an unsuitable suitor?"

Richard's stunned expression revealed his mind clear enough. He shook himself, tugged his sleeves straight, then gestured for Corliss to take his chair. "Please, have some repast. It's been a difficult night but eat while the food is fresh." With trembling hand, he smoothed down his shirt and straightened his shoulders. "It should be a pleasant day."

Has the world gone mad? Adele fought the impulse to scream.

Richard took samples from the different dishes, piled them on a plate, and set the food before Corliss. Then, he did the same for Adele.

Adele watched in fascinated horror as Corliss raised a slice of roasted meat to her lips and began to nibble. Unable to think coherently, she pushed away from the table and started for the door.

Richard ran after her, grabbed her arm, and turned her to face him. "Wait! I know this is all a terrible mess, but you must not leave. Not like this."

Hearing herself laugh, Adele wanted to cry. "A mess? Our trusted servant killed Corliss' mother—for no reason—and you have murdered her espoused husband!" She squeezed her eyes shut to block the images swirling through her mind.

His breath close to her cheek, Richard whispered, "I would not have chosen it so."

Adele backed away. "You're a conqueror from a family of conquerors. It was *our* land that you stole, and this was *our* home, but your family didn't care. Lord Marlow was a brute. What man isn't? Lady Nadine was a bitterly grieved woman, and it was Lord Gerard's fault! Is there no place safe? Must all our steps be haunted?"

Corliss laughed, her voice a high-pitched tinkle. "My good uncle just did what he must. Lord Marlow was not right for me, and my mother's death released her." Corliss' voice cracked. "The poor woman did not have an uncle to solve her problem."

Adele covered her face with her hands.

Richard hissed his words, "I chose to live. That cannot be wrong."

Weak and trembling, Adele gripped the doorpost. "I want to go home."

"I'll take you. Oliver should be at the Widow Brunswick's by now, and surely your father will return quickly. If I know my brother, he will demand immediate justice." Richard glanced at his niece. "I must see Adele home."

Corliss shrugged, unconcerned with company in the face of a good meal.

Adele started along the corridor with Richard at her side, her mind numbed and confused. "Justice?"

"You must remember, I was not brought up here. I was raised in the north. Father always said that if I acquired enough land, he would admit I was worth the effort of keeping alive."

Adele stopped and stared at him. "You never were a part of this family?"

"How could I be? My foster father did not much care

for me either, but he decided that I was intelligent enough to educate, so he brought in a tutor—a priest, more like a father than any other man." Richard sucked in a breath. "My brother will probably demand your slave's head on a platter, but Melchior can defend his own better than any man I know."

Warmth and peace crept back into her at the thought of her father. She walked straight to the front door. "He is no warrior."

Richard called for one of his servants, who immediately came to his side. He gave instructions for the horses to be made ready and three men to escort them to Adele's home, just across the valley. He caught up with her on the threshold. "I know that we are only going a short distance, but for form's sake, I would not have anyone question your dignity."

A tingle ran over her where Richard clasped her arm. As she stepped into the warm sun-laden courtyard, she glanced back.

Corliss stood in the hall, staring after them, her hands on her hips and her eyes narrowed.

Adele recognized the expression, for she had felt it often enough. Jealously burns deep, even when it has no right.

Chapter Twenty-Nine

Caught in a Vice

Melchior awoke before sunrise. A trail of smoke rose from the embers in the firepit to a crisp and clear sky. Men lay motionless and silent on the damp ground, some wrapped in blankets, others slumbering peacefully without. About two dozen in all. While the rest of the traveling party still slumbered, he washed his hands and face in a bucket, then in pre-dawn silence, nibbled a bit of brown bread he had saved from supper.

As the sun crested the horizon, he wandered south of the camp and, after a bit, circled back from the opposite side, where he passed Wilfred breathing softly in his sleep.

The sweep of damp hair falling across his son's face made him look more like a child than a man. A surge of grief gripped Melchior's heart. He reached out, but then hesitated. Wilfred now belonged to another man.

How had it been possible that his son never felt disgust for the men who had forced them off their ancestral lands? How had he been able to sit comfortably at their tables, listen to their barbaric songs, and laugh at their uncouth jokes?

Melchior bit his lip at a memory of Selby chuckling as they watched Wilfred ride off into the dusk. "You'll never keep that one at home, master. He has plans of his own. But don't feel bad...I doubt he's told Lord Gerard either."

Distant hooves pounded across the wide moor.

Melchior looked up to see a speck of a rider pounding his way, the eastern sun glinting off the figure.

The camp started into wakefulness.

The king rose to his feet, his gaze wide and alert. "Who's that approaching with such haste?"

The solitary guard shrugged. "It's been a quiet night. This is the first sign of life stirring, beside Lord Melchior walking about."

The king snorted.

Nikolas threw back his hood and stretched, while Nolan yawned so loudly everyone turned to stare at him. Nolan glared back.

As the rider closed in, the guard called, "Who comes?"

Almost at the same moment, Melchior and Wilfred identified the rider and cried out, "Oliver!"

Melchior jostled men as he made his way through the camp.

Pulling up just inside the camp, Oliver jumped from his horse with a graceful bound.

Melchior's eyebrows rose in surprise. Oliver was different somehow.

Oliver positioned himself between the king and his father, leading his exhausted horse by the reigns. "Hello, father, King Radburn." He bent his head respectfully then searched the men's faces until his eyes alighted on Wilfred. A relieved grin spread over his face. With a brief nod toward Nikolas and Nolan, he shifted his attention back to his father. "I have important news. May we speak in private?"

King Radburn scowled. "Whatever you have to say may be said in front of all. We have spent several delightful days together and have become good friends." He glanced around, challenging. "Isn't that so?"

Nolan bit his lip.

Nikolas shook his head, stepping forward. "It may have nothing to do with the rest of us. Allow them their privacy."

King Radburn stared at the young merchant for a

moment before replying in an icy tone, “If you think you can make better decisions than the king, I suggest you enlist an army to do me battle. But until that time, do not contradict me.”

Melchior raised his hand. “Speak, Oliver, before everyone. What brings you in such haste? We just finished our business at the Widow Brunswick’s, and as Wilfred has been cleared of all charges, we’re returning home. If you had waited half a day, we would have met you at our door.”

Oliver hunched his shoulders. “It’s a matter for everyone’s concern, that’s true, but part is our affair alone. I know who killed Lady Nadine, but the man who did it is old and mad, hardly fit to be tried for his crime.”

A lump rose to Melchior’s throat. He turned toward the king. “Please, let me speak with him alone, before more harm is done.”

His face red with displeasure, King Radburn slapped his thigh. “I will let no more secrets rule my kingdom!” He lifted his hand and pointed at Oliver. “Speak and be quick. I’m in no mood for games.”

Oliver slackened his grip on the reins, letting his horse wander to greener grass wet with dew. “Martha heard strange noises in the night, so Adele and Corliss decided to stay with her to determine the cause of these nocturnal events. They were frightened by the thought that it might be the ghost of Lady Nadine—so they asked me to watch with them. In the dark hours, I saw a shadow move across the hall. I started after it, but then the figure ran out into the night and stopped and swayed and moaned, telling a terrible tale, at the last, stabbing the air and crying out, ‘It’s all you deserve for what you’ve done!’”

Melchior’s heart pinched in a cruel vice.

“It was Selby. He’s been living in a hell of sorts since losing his wife and children, though we knew it not. After his passion was spent, he collapsed, so I took him to his room and left Martha to watch through the night."

Oliver turned toward Lord Gerard. "I saw Richard before I set off—" His voice cracked, and he swallowed hard. "He's watching over Corliss and Adele to keep them out of harm's way."

Oliver faced his brother and braved a smile. "I was concerned that things might not have gone so well for you, so I rode off directly to inform you." Now Oliver glanced around the camp, including everyone in his address. "My brother did not kill Lady Nadine, but the man who did—his mind is altogether lost."

Melchior rubbed his eyes, exhaustion enveloping him. *Selby?* In his mind, he saw his wife's face as she stared intently at her slave—the one who had seen her through every birthing—the one who helped to bring Wilfred into the world. Or so Melchior had thought. She knew the truth, and Edwina had sent her away. Sold her and her children to another estate. *What was her name...Dora?*

In bitter grief, Dora had clutched her husband's hand before she climbed onto the wagon. Selby's hand, his fingers touching, before the wagon jolted forward...

An ache throbbed and pounded in Melchior's chest. His arm grew numb, and his face contorted. The whole world swayed.

Oliver gripped his arm, his eyes anxious.

Melchior tried to smile, but confusion and a strange sense that he had misunderstood his entire life overwhelmed him.

A wave of blackness took him.

Chapter Thirty

Smashed to Pieces

Tarragon sat on a wide bench before the ship's hatch door, bending low and tugging a new boot onto his three-toed foot. He grunted with the exertion, but as it finally wiggled into place, he grinned with satisfaction. "There now, that wasn't so bad, was it?" He lifted his foot and eyed it carefully. "A little snug, but I can—"

A sudden blur rushing past his face, followed by a thud, shook him to the core. He yelped, "Sheesha!" Then he looked down at the body lying at his feet. A scantily clad woman. He frowned. "I know you."

Groaning, the woman rubbed her face and opened her eyes. Amid exclamations of pain and irritation, she struggled to sit up. "You wouldn't be interested in helping me to my feet, Cresta?"

As if to wake himself out of a dream, Tarragon shivered and thrust out a tentacle. "Mauve?" He peered at the ceiling. No hole. He glanced around. The bay door remained closed. "How did you get here? And why didn't you use the door, like everyone else?"

Climbing to her feet, Mauve's eyes widened as her gaze traveled along her nearly bare body. Only a lightweight, shimmering tunic covered her body from shoulders to calves. "That blinking Mystery—What happened to my clothes?"

Tarragon recognized that he was not being asked a question, so he declined any attempt to answer. Instead, he lifted his second boot and shook it in her direction. "Since you are here, I'd appreciate your help."

Mauve slapped her forehead. “I fall into your ship, literally, and all you can think about is your boots?”

With a shrug, Tarragon made his priorities clear. “The sooner I get this on, the sooner I can help you solve your mystery.”

Mauve swept her hand over herself and instantly appeared in a long red dress with wide sleeves, purple slippers, and a black belt. Her hair, arranged on the top of her head in a series of ornate braids, glistened in the garish light. She glared down at him, marring the perfect symmetry of her face. “I found him already. Who do you think did this, idiot?”

With a disgusted harumph, Tarragon tugged on the second boot. It slid into place, and he stood, testing his balance. Once secure, he pointed to the door. “Shall we? These beings not only have power but a sense of humor as well.”

The bay door opened, sending light rays into the ship.

Mauve scowled. “If you think this was funny, I can find ways to tickle your insides.”

Alarmed, Tarragon stepped outside and lifted all four tentacles in an attitude of surrender. “I see how you might be annoyed, but still, you must admit, it was clever. He could’ve killed you. Instead, he merely humbled you.”

Mauve scampered down the incline and pounded across the wet sand to the mouth of the cave. She stared at the ripples of an incoming current. “He’ll have to try a lot harder than that!”

Tarragon plodded up beside her, his tentacles wrapped behind his back.

“Abbas and Omega they call each other. They acted like a father and son. The boy is a fool. The father only plays one. I’d like to know a whole lot more. They could be useful.”

The sunlight sparkled over the water, glorious to Tarragon's eyes. "I doubt you can bargain with them."

With a thoughtful look, Mauve replaced her dainty slippers with tall boots and plodded forward. "I'll kidnap the son. That'll show the oh-so-powerful-one who he is playing with. The fool probably thinks that I'm as weak as a human, stupid as an Ingot, or as single-minded as a Cresta. He has a lot to learn." She slogged toward the shoreline. "Hurry up if you want to watch me take the Mystery Being down a peg or two."

Slapping a tentacle across his face, amazement shivered over Tarragon. He watched her scrabble up the beach and stomp in the direction of the widow's castle. *Of course, I can always offer my services to the winner. Perhaps there could be an exchange—once I save his son...*

~~~

Sterling stood beside Nova in a shadowed corner of the widow's great hall and watched the spectacle, entranced by the crowd's childlike joy yet disgusted by their easy manipulation.

Abbas stood before the great fireplace and juggled three plates before a breathless crowd. To their amazement, he added a fourth plate. He grinned at Cerulean who, in common peasant garb, stood beside the high table. "Toss me that golden vessel!"

Hesitant, Cerulean glanced away from the mistress' gorgeous place setting and grasped a clay mug instead.

Scowling, Nova shoved past him, plucked the golden goblet off the table, and tossed it into the whirling mix.
~~~

Without missing a beat, Abbas caught it and juggled all four objects faster than ever.

The watching throng roared their approval.

Sterling stepped behind Cerulean and gripped his shoulder. He spoke in an undertone. "Now toss in the mug."

Cerulean threw it in a perfect arc, and the mug whirled beautifully before smacking into the goblet, breaking the spinning cycle. The plates and mugs fell to the floor, smashing into uncountable splinters. The goblet rolled to the wall and stopped.

Abbas locked eyes on Sterling, who grinned in return.

A disgruntled woman aired her disappointment. "Good plates ruined. For what, I ask?"

After yanking a colored scarf from his sleeve, Abbas then ceremoniously flung it over the mess. He grabbed a tray off the table, scraped the mess on, held it aloft, and chanted, "Heza, hiza, meza, miza! Be renewed!"

He snapped the scarf away, and the four plates and the clay mug appeared in perfect shape on the tray."

Loud exclamations met his astonishing feat.

Smiling, Abbas placed the tray on the table. "The hand is quicker than the eye. You didn't see what you thought you saw!"

He then bowed, moving backward out the front door into the cool evening air.

Sterling followed with Cerulean and Nova trailing along behind.

Once well away from the well-lit hall and stepping into the long shadow of the curtain wall, Abbas turned and waved his followers along. He snuck inside the doorway of a flanking tower and climbed the steep steps at a faster rate than his apparent age suggested possible.

Anxiety tightening his chest, Sterling's skin chilled in the evening air. *How human.* He lifted his hand, halting

Cerulean and Nova in their tracks. "Stay here. I'll be right back."

Nova challenged, "But what if you're not?"

"Then Cerulean is in charge. Now be a good changeling and obey a direct order from your superior."

Her hands clenched, Nova stomped forward.

Cerulean gripped her arm, shaking his head.

Relieved, Sterling raced up the steps after the only person who had ever made him feel afraid.

~~~

Omega meandered along the edge of the cliff, well aware that the Luxonian woman trailed twenty feet behind him. He had a lot on his mind. His father seemed easily annoyed of late, and that puzzled him. His father adored him. As did his mother. He was a perfect son. How could he not be? Yet, this evening, his father had told him to "go away" for a bit. What did "go away" even mean?

"Hey, you! Boy! Wait a moment. I need to talk to you."

A strange sensation filled Omega. The sun had set and an evening glow still shone over the water's edge, yet darkness filled him. He turned around in the direction of the nasally high voice.

Mauve trotted forward, heaving gulps of air. "Stay put a moment. I had to lose that stupid Cresta to have a private word with you."

Omega peered over her shoulder. There, in the far distance, the Cresta plodded along, stumbling like a newly hatched bird. "What's he done that you should leave him behind?"

Mauve stopped before him, a fierce scowl marring her otherwise pretty face. "He's nothing. Don't bother about him." She repositioned her face and attempted an
~~~

ingratiating smile. “I’ve got a proposition for you, if you’d just allow me—”

“You’re the one who plays with men?”

Mauve snorted, a grin replacing her smile. “I play with them as likes to play.” She shrugged. “Makes life meaningful—to experience everything while I’m here.” She sauntered closer, her hips swaying invitingly.

Omega stepped to the very edge of the cliff.

Her eyes glinted as she slid her hand along his chest.

Repulsed, Omega said the first thing that came to mind. “Father says you’re a leech.”

Her face contorting, Mauve lifted her hand. “I was going to be nice but—”

Suddenly Mauve’s body recomposed from flesh into clay, her face frozen in rage.

Heaving a long sigh, Omega appraised the life-like sculpture and patted the stiff cheek. Then he nudged the composition over the cliff.

As waves crashed ashore, the clay figure whirled downward, finally smashing to pieces on the wet rocks below.

Omega leaned over the edge. He clapped dust off his hands and turned away.

Chapter Thirty-One

Separate but Same

Father Caedmon knelt before the altar, on the chapel's stone floor, his hands folded and his eyes bright with unshed tears.

Father Neumann laid his hands on the old priest's head and murmured the words of absolution that always left both men exhausted, for the words were but the tip of the mystery that delved deep into the heart of a man. To be truly sorry and then truly forgiven was one of the greatest joys in the world, though few cared to know of it.

Father Caedmon made the sign of the cross and then rose.

Father Neumann spoke once more. "Are you sure this is the will of God?"

Father Caedmon smiled in his lopsided way, expressing both humor and compassion. "I don't know; I just suspect. The boy has more in him than he realizes—most men do. Hearing about those families, it haunts me. Sheep led to slaughter while a wolf stands guard over the kingdom."

"Not all kings are wolves."

"No, perhaps not. But too many are. Besides, sheep are not known for leading themselves. They need someone to guide them."

"And you're sure you are that man?"

Father Caedmon's heart clenched. "No, not really, but I fear that God does." He dug his toe into the dirt floor. "He doesn't lead me by bright revelations and loud voices—rather—He simply gives me situations which I must make the best of. Logic and love are my guides."

Father Neumann shook his head, clearly dissatisfied.

"I will offer my services as a tutor. Wilfred is a bright boy, and he's capable of greater things."

"You think Melchior will accept you?"

"I believe he will. Melchior has great learning and faith, but he uses neither. He seems to have succumbed to the degradation of a conquered man—he no longer believes in himself or his sons. In time, they'll all rot on the vine."

Father Neumann sucked in a cleansing breath. He lifted his hands in blessing.

Father Caedmon returned to his humble posture on his knees before his friend. Father Neumann intoned the sacred words in his deep voice. "I bless you in the name of the Father and of the Son and of the Holy Spirit. May you travel safely, may you serve God well, and may you bring His love with you, wherever you go."

Father Caedmon rose again. "If it's any comfort, I won't be going alone. I'm taking young Stephen, and I think I made a friend of one of the king's men—Harold. He begged for a blessing and said he wants to become a Christian, though he isn't especially eager to have anyone else know it."

Father Neumann chuckled. "If you've converted one of those Saxon heathens, then anything is possible!"

Father Caedmon snorted. "I cannot convert a single soul—that's God's work. I just show up for the formalities." He turned but then stopped and turned back. "Oh, you will be sure to check in on the widow? Her faith has been severely tested and her mind nearly wrecked when Demetrius was killed. Please remind her that love is never wasted, no matter how painful this journey may be."

With a murmur of assent, Father Neumann bowed.

Father Caedmon hummed as he hurried off to meet

Stephen by the sheep gate. *Our missions may be along different roads, but we're heading in the same general direction.*

Chapter Thirty-Two

An Unblemished Heart
to Save the King

King Radburn sat upon his throne—which was little more than an oversized wooden chair carved with interlacing patterns and set upon a platform—and stared down at the assembly mulling before him. Yearly reports were to be read in the presence of the king, and he very much wanted to hear them. He just wasn't sure he would live long enough.

He had spent months riding through the various districts of his domain, assuring himself that the throngs which bowed low before him were, in fact, sufficiently terrified to keep his position as king quite safe. He also needed an accurate tally of the healthy, young men who, in time of necessity, would comprise his army. He had to ensure that his personal army outnumbered anyone else's personal army.

There was also the matter of new catapults; he wouldn't mind having more of those on hand. The ability to knock holes in an enemy's defenses from a vast distance offered a distinct advantage. He also intended to see to the matter of foreign tribes who thought, that by merely settling on the outskirts of his land, they could live there free of charge.

As he appraised the throng with kingly dignity, he struggled to ignore the burning nausea, which portended another gastric attack, that would ultimately leave him exhausted for days. He needed medical attention, but his father's physician—the only man he trusted—had drowned. An exceptionally inconsiderate act, considering that he alone knew the recipe to the special brew that made him feel better.

Now, he not only had to sit through several hours of formalities on this bloody uncomfortable chair, demanding that every ounce of taxes be put into his coffers and that every male of fighting age be accounted for so that his men-at-arms could dislodge unwelcome vagabonds from his borders, but he also had to pretend that he didn't feel as sick as a worm dangling on the end of a fishing line.

The pain sharpened.

Breathe slow. Don't vomit!

King Radburn forced his lips to turn up at the corners even as he had to blink back the damnable tears cresting over his burning eyes.

Melchior leaned against the wall, looking as if he were chewing glass. He had not appeared pleased when the announcement of King Radburn's marriage to Adele had been made public. It had taken months for Melchior to heal from his sudden illness in the field, and though he had regained much of his former abilities, he still slouched like an old man.

I better not look like that!

Kind Radburn squared his shoulders, nearly yelping against the pain in his gut.

Adele had done a remarkable job, coyly pretending indifference to their marriage. He frowned. Hopefully, it was merely indifference and not something more obstinate.

Shaking himself free of the unpleasant thought, the king peered at Oliver, who stood off to the side with his arms crossed over his chest.

A new memory flooded his overwrought mind—Oliver escorting Selby to the judgment seat. Such a loyal man. He even stayed for the hanging.

Selby had openly admitted his murderous act, insisting that he was glad he had done it. In the end, the only reasonable course of action was a public hanging.

In a generous act of benevolence and as further proof of his fitness to marry sweet Adele, the king had arrived at Melchior's door to give him the news of Selby's final end personally, even climbing the steps and stopping at his bedside.

Melchior had merely shaken his head in grieved perplexity. "Why did he admit to it so freely? We'd never have known..."

After the hanging, Oliver had followed the king's procession and stood at the foot of his father's bed. "He wanted us to blame each other, but in the end, he wanted to die. His wife and children passed on in an epidemic, so he had no reason to live. Must have seemed like some kind of demented justice to him."

Dragging his mind from this pathetic reverie, the king glanced at Wilfred, who stood at Lord Gerard's elbow, his new clothes displaying his fine form.

Lord Gerard's eyes flashed like fire. Clearly not a happy subject—but what could he expect? Someone had to be king, and it wasn't going to be him.

A sharp pain gripped his intestines, squeezing hard. Using the last bit of his waning strength, King Radburn climbed to his feet, gripping the chair for support.

He waved, interrupting the last report. "That's enough. I wish to make an announcement before I take my leave." He forced a smile. "My wedding will be on the first full moon, the month after next. Everyone is welcome to attend. There will be plenty of feasting and games."

A rousing chorus sprang up at this announcement. Hurrahs and spear butts thumping the floor set off a general hubbub of collective joy.

King Radburn made a hesitant step forward then

thought better of it. “You may leave now...all but Lord Melchior.”

A frown on his brow, Melchior labored forward.

Wilfred stayed behind as Lord Gerard and his men led the throng through the doorway and out to the sunny courtyard.

“My Lord Melchior!” The king smiled grimly as he folded his arms over his aching stomach. “How do you like your new title?”

Grimacing, Melchior offered a hesitant smile. “I’ll need time to adjust. To what do I owe this sudden honor?”

The king gestured for Wilfred to step closer. “Nothing sudden about it. I’ve claimed your daughter for my betrothed for two months now.”

Wilfred jogged forward and bowed.

“Here, boy, I need assistance.”

Wilfred sprinted up the step and offered his arm.

King Radburn gripped the young man’s shoulder and labored down the step. He spoke aside to Melchior. “After the wedding, I will hold another assembly with people of notable worth. We’ll see you made a lord in proper style. But first, I must prepare for my wedding. How is Adele? Has she reconciled herself to her good fortune yet?”

Melchior appeared to have swallowed a melon. “She is surprised by the honor, but perhaps given time...”

The king looked into Melchior’s eyes and saw a truth he did not like. “Be sure to tell Adele that *your* title accompanies *her* honor.” He grasped Wilfred’s shoulder more tightly as he labored down the long hall. “Your boy here has grown on me like a son. Ha! That should amuse you. A boy with so many fathers shouldn’t mind one more!”

As he halted for a breather, he eyed Wilfred appreciatively. “How do you like serving under your father—Lord Gerard, that is?”

Wilfred stared straight ahead. “His men are good to me, and I am learning to be useful.”

King Radburn nodded and gestured toward the stone steps leading to his private quarters. “Help me to my room, Wilfred.”

Melchior mumbled something and gestured to Oliver, who stood by the open doorway. “Come along, Oliver, we have things to attend to at home.” He glanced over his shoulder. “Wilfred, don’t forget your old home. You are always welcome.”

Oliver offered a searching glance at his brother and tipped his head respectfully.

Wilfred returned the nod to both men and then led the King up the stairs, matching his steps to the king’s hesitant movements.

Once in his room, the king fell back on his bed, completely exhausted, sweat pouring down his face. “Find me a doctor. My stomach is in revolt, and my heart is pounding like a hammer!”

Wilfred turned to the door.

“Where are you going?”

Wilfred motioned toward the window facing his home. “There’s only one person knowledgeable enough about herbs and brews to deal with such a sickness: my father’s sister, Martha. I’ll bring her.”

The king groaned at the image of a bulky, old woman feeding him broth. “Bring Adele, too. Tell her that I need her kindness, her unblemished heart to save the king.”

As Wilfred left the room mumbling, King Radburn wondered if death would be more welcoming.

~~~
~~~

Melchior chewed his lip as Adele paced the long room, furious at the request to play nurse to the king, a man she clearly hated.

Wilfred stood aside after repeating the king's request in Adele's, Martha's, and Melchior's presence while they sat before the evening fire in the main hall.

Adele had sprung from her chair like a sapling released from heavy snow. "Would it be murder to simply *not* save the life of so hateful a man?"

Melchior sighed and ordered the horses to be brought out.

Adele wrung her hands as the men made ready.

Martha packed herbs and soothing oils in a satchel.

Melchior appraised his daughter. "Adele, I know how you anguish over matters with the king, but remember, he is a man first and needs our help. Our Christian duty—"

Adele's eyes widened alarmingly. "He needs our help? Where was he when our land and home were taken from us? He was right there working alongside his father and uncles, alongside Lord Gerard and the likes of Lord Marlow, all those who destroyed, burned crops, slaughtered animals, sold children, attacked women, killed innocent men, and left mere scraps for those with wills strong enough to survive. You know this, you've told me the bitter story often enough!"

Melchior's anxiety turned to mild surprise. "I didn't realize you were listening."

Adele studied her father, a breeze blowing auburn locks of hair into her face. "Why did we stop fighting? We should have fought down to the last man."

Humbled by his daughter's bold words, Melchior traipsed through the door and onto the open porch. He scanned the horizon.

Adele strode after him.

"We were nearly down to the last man. Not many left

to resist such an overwhelming force. I decided, along with your mother, that we'd do better to surrender and use what wit and will we had left to preserve something for you children. Your mother counseled patience and measured responses. Martha is much the same. That is why she survived so unscathed."

Adele's expression softened. "But you, Father? You did not survive unscathed?"

Bitter fury seethed through Melchior. He stepped off the porch and stood waiting for the men leading the horses. "My heart was seared but my soul is free." He peered at the setting sun. "I want a better future for you." He gently brushed a stray lock of hair from her face and caressed her cheek. "Adele, is there one man that, given the opportunity, you would like to marry?"

Blushing, her gaze fell to the ground.

Alarm spread through Melchior. Another mystery, and he was beginning to loath mysteries.

Wilfred led the horses closer.

Melchior hurried his words. "What man are you in doubt about...or should I say, what men?"

Shock filled Adele's eyes. She clasped her hands too tightly. "There is a man who has been kind on occasion, but we have never said or done anything to further our friendship. He may not even care for me. It may be all on my side."

"What is his name?"

"He's no one, really, certainly not a lord of great worth. I've never mentioned anything because I know what hopes you hold in store for me. He has little to offer, except his good heart and calloused hands."

"A good heart and calloused hands are nothing to dismiss lightly. I would rather you marry a good merchant than a bad king. If you love such a man, and he loves you, and he had the decency to ask my permission, well, I might not be averse to granting his heart's desire. That is, of course, if he could provide for you. I can't have you marrying a pauper with no skills or trade."

"Oh, no, father. He is a skilled fisherman as well as an excellent merchant. You have said so—" Adele blushed and dropped her gaze.

Wilfred strode forward leading two horses.

Astride a third, Martha followed at an even pace.

Wilfred assisted Adele onto her horse.

When she was comfortably settled, Melchior reached up and took her hand. "I will speak to Nikolas and see where he stands in this matter."

"Oh, Father, do you think that's wise? The king has already made his wishes known."

Melchior grimaced. "Down to the last man, remember? Besides, no one knows what will happen. Why, the king may not survive the night."

Martha snorted indignantly. "I'm not about to commit regicide just for the sake of begging off a wedding."

Melchior smiled. "No, sister, I was not asking *that* of you. Before God, I want you to do your utmost to take good care of the king. Stay by his side, feed him, talk to him, counsel him in your goodness, and by all means, keep him alive! I will come by in a day or two to ask a favor...a favor he will be very unwilling to give, but by your saving grace, perhaps…"

Martha patted her horse's neck. "You are a dreamer, man! King Radburn won't give up Adele easily, even if I do save his life and even if he is honest enough to admit it. But you can try. Just remember, I have my reputation to keep."

Melchior mumbled, "Among other things."

Then he turned to the boy he still thought of as his son, now mounted atop his own horse. "Keep them safe, Wilfred."

Martha kicked her horse and set off towards the king's manor.

Adele stared at her father as she passed, a hesitant smile playing on her lips.

As Wilfred took up the rear, he nodded his head respectfully. "Don't worry, father, I'll protect them with my life." He passed on, upright in new clothes and confidence.

Melchior's heart swelled with joy.

Martha leaned over, said something to Adele, and they burst into laughter.

His sister had been a godsend, and he wondered how he had ever gotten along without her. He rubbed his chin at the thought of her husband, Roland, living in the north and trying to manage his estate without her wise counsel.

Melchior lifted his gaze to Heaven. The quote flooded his mind where it had been silent for months. *"And he showed me a river of water of life, clear as crystal...."* Though he still wished to know the end of that sentence, he was content for now.

Chapter Thirty-Three

The Short Road

Father Caedmon was never one for taking the short road. Undaunted by the sudden illness of his companion who had to turn back early on, he followed cow paths that led him to the homes of humble folk who eked out a living from poor soil and back-breaking work. He begged for a bite of bread and a place to rest, and usually he met with some measure of success, no matter how begrudgingly that success might've been won. He never preached his faith openly, though he was willing to answer any question put his way.

The families that he encountered labored hard, and their children worked alongside the adults from sunrise to sunset.

Father Caedmon maintained a cheerful disposition, smiling and asking the assistance of a youngster while he accomplished some simple job for the family. He preferred to be taught by the children, for they tended to have patience, and they would show him what he didn't know until he could perform to their exact standards...or thereabouts.

In the evenings, he would recite his prayers, which was a new experience for the majority of folks, though once in a blue moon, someone would know a word or two of a common prayer.

On rare occasions, someone would ask a question, and he would explain where the prayer came from or what it meant. The elders would sit apart as Father Caedmon went about his nightly ritual, though the children crouched nearer as if they thought he might call down fire from the gods.

The elders peered cautiously and spoke roughly to the little ones to stay back when Father Caedmon folded his hands and knelt, focusing intently on his devotions.

He prayed memorized pieces that he had learned as a child and as part of his training. If possible, he would celebrate Mass, but usually that was beyond his means, and he had to content himself with a heartfelt observance without the consecration he so loved. He would always offer petitions, asking the angels and saints to beseech the Lord God for the safety and welfare of those who had shared their home with him.

The adults who scoffed or grumbled often stopped then and stared at him.

After the last amen was said—more a song than a word—he would stand and glance around at the assembly. His heart softened at the sight of their filthy faces and bone-thin bodies. In some unaccountable exchange, they seemed to see him in a fresh light, and distrust melted like frost on a sunny morning.

When ready to move on, Father Caedmon would ask directions to Melchior's abode, and they would direct him on the next leg of his journey. Whether he threw his cloak over his shoulder on a warm day or wrapped it around his shoulders on a brisk morning, the parting ritual was much the same. The family would stand in front of their home and watch and wait. He would raise his hand in blessing and, instinctively, they would bow their heads. Occasionally, someone would kneel.

Father would beseech Heaven to remember these people traveling with him along life's journey and ask God to bless them for their kindness.

Then he would smile, wave, and continue on his way.

Sometimes one of the men would jog alongside and offer food or coins or perhaps a weapon to protect him from the dangers that lurked on the road. But Father Caedmon would wave off the gift, saying that he had not earned it, but if they would pray for him, then God would surely watch over him.

As he continued his journey across the moor and up and down hills, avoiding the marshes, the family would stand there watching. He would turn and wave until they were little more than a speck on the land but safely ensconced in his heart.

On the fifth day of his journey, he realized that he must be very close to Melchior's abode, though he wondered if perhaps he had gone just a little too far south.

A horse galloped over the horizon.

Father Caedmon recognized the figure and chuckled to himself. Life could be quite amusing.

Harold slowed his horse as he approached, his face blushing dark red. "Where in blazes have you been, Father? I have been searching high and low!"

Father Caedmon suppressed a grin and forced himself into sobriety. "Why, Harold, I thought we had agreed to meet at Melchior's estate once I made my hopes known to him. Surely, he'll be grateful for a tutor to teach his sons, don't you think?"

Harold's fury deflated like a drained wineskin. "Yes, you said something about that, but any sensible man would've waited for a proper escort or called for assistance—or something."

Father Caedmon rolled his eyes skyward. "I've had plenty of assistance."

"Certainly! You've had a great deal of assistance; I'm assured of that! Your young friend, what's his name, Stephen? Became ill on the first leg of your journey and had to return to the Widow Brunswick's! Even your assistant needed assistance! Out of sheer kindness, I came looking for you. Why, man, I've been up and down these lands so many times I could walk them in my dreams. Where have you been sleeping, in the clouds?"

Father Caedmon swallowed his laughter. "I stopped at farms along the way and partook of folks' hospitality."

"You could've been robbed and left for dead! You should have let me know."

"I was perfectly safe. And, besides, I doubt that Lord Gerard would have lightly parted with your company."

"Oh, that, well, Lord Gerard is preoccupied with other matters. He cares nothing for me. Don't you know? The king is to be married, but word has it, he's ill and may die at any moment."

"It's good you've come along, then. How long till we reach Melchior's estate?"

Harold leaned closer. "*Lord* Melchior, you mean? The king is to marry his daughter, though"—he glanced around at the vast empty lands until satisfied that there was no one to overhear—"word has it that she'd rather die."

"You are a fountain of news. Still, you've not answered my question...how long to get there?"

Harold sat upright and grinned at the humble priest. "By foot?"

Blocking the sun with his hand, Father Caedmon looked at the tall Saxon and smiled winningly.

Harold rolled his eyes and nudged his horse closer. He reached down and gripped the priest's arm. "Get up behind me, and we'll be there before the sun hits the horizon. You're lucky I came along. You were heading right to Lord Gerard's land, and some of his men are not so gentle."

Father Caedmon struggled to get his robes tucked properly around him. He said distractedly, "Like your cousin, Terrill?"

Harold kicked his horse. "He's not my cousin, Father;

he's my foster brother. But, yes, like him. He has no love for men or God."

Satisfied that his robes were properly situated, Father Caedmon gripped the larger man's cloak to stay upright. His words came out jerkily as the horse adjusted from a trot to a canter. "He-must be-a lonely-man."

Harold, gripping the reigns, spoke with sudden honesty. "He wouldn't be the only one, Father."

With a sigh, Father Caedmon tightened his hold. "In that case, take the short road, son."

Chapter Thirty-Four

A Delicate Matter

Richard gave up all hope of becoming anything more than a stranger to his brother. Once the shock of Lord Marlow's death had settled into acceptance and all the burial duties had been attended to, Lord Gerard closed himself off from the world—especially from Richard. He announced every action with curt resolve, saying things like, "I'm going on a hunt. Don't look for me," and, "I'll be checking the western border, I don't need help."

When Richard had first detailed Lord Marlow's attack and his subsequent death, Lord Gerard's attitude changed from amazement to fury. To Richard's bafflement, he stomped off in fuming silence. That night at supper, he refilled his cup so often that alarm filled Richard. When he advised caution, his brother lurched forward, cursing and waving and sloshing the dark brew onto the straw-strewn floor.

"By the gods! I am sick to death of you telling me what to do! What has caution done for me? I've more trouble now than I've ever had in my life!" He counted on his fingers. "My wife is murdered by a wretched slave. The son I thought dead and buried has been living as another man's son. Then, to fill my cup to overflowing, you tell me that my friend attacked you, and you were forced to kill him.

"Bloody damnable trouble everywhere! Evil hounds my steps." He looked over his shoulder. "I'm a haunted man." Gesturing, he dismissed all objections. "It's the unquiet dead and avenging spirits. They're tracking me."

Fighting the urge to retreat north, Richard stayed to watch over his family, though he took to hunting in hopes of alleviating his pent-up frustrations.

He returned home, tired but relieved that he had managed to bring down a large stag. As he finished the arrangements for dressing the meat, Corliss appeared in the kitchen, smiling as innocently as a spring morning.

"My dear uncle, I have ill news, and I don't know who else to trust—you're my best advisor." She paused while he led her to a seat in the main hall.

He wiped his hands on a wet cloth, a gut-wary warning alerting him to any sign of falseness.

"My father has been so very angry; the matter concerning my mother's death did not end to his satisfaction."

Richard's first flush of pleasure at being thus consulted was drowned in confusion. "But the boy was clearly innocent. Gerard did not wish to kill an honest man, surely?"

Corliss languidly fanned her face with her hand as if to cool a blush. "Not at all! But as it stands now, all his past friends are at odds with him. If you two could work toward some common good, then perhaps everyone would remember their better selves."

Richard wondered what Corliss was maneuvering toward. "Any suggestions?"

"There is a danger that threatens the king, and I cannot imagine a better man than you to deal with these...delicate matters."

Richard rubbed his chin. "To what *delicate matter* are you referring?"

"Adele's aunt, Melchior's sister, the loud woman who came to live with them…" Corliss shivered. "She hears voices and speaks to the spirits. She's in league with the dead! If Adele were to marry the king, he'd be ruled by her, and if Adele were under the power of her aunt, who is under the power of the angry dead—well then—where would *we* be?"

Alarm spread over Richard. "Does Adele know of this woman's ways?"

"You don't think two women live together without knowing such things? Adele seems mild-mannered, but I assure you, she's quite independent. You've heard the way she speaks to her father! Goodness, I would never speak so to my father. But what do you think, uncle? You dealt with Lord Marlow's treachery so valiantly. Do you dare face the king with this ill news? Or should I speak with him directly? I'd be glad to offer my servant's healing services and comfort the king in his hour of need."

Richard stared at the far wall, his mind whirling. He didn't want Adele, with her honest and gentle heart, chained to the king, and if he could save her from such a fate by bringing forth some minor concern that she could be cleared of later, then it would be worth the risk. Clearly, Corliss wanted the king for herself. A perfect match! Thus tethered, they would keep each other on short ropes, beneficial for everyone. "I see what you mean, but you should stay clear. I'll speak to your father, and we'll approach the king together. When the opportunity affords, we'll offer your assistance. Frustration makes him ill, and surely you could cure him of that."

Corliss blushed.

With a nod goodbye, Richard sought out his brother. After a short search, he stopped in the shadow of the courtyard wall and watched Gerard overseeing the care of the horses.

What had happened to the bold youth of their childhood? Gerard could fight and hunt and curse with the most stalwart warriors and then sit with their father and speak like an equal.

But now Richard pitied his brother. since He lived in mortal fear for his soul. Perhaps in their joined opposition to Adele's marrying the king, they would find a means of reconciliation.

Richard stepped into the light. "Gerard, we need to speak."

Lord Gerard sighed. He motioned towards the gate, yelling over his shoulder, "No one follow us, you hear?"

The two brothers walked side-by-side to a copse of trees and strolled under the canopy of oak and elm.

Once safely enveloped in the shadowy woods, Richard faced his brother. "Corliss is concerned that Adele is not the proper woman to marry the king. She fears that the aunt is in league with unnamed spirits, and if Adele marries the king—"

Lord Gerard could not have turned any paler. He stared at his brother with wide, horrified eyes.

In the distance, a figure ran swiftly toward them.

Lord Gerard raged. "The dead are about to possess the kingdom, and now someone is disobeying my direct orders!"

The man called between panting breaths, "Lord Gerard, I have a message!"

"Tell me the news, fool! Every man in the kingdom can hear you!"

Terrill stumbled to a stop before Lord Gerard and gasped for breath, then he threw back his shoulders and lifted his head. "Harold has intercepted Widow Brunswick's priest as he traveled on our lands. The old man comes to offer his services to Melchior, but I sent word to the king to see if he was content with a meddling priest preaching and converting people to his ways. Even Harold has fallen under his spell! But the king was indisposed, so he appointed Robert to look into the matter. Robert has ordered me to ask if you would hold the man until we can ascertain the truth."

Lord Gerard bellowed, "Bring the priest to me!"

Terrill turned away, but Richard held him back. "What do you mean that Harold is under the priest's spell?"

"Harold says he wants to leave your service and join the Christians. 'Take up his cross,' he calls it. I call it madness, but you decide. Maybe you want all our men converting. Warriors turned milksops."

Lord Gerard dismissed Terrill with a curt wave, a flush working up his neck and seeping onto his cheeks.

The priest is in mortal danger. I've said too much, linking Adele to this very thing—trafficking with the spirit world.

"My brother, do not be too disturbed by what that fool said. The kingdom is safe. We are men of reason—we do not allow ourselves to become possessed by spirits. But we should speak to King Radburn about his marriage. Adele is not the woman for him. I think there's another—"

"What are you saying?" Lord Gerard blinked, and his face turned ghastly white. "Of course, Adele is not the right woman. She never was, but the king thought he saw innocence where there was really deceit. I'll lose no time opening his eyes."

Horrified by his mistaken judgment, Richard gripped the tree trunk.

Lord Gerard's eyed glimmered in madness. "It's no surprise their priest has arrived. He wants our land. They want it *all* back. They think they can rule from the other side, but the land of the living is for the living alone! I'll have Adele and her aunt and that priest hung from the highest limbs, and then I'll see their bodies burned. By all that is sacred, I will end this!" He clutched Richard's hand fervently. "Thank you, brother. I was wrong to doubt you."

In that admission, Richard realized a grim truth. *I can*

no longer trust myself.

Chapter Thirty-Five

For the First Time

Zuri stomped forward and grabbed the Cresta by his bio-suit. "Where is she?"

Melchior's house stood silhouetted against the late afternoon sunlight,

With a line of sweat dripping down the side of his face, his golden eyes red-rimmed, and his suit smeared with road dirt, Tarragon reared back. "Don't handle me!"

Abashed at his impetuous move, Zuri clamped down his anger, released Tarragon, and tried to form coherent words. "Where is my daughter?"

Brushing dirt off his front, Tarragon shrugged. "How should I know? She was playing servant girl with Sterling and that Luxonian boy last I saw."

A group of men tromped out of Melchior's front door and pounded down the steps. In boisterous conversation, they headed toward the stables.

Zuri motioned Tarragon around to the far side of a shed. The scent of dried hay drifted to his nose, making him sneeze. He clapped his hand over his face, muffling the sound.

Tarragon snorted. "And you complain about my native sensitivity? At least I can control my bodily functions."

Wiping his face with his arm, Zuri glared at the rotund Cresta. "So, she was all right when you saw her?"

"She was fine."

"I don't understand. She hasn't answered one of my messages."

With a surprisingly elegant eye-roll, Tarragon started toward Selby's old hut. "We can discuss matters in there. Knowing how superstitious these people are, they probably won't use it again for a long time."

Zuri strode at the Cresta's side, his anxiety settling into mild concern. "They're going to burn it down tomorrow."

Tarragon ducked his head as he entered the front doorway. "We have it for tonight then." He stretched and sighed, staring longingly at the bed. "I have endured much to find you."

Alert again, Zuri fixed his gaze on the Cresta. "What?" Alarm spread through him. "You said that Nova was fine!"

"She is." Tarragon flopped down on the rickety bed. "But Mauve will never be the same."

"Mauve? I thought she was at the widow's place."

"She was. Until she got a little too inquisitive and discovered the Mystery aliens playing fools in front of everyone."

"She found them?"

"And they, or he—the younger one—found her annoying. She was rather. But still. He took justice a tad far, me thinks."

His heart pounding, Zuri stepped further into the dim interior, wishing he still had night vision. "Where is Mauve now?"

"Shattered to pieces on the rocky coast. Not a chance she can be put together again. I checked."

Caught off guard by the violent image, Zuri fell back and sat down hard on a stool. "She's dead, then?"

"Even a Luxonian couldn't fix her. After an embarrassing incident, she planned to take revenge, so I followed and watched her saunter up to the Mystery boy on the edge of the cliff. They chatted for a few moments, but even from that distance, I could see that he wasn't the fool she was. Poof! She was turned into a statue, and he nudged her over the cliff. People say Crestonians are cold! This was positively arctic."

"Oh, God, what about Sterling?" Blood rushing to his ears, a faint dizziness swirled the room. "If they are that dangerous, we need to get off the planet. We must get the children!"

"Calm yourself, Ingot. I don't believe that the Mystery Being meant any harm. She planned to kidnap him, you know. Maybe he was just protecting himself. In any case, they haven't injured anyone since we've been here, but they could have long ago. And they did try to warn her; she just wouldn't listen."

Exhausted but more determined than ever, Zuri pulled out his datapad and tapped it to life. "Start from the beginning, from when you first met Mauve, and tell me what happened. As soon as we have this on record, we're heading to the widow's castle to get Sterling and the children."

Tarragon waved a tentacle in the air. "I'll make the report, don't worry. But we're not going anywhere. Everyone is heading here. All we have to do is wait for the family reunion."

~~~

Teal braced himself as Kelesta sat on the edge of his bed. She scooped strawberry ice cream from a bowl and held the spoon invitingly before his face.

Teal waved it away. "I'm not hungry."

"You need to eat."

"No, I don't."

"All right, you don't, but it would be good for you, anyway. You're not going to get over your depression
~~~

until you start inviting cheer into your life. And there is nothing more cheerful than strawberry ice cream."

Teal stared at her.

Kelesta set the bowl aside and rose. She stepped to the window and lifted the white curtain aside, peering into the distance.

The simple stone cottage hugged a niche in the cliffside, protected, yet facing every storm head-on. The sound of surf rolling on the shore repeated in rhythmic rounds as two birds soared across the sky.

Teal tossed back the sheet covering his body and then, as embarrassment flooded him, shrank back. "Where are my clothes?"

Kelesta padded to a shelf, bundled rolled-up pants and a shirt into her arms, and carried them to the bed. She placed them next to him and strolled back to the window.

Discombobulated by his unaccustomed blushing reaction, Teal unrolled the baggy cotton pants and tugged them on. Then he pulled the matching cream-colored shirt over his head. With a deep breath, he steadied himself and paced to the window. "Thank you." He glanced aside, startled at the somber look in her eyes. "For everything." He shrugged. "I'm not a very good patient, I'm afraid. Not used to being taken care of."

"You're a parent. Being helpless isn't comfortable."

Teal pressed her arm. "Nova will be all right. Zuri knows what he's doing."

Kelesta shook her head. "We're past our time—Nova will have to take care of herself soon."

Teal swung aside, facing her more directly. "What does that mean? You have countless ages ahead of you."

Kelesta gripped the window frame, the breeze blowing tendrils of hair off her face. "There is a price for everything. Zuri refused his neuro transplants, all the attachments really, for too long to turn back now. I took on human form to have a child—and it has cost much."

Tears stung Teal's eyes. "But Song, surely she can help you—like she helped me."

Her lips wavering, Kelesta met his gaze. "Song revived you. She can't cure you." Taking his hand, she led the way to the door, the rolling ocean waves, and bright sunshine.

Teal let himself be drawn along and understood for the first time what death really meant.

~~~

Omega picked up a slimy piece of broken clay from the foamy sea waves and stared at it. Overcoming a surprising revulsion at the slick sensation, he pinched it tighter in his fingers. A strong wind blew over him, tossing his hair into his eyes. He picked up another piece and placed their jagged edges side by side. They didn't fit together at all.

On impulse, he waved, and a cloth bag suddenly hung limp in his hand. With another swift motion, the clay fragments floated to the surface of the water. He opened the mouth of the bag and used it to scoop up the pieces, like a net capturing fish from the sea.

Once the bag was full, he splashed ashore and dashed up the trail.

In a quiet corner of the courtyard, he spread the broken pieces in the sun and laid them flat. He chewed his lip, perplexed. What to do next? He had never done anything like this before, and he wasn't sure how to start.

"What've you got there?" A burly soldier tromped forward and stared over Omega's crouched figure. "Oh, you broke something, eh?" He whistled low. "No putting that back together, son. It's ruined, see?" He patted
~~~

Omega's shoulder. "Best to man up and face the wrath of the owner than try to hide the mess out here. She'll figure it out eventually."

Further disorientated but hopeful for some direction, Omega shielded his eyes from the glare of the sun and squinted at the older man. "How do you know I can't put her back together?"

A snort and a chuckle accompanied the man's grin. "It's clay, young fool. It dissolves in water—saltwater most assuredly. I've never been so partial to a clay vessel that I'd called it a *she*, but my captain and I loved our ship; *she* was a beauty in our eyes."

With a shake of his head, Omega rose to his feet.

Abbas marched across the hard ground with a stern look in his eyes.

"My father is coming; I best meet him." He scattered the broken pieces.

The soldier turned and faced the white-haired man coming his way. His face crunched in concentration. "Ah, you be the fool then that entertained us. I only got to see you once—duty calls at unfortunate moments." He smiled as Abbas stopped before him. "Good evening."

Abbas offered a quick nod of acknowledgment then stared at his son. "Where have you been?"

The soldier lifted his hand like a benevolent referee. "Don't be too hard on him. Been trying for a long while to put the thing back together, but it's a lost cause; he knows that now. So he'll pay restitution and be done with the fear and guilt of it."

With an obvious swallow, Abbas choked out his question. "What did you break, son?"

"Mauve."

Clenching his jaw, Abbas gripped Omega's arm and nodded a polite goodbye to the warrior.

Omega trotted at his father's side across the battered earth. "Where are we going?"

"To join the others—and away from here."

"You don't mind about Mauve? She was being annoying."

Abbas dragged his son into the shelter of a dark corner and shook him by the shoulders. "You have no idea what you've done!"

Grieved by his father's fury, Omega whined, "But I tried to put her back together."

"If you thought putting her together was hard, you have no idea what you've just shattered. Our whole existence is based on absolute secrecy. You can be sure now that, not only are we known, we are hated."

Feeling the slime still on his hands, Omega wrinkled his nose. *Hated? What did that even mean?*

Chapter Thirty-Six

To Get Stung

Roland, lord and master of his own small estate and exhausted by troubling affairs, decided to send three men to bring his wife home to him. But before the day was half over, the first man returned with a limp, explaining that he had fallen out of a tree trying to reach a late apple. Though put out, Roland figured that two men could still manage what three had set out to do.

By the next morning, the second man returned, holding his hand over an oozing wound on his thigh. "I've been bitten by the largest snake ever seen by man," he'd wailed, "and I can't leave this Earth without seeing my wife and child once more."

Roland sent him out the door with the injunction to "Put a hot poultice on it and drink some strong beer—you'll feel better by evening." The only thing that kept his temper in check was the thought that he still had one more man to accomplish his goal—only to find that last man in the kitchen, tucking into a large loaf of brown bread and hot stew.

"What under the great sky are you doing here? I sent you to fetch my wife! I need her more than ever, and I find you returned without her! I've already lost two men to ill-fortune and now you...you...insect...sit here as comfortable as a toad! I ought to have you whipped!"

The servant managed a good-humored grin.

Roland could no more have a man whipped than he could embroider a shirt. In fact, he was much more likely to embroider a shirt, and they both knew it well.

The servant rose languidly and bowed. "I couldn't just

leave a good man to die in the mire, could I? Why, the mistress would have my head if I ever did such a thing! Besides, my own wife is nearing her time, and I saw this as an act of providence to turn me home again."

Roland slapped his hands together in impotent fury. It was no good! He couldn't manage another day without his wife. For some reason he could not fathom, all good habits disintegrated when his wife was gone. When Martha was around, everyone behaved. Babies never arrived at inconvenient hours, snakes didn't bite, and men rarely fell out of trees. Roland was free to pursue his interests, which involved collecting and mounting every species of insect he could find, recording bird calls, and measuring the sizes of various dams, beehives, and other natural habitats to see if they foretold some coming event—a hard winter, a sudden storm, or perhaps the end of the world.

The things he studied and recorded were of invaluable importance. If mankind did not realize it now, they would someday. In the meantime, his schedule had been thoroughly disordered by daily affairs, which kept intruding because his wife was not around to manage them.

"Oh, honeybees and hot peppers! If there are no men capable of seeing to this matter, I'll go myself!"

With dreams of undisturbed days of natural investigations floating about in his mind, Roland set out.

For three wandering days, he had stopped so many times to take notes on the abundant insect life and catch a few interesting samples that his traveling speed had dropped to a snail's pace. Sitting astride his humble mount, he let it mosey along as it pleased. Content with himself and all the world, a song bubbled like a summer brook from his soul. "A humble and a bumble and a buzzing bee, humming through the forest, Lord, watch over me...hmm and a hmmm and buzzing bee—" The rhyme was cut short, his mouth fell open, and his eyes bugged. "Holy heathens!"

Three mounted men emerged from a large grove of trees. At the crossway, they surrounded his horse with their pike staffs pointing directly at his ample middle.

Roland saw no need to return their silence or the grim attitude. He offered the sweetest smile from his face that he could manage. "Sirs, I implore you, do nothing foolish. I'm a simple traveler—a landowner looking for my wife to bring her home again. She's now residing with her brother, Melchior. Perhaps you know him and could point me in the right direction? I was pursuing the most spectacular butterfly—"

Without warning, one of the warriors, a rather thin but cocky fellow, grabbed Roland's horse and took possession of the reigns. "We're Nolan's men, and he doesn't like trespassers. But since you are a landowner, I suppose he'll be glad enough to invite you to dinner. But beware, you'll not be the same man when you leave." The warrior turned and motioned his company to follow.

Roland slouched in doomed silence.

~~~

Nolan greeted his newest guest at the doorway with all the exuberance of a man ready to enjoy a sumptuous feast. He thumped Roland on the back, asked after his family, and listened patiently to Roland's catalog of troubles.

Roland grinned as he plunked down at a well-laden table. He pouted about his wife's absence for a moment or two longer and then partook of the delicious offerings. He drank liberally and ate everything put before him. He
~~~

glanced around at the men enjoying the feast and chuckled, "Your man was out of line when he met me, Nolan."

"Oh, how so?" *He brought me another fool, so he can't be too off the mark.*

"He said that I wouldn't be the same when I left here. Ha! On the contrary, I shall be twice the man that I was!"

Nolan smiled and beckoned for more mead.

In the wee hours of the morning, stretched out on a couch with his fat stomach bulging from under his rumpled shirt and his face red as a lobster, Roland was in such an agreeable mood that he soon acquiesced to a series of reasonable requests. He would let Nolan take a bothersome section of woodlands off his hands and pasture a herd of sheep on his southern fields, free of charge.

For the rest of the night, Nolan rested in front of a blazing fire slowly sipping his cup of mead, which he never refilled, and hummed a very happy tune indeed.

In the morning, when the agreement was referred to and an embarrassed Roland recalled the arrangement, he pursed his lips, slung himself onto his horse, and muttered, "No need to see a bee to get stung in this world."

With a happy sense of accomplishment, Nolan sent Roland away with two of his best men-at-arms so that the wandering scientist would make it to Melchior's manor without any further incident.

Roland tipped his head goodbye and turned his horse to the road. A new hum issued from his depths. "Zigging and a zagging across the way, through the heather into the hay. Nolan nearly stole me blind; it's not my fault; I don't mind. Zigging and a zagging throughout the day, Martha shall hear of it! Oh, what'll *she* say?"

Nolan laughed and turned indoors, new plans dancing in his head.

Chapter Thirty-Seven

Need a Miracle

Adele sat astride her horse as it ambled along the path toward home and considered her day. She had never in her wildest dreams imagined that she could sit comfortably in King Radburn's room and laugh with him, but that was exactly how she had spent the afternoon. Even more surprising, the king himself seemed pleased.

Apparently, in kingly circles, laughing was frowned upon. Though he hadn't known many kings in his lifetime, he had acquired the belief that kings do not laugh—except perhaps at the execution of a loathsome enemy. But even then, *that* was the exception to the rule, he had explained.

From the depths of her bag, Martha had brought forth healing potions and powders, soothing teas and calming oils. With smiles and her voice full of warmth and amusing exaggeration, she told funny stories, made droll jokes, shared anecdotes of when Adele was a baby, and all the while plied the king with chamomile tea and hot biscuits with honey. She arranged resin-laden pine logs in the fireplace and oversaw a servant who gently rubbed the king's noble neck with an oil that smelled like luscious fruit. She nudged Adele toward the king until she perched on the edge of a nearby chair, close enough to be alluring, yet just out of reach.

At first, the king endured Martha's cures-all through clenched teeth. After a bit, he began to look her way, and astonishingly soon, he began to stare at her as if she were a caterpillar transformed into a butterfly.

Martha darted about the room, arranging this,

straightening that, making faces that would make anyone laugh, all the while keeping up humorous commentaries.

From his bed, the king watched Martha roam about, his eyes flickering toward Adele only infrequently. Then as one absurd comment made him smile, he looked at Adele, and as she was smiling too, his smile grew.

When their gazes met, a flush heated her face, surprising her. This encounter did a great deal to bring life and vigor back to King Radburn's languid body.

"By God, I feel better already! My heart isn't beating a hole in my chest. My head stopped aching. Even my arms and legs feel renewed." He stopped watching Martha altogether and focused on Adele.

At that point, Martha began to tell an exceedingly embarrassing story about something Adele had done as a baby—running naked into the courtyard—forcing Adele to her feet, laughing and nearly crying. "Aunt, please! You can't tell that story!" She waved her hands frantically, trying desperately to shush her aunt, who clung to the story like a sailor gripping a lifeline.

King Radburn burst out laughing.

Caught off guard by the unexpected sound, Adele and Martha froze. For a moment, there was no sound in the world except for the king's joyful laughter.

As evening came to a close, Martha gathered her herb bags and bottles. "It's time we headed home. Melchior will wonder what's happened to us. I'm afraid the servants may not see to his needs properly. You know how servants can be. They're not like family."

All happiness on King Radburn's face fell away. He quickly replaced it with stern acceptance. "I appreciate all you've done, Martha. You, too, Adele. You've brought me joy—truly the work of a queen."

Adele blinked, her heart clenching. *He's lonely?* Conflict reared its ugly head. Though it had been a more pleasant afternoon than she had expected, and she no longer wished him dead, she could *only* wish him well. That had to be enough.

~~~

Melchior sat at the table in the main hall with Nikolas in companionable silence before gathering his courage to broach the tender topic. He took a gulp of his thick beer and wiped his mouth. "Did I tell you that Martha and Adele went to see the king today?" Melchior winced in the remembrance that he had already mentioned the fact, but he couldn't think of another way to open the subject. "He's been ill and needed someone to make him feel better."

With his shoulders hunched and his gray tunic rumpled, Nikolas looked mighty forlorn. The young man shoved his beer away. "Kings have all sorts of doctors and men of learning to see to their needs. Why does he want the services of your sister? And surely Adele didn't have to go."

"Martha knows her herbs, and he asked specifically for Adele."

"He would, the villain!" Nikolas snapped and clenched a fist, muscles rippling under his skin.

Melchior nodded through a smile. "I'm glad to know your opinion."

"Why? To make sure that I don't challenge the king?"

Melchior's eyebrows rose. "*Are* you thinking of challenging the king?"

"I'd just get myself killed. Oh, it's no use." He slumped in his seat and shook his head, his dark brown hair falling over his face. "I'm not fit to claim Adele's attention. I
~~~

can't win her from so formidable an adversary."

Melchior's grin widened. "Glad to know your true intentions."

Nikolas slapped the table. "Intentions? I'm a poor merchant in a world of warriors and conquerors. I'm lucky to be alive. I have no *intentions.* My life is directed by superior fates, not by any will of my own."

Melchior sighed, rose from his chair, and paced across the room. After a few turns, he stopped beside Nikolas. "I don't agree. Just because you are poor doesn't mean you have no influence. It's true that you, like me, have to accept certain limitations. We're not God, we're not large landowners or kings—but we are men. And as men, we have something that makes us all the same. As Saint Peter said, 'In very deed, I perceive that God is no respecter of persons.'"

Nikolas dropped his head onto his folded arms. "Please, don't quote scripture."

Melchior's eyes traveled from his friend to the fire. "We're sons of the same God, and we're all infinitely less than God. Kings overrate themselves because they have power on Earth; while men like you undervalue yourself because you have little influence. But really, we're all alike. Don't you see, Nikolas? If you give up, then you are giving in to that deception—that man's power is greater than God's plans."

Nikolas raised his head a few inches and spoke to Melchior's ample middle. "As I remember the story, your God got himself killed. Begging your pardon, but I'm not interested in getting hung just to see if someone will raise me from the dead." He sighed and propped his head on his hand. "Remember Selby? Even when he tried to exact revenge for the wrong done unto him—and there was wrong done to him *by your hand, Melchior*—even still, he could not change his fate. He was hung without mercy."

Melchior stared at Nikolas, a frown building an ache between his eyes. "You're right. You're not the man for my daughter. It would take a man who believes in himself to intervene on her behalf so that she would not be forced to marry a brute and a fool. But instead, you are quite reasonable. Not passionate, just very reasonable. I hope your good sense will keep your bed warm at night and provide heirs for your few earthly possessions!" Melchior stalked across the room.

Nikolas sat with his head propped on his hand, speechless.

Lifting his voice across the open space, Melchior let loose his decided opinion. "Some men are doomed from their first breath, born into a terrible world. But *even then*, we do not see all. Selby had choices and opportunities we know nothing of, and he suffered grief and terror I cannot imagine, but God's world didn't stop at the end of that rope! And Selby's didn't either."

Nikolas lifted his head and gazed through sad eyes.

"How *passionate* are we? Not just to live but to die to save someone we love. Selby was wrong in his murderous hate, but he was right in his passionate love. Good heavens! We are men, and we're all mixed up, but God helps us, if only we ask. He won't perform a miracle unless we're willing to need one."

Nikolas sighed and folded his hands in his lap. "I do care for your daughter, and if I knew of a way to free her, I would do it. But King Radburn is a powerful man, and he already dislikes me. I'm poor, and few would mourn my passing if I were to die. Even Father Caedmon wouldn't worry about my poor corpse."

Melchior snorted in derision. "You're weak. I never thought I'd see the day when the son of Osborn would shame me. I'm not asking you to go to the king and demand that he gives up Adele. I'm simply asking you to admit that you want to marry her and let me tell him that I'm in favor of the match. Who knows, perhaps he doesn't enjoy her company so much, and he's already casting his eyes in another direction. In any case, my sister's ministrations must have done some good, and he'll be in a better mood than he was this morning. Let's go and see how things stand with him tonight."

Nikolas rubbed his face, stood up, and squared his shoulders. "I must face this. I can't run away just because I can't win. Where is the nobility in that? Perhaps your God is real, and He does grant favors to the hopeless. At least, Adele will know I tried."

Melchior scratched his chin. "Not the most rousing speech I've ever heard, but it'll have to do."

Pounding hooves sounded in the distance. Melchior smiled. "They're back. Let's acquaint them with our plan, then we'll be off."

A large man with shoulder length brown hair and a muscled build barreled into the room. He strode up to Melchior, clutching a pair of worn gloves, a fierce scowl etched across his face. "My Lord Melchior, my name is Harold, and I'm here on behalf of a friend of yours who has been wrongfully detained. Father Caedmon was coming here, to your manor, to offer his services to your sons, to educate them in the arts and letters, when he was waylaid by one of Lord Gerard's men. Since the king has been indisposed, Lord Gerard's nephew, Robert, scoundrel if ever there was one, has seen to matters. To get to the heart of things, he directed Lord Gerard to take the priest to his manor house and hold him there for safekeeping until the king can make his wishes known. But I fear for the priest's life."

Melchior clapped his hand to his forehead and laughed, staring at Nikolas. "My, but God has a way of making us eat our words!" He signaled to his men. "Get to your horses!" He turned to Harold and beckoned Nikolas with a wave. "Come, I'll need every brave man I can find."

As Melchior mounted his horse in the warmth of the stable, his sister and daughter, still on their horses, were led forward by their men.

The moon, only half full, cast a dim light, and cold stillness pervaded the air, but the horses' eager snorts and plodding steps warmed Melchior's heart. Gladness filled him at the sight of his sister. "Welcome home, Martha. Get inside and warm up. We'll discuss your visit as soon as we return. Nikolas and I are off to Lord Gerard's to see after the welfare of a good priest waylaid as he journeyed here. I must look into the matter, for Lord Gerard has no reason to love me or this priest."

Martha's tired voice broke through the gloom. "Thank you, brother. It's been a long day, and I'm worn to exhaustion. Who knew playing the jester could be such hard work? As for Lord Gerard, what a strange family! His nephew, Robert, was just going in as we were leaving, perhaps about this same matter. His rudeness towards Adele was unparalleled—"

Martha's complaint was cut short by pounding hooves.

Melchior bit his lip as he mentally tried to place everyone. Wilfred had returned to Lord Gerard, Martha and Adele were before his eyes, Oliver and the others were eating supper, and all the men who were not acting as escorts were at home. Who could possibly be riding in at this hour?

A loud voice called out, "Lord Melchior!"

With little moonlight shining through the stable door, Melchior could see nothing beyond his horse's head. "Yes, who's there?"

"It is Giles, one of Nolan's men."

"Nolan, yes, I remember him. Is your master well?"

A rueful laugh brought smiles all around. "Aye, my

master's never been better. He just met up with one of your own—your sister's husband, Roland, wandering alone and unprotected, so he gave him shelter for the night, and I was told to bring him here. We'd have been here earlier, but the man likes to go off like a hound after a fox! He claims that he's a man of science, but he led us all over the kingdom today. I never knew such a short journey could take so long!"

Riding up from behind, Roland exploded in exasperation. Wet and shivering, with dark circles under his eyes, he shook a clenched fist. "Be off with you then, you and your helpless brother. I've never seen two grown men so frightened of a snake in all my life. Idiots acting like I was putting my head in a lion's mouth." Taking a deep breath, Roland addressed Melchior. "Now, good brother, I am exhausted and very dirty, and I want my wife!"

Martha directed her horse to approach him. "Good Lord, Roland! What under the great sky has induced you to leave home and follow me here?"

Roland's voice changed from a commander's to a child's whine. "Oh, Martha, is that you? Please, do something! I'm wearied to death."

Martha's laugh rang out as she slid from her horse. "Follow me, husband. I know this place like the back of my hand. Good people all around. You need a bath and a warm drink to soothe your nerves. It must have been a frightfully long journey! Why on Earth did you come all alone?"

Roland nearly fell off his horse in his eagerness to relate all. "I sent out men to get you. You have no idea..."

Melchior directed his horse into the open air, and all conversations faded to the background. He grimaced at the thought of Roland at the supper table. Or any table, for that matter. The fool spoke of nothing but his insatiable interest in insects and other deplorable creatures. Though he was also a man of science, *Melchior's* science actually mattered. It was not a bunch of stupid musings about creatures God only made to test the patience of men.

He waved back at Nolan's men. "Thank you for your trouble. Go inside and get something to eat before you make your return journey. I must go, but I'll be back soon."

Nolan's men looked at each other then shook their heads. Giles spoke up. "No, thank you, Lord Melchior. We've been gone long enough. We must return at once." With that, they turned and vanished into the black night.

Nikolas urged his horse forward. "They're afraid of meeting up with that fool again."

Melchior snorted and nudged his horse along. "No doubt, but let's hurry and save Father Caedmon. Then we can find out about Martha's visit with the king. All must've gone well, or she would have told me at once."

Adele appeared astride her horse in the darkness and spoke softly. "It went well, father. Too well, I'm afraid. You'll find the king more determined to marry me than ever."

Caught off guard, Melchior pulled up sharply. "Oh, Adele, I almost forgot you. It's so blasted dark outside! We must see to Father Caedmon first, but Nikolas is coming with me, and we'll speak with the king soon."

Hidden in the darkness, Adele's voice seemed to come from the very air. "Thank you for keeping my father company, Nikolas."

Nikolas nudged his horse forward. "Don't worry, Adele, no matter what happens—"

"No more of that!" Melchior squinted into the darkness, trying to glimpse his daughter. "Come from the shadows; I can hardly see you."

Adele moved forward, and Melchior leaned in, finally catching sight of his pale, weary daughter. "I'll get things arranged, have no fear, but we must have things done properly."

"The king will not listen, Father. He's lonely and imagines that I can bring him joy, but really, it was Martha. She soothed and amused him, not me."

Melchior snorted. "She can be an amusing woman! How she has managed that fool all these years...but never mind. Go inside and warm yourself. See that everyone is safe and sound for the night. We'll be back soon."

"Yes, Father." Adele looked to Nikolas, and their gazes held for a moment.

Cruel foreboding filled Melchior. He swung his horse away.

Nikolas, Harold, and two other men nudged their horses up the slope behind him. They galloped across the valley by the light of the moon, only reigning in when Lord Gerard's mansion came into sight. The fortress-type manor was ablaze with light.

Melchior sighed as he urged his horse forward once again. "Come now, only a little further."

Once at the gate, Nikolas jumped down and pounded on the hard wood.

A soldier from inside the tower behind the gate called out, "Who goes there?"

"Your neighbor, Melchior would like to speak to his Lordship."

Melchior and the men slid off their horses and stood alert, ready to enter.

A heavyset man wearing a leather jerkin marched forward with a torch and called for reinforcements. "Come, men. Here they are!" He peered at Melchior through the smoky gloom. "Lord Gerard just told us to retrieve you, yet you've come to us."

Suspicion and alarm spread through Melchior. "Why? What does he want with me?"

"He's ordered your arrest."

Harold cursed, and Nikolas spluttered, but Melchior thrust out his chest in fury. "Arrest?" He dropped his voice to a growl. "Who is he to arrest me? On what charge?"

Seven soldiers surrounded them, their weapons ready. The gatekeeper lifted his chin in defiance. "On the charge of witchcraft. I'm to retrieve your sister and daughter as well. He says you're all in league with the devil."

Stupefied, Melchior hardly moved as the warriors surged around him.

Nikolas edged up closer and whispered in his ear. "Anytime, Melchior, anytime..."

Without taking his eyes off the gatekeeper, Melchior snapped, "Anytime what?"

Nikolas followed Melchior as they were hustled into Lord Gerard's castle. "One of those miracles you mentioned."

Chapter Thirty-Eight

I Offer It Freely

Richard used every ounce of his strength, his arms wrapped around Lord Gerard, to keep his brother from attacking Melchior.

Clearly bewildered, Melchior stood in the middle of the great hall surrounded by guards.

Lord Gerard screamed, "The devil take you, spawn of hell! You thought to plant your daughter into the heart of our land, her lying tongue whispering into the king's ear! I know all about your plans. Fool, did you think the priest would defend you? He told me everything. I know his plans, your plans, Adele's plans, and even your little minion's plans." He glared at Nikolas, the young man standing at Melchior's side. "Don't think I haven't noticed how close you stick to him. Leeches could take lessons from you, merchant!"

Nikolas jumped forward but was held in check by Harold.

Terrill guarded the doorway, his pike staff lowered and ready for action.

Richard's arms felt leaden even as he loosened his grip. Had his brother gone completely mad? He certainly looked the part, his hair disheveled and his clothes dirty and rumpled.

Melchior stomped forward, rage replacing confusion in his eyes. "I demand the right to be heard. Where's my son, Wilfred? Where is Father Caedmon?"

"Ha! *Your* son? You have no son named Wilfred, Melchior; it was all a lie. You were sadly deceived! But I have fixed the matter. Wilfred is my heir. He'll inherit all.

But your wretched daughter associates with the dead. Your own sister told Corliss. Corliss told my brother, and he told me. I had the priest interviewed, and he told me everything, even about his mission to train men in his work. He had his eyes on Wilfred; you know he did. Twice now, the devil has conspired to take my son from me, but I have snatched him back. He is mine, and no other will have him."

Melchior stood his ground. "You've lost your wits! Wilfred is his own man, and Adele is innocent of all witchcraft! Whatever Corliss told you is a lie. Now, where is my son?"

"Your sons are your own business."

"I mean Wilfred!"

"Wilfred is upstairs keeping watch. Fate gave him back to me, and he'll protect me."

"Where is Father Caedmon, then?"

Lord Gerard strutted about like an angry rooster while every eye followed, every muscle taut. "Your priest is below. I'll have him brought up, but don't think I will give him to you." Lord Gerard barked an order to a nearby guard, who turned and slipped away.

Richard's heart raced at the thought of what the priest might look like after Lord Gerard's men had had their way with him.

Glowering, Lord Gerard stepped up to Melchior and pushed his face close. "You think I was a fool? That since my wife had tricked me once, you could trick me now? I've heard about your priests. I know what they are about—eating flesh and drinking blood."

Grimacing, Melchior stepped back.

"Don't bother to lie. I questioned him myself."

"Questioned him or tortured him? Who gave you that right?"

"Right? Does a man need permission to protect his

family? I sent Robert to inform the king but he—" Lord Gerard's face flushed. "He ordered my nephew away and questioned my sanity!" Lord Gerard's eyebrows rose as his voice fell. "He's already possessed. But no matter, he'll not remain king for long."

Melchior swallowed, and his pale face blanched. "Why do you say that?"

"I will take the kingdom. I've sent word to all worthy men in the area to join me. I'll show no mercy. There cannot be two kings ruling these lands."

Melchior's gaze strayed to Richard. "And where do you stand? Are you for your brother's plan?"

His throat constricted, Richard forced out his words. "I agree that a marriage between Adele and the king would be unwise, but there is no—"

Melchior shouted, "Will you fight your brother's battle?"

"Surely we can find another way."

Lord Gerard smirked. "As you did with Lord Marlow?"

Richard turned on his brother, his temper flaring. "I was attacked—I had no choice. But now we have time, and choices are yet before us!"

"Ahem." Lord Gerard's man marched forward, leading a stooped figure.

Tears sprang to Richard's eyes.

Melchior's voice rose loud and angry, "My God, what have you done? He's just a poor old man who could do you no harm!"

The priest's right eye was swollen shut, and his cheeks showed the abrasions of a man who had been forced to the ground and beaten while his face was pressed against the hard ground. Sickened at the sight, Richard exhaled a long breath to relieve the bile rising to his throat.

With his chest thrust out, Lord Gerard circled around Father Caedmon. "It took some convincing, but I got the truth at last. He admitted that he eats the body and drinks the blood of his God and that he was coming here to teach, not just your sons but all men, lords and slaves alike, so that they could all call Him master and serve Him. Those were his words. Deny it as you please, Melchior, but he said he would die to defend this belief. And he *will* die defending it, for I will not let him live much longer. I'm glad that you came, for I wanted you to see what happens to men who traffic in such idiocy. And you!" Lord Gerard turned, his gaze piercing Harold. "I can think of no better cure for what ails you!"

His teeth clenched, Richard trembled with rage. *God, give me strength!*

Terrill barely suppressed a smile.

Nikolas gripped Harold's arm.

Father Caedmon's voice barely rose above a whisper. "It is true—a kingdom cannot have two kings, but you cannot take my life; I offer it freely."

Melchior charged forward. "Don't think that you can kill this man with impunity. Wilfred cares for him, and he will hate you for this brutality."

Lord Gerard spoke aside to one of his men.

Before the soldier took two steps, Richard intercepted him. "Wait," he commanded. Then he approached his brother, who glared at the interference, and he whispered in his ear, "Killing the priest is not wise." He pressed Gerard's shoulder and led him to the far side of the room. He imbued his words with the authority of the angel of death. "The spirits of martyred priests rise to haunt those who killed them."

Lord Gerard blanched. Suddenly, he marched back toward Melchior. "For *your* sake, Melchior, for the sake of your family and our long friendship, I am willing to spare the life of this priest. He can live out his days in my dungeon, where he will never menace anyone again." He waved Melchior and his men off. “Go on now! Bother me no more. I must see to the needs of the kingdom.” He gestured for his men to take Father Caedmon away.

Harold gripped Melchior’s shoulder and walked with him out the door and into the cold night.

Richard dearly wished he could follow.

~~~

Harold followed behind as Nikolas and Melchior returned to the manor house. Uncertain what else to do, he stepped to the glowing fire in the hearth and warmed his hands, pondering life’s twists and turns. How could a good man go so wrong in such a short time? *But was Lord Gerard ever truly good?*

Once inside, Melchior said nothing. He only started for the stairs.

Nikolas called after him, “Where are you going?”

Slowing his steps, Melchior waved his friend off. “I don’t know what to do. I need to think.”

His face flushed. Nikolas pounded the table. “I know what I’m going to do! I’ll tell the king what Lord Gerard is planning.”

Melchior turned on the first step. “Yes, of course. But let me rest now. We need to think this out carefully.”

His heart squeezing into a painful fist, Harold stepped forward. “Begging your pardon, sir, but we have no time. Lord Gerard is mad. If we don’t act quickly, it’ll be every man for himself.”

Melchior’s shoulders slumped. “True, but the news shouldn’t come from me—”

Nikolas brightened. “I know just the man!” He turned to Harold. “Remember Nolan? He’s the perfect man for
~~~

such an occasion."

Climbing the last steps, Melchior shouted back, "King Radburn is volatile at the best of times—don't tell him too much too soon."

Nikolas waved Melchior's fears away. "You said I should follow my passion. Here I'll be approaching the king with vital news—he'll be grateful." His grin widened. "Now, he'll have something to think about besides a wedding."

A flush rose in Melchior's cheeks as he ascended the last steps.

A moment later, the sound of pattering steps was followed by two disheveled people entering the room.

With eyes wide and hair mussed, Oliver hurried into the room.

Adele, in a nightdress and a stocking cap, trotted close on his heels. Looking like a young girl, she called out, "What's happened? Why are you shouting?"

Harold retreated to a dim corner, uncomfortable in such an intimate family scene. *I shouldn't be here. But then, where should I be?*

Nikolas dragged his fingers through his hair. "Lord Gerard has gone mad. He tortured an innocent priest because Corliss told Richard that you and Martha were in league with the dead and that you're planning to take over the kingdom when you marry the king."

Adele's eyes widened as she spluttered, "He must be mad then! I don't even know this priest. Why did Richard listen to such talk? Did the king agree to this madness?"

"Not yet. But Corliss told Richard some absurd tale about Martha speaking to the dead. That story has Lord Gerard thinking the worst of you—of all of us."

Adele wrapped her arms around her middle, trembling. "Why would Corliss do such a thing?"

Harold stepped from the shadows. "It's the oldest

reason in the world. She lost her betrothed while you found a king. There's no mystery in jealousy."

Like a man overcome in besotted love, Nikolas clasped Adele's hands in his own. "Melchior accused me of being weak when I was afraid of confronting the king, but I'm no longer afraid. Even after being tortured, that priest was still determined. I'm no less a man than that priest. I will go and set matters right."

Adele pulled her hand free. "I don't want to marry the king, but I most certainly don't want anyone thinking I am in league with the devil—oh!" Her hands clapped on her face, and she turned away. "I told her of the saint carvings on the door!"

Nikolas looked at her, his brows furrowed.

Oliver's expression darkened as he darted a glance at Nikolas.

Glancing around the room, alarmed at the petulant expressions, Harold pushed for action. "We'll go see Nolan, then."

Stepping between Nikolas and his sister, Oliver wrapped his arm around Adele's shoulder. "Don't worry. God will take care of us."

Adele stared into her brother's eyes. "You really believe that, Oliver?"

He shrugged. "They may settle things peacefully."

Adele stepped out of Oliver's embrace. "Everything comes at a cost. It might work out for you, Oliver. You won't have to marry the king."

His heart sinking, Harold pounded to the door.

Chapter Thirty-Nine

Lost Home

Nolan brought his guests to his warm chambers, sat them on a wooden bench, and listened to the sorry tale. When they had told all, he insisted that Nikolas and Harold partake of a little nourishment and wait for the morning before confronting the king.

Soon, bowls of hot pea soup, bread, and wedges of cheese were laid before them in the main hall. Comfortable beds overlaid with thick furs were assembled in a guest room.

Despite the food and comfortable bedding, no one rested easily. The night grew cold, and outside, the air filled with thick, white flakes.

When at last the morning light made travel safe, all three men dressed in haste, gulped down half a dozen boiled eggs, and galloped to the king's gate, expecting to be received at once. Though they sent a message warning the king of serious news, they were kept waiting until nearly noon.

When their turn finally came, Nolan charged into the main hall, which was filled with watching attendants and a handful of wary soldiers. In his flowing purple robes, the king sat on his accustomed throne. Using his most authoritative voice, Nolan bellowed, "King Radburn, why do you make important news wait on your doorstep? That is not the act of a wise king! Listen now, or you'll live to rue your foolish pride."

The king offered Nolan a disgusted look.

Undaunted, Nolan continued with his mission. "Lord Gerard is mad with fear and believes that the dead will overthrow the kingdom through the powers of a priest and your lovely bride-to-be!"

Blinking like a sleepy cat, the king grinned.

Nolan pushed on. "Apparently, Adele's aunt spoke foolishly and sent Corliss' young mind into a terror. She, in turn, told her uncle that Adele's family traffics in the spirit world. Of course, you know that's not true, but Lord Gerard's mind has been overstrained—he fears his own shadow."

The king's abrupt laugh echoed in the large hall, further straining the nerves of everyone present. Even the soldiers appeared startled.

Nolan composed himself for another try. "His recent actions reflect a man on the brink of disaster. He's raising an army against you! You must act soon to prove that you'll not allow the kingdom to be taken over by any force—spirit or otherwise."

King Radburn's gaze could have cut stone. "Your skill in stating the obvious is unparalleled. I, too, have eyes, and I see better than you think."

Nolan took a step back, his face hot and his fury mounting.

Rushing forward, Harold stepped into the breach. "But, my Lord King, he has already tortured an innocent priest, Father Caedmon, who only came to offer his services to Melchior's sons to teach them their letters and things—"

"Yes, and *things*! That is what I've been told, too." King Radburn climbed to his feet and stared down at the three men from the dais. "I'm not interested in priests and their teachings. But I am interested in what my people believe. If men believe that there is an all-powerful God who looks after them, well then, what do they need with a *king*?"

Silence pervaded the room.

King Radburn rubbed his chin as he seemed to consider

his own puzzle. "The Israelites' God advised them against choosing a king—as I would have done if I were He—gods and kings don't mix well. But the Israelites scorned this good advice, and they regretted it ever after."

Nolan's hands itched to wrap themselves around the king's throat. *Dare he play the philosopher, now, when there is not a minute to waste?*

With new agility, King Radburn stepped down from the dais and paced toward the kindled hearth at the east end of the room. "I don't care what happens to the priest. In fact, I would advise Lord Gerard to kill the man to erase any future complications. But as for the other matter, I am a new man by Adele's hand. She has the power to make me feel well, and *that* I will not lightly forgo. I have seen into her soul—beautiful and innocent. Difficult qualities to find in this world. I will marry her; Lord Gerard has nothing to say in the matter."

Dashing forward in haste, Nikolas stumbled and fell at the king's feet. "Sir, you cannot marry Adele. Her heart is divided. Though she cares for you as a king, she does not look to you for a husband. She and I have discovered that we—that we hope for the same thing. We wish to be free to marry—with your blessing. We'll be poor, but many men live happier in their poverty than kings." Blushing, Nikolas rose to his feet.

King Radburn's smile was replaced by a wince. His hand traveled to his chest, clutching his cloak. "You love Adele?"

"Yes, and she loves me. We would've told you sooner, but we didn't discover it ourselves until recently."

"*How* recently?"

Nolan heard the warning in the king's voice and stepped forward to intervene, but the tension in the air nearly took his breath away.

His chest out, like a man ready to take a sword thrust,

Harold did the needful. "King Radburn, Lord Gerard is planning an attack!"

"I am the king, and I know my business. Go outside and wait."

Harold glanced at Nikolas and Nolan, bowed formally, and marched to the door.

The king returned his attention to Nikolas. "You're a shopkeeper, correct? You're right; you will be poor. Always. Remember, you live by your king's pleasure." His eyes strayed to Nolan, and the cat-smile returned. "Let me propose this. Nikolas can marry Adele—over my dead body. I will gladly engage Lord Gerard in battle and kill him at my leisure." His gaze focused on Nolan. "You defraud innocent men of their land under the pretense of doing them a favor."

Nolan forced a tight smile. "I have many friends. If they choose to be generous, who am I to argue?"

"*That* generosity stops today, or I'll take all of your lands as bounty. A portion of your gifts, however, I will accept as the king's due. My men will make an account of the district, and all misunderstandings will end."

In seething, helpless fury, Nolan glared at the man before him. "I don't remember us having any misunderstandings, King Radburn! We once got along quite well."

"As you stole men blind, you became blind yourself! My men outnumber yours four-to-one. I also have an arsenal of the finest weapons in the land. Make no mistake; you will abide by my decision." The king forced his grimace into a twisted smile as he waved toward the door. "You don't want to suffer the same fate as the unfortunate priest."

Nikolas gasped, turned on his heel, and stalked toward the door.

Nolan turned stiffly, gritting his teeth. He marched into

the courtyard, followed by his companions. He knew where his allegiance lay, and it was not with the king.

~~~

Harold arrived at Lord Gerard's estate at mid-day and immediately asked one of the guards about the priest. Learning that Father Caedmon was still alive, he stormed into Lord Gerard's private quarters, a luxurious room with plush furniture, hanging tapestries, and a boldly patterned rug. He knelt before his seated lord, who relaxed with a simple meal close at hand. "My lord, I've always been your good servant, and I know that you have treated me better than I deserve, but I beg you to release me from your service, for I will never be of any use to you now."

It being obvious that he was in no danger, Lord Gerard took the affront with benevolent understanding. He sat on a well-worn chair and waved Harold to state his case.

"I know that you hate the priest, but I assure you, the man is harmless. He's old and weak. Allow me to take him to Melchior's estate so that he may die in peace. I promise, on my life, that I will never allow him to harm you or your estate. I'll watch him closely and if I ever have any reason to doubt him—I'll kill him myself."

Without a word, Lord Gerard rose and paced to a larger room across the hall. A table was spread with maps and charts, and men-at-arms leaned in discussing matters. All conversation halted as Lord Gerard and Harold entered.

Lord Gerard stared at the maps and wrinkled his brow. "I've no more use for the wretch. Take him and do as you please. I had to send Wilfred off on account of the fool. Heal him or kill him, makes no difference to me. Once I have the kingdom in order, there won't be a man alive
~~~

who can challenge me." He turned and glowered into Harold's eyes. "But if I ever find him wandering loose, I'll bury him with my wife so they can keep each other company!"

Harold bowed and retreated into the main hall.

A moment later, Terrill strode into the room, leading Father Caedmon with a rope about his neck. Terrill sneered. "How now, brother-of-mine? Have you remembered your duty and come to offer service, or are you still hell-bent on self-destruction?"

Father Caedmon's breath rose and fell in ragged huffs, though he lifted his gaze to meet Harold's.

Harold's eyes swept over the priest, appraising the damage done to the frail man, before he glared at Terrill. "I've been released from Lord Gerard's service and have come to take the priest away."

Terrill jerked the rope, knocking Father Caedmon off balance. "No, you don't! This man has been charged with consorting with the dead and threatening the kingdom. You're no match for the likes of him."

Hot fury flooding his body, Harold gripped Terrill's shoulder, digging his fingers in. "Lord Gerard released him into my care, and I'm taking him to Lord Melchior. You've nothing to say in the matter. Now let go, or I'll—"

Terrill wagged his fist. "Traitor! I was told to bring him up for questioning, and that's what I aim to do. Your father would disown you if he were alive!"

Harold jerked Terrill's arm back, forcing him to drop the rope. "Listen to me, little brother, you use words you don't understand. Serve Lord Gerard as you wish, but I claim the same right to serve whom I choose." He shoved Terrill away, sending the man flailing across the stone floor.

Turning to Father Caedmon, Harold widened the loop and swung the rope from around the old man's neck.

Terrill rose to his feet, lowered his head, and positioned himself for a charge.

Appearing in the doorway, Lord Gerard bellowed, "Terrill, you idiot! Get in here. I have work for you." He gestured to Harold. "Get that maggot out of here! I don't want his foul body stinking up my home!"

Terrill stood with his legs spread wide, sucking in bursts of breath. "But you wanted him for questioning!"

Lord Gerard propped his hands on his hips and cursed, "Damn your eyes, I never said any such thing." He looked once more upon Harold. "Go, before I kill you both!" He glanced at Terrill. "Listen to me, fool. I want to assemble every available lord. Get your men and go!"

Harold led Father Caedmon into the fresh, wintery air, helped him mount his horse, took the reins, and gently led the animal onto the path leading to Melchior's estate.

As they walked, Father Caedmon's voice rose shakily. "It's beautiful. The rolling hills. White snow and blue sky. Untouched by malice."

Swallowing back bile, Harold nodded. Images of his brother's fury-twisted face floated before his eyes.

Father Caedmon sighed. "This present trouble will not last."

Harold shook his head. "It's more the past that troubles me."

With honest concern in his voice, the old priest asked, "Why?"

"Terrill was my foster brother, yet now, we're as good as enemies. I wasted my youth being his friend. Why were we ever brought together? We might as well have been strangers all these years."

Father Caedmon stroked the horse's mane. "Never regret a kindness, no matter how it's taken. In the end, our kindness cures us."

Blinking back tears, Harold lifted his head as he trudged forward, his prints leading further from home with every step.

Chapter Forty

I Can't Lose

Sterling let Nova and Cerulean lead the way across the dark terrain, his hands clasped behind his back, a frown exasperating his throbbing headache. *These infants will soon drive me mad! Just get through this meeting, reunite with Mauve, make the stupid report, and return to Lux and a life of sanity. It's all I ask!*

Nova seemed unable to stop talking. A child endowed with hypersensitivity who actually thought he cared how she felt and so was taking the long road through her emotional state.

He glanced up. Cerulean held his head bowed low. *Probably trying not to trip over this blasted uneven ground.*

Melchior's abode stood silhouetted against the moonlight, forlorn, like a child's toy left upon the landscape.

Sterling shivered. Mauve would certainly be waiting with open arms. So ready to embrace— His thoughts tripped over themselves, and he grimaced. *Pretty much anyone.*

Did that bother him? Of course not. He wasn't possessive. Or territorial. Like one of these human barbarians. Though, the king's nonchalance toward his own son did seem a bit too detached. Surely, it would be upsetting to murder one's own offspring, even by accident. Especially—one would think—the son of the woman he professed to love.

Nova stopped in her tracks, slapping one hand into the other. "That's it!" She grinned at Cerulean and then shouted, "They don't mean to control me—it's just that they have invested so much of themselves that if something happens to me, it happens to them!"

Cerulean peered over his shoulder and met Sterling's direct gaze. *Took her long enough.* He cleared his throat and pointed ahead. "We should find them in Selby's old home. It's beyond the main house by—"

A group of horsemen exited the barn and sped into the valley, heading their way.

Ducking into a ditch, Cerulean dragged Sterling by the arm.

Nova scuttled up close behind.

The murmuring voices faded, and Sterling shook himself free. He straightened and pursed his lips. "You forget yourself, Cerulean. I am the leader here. I tell you what to do. You don't drag me out of the way of stupid animals."

Nova smirked. "You'd have hated being trampled, even if it didn't kill you."

Cerulean faced his superior, ever the proper guardian. "I apologize. I was out of order, sir."

With a huff, Sterling waved toward Selby's hut. "Hurry up! I hope Mauve has arranged some decent comfort for us. I'm completely drained."

Nova laughed. "She's never cared for anyone's comfort before. Why would she start now?"

Cerulean shot the mixed-breed a warning glance.

Sterling's nerves began to tingle. He wiped his brow. *She's two for two. I'm beginning to hate this—*

A figure pelted out of the hut and raced across the hard-packed earth with his arms outstretched. With the muscular build and pounding steps, it definitely wasn't Mauve. A few more steps and the figure clarified itself. Sterling sighed. *Only Zuri.*

Zuri caught Nova in his robust arms and swung her in a circle.

At first, she yelped and struggled, but then she plunged her head onto his shoulder and hugged back.

By the Divide! They'll hurt each other holding on that hard. He rubbed his upper arm where Mauve had left bruises. Sadness pressed on his shoulders like a heavy weight. *This is nothing like that.*

The outline of a Cresta blocked the doorway to the hut. "Hurry and get inside!"

Being jostled along by Cerulean, Sterling followed Nova, who clung to her father's arm as if she had been lost at sea for a week rather than in his competent care for two days.

As his gaze swept the interior, Sterling's insides dropped to nether regions. *Where is she?* He gritted his teeth. *Not with another man, surely. Not now! After I explicitly told her—*

"Sterling." Zuri stared at him, beckoning to a chair beside a rickety table. His gaze had gone from ecstatic to pathetic in a remarkably short time.

Sterling blinked in the wavering light. A fire flickered in the tiny hearth. Exhaustion seeped over him. "Won't someone see the fire and investigate?"

Zuri glanced at Tarragon. "We dressed like beggars, and I was given the night to rest with my *sick* friend."

Tarragon dangled two dirty cloaks before them. "Amazing what humans will believe when given a glimpse of off-colored flesh."

Since Sterling hadn't taken it, Nova plopped down on the waiting chair. "Well, it's good to stop stomping all over the kingdom. I thought we'd never get here." She spoke to her father, jerking her thumb backward. "These two could've blinked here in a second, but they were nice enough to go with me every step of the way."

Shocked by this true—but kind—assessment, Sterling wouldn't be left behind in generosity. "She's a good companion. Shared a number of personal insights as we traveled." He shot a glance at Cerulean, who kept his gaze focused straight ahead. Sterling rubbed his hands together, ready to move on. "So, what's next? I assume that Mauve has prepared proper accommodations and perhaps even a few refreshing—"

"Mauve is dead." Tarragon stared fixedly at Sterling. It was an announcement. A fact. The moon is high. The floor is dry. Nothing more.

Nova gasped, her hand flying to her mouth in perfect imitation of shocked human grief.

Cerulean dropped his gaze and shook his head. Another legitimate sign of grief.

Zuri gripped Tarragon's shoulder above his right tentacle. "You don't tell someone that the love of their life is dead like—"

"She wasn't!" Sterling heard the words but wasn't sure they had come from his mouth. But they must have. Everyone was staring at him. He shook himself. He was still here. In this shabby hut. On Earth. With these idiots. "She wasn't the love of my life."

Silence dragged on.

An owl hooted.

Nova shuffled her feet, staring at him with those perfect almond eyes of hers.

Cerulean looked up but said nothing, his expression properly grave.

Another owl hooted back. Nature was having a polite conversation in the night.

Zuri stomped up and gripped Sterling's arm much too hard.

To his surprise, Sterling let the Ingot lead him out the door and into the night.

After they had wandered into a barn where a cow and calf lifted their heads in mild interest, Zuri leaned against the wall and crossed his arms.

Moonbeams slanted into the room, highlighting the mama cow's eyes, making them glitter.

"She thought that she could bargain with the mystery boy—even blackmail him. I guess he played a trick on her. Dropped her half-naked into the Cresta's ship. So she planned revenge. But he didn't appreciate her attempts to allure him into her embrace."

Is this nausea? Sickness? What humans are always ranting and raving about? Before he knew what was happening, Sterling vomited the bread and ale he had eaten at mid-day. It didn't taste any better the second time around.

He felt Zuri's hand on his shoulder. The instinctual desire to brush any gentle touch aside was halted by the mere fact that he felt too weak to brush a fly aside. Once he was certain that he could manage it, he straightened and wiped his mouth with the back of his hand. Then he instantly changed into fresh clothes.

Zuri stepped aside and leaned on the wall again. "I'd thought I lost Kelesta, remember? The worst hell I could imagine. Not having a chance to tell her that I loved her before she departed."

Sterling sucked in a deep breath. "But she didn't die. And she loved you without being told." Something deep inside broke—free. "You have a remarkable daughter. I'd thought all mixed breeds were doomed to narcissism. But she shows true spirit. She actually cares about her parents. She just didn't know it."

Zuri shook his head. "I thought I was helping you deal with your loss."

Sterling stood in the doorway and stared at the moonlight. "I can't lose what I never had."

~~~

Abbas, in his human form and dressed in a long white tunic, paced before a shimmering essence in a brilliantly lit space. Rainbows glinted from a million facets surrounding them.

The shimmering form expanded as it spoke in a high dulcet tone. "You take these experiences too seriously. He'll outgrow his mischievous nature. Just give him time."

Halting, Abbas turned and faced the light. "You're his mother, and you see nothing ominous in his murdering an innocent being without thought or repentance?"

A charming laugh tinkled like a small bell. "I was watching—everything! I saw the creature Mauve, and she is no loss to anyone. No caring parent, fond sibling, adoring lover, or needy child will miss her one bit. Even the Luxonian who kept her company cares little. Don't worry."

The tolling bells of doom rang in Abbas' mind. "It was still wrong. He must not murder other beings."

"You will teach him all he needs to know in time. Now come and rest with me. I've placed him into the care of others for now. Humanity won't change a whit before you return."

Against his better judgment, which he could not explain even to himself, Abbas let himself be drawn into her brilliant embrace.

His human figure dissolved, and the two beings shimmered like raindrops on a spring morning.

She cajoled him in merriment. "Stop brooding. No one will be upset. She was always thrusting herself into every experience simply to satiate her covetous desire for
~~~

whatever pleasure she saw others having. She thought only of herself, a complete narcissist."

In an unprecedented move, Abbas buried his next thought deep in his interior. For if she knew the truth, it would destroy her happiness. *You just described your son.*

Chapter Forty-One

Powerless

Richard returned from his latest hunt and found his brother, Nolan, and an assembly of landowners in the main hall, arguing and hammering out their battle strategy. Rough-drawn maps lay strewn across the central table.

Clearly, I've been left out of all plans. He stood in the entranceway and cleared his throat.

Lord Gerard glanced his way and tossed off a curt gesture. "This doesn't involve you."

Richard charged to the table and inserted himself between Lord Gerard and his men. "But I have some part to play, nonetheless."

A grimace interrupted his brother's look of concentration. "You're not going to fight, so you needn't concern yourself."

With that dismissive remark, Richard turned and considered the room full of men. Standing next to his brother, Nikolas shuffled his feet, an uneasy look on his face. Twenty other men stood around. *They will follow their leader with blind faith.* Sick foreboding filled Richard. *Necessity makes for strange alliances. Which rarely works out well.*

Adele's sweet face rose in Richard's mind. The air grew thick and hard to breathe. Without another word, he strode from the room and hurried outside into the crisp winter air. He ambled down the hill on a frozen well-trodden path, past a snow buried garden, and straight to Melchior's home.

Then he saw her just outside the house, and his breath

escaped him. Bright-cheeked and laughing, Adele played with little Thomas. Sunlight streamed over her dark hair, which swirled about her hood and cape.

She looked up, and when their gazes connected, she blushed and smiled. After dragging strands of hair from her face, she took Thomas' hand and swung it playfully. "Hello, Richard, it is good to see you looking so well. Have you come to see Father?"

Richard smiled stiffly, his words sounding harsh and impersonal. "Yes, on a matter of some importance."

Adele nodded and turned toward the house.

Richard swallowed and marched at Adele's side. "How is the priest, Father Caedmon? Has he recovered from my brother's justice?"

Adele turned, scowling.

Thomas whined and wrested his hand free like an escape artist. Then he scurried around the back garden and slipped in the kitchen door.

Adele barely darted a glance after him before she narrowed her gaze at Richard. "Justice?"

Disturbed by his misstep, Richard winced. "My brother has always been terrified of ghosts, and he believed that Father Caedmon was capable of calling up spirits. He thinks Lady Nadine plans her revenge."

Adele shook her head, her eyes wide in bewilderment. "Monstrously absurd! Besides, how could a priest summon the dead? He is no conjurer! Your brother did evil in thinking evil of him."

A heavy sigh left Richard feeling weak and confused. "You're right, but I fear his evil is not over, and I'm powerless to stop him. I had hoped that he would be content once the priest was gone, and he learned that you didn't wish to marry the king, but that was not enough. Ambition is replacing anxiety." Anguish rose like an overpowering demon. "This coming battle will be in vain."

Fresh snow began to fall, snowflakes swirling like sparkling dancers in the air.

"Your brother will fail?"

Richard's shoulders slumped. "Gerard mismanages everything. He let his wife's love languish and turn bitter. His daughter was born innocent, but now she connives to no good end. I'm his brother, yet he cares nothing for my opinion. His son, by nature only, will not stay under the shadow of such ill will. Even his own men will turn away when his pride costs the lives of their fathers, brothers, and sons."

Adele's brows rose, making her seem genuinely interested in his opinion. It had been many years since anyone had shown any interest in his thoughts.

"What drives him so?" Adele shook her head like a bewildered child.

"The same forces that drive us all, the ones we hide behind and pretend not to see."

A commotion in the doorway caught their attention.

The large front door swung open, and Melchior stomped onto the threshold. "Adele? What are you doing in the freezing cold? Come in here before you take sick."

Adele waved to her father. "Coming, father. I'm speaking to a friend." She turned back to Richard. "Please stay for a while and eat with us." She hurried up the steps to her father.

Richard trudged along behind.

As the two arrived, Melchior rubbed his hand across his face and stepped aside. He bowed respectfully and gestured for his guest to follow him into the main hall.

Adele nodded goodbye and retreated toward the kitchen.

Once before the large fire, Melchior inhaled a deep breath and faced his neighbor. "Please, sit. Make yourself comfortable. Adele will bring some refreshments."

Uneasiness swamped Richard's mind, distorting his thoughts and setting his heart to pounding for no good reason. In a desperate need to keep busy, he strode to the blazing fireplace and rubbed his chilled hands together. "No, I cannot stay. My brother wouldn't be pleased to know that I'm seeking your counsel, but I'm in a terrible position. I don't know where to turn."

Melchior stepped closer. Gesturing for Richard to take a seat near the fire, he took the chair opposite him. "I can only imagine. Family loyalty offers brutal rewards!"

Perched on the edge of the seat, a wry grin cracked the fierce hold on Richard's composure. "That's why I've sought you out. I'm not like my brother. If I had my way, you'd have all your possessions back, but that's another story. It's your son I am worried about—your son and your daughter."

Melchior's shoulders straightened, and his eyes narrowed. "I understand your concern about Wilfred—I'm concerned myself—but he was to be a messenger, nothing more. Has that changed?"

"No, but Wilfred has been among his old friends. He's beginning to swagger again, if you know what I mean."

Melchior dropped his gaze. "Father Caedmon offered to teach Wilfred, but the foolish boy declared that he didn't need to read and write—he would prove himself through *manly* skills." He lifted his eyes and met Richard's gaze. "Is he in trouble?"

"Not yet. But he plans on heading into foreign parts if this first battle goes ill, which I'm certain it will. He has befriended the wrong men. Men who hire themselves out to do other men's dirty work.

"You've spoken to him?"

"He won't listen to me. But I thought that perhaps you or Henry—"

"Wilfred has made it clear that he doesn't need us."

Defeated, Richard rose. "I just wanted to warn you. If Gerard loses this battle, Wilfred will leave. Where he goes and what happens to him, I cannot say, but I am certain it will not be good."

Melchior struggled to his feet. "Stay a moment. Let me get Father Caedmon; he's wise and may have good advice. I'll call for him." Melchior hurried through a doorway, calling for Oliver, who came directly. After a short consultation, Oliver jogged away, and Melchior returned to Richard.

Impatient to leave now, Richard tapped his thigh. His eyes darted to the door as Adele passed by.

Melchior edged closer and dropped his voice low. "You said you were worried about my daughter...I assume you mean Adele?"

"Yes…I…" Richard's mind drew a blank. What had he intended to say? Everything about her muddled his mind. "Yes, I'm concerned that young Nikolas may not be able to protect her. Or himself, for that matter. He's not a soldier, and this battle will be fierce."

The frown on his face fading, Melchior sat back in his chair and relaxed. He smiled. "Of course, you would see it like that. But God will look after the young man and bring him through unscathed. He has a noble heart. If any man should be protected by the Almighty, it would be him."

Oliver stepped through the doorway, leading Father Caedmon with care.

Melchior jumped up and assisted the crippled priest further into the room, his smile widening in pride. "Father Caedmon did not come in vain, for Oliver has begun to study under him, and he reports that my son is an excellent student."

Father Caedmon laughed. "His father's example, surely. Ripe for learning! I'm glad I came, or the fruit might have withered away."

Oliver offered a brave smile and blushed.

Melchior gestured toward Richard, who immediately rose from his chair. "Here, let me introduce you."

Father Caedmon waved. "No need. I know Richard well. He tried to intervene on my behalf but sadly to little success. Still, I never had the opportunity to thank you. It was gallant of you to risk your brother's wrath on my account. Your brother's former servant, Harold, has also become a student of mine. With these two young minds, God will change the world. See if He doesn't!"

Adele passed by the doorway, flashing a smile.

Flummoxed, Richard cleared his throat. "I must return or my brother—"

Melchior waved in protest. "No, wait. Let's ask Father."

Richard shrugged in resignation.

"Richard brings ill news about Wilfred; after the battle, he will likely follow his old passions."

Father Caedmon gestured to the chairs. "Please, if we may?"

Oliver pulled forward more chairs, and the four men made themselves comfortable.

Father Caedmon rubbed his grey beard. "In scripture, there are many examples of men who make bad decisions early in life but repent and become holy souls. We are born into a broken world, and Wilfred is beyond our counsel now. But experience will teach him much. We must pray, asking the Lord that he not be killed before he has an opportunity to learn God's will."

Richard shifted uneasily. "Sir—Father—I'm not a praying man, not knowing your God. When you told my brother that you eat your God and drink His blood, I thought that you were as mad as Gerard. But Wilfred explained you meant the words as symbols, and I was relieved. Your Jesus was a wise and holy man. I wish more men cared as He did—but as you said, we live in a broken world. Wilfred is beyond our reach now."

Melchior's head dropped, his gaze swept the ground, and his lips compressed tight.

Father Caedmon grinned good-naturedly. "I understand your confusion, for there are many who misunderstand. When Jesus said, 'This is my body, this is my blood, eat and drink,' He meant it. We need constant help not to fall into darkness. So, God feeds us of Himself."

Disgusted, Richard spluttered, "Can we eat a spirit? Eat God? Impossible!"

Father Caedmon laughed. "You are right, and that is why I know it is true. Because God delights in doing the impossible!"

Richard sprang to his feet.

Father Caedmon reached out imploringly. "Don't you ever tire of telling God His limits? Ordering Him by our standards? Where does grass that feeds the cattle come from? Do you think that every fruit and flower springs to life of its own will? Who else has been feeding us but God?"

Exhaustion seeped through Richard. "I see now why my brother feared you. You're not dangerous as most men would define the word—but dangerous still." Richard nodded to Melchior. "I must go. I wish you and your family well." He nodded briefly toward Oliver and strode to the door.

Father Caedmon called after him. "Richard, don't forget—every act of love is an act of God."

Adele padded into the room bearing a tray laden with refreshments. She'd scooped her dark hair up in a bun, but several strands hung loose, framing her face in a golden glow.

Richard froze, staring at her. Brilliant clarity nearly blinded him. He fled from the room.

Chapter Forty-Two

Threshold of Eternity

Nikolas sat awkwardly on his horse in the middle of the wide field before the King's castle, embarrassed by the privilege of steed under him but glad for the safety. Amid Lord Gerard's men, he sat high and almost mighty. But the King's men ranged before them looking much too impressive for comfort.

Though the season was ebbing away, the air was still frosty. Aging winter was loath to lighten her grip.

Despite the chilly air, drops of sweat rolled down his back, and a damp lock of hair stung his eyes. A crowd of battle-ready men stood near his horse. He must stay focused, and he definitely could not loosen his grip on his sword. It was not a great sword or even a good sword, but it was the best a man in his position could own. What he lacked in quality, however, he made up for in quantity. He had two knives tucked in his belt and a mace looped to his saddle. His greatest fear was being knocked off his horse amid all the jostling and shouting and then being stomped to death.

Surprisingly, the scene unfolding before his eyes reminded him of battle scenes he'd heard about as a youth. Eloquent descriptions rarely bore resemblance to honest facts, but in this state of heightened concentration, every detail flushed with vivid colors, and each movement slowed to a dreamlike state, he found himself flummoxed by the familiarity of it all, as if every ancestor who had ever fought in a battle had somehow transmitted that experience into his brain.

His horse snorted, as if just as uncertain of entering a

battle as Nikolas. It shied from the men's horrific language and rude gestures.

King Radburn's villa, not made of stone but of thick timber, with layers of ornate carvings and a high peaked roof, perched on the top of a low hill in the center of a rectangular field. A broad wall protected the property. A moat encircled the wall, while a bridge stretched across the moat from the turf to the entrance of the estate.

One fool tried to swim the breach until an arrow arched from a high window and pierced his back. He screamed only once before slipping to his watery doom. There were no further attempts to follow the pathetic warrior.

Lord Gerard did not appear to notice the loss of a man so early in the battle. His horse cantered forward so everyone could see him, including the enemy, while his men lined up haphazardly on the field behind him. Five hundred footmen with spears, knives, swords, maces, and bows and arrows were a formidable sight. The king, however, sitting serenely on his magnificent steed with his men ranged on a line of turf before the bridge, also made a nice show. The king could afford to mount numerous men, whereas Lord Gerard only had himself, Nolan and his men, and a hundred other mounted soldiers.

Nikolas' gratitude for the aide of Melchior's horse was tempered when he realized that sitting above everyone else, he made an outstanding target. He ought to be on foot, charging into the battle with the fury of a man facing death or glory, not carried like a high and mighty warrior on another man's horse.

Nikolas adjusted his weaponry, reassuring himself that every weapon could be thrust into action at a moment's notice. He patted the horse and murmured comfort, which dissipated into the air as a cold cloud.

Apparently, the king felt little apprehension, for he and his retinue trotted across the bridge at a calm pace.

The dark villa loomed in the background with faces appearing at every window hole, like a monster with a hundred eyes.

Not to be outdone in arrogance, Lord Gerard started forward, matching the king's methodical gait. The opposition drew closer like a tightening band.

On the far-left flank, Nolan marched swiftly, apparently eager to outdistance everyone.

Nikolas' horse whinnied as he and the men marched forward, keeping pace with Lord Gerard. Memories flooded his mind: Melchior's assured goodwill as he said goodbye and Adele facing him with flushed cheeks, while little Thomas tugged relentlessly on her arm. All his intended words had lodged in his throat. The brat vanquished Nikolas' desperate attempt to proclaim his love.

The faces of the enemy became discernable. Did he know any of these men? Would those who shot at him know who they were shooting?

A man to his left screamed and fell backwards onto the hard ground, an arrow sticking grotesquely out of his chest.

The king shouted, "Wait for my command!"

The tension mounted unbearably, the soldiers eyeing one another with unease

Terror seized Nikolas. *Why do men have to die today?*

The king sat high on his horse, motionless now, his men still ranged behind him. That smug, inscrutable face, those disdainful lips.

They would never possess Adele! She would *not* be forced to marry that man. *I must save her, at least. For the kingdom! For Adele!*

A man on the king's right carried the standard aloft—a bull with fierce horns standing atop a hill.

With a surge of passion, Nikolas felt drawn forward.

He massaged the handle of his sword.

Ever fearless, Nolan called out, "Kingship be dammed!" and he galloped forward. He and his horse flew across the barren field, a resin-soaked torch lifted high in his hand. He headed straight for the castle.

On the right, Lord Gerard charged full tilt at the king.

Nikolas kicked his horse into action and aimed for the standard-bearer.

King Radburn sat serenely on his mount, apparently unconcerned that a battle-eager army approached only a hundred yards away.

With a burst of speed, Lord Gerard advanced upon the king, swinging a weighty mace. As he did so, another man came out from behind the standard-bearer. This new man . . . his face . . . but for his simple attire, he looked like the king. *No, it couldn't be.*

For a deadly moment, Lord Gerard hesitated, not knowing which man to pummel. He spurred his horse toward the more ornately dressed man, when a shout rang out. Nolan was being beaten back. He cursed mightily. Alone, Nolan would never reach the castle.

A wall of men encircled Lord Gerard.

Nikolas stopped. He sat, staring at the scene as if from a great distance. It was so inevitable, so obvious, being outnumbered with such poor leadership, that he was surprised by his surprise—the whole thing would be over before it had properly begun.

Lord Gerard's warriors surged forward, swords clashing, in a fruitless attempt to reach him.

Why fight a lost battle?

Yet, his heart defied his reason. After slipping his knife from its sheath, he charged directly for the humbly dressed king. A scream rose from his throat, forcing an opening in the wall of warriors. With all his might, he threw his knife directly at the king's chest. The knife twirled through the air, but Nikolas had no chance to see where it landed, for out of the corner of his eye, he glimpsed a spear flying through the air towards him.

A sharp pain and a rush of blood. Nikolas instantly lost his breath, his body recoiling. Trying to maintain his balance, he reached for something solid but grasped only air. His horse reared up, and he fell heavily on the ground.

For a moment, Nikolas feared that his horse would crush him, but the mad animal lurched and ran off.

Shouts and clashing of weapons and confusion blended into a haze.

Distant screaming tore through the air. Pounding boots raced past on either side as arrows rained down from the sky. Nikolas blinked and tried to breathe, but he would never enjoy the scent of fresh air again. The metallic taste of blood filled his mouth. His head hit the ground. He turned his gaze away from the massive wood piercing his chest. Sky and the earth, soldiers and blood, melted into one chaotic swirl of color.

Suddenly, Nolan's face appeared over him, tears streaming down his mud-streaked face.

Nikolas tried to speak, but only a grunt met his ears, and his chest ached so. No strength to suck in a breath. Blood filling his mouth. That spear sticking from his chest.

Nolan crossed himself, his lips moving, his eyes blinking rapidly.

In the far sky, a bird flew overhead, wings flapping as it sliced through a ray of light.

The light grew, and a melody rose from the ground. A gentle rhythm called him.

Colors swirled, and the pain slipped off like a ragged coat. A fresh breeze blew. The scent of the sea in his nose. A glorious wave rose and lifted him from the hard, cold ground.

In a green field before the ocean where waves lapped the shore stood his father. His face gentle and eyes sparkling…his hand outstretched…

Grief died, and joy breathed new life.

Dad, I'm home!

~~~

Melchior sat on the edge of his bed, staring out the west window. The sun had settled on the horizon, and twilight loomed, leaving all in drowsy stillness.

He felt too weary to work, but it was not quite time to sup or sleep. It was a lost and lonely time when a man might hum, but no one sang.

Melchior held a letter in his trembling hand. It had arrived only a few moments before, and he had retreated to his room to read it. *Lord Gerard has been taken, and Nolan retreats with as many men as he can claim. The castle and all the king's land remain undisturbed. He is in full possession of his kingdom.*

No mention of Nikolas.

A few hours earlier, Melchior had sat at his desk, attempting to remember once again the words that had comforted him so long ago. But then, as now, he was struck dumb, staring at a mostly blank page. Anxiety crept over him, a chill spreading across his body as a portent of some dreadful reality.

He remembered when his wife had died. He'd sat by her side, holding her hand as her lifeblood stilled and cooled. He cried silently as the children wept aloud. He remembered the sensation of her spirit was floating near him, reaching for him, and he could not cross the divide. The horror of his loss choked all thought and action.

This time, he was not yet sure who had died. He
~~~

guessed there were many, and the horror of it numbed him in much the same way as it had when his wife passed. Every death changed the world, however mysteriously. All his hopes scattered before a scorching wind.

Melchior sighed and shrugged his weary shoulders. Life had never been under his control. He'd understood that from the first time battle-hardened warriors stepped onto his father's land. But he still felt the sting of loss—a future that would never be. He'd wanted peace. He'd wanted a good husband for his daughter. He'd wanted to hold grandchildren and laugh in his old age with the joy of a man who could die without worry. But callous mischance arrived instead.

Tears coursed their way down his cheeks as the last ray of light winked out. The sun eclipsed, once again, behind a bold horizon line.

A presence hovered nearby.

His skin prickled. He surveyed the room.

No one.

The world held its breath in silence. Too solemn a day for banter or cheer of any kind. Even the meals had been reduced to bread and water.

Suddenly, Nikolas' honest face and form appeared before his eyes, standing, as he often did, with rounded shoulders and a far-away look in his eyes. *Thinking of his father and the sea?*

Heartbroken, a chill swept over him. Then, just as suddenly, his agony subsided. A wave of warmth tingled through his limbs. Without a doubt, Nikolas would be no man's son-in-law, and he would be no woman's husband. Still, he lived. In another world. Melchior's mouth fell open as he marveled.

~~~
~~~

Adele's gaze remained fixed on the straw-strewn floor in the hallway as her family received the news that Nikolas had fallen in battle. She did not respond to any sympathetic glances of comfort. She merely stepped past the messenger, walked out the door, and wandered to a sheltered spot—a meadow surrounded on three sides by an ancient forest. Adele perched on an old log that jutted out of the forest like a broken finger, while cardinals and sparrows sang in the dappled light. The frozen air chilled her breath despite the sun, but she felt nothing.

The news of Nikolas' death did not surprise her. For a reason she could not explain, she had always doubted that she would be Nikolas' wife. Fate had decreed that rather than marrying a gentle man, she would become the wife of a powerful, ambitious king.

Adele pictured King Radburn's face and found that she no longer hated him. She knew Corliss had spread the rumor that sent Lord Gerard into madness, touching off the sparks of fury that were the precursor to a pointless battle. She had peeked into the king's soul when he was hurting and vulnerable, and that had done much to heal her hate. The fact that Nikolas had died in battle against him only added to her exhaustion. Why fight for something that few women ever truly experience? Nikolas' love would remain untarnished in her dreams.

She needed to adapt to the world as it really was. She had two options: she could attempt to dissuade the king and beg to stay with her father, so she could care for her brothers and sisters with only her father's feeble support, or she could accept the king's offer and aid her entire family. She leaned back against the trunk of a tree that continued to stand even after its match had fallen. Nikolas' face rose sharp and clear before her, while tears mixed with passing dreams, slipped down her face.

~~~

Father Caedmon's forehead rested on the edge of his bed as he knelt against it. His injuries did not allow him the luxury of kneeling for long, but he could manage for a short while, leaving the present world for the life of the spirit.

The battle's conclusion had been reported far and wide, and he knew that Nikolas was now beyond his reach, but he did not grieve. Had Nikolas been luckier than Wilfred? Of the two, Wilfred was still a babe amid wolves while Nikolas, with his brave love, most certainly kept better company.

Young Adele would soon wed in pomp and kingly ceremony. Father Caedmon grimaced. Surely, there would be a battle of wills in their marriage no less fierce than the one fought on the open fields. The old priest pitied the woman who must take up this particular cross.

He shifted his weight and pressed his head more firmly against the wooden frame. He did not fear for Nikolas' soul. He had spoken with the young man shortly before they left for battle, and he had seen the eager, honest glint in his eyes as he leapt astride his horse. "I will most certainly win, for my heart is true and my cause is just!" He had not realized that winning was not a matter of defeating an Earthly king but of enduring beyond despair. In that respect, Nikolas had won.

Father Caedmon made the sign of the cross, stood, and rolled onto his hard bed. He lay down, folding his hands over his chest. Nikolas was beyond all care, but anxiety still slithered into his mind. The image of Wilfred riding toward the horizon filled his mind. From his vantage point, it looked as if his young friend was in a heady flight straight toward the edge of a cliff.
~~~

Chapter Forty-Three

Far from Sight

Oliver sat by a roaring fire in the kitchen as the early morning light slanted across the floor. He chewed methodically, holding a coarse hunk of bread in his hands absently, while men and women bustled about him as on an ordinary day.

They had accomplished so much dreary duty, and now everyone returned to the routines of life. How was it possible that he had directed the burial of twenty-two bodies, arranged for the burning of slain horses, seen to the repair of damaged tools, done sundry other painful duties, and yet, after a wash and a fresh change of clothes, he now sat eating breakfast, expecting to spend the forenoon seeing to the care of the livestock and the afternoon learning his letters with Father Caedmon?

He raised his head at the sound of his name.

Wilfred stomped across the kitchen.

Oliver had expected Wilfred to flee when Lord Gerard had been taken captive. Instead, Richard ordered his nephew to see to the care of the estate despite his father's degradation.

The king had not been gentle with Lord Gerard, and if the prisoner lived, he would never be the same. Everyone murmured in great surprise that King Radburn had not summarily killed Lord Gerard. But Oliver considered the case from King Radburn's view.

The king wanted no martyrs. Rather, he wanted to silence his opponents. How better to do that than to put on display a broken man? No, if one really wanted to defeat an enemy, it would be better to break his spirit than his body, and by all accounts, King Radburn had accomplished both.

Wilfred strode forward, his eyes over-bright. Upon reaching the table, he leaned down and whispered, "Corliss has declared that she'll kill herself and has run off to the sea. We must find her"—he swallowed and glanced around the room, then locked his gaze on Henry—"before someone else does. Many men would not think twice about taking out their revenge on Lord Gerard's daughter. Please, Oliver, Melchior's servants will only look for her if *you* send them."

Oliver stared at his brother's earnest expression. He could see the sweat of fear forming on his brow and smell the blood, which still clung to his one good suit of clothes. Oliver swallowed the last of his bread and stood up, brushing his hands free of crumbs.

This would not be an ordinary day after all.

"I'll explain matters to father and then inform Father Caedmon but go ahead and tell the men to wait on the cattle; I'll get to them tomorrow. Leave the boys to their usual labor. If anyone questions you, say I ordered it so."

Wilfred stared, his fists clenched. "Yes, I'll tell them. Meet me out front with your best horse, and let's be quick about it!" Wilfred turned on his heel, blushing, ready to stomp off the way he had come.

Oliver rose from the table. "You took our best horse some time ago, and there are few who can be quick about anything. But for Corliss' sake, we'll do our best. I pity the fool who thinks he can manage her."

Wilfred stomped outside and mounted his horse, kicking the animal viciously. He rode off Melchior's lands in much the same way he had raced off months earlier.

After a long search, dusk arrived on the broad moor. Oliver patted his horse's neck as a messenger relayed the news that Wilfred had found Corliss. He turned his horse and called to his men.

The men gathered close as the messenger, a short and thickset man, recited events. “Corliss stood on the edge of a cliff, apparently waiting for someone to rescue her. She made no effort to refuse Wilfred when he arrived and settled her on his horse. Neither did she fuss when they headed, not toward their father’s estate, but toward the port city. I followed as far as the edge of town, where Wilfred took Corliss to an inn. They were laughing like children. He’s probably filled her with stories about how he’ll find her a rich lord in a distant land.”

A balding man with a round belly at Oliver’s side grimaced in disgust, while another servant, smaller but sinewy, shook his head. “She’ll believe what she wants for as long as it suits her. Once she meets a man with wealth and power, she’ll abandon her brother. He’ll wonder what he risked his life for.”

Oliver narrowed his gaze. “You think he is risking his life?”

“Lord Gerard isn’t dead. The king tortured him all right, but he’ll recover. And when he does, he’ll hate not just the man who beat him in a fair fight, but the man who took his last possession—the only person that he ever really cared about.”

Oliver sighed. Wilfred had shown promise but never stability. Corliss was a woman of beauty but never wisdom. They would end up taking each other into dark territory. Relief filled him at the realization that, in their heady flight, they would be far from his sight.

Chapter Forty-Four

Marriage is as Marriage Does

Adele shuddered as King Radburn's sweaty hand clutched her own. She wanted to pull hers away and wipe it dry, but that would be a breach of decorum too great to overlook.

Sitting high above the crowd on a dais, enthroned as queen, she saw no reason to make her life any harder than it already was. Strictly speaking, her hands were as spotless as the rest of her body, though she yearned for a bath. Never before had she been allowed the luxury of being clean for so long. Still, the sensation that she was not really clean kept her head bowed.

The first night with her husband had been an unpleasant shock, not because he was intentionally cruel—he wasn't—but because she was unprepared for the combination of intimacy and her own emotional distance. Confusion and disappointment muddled her emotions.

The king released her hand, and they took their seats on royal chairs at a table as long as her father's entire hall. He was fully prepared to enjoy an evening meal with a variety of guests and men-of-arms. Even her father and brother sat in attendance at a lower table. The fire roared cheerfully, but King Radburn's too-perfect smile could have chilled the beer.

Adele placed a few nuts, one boiled egg, and a thin wedge of cheese alongside a small piece of brown bread on her plate.

The king looked over and frowned. "Can I afford nothing better than measly scraps and a few hard nuts? Are you ill?"

Adele hardly dared to look up. His sarcastic tone bit into her mind. She was a mere child, a foolish girl, and all her years of managing her father's estate were mere nothings to him. "I'm fine, thank you. I am just not used to this rich food. We did not eat meat every day, and I'm afraid—"

"Afraid? Do not be afraid of a little quail! Why, the poor bird gave its life for you, and yet you sit there acting as if I would have done better to let you forage the forest floor for your dinner."

Adele's head rose, and her hand flew to her cheek. "Oh, no, you don't understand. It's just that I don't—"

Heads lifted and eyes stared.

Her words lost, Adele's color deepened.

The king's smile warmed. He spoke in his most tolerant fashion. "No, I understand better than you realize, simple girl. Do not be embarrassed. That's why I chose you out of all the highborn maidens I could have had. You are new to luxury. It's a forgivable failing, but understand this: you will be the mother of my children, and it's my duty to see you well fed."

He waved at the attendants, signaling them for them to pass various viands forward. "Here, take some of this delicious venison. It is roasted to perfection, and a little of that bird there, and here, have some ale. Don't be shy! Why, woman, a little fat on your bones would be good for you. No man wants a bony wife in his bed!" He smirked. His eyes roamed over his audience.

His men leered appreciatively. Rude laughter rumbled in undertones.

Adele wished she could melt into a puddle.

Grinning, King Radburn lifted his cup high. He saluted the assembly. "Glad I am to see so many of my friends in attendance. Let us enjoy this rich bounty, remember our valiant victory, and know that the kingdom is safe for generations to come. My wife"—here King Radburn smiled upon Adele's bowed head—"is delighted to have such distinguished lords and mighty warriors celebrating with us, and though the honor is great, she humbly wishes for you to eat, drink, and, as the Romans say, be merry—for who knows when we'll all die."

A deafening silence filled the hall. One should not speak of death at a victory feast.

Adele clenched her hands in her lap. She hated to look up and see her father's expression, for he had quoted the pagans often enough—in derision. She knew what he must think, and she dared not meet his gaze.

Oliver sat at his father's side, gripping his knife in one hand and scooping food onto his bread plate. He glanced at his father as if watching for any sudden moves.

Father Caedmon sat opposite them.

Martha and her husband, Roland, sat with the younger children further away. Martha flushed, but Roland continued to eat with great relish. He reached over another man for the flask of ale.

As if on cue, King Radburn gazed over the assembly and waved his hand benevolently, signaling for Melchior to stand. "I would have you all acknowledge that Melchior, the father of my bride, is now *Lord* Melchior, for I have reinstated much of the land he lost when Lord Gerard—alive by my mercy—stole his lands unjustly. In consideration of Gerard's treachery, I have returned both lands and title to Lord Melchior, now no longer a thane but elevated to honor worthy of respect among men."

There was much scuffling as everyone stood to do proper honors.

A drunken soldier raised his cup in salute and cried out, "A toast to Lord Melchior!"

Deep drafts were drunk.

The king acknowledged their acceptance with a loud

clap.

The assembly quickly echoed the clap with thunderous applause. Enough ale, mead, and beer had been drunk to make any small moment boisterous, so in addition to the clapping, there were soon shouts and stomping of feet.

The drunkard followed up his success with a command. "Lord Melchior, speak to us!"

His face scarlet and eyes flashing, Melchior stood and forced a smile. "Greetings to my neighbors, friends, relatives, lords, and men-at-arms in service of our *mighty* king." The fact that he was now a lord was lost in the sea of tumultuous emotions. "*Lord Melchior* sounds too grand for a man who simply loves his family, his land, and words." Melchior's gaze shifted from his daughter to his king's smirking face. His lips trembled. "For words have the power to *lord* over us, for *truth* is bigger than men, even a king."

Roland's chewing became audible in the otherwise hushed room. A dog growled for possession of a bone, then yelped as an irate listener kicked it into submission.

Melchior lifted his arm. "Before God, I salute my king, husband to my most precious daughter. May he be worthy of her."

Good enough—no one wanted a long speech. Exuberant warriors cheered, calling for the king to prove his love. "Show us how much you love the queen!"

King Radburn surveyed his assembly with a satisfied smile. He turned to Adele, bowed, and took her hand.

Frozen in fear and humiliation, a mere toy for these men's base pleasure, Adele stiffened, unable to return her husband's mischievous grin.

The king rose to his feet and reached for her.

Aghast, Adele realized that he meant to show her off before the assembly, before all the leering eyes, her own father and brother, and even before the priest, for God's sake! King Radburn wanted her to act like the possession she was. Shaken, she stood and let the king raise her arm, waving it like a banner.

Another cheer rang out. The floor stomping and yells grew deafening.

A shiver ran down her back. These were the same men who slapped her buttocks when she passed in the hall or slid a hand along her leg pretending innocence, or stumbled against her on purpose. Bile rose in her throat.

Her husband, king of a mindless throng, gripped her hand in his own sweaty palm and showed her off as his prize. He might have won her in battle. Adele felt a lump rise in her throat. He *had* won her in battle. The king had wanted Lord Gerard and Nolan and Nikolas to try their might against him—he'd wanted to prove he was the king of the land and take his prize.

The yelling grew to a roar, shaking the rafters.

Adele's ears pounded to the drunken beat.

King Radburn bent over and clumsily attempted a kiss, but Adele reared back.

The cheering halted as suddenly as it had begun. Snorts, derisive comments, and open laughter filled the air.

King Radburn's face turned scarlet. He jerked Adele into a painfully tight embrace.

Melchior, followed by Henry, shoved forward.

Father Caedmon stood and—though he did not shout—his gravelly voice carried weight. "All the king's *men* must foremost honor the king's *wife*. To dishonor the queen is to insult the throne!"

This chastisement was met with astonishment.

Father Caedmon spread his arms wide and, smiling in benevolence, he swept his steely gaze from one side of the room to the other. "It has been a long day, and it would be best if old men and young queens leave now, for we are too weak in the face of your manly vigor and spirited feasting."

Father Caedmon shuffled past Melchior and Henry, stretched his bony hand up toward Adele, and then clasped it in his own.

Gratitude flooded Adele.

The old priest offered a stern nod to the king, who glared back through angry eyes.

Adele shivered as she stepped off the dais and wended her way through the packed hall, followed by her father, Oliver, and a few attendants.

The assembly returned their attention to the spread of food and seemed pleased for the opportunity to refill their cups. The rumble of conversation returned to its loud and jovial frivolity. Boisterous laughter echoed against the walls.

Though Father Caedmon still gripped her hand in his, Adele felt no revulsion, only immense relief.

The king's voice rose as she exited the hall. "Here is to old men and wives. May they always go to bed early!"

Riotous laughter burst forth.

Adele followed the old priest blindly, for she could only see the furious gleam in her husband's eyes.

Chapter Forty-Five

A Worthy Calling

—OldEarth—

Teal, dressed in a merchant's tunic with a cloak wrapped over his shoulders, exhaled a white bloom of fresh air and crossed over the frozen earth. He grinned. *I made it back. On Earth again. Finally!*

He glanced over his shoulder at the small ship bobbing on the lake and sighed. Uit, a leading Ingal from Cresta, had come along to interview Tarragon and get a first-hand report. But he didn't like long-distance travel and had put himself into a trance that would not end for another twenty-four hours.

Wearing a peasant's coarse woolen tunic with wide sleeves, Kelesta marched at Teal's side and stared at Melchior's estate—a sloping structure in the distance. "Let's hurry! It's been so long. I'm not waiting for that lay-about to wake up."

In full agreement, Teal clasped her hand, and they raced like children across the snowy ground.

Leaving a sheltered grove, Cerulean and Nova jogged forward to meet them, laughing.

Nova bounded ahead with a smile spread wide across her face and nearly fell into her mother's waiting arms. "You two looked so silly, running hand in hand. Zuri will be jealous!"

Teal halted, his heart lurching. "He has nothing to be jealous about." He frowned at the memory of Kelesta feeding him while he lay weak in bed. *She's a good friend. Zuri knows that better than anyone.*

Nova grinned as she swung her mother's arm high and waved to two other figures now emerging from the woods.

Tarragon's rotund figure clearly set a sedate pace. And for whatever reason, Zuri didn't race ahead.

In the background, Melchior's home stood silent with no one bustling about. Grey clouds deepened, and the wind picked up.

Teal's gaze ran from Melchior's charming abode to his son, Cerulean, standing at his side. Relief and joy mingled, and a smile wavered on his lips. "How are you, Cerulean?"

Cerulean completed a formal bow and straightened. "I am fine, Father. Though Sterling has endured much."

Not what he had expected to hear, Teal leaned in and pressed his son's shoulder. "We should speak privately."

Cerulean nodded his agreement.

Zuri stepped up and stopped before his wife, his features placid, almost solemn.

Poor Zuri, always taking his responsibilities to heart. So very un-Ingot of him.

Alarm sprang into Kelesta's eyes. She stumbled to her husband, her arms reaching out. "What's happened?"

Zuri stiffened and made his report. "An innocent man was accused of murder then cleared of the charge. The guilty man, a victim of cruel fate, never received justice. The king murdered his son and took an unwilling woman to wife. Melchior's neighbor, Lord Gerard, deceived by the wife he never loved, is the true father of Melchior's second son. Lord and king fought a battle where many died for no good cause. A generous priest served in kindness but was rewarded with cruelty. And Lord Gerard has lost all, even his feeble mind."

Kelesta slapped her forehead. "I didn't mean here! I meant with you." She scowled. "Aren't you glad to see me?"

Wincing against something akin to pain, Zuri embraced his wife in a gentle hug. "Sorry. I don't know what's wrong with me. Trying to send reports but my system seems off." He offered a half-smile. "I can't get sick officially. But I might be broken somewhere."

Horror swept over Kelesta's face.

Nova scowled, her eyes darting from her father to her mother.

A sinking sensation drowned Teal's joy.

Tarragon cleared his throat noisily. "As I am the closest thing we have to a doctor here, and I am the highest-level scientist, I will take a look after we get properly settled."

Kelesta peered over Zuri's shoulder. "Where's Sterling and Mauve?"

Cerulean and Nova stood stock still, only their eyes locking in mutual understanding.

With an irritated harumph, Tarragon slapped Zuri's shoulder. "I thought you sent reports."

Zuri rubbed his eyes. "I can't remember who I sent reports to, and though everything should be stored in my memory, there are gaps." He yawned loudly. "I'm not sure what's going on."

Kelesta linked arms with her husband and led him toward Melchior's home, glancing over her shoulder. "Can we slip inside and blend in as poor guests in need of shelter for a bit? We need rest before hiking back to the ship."

Cerulean, striding after them with Nova at his side, called out, "Soldiers still recovering from the battle are in the main hall, so we might be able to claim a sheltered corner for mercy's sake."

Slapping his tentacles against his hips, Tarragon stood his ground. "Uit is awaiting my report back at the ship. I have no interest in wasting time. I'll take Zuri and his family with me." His gaze slid from Zuri to Kelesta and finally focused on Nova. "You will be much more comfortable on board, and I can analyze Zuri's condition using the proper tools."

Zuri turned around and nodded. "Yes, that makes sense." He peered at his wife. "Don't worry. It's probably nothing. I'm just getting old." He wrapped his arm around his wife and started back the way she had come, chuckling. "The best thing about having a mixed-breed daughter is that she gets the best of both of us—patience from me and perfect health from you."

Kelesta met Teal's gaze as she passed with her family at her side.

Teal's heart twisted from the grief he saw there. He watched Tarragon lead the small family up the incline and around the bend. Then he refocused on his son, who stood waiting at his side. "Where are Sterling and Mauve?"

Cerulean pointed to a burned-out hovel. "Sterling is over there. Mauve…she intercepted a member of the Mystery race and tried to manipulate him the way she did most humans." He paused, his gaze dropping. "She didn't survive the encounter."

Teal swallowed back a bitter taste. "Luxonians rarely experience death up close and personal. This must be a painful blow."

Cerulean led the way across the short grass toward the hovel.

The wind blew in their faces, tossing their hair and howling in their ears.

Teal plodded along desperately trying to think of what to say to Sterling that wouldn't sound like a ridiculous platitude. *Mauve was too selfish to love. Love would just roll off her like rain pouring down a rocky hillside.* He huffed. *But I can't very well just say that, now can I?*

Cerulean glanced at his father several times as he kept pace. "I have some questions."

Teal nodded. "Yes?"

"A man named Nikolas died in a meaningless battle, so where does his spirit go now? Did he cease to exist, or is there some place of justice I can't yet see? And Adele was forced to marry a man she didn't love. How could that happen since it could never be a real marriage? And why doesn't Melchior change the customs he doesn't like instead of just complaining about them? Father Caedmon calls himself a priest. What is a priest? Who is this God that he speaks of? I can't see him or hear him. Where is he?"

Teal felt the ground fall out from under him. He stopped before Selby's burned-out hovel and stared as flakes of snow fell from the sky, adorning the grotesque structure in simple glory.

Death took many forms.

~~~

Tarragon could hardly believe his luck. He had the entire family completely at his disposal on a ship with all sorts of wonderful medical tools. And the perfect excuse to use them! He had to tamp down his glee. But then, the sight of Uit as he entered the bridge, with his slime-green cilia and matching eyes, burst the bubbles of his joy.

Never disposed to humor, Uit traipsed across the deck and raised a tentacle with an oblong chip pinched dexterously. "Please, do hurry along. I've serious matters
~~~

to attend to and three more visits to make before I can return home."

Tarragon shrugged. "You could've just asked for a virtual visit. I would've given you the same information, and you wouldn't have had to come all this way."

"Ah, but now I can see the truth of the matter and investigate if I have any suspicions of wrongdoing."

The cilia on top of his head rising, Tarragon felt his internal temperature rising. "Wrongdoing? What could I possibly do wrong?"

A young woman's voice called, "Tarragon?" Nova stuck her head through the doorway. "Zuri is ready for you whenever you are. Kelesta gave him something to help him relax, so he's pretty sleepy. If you have any tests to run, you'd better do them soon."

Uit's golden eyes widened.

Tarragon attempted an innocent grin. "An Ingot that has malfunctioned. I'm doing a simple system's check to discover the problem."

Uit rolled his eyes toward Nova who still waited with only her head showing through the doorway.

Blast it! "That's his daughter, Nova. She and her mother are assisting in the human assessment."

Uit snorted through his breather helm and wiggled a tentacle in Nova's direction. "He'll be with you in just a moment. Thank you."

Nova scowled but took the hint and left.

Uit gripped Tarragon's shoulder and peered directly into his eyes. "That girl is not an Ingot."

On impulse, Tarragon plunged into honest mode. "Nor is her mother. Kelesta is Bhuaci, and Nova is a mixed breed."

Two tentacles flew to Uit's face. He was the picture of a scandalized elder. "A mixed breed? They're not allowed!"

"It is allowed if the participants are willing to pay the price."

Uit fixed his gaze on Tarragon.

"Zuri offered up his technology, and Kelesta offered her immortality."

"For what purpose?"

"Love."

A smile crept across Uit's face. "But we know better?"

"We don't know anything yet. Give me the proper tools and a good excuse, and I'll know a great deal more before the day is out."

~~~

Omega, invisible to the world at large, stepped out of the barn and stopped only a couple of feet before Teal. Teal stood before Cerulean. Omega had heard every one of the boy's questions, amazed that the youth had the same thoughts jumping around in his mind.

A hunched figure stumbled forward from the burned structure. The older Luxonian. An odd one. With his authority, he ought to be more self-controlled. Yet he appeared to be as unbalanced as a tree standing on its crown.

Teal grabbed Sterling and wrapped an arm around him, leading him to the open-sided, blackened hearth. He let Sterling slip to the ground, hunched with his head in his hands.

Cerulean followed at a distance.

What a strange group!

Teal spoke first, staring at Sterling's bowed head. "What are you doing? We have a job to do, and you must report back to the—"
~~~

"Oh, blast! Leave me be!" Sterling struggled to his feet and glared at Teal, shaking a finger at Cerulean. "Your son is quite capable of taking care of himself." He gripped Teal's arm. "Take me home! I'm no use here. I just came to make Mauve happy. And that's impossible now, isn't it?"

Cerulean glanced aside, his eyes wide as he stared.

At me? He's much too perceptive.

Omega reviewed his presentation. He ought to blend in with the environment perfectly. It's how Abbas always did it when he didn't want to be seen.

Cerulean tapped his father's arm. "Father, the Mystery Race is nearby. I can feel him."

"See, Teal? I told you! He doesn't need me. Or you. Cerulean is too smart for either of us."

Outrage colored Teal's face. "You can't be this weak! You're supposed to be a leader—you're a member of the Supreme Council, for God's sake."

Omega's whole being shimmered in delight. There was that word again. That powerful thought. *What did it mean? If only I—*

"Don't you invoke God, Teal. I could show you a hundred glorified statues here and other places too, making the whole idea ridiculous."

Cerulean stepped forward. "But there is only one Creator. Humans know the difference, even when they pretend they don't."

Stunned, Omega floated into the sky, beyond the atmosphere, and closed in on the stars. *A Creator? Ah, now there's a worthy calling. Won't Father be pleased?*

Chapter Forty-Six

Lord Gerard's Passion

Melchior stood before the king, his hands folded in front of him, his head bowed. "Sir, you've no reason to please me and even less reason to go to the trouble of killing the man. Let Richard take him. I'll bear the responsibility."

The king looked down upon the older man, a sneer curling his lips. "Bear the mangy dog to your den, if it pleases you. Take him and spare me the chore of disposing of his useless carcass."

Exhaling a relieved sigh, Melchior bowed low. "Yes, my king." Then he pointed Richard to the dungeon.

~~~

Richard's heart squeezed painfully at the sight of his brother lying sprawled across the hard-packed dirt floor, unresponsive to his call. He ignored the hard clumps of straw and filth all around. Even the stench did not bother him as it had on former visits. "Gerard, it's me, Richard. Can you stand?" He shook his brother's shoulder vigorously, his own hands trembling.

Gerard stirred and thrust his arm over his blackened eyes. "Go to Hades! Stand, you say? I'm barely alive. You'll ask me to dance next."

Richard knelt in the stinking straw. "You're released. The king has given you into Melchior's hands."

Gerard uncovered his face and stared through puzzled eyes. "I'm a dead man. Why give me away? Why do
~~~

anything? Damn that accursed man...calls himself a king! He could have killed me right off, buried me alive, burned me to cinders, or drowned me like a cat in that pitiful moat of his, and it would've been over. What's he waiting for? Damn him!"

Richard darted a glance behind him and hunched his shoulders. "Don't you understand? He's letting you go. Melchior will let us stay with him until—"

Using his good arm and with his brother's help, Gerard heaved his body forward and struggled to a sitting position. "By the blade of Woden's sword, I'm to leave here...alive?"

Richard tried to shush his brother. "That's what I've been saying. Now, please, get up. If you can't manage it, I'll carry you."

"Son of thunder, you'll do no such thing! That damnable brute may have tortured me near to death, but the grim reaper hasn't had his way yet. I'll walk out on my own power."

Richard's jaw hardened, but he kept his hands at his sides as his brother struggled to his feet amid muffled groans of pain. Once upright, Gerard's legs buckled, making it clear that he could not walk without assistance. Richard stepped alongside and gripped his brother around the waist.

Gerard bounced explosive oaths against the crumbly walls. The two inched their long way to the entry and outside.

Harold strode forward with a horse.

When Gerard was finally seated with his body slumped forward only half-conscious, Richard led the animal south toward Melchior's estate.

After an arduous journey, they neared their destination. Gerard awoke from his stupor and blinked at the wooden structure looming in the distance. His gaze slid past it to the path that led to what had once been his home. "Who'll live there now, I wonder?"

It was a croak more than a question, but Richard understood. "The king has bequeathed it upon his bride's family."

A gurgle rose in Gerard's throat.

Richard looked up, alarmed, until he recognized the bitter chuckle.

"He's got his own lands back?"

Richard surveyed his brother's blackened and broken teeth, made all the more distinct by the purplish circles around his eyes. "You could say that. Though I doubt he'll ever get the use of them. King Radburn's men are already installed and taking full advantage of everything they can lay their hands on. Melchior may have the title, but he'll never have the pleasure."

Gerard nudged his stationary horse into motion. "What do I care for another man's pleasure?"

Richard swallowed back bile as memories of the bloody battlefield rose in his mind.

~~~

Melchior greeted the new arrivals in the main hall.

Most of Gerard's men had fled, and those few that remained looked for work. Melchior made it quite plain that he had no need of need men-at-arms, so those who had sufficiently recovered retrieved their families and rode off in search of other employment.

Only Terrill had the loyalty to stay, or the lack of imagination to find any other option and remained at Melchior's abode, perhaps in the vain hope that his master would return to his former glory. He merely existed on
~~~

the boundaries of decency, which meant that Melchior could not throw him out.

Melchior stroked his cheek as he stared at the former Lord Gerard, a man long despised, who now depended upon his mercy for mere survival. Listing on one side, Gerard appeared as a picture of human misery. But once he spoke, all Melchior's sympathy vanished.

"I hear the king has granted you great rewards, Melchior. Your daughter is queen and your estates returned. The gods must be pleased with you!"

Melchior froze; only his eyelids lowered. Of course, Gerard would see it that way. He would see it as good fortune, as would most men in the world. Melchior's words rode on an exhausted breath. "I do not measure my wealth on your scales, Lord Gerard. Do not overestimate my fortunes."

Richard led his brother to a wide bench next to the largest table in the main room.

Tapestries draped the room in solemnity. A fire crackled in the expansive, well-stocked fireplace. In the background, men and women crossed through doorways and passed open windows in business-like bustle.

Gerard slumped heavily onto the bench. His grotesque face peered at his benefactor icily. He attempted to wave his good hand, but it fell to his side in defeated exhaustion. "Do not call me *lord*. I'm lucky I'm not a slave or worse. I am, perhaps—considering the situation—your servant now." He glanced aside.

Terrill stood hunch-shouldered in the corner.

"Oh, here is one of my own, at last. A man I once called mine...but now, I suppose, he's yours, too? Like everything else."

Melchior's teeth clenched so tightly that his jaw ached. He forced his lips to part. "I own little more than you, my friend." He gestured toward Terrill and bid him come forward. "Here is your man. A most loyal servant, this one. He would not leave, not until all hope was lost."

Coughing convulsively, Gerard bent double. He struggled to catch his breath. "All hope is lost, man! Lost on the day that shrew cursed me."

Melchior swallowed. His bitter mood further soured. *Kindness is wasted on this horrid creature.* "If you do not like—"

Richard sped forward. "Please, Gerard. Remember by whose benevolence you have been rescued. The king did not have to release you. He could've made a different decision."

Gerard groaned as he leaned against the table. His head fell forward, touching the tabletop. "You're right. I'm mad with pain." He lifted his head with trembling effort. Pools of grief welled in his eyes. "Those hellish beasts. It would've been so much easier to kill me. But since I live, I must be grateful. The gods know you have little reason to love me."

Melchior sucked in a shuddering breath and blinked back the damnable tears that formed in his eyes. "I didn't rescue you; your brother did. He's the eloquence. I merely repeated his words, and the king saw fit to show benevolence. I have little enough to offer, but you are welcome to recover your strength here." He waved toward the south wall. "You'll find a private niche in the back, out of the draft. My sister is still with us. She is a trained healer and may have some viands and poultices to assist you. If you need anything, just send your man. I'll be as good a host as my meager means allow."

Gerard smiled crookedly. A thin strand of drool dripped onto his bloodstained cloak. The broken teeth accented the ghoulish effect. "I owe you an apology, Melchior. Look at me, half-dead, succored by your kindness. And where is my daughter? Fled to the sea, I hear. And my new son? Gone, too. Flesh and bone abandoned me. At least, you have one grown son that has stayed by your side."

Melchior followed Gerard's gaze.

Oliver stood in the doorway, beckoning him.

Melchior nodded. "I must go. Send your servant for food, and your bed will be made ready." He bowed stiffly and turned toward his son. He had wanted justice for so long. But he never imagined that it would taste like this.

~~~

Gerard laid his head down over his crossed arms and closed his eyes.

Footsteps advanced, uncertain.

Gerard peeked through one eye.

Terrill drew near.

Harold emerged from the shadows and intercepted his foster brother. Ink stained his fingers and where he had rubbed his nose. "Martha's got hot soup and bread in the kitchen. Go eat while I get him settled. When he's ready, you can bring something out."

Terrill glared through narrowed eyes. "Why are you so generous all of a sudden?"

Harold shook his head as he shoved his brother in the direction of the kitchen. "Don't ask. I can't explain."

As Terrill moved off, Harold tromped closer.

Gerard closed his eyes and feigned sleep.

Harold lifted his former master into his arms, carried him to a quiet corner, and laid him on a bed of fresh-smelling straw.

Gerard rolled onto his side and groaned, exhaustion
~~~

enveloping him.

Harold muttered, "God, why do we do this to each other?" With a heavy sigh, the man lumbered away.

Gerard slid in and out of consciousness as the household bustled about, ignoring him for the most part. The few times he opened his eyes and followed the typical antics of the household members.

That evening, Martha hurried from room to room, trying to do everything at once with busy-bee activity. Annoyed at her bustling noise, he hissed at her. When she approached him with a basin of hot water and a clean cloth, he cringed. He was in no mood to be coddled. He would not be bathed like a baby out in the open. "Get your ugly carcass from my sight, you old hag!"

Martha absorbed the insult and stared at him, tight-lipped. "Well, you are no sight for sore eyes yourself. You've lost a battle and been beaten until your bones snapped, but you've no reason to hate me. I've done all I can, but if you want to remain filthy—"

Gerard leveraged his weight on his good arm and tried to rise from his bed, but pain crippled him. Frustrated, he merely swung his arm out and slapped the air. "I said, get yourself gone! I don't need a woman haunting my day as well as nights!"

Martha's eyebrows rose at this. "Hmmm, that's an honest request. But listen to me—"

Little Martha, Melchior's daughter, tiptoed to her aunt's side and tugged the woman's ample skirt. "May I help?" She faced Gerard. "I'd be happy to give you what you need."

Gerard's eyes darted between the two Marthas, one big and imposing, the other small and yielding. He jerked his snarl into a lopsided grin and heaved his body into a sitting position in order to appraise the child more carefully. "Yes, she'll do. She looks like my Corliss. You haven't told me where she has gone, but I'll find out."

"She and Wilfred went on an adventure." Little Martha sighed. "Wish I could've gone."

Gerard glanced up at the older woman.

Martha nodded in affirmation. She still held the basin of water with the towel hanging over her arm.

Gerard's eyes skipped over the bathing basin as he lowered himself on the bed and let a defeated sigh slip between his trembling lips.

Little Martha frowned. "Would you like me to get father? He sat up front at the king's wedding, so I'm sure he's heard all the news. We sat way in the back, and no one spoke much to us."

Gerard's eyes darted toward the larger Martha once again, and once again, she nodded. Gerard wiped his dirty face with the back of his hand. "I've been in the fire of Hades. I know nothing." He raised himself up despite the protest from his aching body. "Yes, little one, get your father." His gaze shifted to the woman. "Where's my good-for-nothing brother?"

Martha sniffed as she placed the water basin on a nearby bench. "If you call the man who saved your life and worked like a beast of burden to keep you alive a 'good-for-nothing,' well then, you hardly deserve the power of speech. You're lucky they didn't cut out your tongue to keep you from any more mischief."

The smaller Martha's eyes widened in horror. "She didn't mean it, Lord Gerard. She's been overworked and very worried." Her eyebrow rose as she turned to her aunt. "May I get father?"

Martha shrugged and laid the cloth within Gerard's reach. "Go ahead, child. For all the good it'll do." Then turning to Gerard, she pursed her lips. "Here, clean yourself as best you can. I've no great desire to earn any more of your wrath."

She stepped away.

In a flash of unexpected honesty, Gerard shot his words like arrows to land where they would. “I hate that I’m still alive.”

Martha stopped in mid-motion, smoothed down a stray lock of hair with trembling fingers, then continued towards the kitchen. “Yes, and considering your situation, I can’t blame you.”

Chapter Forty-Seven

Places I'd Rather Not Go

—Six Months Later—

Oliver sat hunch-shouldered, gripping his pen as if it might fly from his fingers.

Father Caedmon grinned as he looked over Oliver's work, his hand resting gently on the man's shoulder. "We've only a few pens at our disposal, it's true, but you need not fear dropping this one. With a grip like that, it'll never be lost. Crushed maybe—but not lost."

Oliver exhaled, relaxing his shoulders. His eyes darted to the other men in the room intent upon their work. "I wasn't afraid I would lose the pen, but rather that the pen would take me places I didn't want to go."

Father Caedmon chuckled. "You have my sympathy. I remember my first attempts at writing—they were no better than yours, be assured of that. I was a grown man, only learning at the insistence of others who thought that it would make me a better priest and a better man. At the time, I believed that my service to God was a simple matter between me and God, but I was soon to learn differently. When you serve God, everyone has an opinion." Father Caedmon shifted his weight, dragging his weak leg across the room to the tall desk in the center.

"It is time to pray and rest now. You've worked long enough." Father Caedmon surveyed the strained faces of his four weary students and smiled encouragingly. "God bless your efforts. I know it's hard, but writing is one of the most marvelous skills known to man, and few have the opportunity to learn. Surely, the first person who made his mark in the sand, or scratched on wood, or chipped at stone, must have felt a thrill to know that his mark, however simple, would speak to others. Writing must always be revered as a holy enterprise."

Father Caedmon lifted his hands in blessing. "Come now, let us refresh ourselves, first with prayer and then with nourishing food and drink."

A long, heartfelt sigh from one of the younger apprentices brought a smile to Oliver's face. He tapped his quill against the inkwell and wiped it carefully. Rubbing his cramped fingers together, he stretched to ease the crick in his back. Finally, he stepped away from the high desk and looked around.

Oliver's gaze met Harold's chagrined face.

Harold lumbered in his direction. "You've moved on to pen and ink quickly, but me, I am stuck using these cursed styluses. Like a babe, I'm choking on porridge."

Joy in this new friendship lightened Oliver's heart. "You'll catch on. It's like lighting a fire. It must spread from your mind through your arm to your hand. I thought I would break more implements than Father could afford to replace before I learned to grip one correctly."

"Yes, but you did learn, and it will have value for you. You'll become a priest, but me, well, this learning is a waste. I'd rather stand guard and protect those who need protecting." Harold's voice dropped to a whisper. "I wish Father Caedmon could accept that."

Rubbing his chin, Oliver studied the hunched priest as the old man limped from the room. "He understands more than you know. Besides, I may not become a priest. I can't lead men, not like Father Caedmon. But when I listen to him, I become bigger than myself, and that makes me feel—" A new fire flickered in Oliver's soul.

Harold's eyes softened. "I see it in your face. All this learning agrees with you. But Father Caedmon doesn't take proper care of himself. Someone must watch his back."

Oliver started toward the door, and the two men walked out onto the courtyard green.

Father Caedmon stood waiting by the chapel entrance.

A young boy bounded forward. "Father Caedmon, come quick. Men have ridden in haste with urgent news. They say there's been an attack in the north, and Lady Martha's husband had something to do with it. The whole household is astir."

With a grimace, Father Caedmon gestured to Oliver and Harold. "Your repast will have to wait. Go, talk to the soldiers—find out what is going on. I'll be there shortly."

Oliver and Harold strode off in tandem.

As they came through the front door, Melchior's voice rose in irritation. Three heavily armed soldiers, weary and impatient, stood in the middle of the hall.

Martha stood beside her brother, her arms akimbo and anxiety chasing anger across her face.

The largest of the three soldiers, a bull-faced man, spoke heavily, dutifully making his point. "We intend no disrespect, Lord Melchior, but this matter with your sister's husband is serious, indeed. We've been ordered to interview her, and we mean to do so."

Melchior jutted his chin forward. "My sister's fool of a husband is accused of a crime, and you've come all the way down here to interrogate *her*? What nonsense! It's Roland you need to speak with. She has little to do with the affairs in the north. Save your breath, turn around, and go home!"

The bull-faced soldier snorted and clenched his fists. "Man, the lords of the north are in an uproar! There has been an invasion, Picts from the eastern sea. And a very successful one at that! Only two of five landowners have escaped with their lives. Your sister's husband was not one of the lucky ones."

Martha clutched her heart and swayed on her heels.

Grief stabbing his chest, Oliver ran to her, as did Gilda. They each grabbed an arm and drew her to the main table.

The three warriors followed close behind, apparently fearing that she would be spirited away.

The first soldier leaned in and spoke to her directly. "My lady, I've been in the service of Lord Morven for most of my life—he was like a father to me—but now, he is wounded almost to death, and it happened during a feast which *your* husband arranged. It was at your home that this mad slaughter took place. And I, among others, demand to know what part your husband had to play in this tragedy!"

Oliver could hardly believe his ears. How could anyone believe that Roland was capable of such evil deeds? He couldn't hurt a fly. Literally!

Martha leaned heavily against the table, her hands over her eyes. "He's dead then? Roland is dead? Are you sure?"

The warrior glanced away. "Yes, he's dead. If he weren't, I'd have driven him through myself! Your husband arranged a festive dinner where thieves and bandits murdered all who opposed them! They set fire to the premises as they looted. I was there; I saw it all!" The warrior stared down at Martha's slumped figure, slapping his fist into his hand. "Barbarians are now eating and drinking with damnable joy at their mighty conquest, and I want to know what part your husband had to play in it. What did you know of his arrangements?"

Fury at this unjust questioning filled Oliver.

Melchior strode forward, forcing himself between his sister and her interrogators. "Good Lord, man, have you no sense? She's been here helping me while her husband entertained his guests! If Roland died in the exchange, then he, too, was a victim. Why lay blame at his door when his whole household was destroyed?"

"Many a fool has made a treaty with an enemy only to be deceived and killed in the process. Roland arranged the festival that gathered all the great men of the surrounding districts at one table. The advance of the enemy was too perfect, too well executed to be mere chance."

Melchior tugged at his hair in sheer frustration. "Get out of my house! My sister had nothing whatsoever to do with this tragedy, and she's been told the worst of news. You can blame Roland for many things—stupidity, selfishness, even foolish pride—but you cannot blame him for duplicity. He didn't have it in him. If he thought these men were going to give him a rare butterfly, he would have arranged a feast in their honor. He was that kind of fool. You can look no further for justice here. Go, and tend to your master, and leave this poor woman to her grieving!"

Oliver braced himself, prepared for a struggle.

The warrior's jawline hardened, and his gaze turned icy. "I will return north and tend to my lord. But if I ever lay eyes on you again, you'll pay the price for being a relation to a liar and monster of no common stripe. All the lands that now lay in the hands of marauding barbarians will be recaptured, and when they are, not one foot of them will fall into your family's hands. Our wrath will not soon die!"

Martha's weeping choked her feeble attempts at speech.

In true form, Harold intervened, his soldier's stance and a commanding gesture ushering the unwelcome guests to the door.

Father Caedmon shuffled toward Martha, his hands clasped and his eyes beseeching Heaven.

Grateful for the closure of so dreadful a scene, Oliver ushered the watching crowd back to their duties.

Father Caedmon beckoned Melchior. "She needs you

now like never before. You must be her strength until she finds her own again."

Melchior nodded absently. "Yes, of course." He stepped forward, muttering under his breath, "But who will be my strength?"

At that moment, Oliver knew his duty. *I will, Father.*

~~~

Melchior ordered two servants to assist Martha to her chamber. Once there, he arranged her on the bed and drew a large blanket over her shivering body. "Rest, my dear. You must regain your strength."

After tossing and turning, Martha finally fell into an exhausted sleep, lying like a dead woman, pale and gaunt on her bed.

Melchior left the servants to watch over her and meandered back to the main hall. He slumped in a chair by the fire.

Richard strode into the room. A glimmer of the firelight slanted across his somber face. "I just heard. So very sorry. Is there anything I can do?"

Melchior stared into the flames. *Not unless you can bring the dead back to life, mend a broken heart, or find a lost son.* "No, there's nothing anyone can do."

Richard's gaze flicked to Melchior. "Are you going to see the king?"

His mind cloudy and weary with grief, Melchior shrugged. "Why?"

Breaking away from the fire, Richard paced across the room. "The king should know what happened. It concerns him, certainly."
~~~

Melchior clasped his hands. "He probably knows more than I do."

"Perhaps he doesn't know enough."

Melchior sighed. "Martha should not lose her lands, though I doubt he'll take her side." Melchior peered over at Richard "You'll go?"

Richard nodded.

Melchior sighed. "I'd like to see Adele. She's the only one who can comfort me now." He pushed himself from the chair and shuffled toward the dim stairway.

Richard stepped aside. "I'll wait for you here."

In mild surprise that his spirits could be lifted even a little, Melchior ascended the steps.

~~~

Adele knew that she had to inform her husband, but she dreaded the moment. She surmised that he would be pleased, but how did she feel? Her own joy at the realization that she was with child was tempered by the fact that her husband would rule the child as he did his kingdom. She would have little to say about the child's upbringing. Nausea burned her throat.

When a servant bowed into the room and informed her that her father and Richard had arrived in the forecourt, her heart constricted. *Will father be pleased—or grieved?* She sighed and hurried to finish dressing. Confusion and nausea could not rule her now.

As she rushed down the steps, Melchior and Richard stepped into the main hall. Richard looked unusually handsome. His somber expression belied his gentle, self-effacing heart. She almost stumbled at the sight of him but righted herself. Shaking off her lightheadedness, she
~~~

rushed to her father with her arms outstretched. She was about to take his hands while darting a welcome glance at Richard when someone cleared his throat loudly.

King Radburn swished into the room, his robes flowing like water rippling along a brook. “Lord Melchior! To what do we owe this *early* surprise? Why, I’m just barely out of my bed, and my wife is not yet properly dressed.” King Radburn’s eyes roamed from Adele’s pale face to her stocking feet. He twisted his grimace into a lopsided smile and closed the gap between himself and her. Then he thrust his arm about her waist.

Adele clenched her teeth.

Melchior’s eyebrows rose, and his lips pursed tight. His gaze shifted from Adele to the king. “I have come to see my daughter first and foremost, but also to inform you of serious news. My sister’s husband and several landowners have been attacked and their lands stolen.”

King Radburn brushed off the announcement with a languid wave. “Yes, I know of it. I sent my men to learn the particulars. But it has little bearing on us here. Marauders ravage the coast because it is vulnerable, and they can run away quickly. If they had met with a formidable defense, it would’ve been a very different story. Your sister’s husband was unfortunate, at the wrong place, at the wrong time. Though rumors claim that he hoped to gain something.”

King Radburn surveyed Adele’s trembling body and frowned. “You don’t look well, my dear. Return to your room and stay there until you can make yourself presentable.”

Horrified at the news, Adele hesitated before she bowed, blinking back tears. She turned and scurried from the hall. As her nausea demanded release, Adele knew she would not feel presentable for quite some time.

~~~
~~~

Melchior bit his lip and clenched his hands as he suppressed his fury. "Since my daughter is no longer welcome to enjoy my company, I fear I must turn home again. My duty is accomplished, and my principal joy is gone."

Richard's gaze followed Adele.

King Radburn sniffed as he appraised Richard. He flicked his hand toward the main dining room. "You just got here, and I'm in the mood for a hunt. It's early yet—eat something, and we'll go out. Adele will have plenty of time to make herself more favorable."

The king had clearly planned their day. Melchior sighed.

Richard nodded his acceptance of the King's command.

By early afternoon, the three men set out with a handful of soldiers to hunt down what the great forest had to offer. Richard was in his element. He rode with the host of men deep into the woods, leaving Melchior with the king.

King Radburn sat astride his horse and pulled his gaze from Richard's retreating back to Melchior's forlorn face. "What do you know about that man?"

Melchior patted his horse's neck. "Richard? I know what you know—he is brother to Lord Gerard."

"Yes, of course. I'm not an idiot. *I* gave his brother into your care. You're still hosting him, I suppose?" He didn't wait for an answer but rose higher in the saddle, like a man preparing to proclaim his insightful knowledge to the world. "Lord Gerard was a braggart and a fool who inherited his power from better men. But this one, this brother of his, I've heard that he killed Lord Marlow when attacked from behind. That's no small feat. He's strong and well-endowed and loves the hunt, yet his brother despises him. He lives up north, but his lands have never been attacked."

Questions underscored his last statements.

Melchior rubbed his temple. He pictured Adele's pale face, and dizziness clouded his mind. He had to force himself to stay on his mount. "It is true, Richard's lands have remained unmolested, though that can change in a moment. He's an honest, intelligent man with more decency than—"

"Us Saxons?"

Melchior shrugged. "Most Saxons I've known are brutes from first to last. But even when attacked, Richard was reluctant to kill his enemy."

King Radburn smirked as he kicked his horse into motion. "I hardly see that as intelligent."

Melchior forced his mount to pace alongside the king. "You wouldn't. You've been raised to honor the glory of battle and men who can win. But an educated man raised Richard. As a boy, he learned that there is more to conquer in this world than other men."

King Radburn spurred his horse into faster action. "You chase idle fantasies. I, too, was educated, though late in life, it's true. But I never forgot my earlier training. Kings have strong wills and lead others. Weak men are led, and their passing is not remembered."

A hot flush crept up Melchior's cheeks as his mount kept pace. "What will you be remembered for, King Radburn? Will anyone mourn your passing?"

King Radburn turned his horse sharply around and stopped Melchior's steed in its tracks. "My *son* will remember me, and he will know that it is better to be respected than loved."

Melchior could not resist an honest quip. "You ran your son through."

King Radburn's lips quivered into a twisted smile.

"Adele is with child. She will have a son, and he will grow into manhood and be just like me."

The reins in Melchior's hands trembled. "She would've told me!"

"You are worse than a woman, Melchior, waiting to be told. The signs are obvious. Did you honestly believe that you were giving me news when you came here today? Did Richard think that his passion for my wife has gone unobserved?"

Cold seeped through Melchior.

King Radburn snorted and turned his horse. "I'm going to check on my men. Stay here. I'll return and lead you home since I doubt you know your way." He kicked his horse, directing it into the woods.

Melchior watched the king disappear into the forest. He slid off his horse and tied it to a branch by a bubbling stream. Then he strode along the water's edge, his eyes sweeping the ground. A round black stone lay half-buried in the bank. Melchior pulled it free of the muck and rinsed it in the water. He wiped it clean with a corner of his cloak, rubbing it between his fingers. Its smoothness warmed his chilled hand.

The sound of pounding hooves sent him into the shelter of a hedge.

Richard galloped across the stream with several men following, three with deer carcasses hanging astride their saddles.

From the shadows, Melchior peered after Richard. Then the king's horse trotted up. At the stream, the animal hesitated, neighing.

Melchior passed the rock from hand to hand. Suddenly, Melchior arched his arm back and then threw, whipping it into the air and hitting the king's mount under the eye.

The horse reared up, throwing the king to the ground. In a frenzy, the animal scuffled along the bank until it found sturdy footing and trotted off in furious haste.

Melchior stared at the body of the king as it lay twisted in the muck. Swallowing, he stepped forward. *Oh, God. What have I done?*

The body did not move.

Melchior inched forward and nudged his toe against the head of his august leader. In the immediate silence, Melchior's heart rejoiced at one thought—*freedom!*

King Radburn groaned.

Melchior's spirit responded in echo.

Chapter Forty-Eight

One of Us

—Seven Months Later—

Adele lay in bed, her baby sleeping in the crook of her arm. She stared down at him in wordless admiration. So relaxed yet vibrant.

The front gate slammed shut for the night.

The baby's tiny hand reached out, startled at the distant boom.

Adele closed her eyes. King Radburn would return soon. He had made the formal birth announcement, and now the entire world knew that the king had a son and heir.

King Radburn. Adele shook her head, a smile tugging at the corners of her lips. Now that she had given birth to his son, must she still call him by his formal title? She closed her eyes and drifted off to sleep, her baby nestled snugly in her arms.

Sometime later, Adele awoke. Gloomy darkness surrounded, her and candlelight flickered by her bed. Night had fallen. Her arm ached, but when she tried to move, the baby cried out. When she inched her body upward, a cramp seized her muscles. The baby screamed lustily, and Adele panicked. Her full breasts ached.

King Radburn limped into the room, leaning on a cane. In his free hand, he grasped a steaming bowl, and the aroma of broth and meat traveled to her. He smiled. "I sent the servants to bed. They must be fresh in the morning." He carried the bowl forward. "Thought you'd be hungry. The boy needs to grow, and you've not eaten."

He managed to set the bowl on the table without a spill before he stared down at his son. The baby plaintively sucked his fist. The king's eyes shone, and his smile broadened. "Magnificent."

For the first time in her life, Adele wholeheartedly agreed with the king. Joy swelled in her heart. She did not like her husband, but she might love him.

King Radburn beckoned, his fingers wiggling at the baby. "May I?"

Adele loosened her grip.

Perching on the edge of the high bed, the king gently scooped his son's bundled body from his wife's grasp.

Adele rubbed her arm as she watched her husband hold their son. Her heart softened as she whispered, "What shall we name him?"

King Radburn hummed a little tune.

The baby opened his eyes, his brow furrowed, and his gaze seemed to fix on his father.

King Radburn lifted a finger, which the baby grasped. "I announced it today. James Radburn."

Fury rose and tears sprang to Adele's eyes. "You named him without asking me? And announced it too? Am I not his mother?"

King Radburn's shoulders hunched around the child as if he were protecting him from Adele's lament. He shifted his weight, his gaze fixed on his son.

The baby drifted off to sleep.

King Radburn slid his gaze to his wife. "My given name is Jarvis, but I hate the sound of it. I like James, a proud name, perfect for my first son—James Radburn."

Adele bit her lip. Her frown relaxed at the sight of him gently rocking their baby. She sighed. James.

Baby James stirred, a pout working into a perfect storm.

The king flicked an anxious look at Adele. "You'd

better eat up. He's surely hungry and,"—he shrugged—"I don't have what he wants."

Grinning, Adele reached for her stew, a happy thought soothing her wounded spirit. *A mother always has what her son needs.*

~~~

Melchior winced as he dismounted his horse. *I'm old. Very old.*

Oliver and Richard stood by, ready to enter the king's castle.

He remembered how he had felt when his first child was born. He had been frightened but also very proud. Edwina had been a wonderful mother, and though he had not been a perfect father, he loved his children. Would King Radburn do as much? He would provide a home, wealth, honor, and power, but would he *love* his son?

Oliver glanced about, chewing his lip like a man preoccupied with many concerns, while Richard seemed ill inclined to speak. It was a somber trio that marched into the king's hall.

King Radburn approached, limping clumsily even with the aid of a cane, but his face beamed with joy. "Lord Melchior, come greet your first grandson! And, Oliver, it's good to see you looking so well." His eyes flicked to the third man. "Richard."

The three bowed in formal courtesy.

King Radburn lifted his hand. "Supper is ready, and Adele is resting, but I will have one of the servants bring James to us. You'll be amazed at his great size, Melchior, quite robust."

Melchior stepped mechanically beside the king as they
~~~

strolled to the dining hall.

The kings' men, peasants, merchants, farmers, blacksmiths, soldiers, and others filed into the hall for their evening meal.

Oliver and Richard sat down at the offered seats. Melchior sat beside the king as his honored guest. The king gestured toward a variety of viands, so Melchior accepted a breast of pheasant, bread, and a piece of fruit to please the king, but he had to force down every mouthful.

As soon as the meal was over, the governess, a white-clad figure with a wrapped bundle in her arms, approached with the new babe cradled in her arms.

Melchior shivered. He didn't want to care too much for a child the king would rule so completely.

Padding down the long hall, the governess clutched the bundle tightly.

Melchior's heart rate quickened.

The governess stopped before the king and unwrapped the baby from his swaddling clothes for a closer inspection. James wailed at the sudden light and cool air.

Melchior's heart leapt, compassion breaking his last reserves.

With a sudden scowl, King Radburn snatched his son from the governess. "Clumsy idiot, you've awakened him, and he's cold. He'll get worn out with crying and take sick." King Radburn rewrapped the infant, cooing in an attempt to calm him.

James screamed more plaintively than ever.

The king gestured to the governess impatiently. "Take him back to his mother. He's probably hungry now." Huffing as he sat back down, the king offered a lopsided grin. "It takes powerful lungs to scream like that. A lusty lad, I tell you!" The king surveyed the quiet assembly. "He'll make a strong ruler."

Melchior rubbed his aching head. "Could I see Adele tomorrow? I'd like to speak with her."

King Radburn took a swig of his wine and nodded. "Certainly." He looked at Oliver and Richard. "And I suppose you two wouldn't mind spending the day hunting with my men? They need to fill the smokehouse."

Oliver nodded in agreement for the both of them.

Over the next three days, Melchior visited Adele several times. On the last day, he sat at her bedside as she leaned against pillows on her large, comfortable bed.

James slept peacefully in her arms.

Melchior frowned at her silence. "Are you not recovered yet, my dear? You still seem overtired."

Adele brushed her hand over her baby's fuzzy head. She darted a glance at her father. "Don't worry so much, father. I'm fine. James is healthy, and Jarvis is healing well despite his injuries. Everything is well."

Melchior eyed Adele carefully. "Are you content, then, with King...with Jarvis?"

When Adele stared at him, her brows furrowed.

Abashed at the silent interrogation, Melchior lowered his gaze. "He could have died, and perhaps things would have been easier—"

Adele gasped. "If King Radburn had died, he would never have known his son. This child is the best thing that ever happened to him. James is God's merciful grace to us both!"

Melchior swayed as he stood. "It was a stupid thought."

Adele stared at him, fear in her eyes. "You haven't been wishing for his death, surely?"

Melchior pressed her shoulder then turned away. "Get your rest, my dear. Oliver cannot stay away long, and Richard is needed at home as well. I'm glad you are content."

Adele attempted to rise. "I will see you out."

"Please, stay where you are; you look so comfortable. Enjoy your baby. I will return to see you again soon."

Adele reached out and grasped her father's hand. "James must know his grandfather and learn the stories of our family. He is *one of us*."

Melchior embraced his daughter, kissed the top of his grandson's downy head, and stepped away before tears could fill his eyes.

~~~

Adele started at the strange sound, a man clearing his throat in polite announcement of his presence.

Richard stood in her bedroom doorway, his hands clasped before him.

Comprehending the fact that the door had been left open when the servant took her breakfast tray away, Adele handed her baby to a servant and flipped back the bed covers to rise.

Richard strode forward.

Adele gestured to the governess. "Take him downstairs, and I will follow directly."

Her eyes fell on Richard's strong and perfect figure as he marched to her bedside. Once again, she attempted to rise, but Richard gestured for her to remain seated.

His gaze darted to the chair Melchior had been sitting in a few moments before.

Adele nodded.

With utmost care, Richard perched on the edge. "I want to thank you, personally, for allowing me the pleasure of visiting with you and your family." He glanced about the spartan room. "I've already taken my leave of the king." He clenched his hands in his lap as his gaze fell on Adele.
~~~

Adele tugged the cover over her lap and tilted her head. She should be afraid, or at least uncomfortable, to have this man in her room, but she wasn't. Not in the least. Rather, curiosity thrilled through her.

Richard leaned forward and said in a low voice, "I pray that you are happy." Abruptly, he rose and paced in front of the bed. "You know how it was with Lady Nadine. She was not happy. I'd always wished I had done something. Though a man may not intend to, he can hurt a woman beyond repair. And I've feared that perhaps—"

Adele forced a lighthearted laugh. "You and my father have much in common. You both worry too much." She looked into Richard's grieving eyes and instantly felt contrite. "I do not mean to belittle your concern, but I married the king, and I will make the best of the situation."

Richard snorted. "As if you had a choice! Good God, woman, don't you see, though I have no right, I worry about you. I know you are capable; that is one of your charms. You are capable for everyone who needs you—even a man who can't possibly see your worth."

Adele's eyes darted toward the doorway, and she wrapped her blanket more tightly around her. Her voice fell to a whisper. "I'm a married woman, no matter how you feel. I thank you for your concern, but I must see to my son. No worries, I am perfectly fine. You can ask my father if you don't believe me." Without further ceremony, Adele called for the servant.

Richard ran to her side. "Adele, wait, listen. I'm sorry. I spoke in haste, and I've put you in a difficult position, but I'm only asking that if ever you need help—any help at all—you will call for me. If only I knew that you would ask and trust me to come to your aid."

Adele stared into Richard's anguished eyes.

The servant bustled through the doorway.

She lowered her gaze and whispered. “If ever the need arises, I will call for you.”

Richard bowed stiffly. “Thank you. Now, I must take my leave. I’m taking care of my brother, and it has not been an easy task. Thank the king again for his hospitality.”

Adele nodded.

After Richard departed and the servant had left to arrange her clothes, Adele slipped from her bed and hurried to the window.

Three men rode through the gate, gusting wind tugging their long cloaks as if to snatch them off before they left the kings’ lands.

A breeze blew through her hair as she leaned against the window frame, watching the three men she loved best in the world gallop over a hill and beyond her view.

Chapter Forty-Nine

Stand Aside

—Five Years Later—

King Radburn leaned heavily on his ornate cane, studying his young son's attempts to impress him.

Thwack, crack, thwack, crack. A swift succession of hits, wooden sword against wooden sword, rang through the air. The sword master, a middle-aged man, heavy around the middle with thick arms and legs, struck like lightning. He had been considered a formidable adversary in his day, but as his day had turned to twilight, King Radburn had appointed him to teach little James how to ply the warrior's trade.

"Keep your arm up, young master. Don't look away! Focus on me—try to anticipate my next move. Block me! Don't just stand there! Be quick about it. Follow up with a thrust of your own. Step into your move. Show your mettle, boy, show who's master here!"

James, short and stout, panted with exertion. Perhaps because his father was watching, he redoubled his efforts and countered every move his teacher made.

Adele sat on a beautiful wooden bench that had been built especially for her so that she could sit in the fresh air sewing her embroidery and watching the children play.

A cloudless sky reigned over a hot day, though a steady breeze blew across the land, easing the summer's heat. In the background, strands of cobwebs shimmered across the tops of blackberry bushes dappled with juicy fruit clusters. Birds twittered and chirped to each other in the open sky.

Adele's daughters, two-year-old twins, tottered across

the soft grass, chasing a butterfly.

Adele glanced from her daughters to her son, and her happiness faded, though she adroitly adjusted her smile. She blocked the sun with her hand as she watched his progress, nodding encouragement when her son glanced her way.

King Radburn turned from his son's valiant efforts and hobbled over to his wife. A slur had entered his speech since the day he broke a molar on a cherry pit, and an eyetooth had been knocked out while racing his horse through the woods. He leaned on his staff, which was carved with intertwining spears that reached toward a fierce boar's head. It was sometimes used as a weapon to punish a servant's lapse of attention or to nudge someone when he wished to make a point exceptionally clear. "Well, he's young yet. There's still time enough."

Adele shook her head sharply, and a flush heated her cheeks. "He's only a baby, yet you demand *manly* qualities."

The king stared down at his wife and pursed his lips. "Perhaps I do. But if I do *not,* he will never become what he must to hold this kingdom together. Don't forget, there have been marauthers—" He paused, his jaw clenched, and he began again coolly. "Marauders have successfully divided many kingdoms larger and better equipped than our own. If I were not constantly on my guard, making every effort to hold onto what we have, we, too, would have been conquered. Remember last year—"

Adele huffed an exasperated sigh and dropped her sewing in her lap. "You need not recite the troubles of our times; I know them well enough. James is but a boy, and yet you have him working with a grown master when he should be playing with children his own age. Once childhood is gone, it cannot be retrieved."

The king clutched his staff, and his careful speech

slipped into lisps. "Do not lecthure me, woman! I know better than you. I was never granted the luxthury—" He swore under his breath, exhaled, and forced himself to speak more distinctly. "The luxury of a childhood myself! But it was in that early training that I learned what's needed to become a king!"

An awkward silence ensued as Adele once again bent her head over her sewing.

The king dug his staff into the ground.

The trainer gestured abruptly, and he and the boy raised their swords in salute, thus formally ending the practice.

James ran to his father, nearly tripping in his excitement. "Did you see? I'm better, aren't I? Master Raymond says that I'll be the best swordsman in the whole of the kingdom. He says I have a strong arm and a sure eye." The little boy clambered over to his mother and snuggled under her arm. "I'm getting better, don't you think?"

Adele put her sewing aside and pulled her son higher onto her lap. "Certainly. You're better than you've ever been, and I agree—you'll be the best this land has to offer. I don't know any other boy who practices as hard and faithfully as you. I shouldn't wonder that you'll teach your master a few new tricks in time. Now, come. You must be starving." She looked over to the instructor. "Master Raymond, you must be hungry as well. Come in and eat. It is well past the usual hour."

Master Raymond bowed in gratitude. "No, thank you, my lady. I'll be off to my other duties. I have other men to train, and I mustn't neglect them." He bowed to the king and turned away.

James watched him go and then, sighing, climbed off his mother's lap and began to whine. "I'm hungry! Let's go. Grandfather is coming today, and I want to be fit for the festival."

As if stung, King Radburn gave way to irritation. "Were you invited?"

James turned, a fierce scowl twisting his boyish face. "You said that if I did well in practice and my studies, I could go. You did!"

Adele gripped her son's shoulder, a disapproving frown knit across her brow. "James! You mustn't speak like that. He's your father and the king besides."

James' glare darkened, darting from his father to his mother.

Gratified by his son's impetuous spirit, King Radburn lifted his hand. "No, it's true. I did promise, and if I did not keep my word then I would be no better than some others I could name."

Adele's heart clenched as she assembled her sewing. She called to the twins. "Katie...Kimberly, come now! It's time to sup."

A servant rose from behind, ushering the children forward with a sweep of her hands, while another servant took charge of the queen's embroidery. A third took a position behind the king. They all processed forward in slow, stately dignity.

James marched forward, his head high and his chin set in determination.

King Radburn glanced aside and gratefully perceived a shadow of himself in his son.

That evening after a wash and a change into fresh clothes, King Radburn stood on his dais in the great hall looking down at the happy throng, an assembly of his men and merchants and folks from the surrounding villages. The warm day had fallen into the clutches of a star-bright night. The whole villa and surrounding keep stirred with the multitudes celebrating midsummer's eve.

The large front doors had been flung open to the exuberant crowds, who jostled together under the stars.

The bustle of merry, chattering voices filled the night air. Torches hung from posts or stood perched on stands in the middle of loaded tables.

King Radburn stood with a full cup clasped in one hand.

A strange familiarity filled him. He vividly remembered the day he'd announced his engagement to Adele and the day he made Melchior a lord. Now, only a few short years later, he had given Melchior three grandchildren and permission to build a magnificent church on his land. Though he had no personal interest in the matter, the Church did have its uses, and he was willing to allow Father Caedmon to educate chosen men in the science of arts and letters. There was power in words and especially in recordkeeping. Who better to write important words and keep good records than those otherwise useless priests?

There was something to be said for having scribes, as well as warriors, sweating and toiling for one's purposes. Recently, he had been able to prove, through various written records, that he owned much of the land that Nolan once thought belonged to him. The fact that the records had been drawn up under his eye did not change the power he had to enforce their testimony. He was a much more powerful man now with records than he had ever been without them.

Melchior plodded into the hall.

King Radburn observed him with a small lift to his lips.

Dark circles underlined Melchior's eyes, while a tight frown appeared embedded in his forehead.

James, followed by the twins, scampered through the main hall behind their mother. Despite the noise, clouds of smoke, and general confusion, Adele stepped gracefully up the dais and settled the children with their attendants. She nodded respectfully to her husband, her mouth a stiff, thin line that only broke when she saw her father approaching. She waited with her hands clasped in front of her.

Melchior reached the table and bowed formally with an appraising stare at his daughter and a mere flicker toward the king.

Adele's cheeks flushed.

Well-lubricated with two drinks and in a benevolent mood, King Radburn attempted a welcoming smile, lifting his cup and sloshing it a bit. "Here you are! I was worried we'd have to begin without you. The children have been demanding to see their grandfather all day. Please, don't think of sitting with the others. Honor us here at our table."

Melchior rubbed his chin. "Whatever you wish, but first, I need a private word. Could we step aside a moment?"

Flummoxed by the suggestion of a change to his perfect plans, King Radburn felt heat creep up his cheeks, and embarrassingly, his speech faltered. "Leathe my own assembly at festhival thime?"

Melchior rubbed his temple. "It's an important matter. What I have learned will affect many people, and it would be best if you knew of it sooner than later. For if—"

A shout rang out.

Both men looked up.

The crowd grew boisterous, jabbering noisily with minor skirmishes, as men and boys vied for attention.

King Radburn gestured with his cup, sloshing wine onto the floor. "You worry too much! Everyone is waiting for me to offer the first toast and begin the entertainment." The king lurched forward, saluted his wife, and then lifted his glass to the crowd, shouting above the loud throng, "I give you the queen!" He drank deeply.

Adele took up her cup and sipped.

A cheer rose and then conversation settled as most everyone drank deep.

King Radburn followed up with another toast. "To the gods! May the crops grow bountiful, our children grow strong, and may vengeance always be ours!"

Loud stomps and yells pummeled the air.

Surveying the heightened tension, the king grinned in boyish pleasure. He glanced at his son. "Send in the jugglers and fire dancers!"

From the midst of the throng, a multitude of grotesquely dressed men burst forth, jumping, hopping, and flipping themselves across the hall, throwing burning brands high into the rafters and catching them. Applause mixed with oohhs, aahhs, and shrieks, as the children were overcome by the exotic excitement, lifting the general bustle to a riot of sound.

The crowd ate and drank happily while entertainers ran back and forth in outlandish costumes with frightening masks. They laughed at some and taunted others as they recited poetry, lewd and humorous; imitated a bear baiting; and juggled plates, bowls, and eggs, dropping not a few. The crowd roared in boisterous approval, and when it was announced there would be *a real fight to the death* outdoors, the crowds poured into the courtyard, encircling the contenders.

Taking up his position front and center, King Radburn stood with his wife and children at his side.

Two men, stripped to the waist, lunged forward brandishing knives and shouting oaths to Thor and Woden, and even to Tiw and Wetlund, brandishing their knives. They quickly convinced the audience that they were in earnest. The crowd pulled back, the children were banished to the back, and men leaned forward with mad gleams in their eyes.

While engrossed in the spectacle, hot blood coursed

through King Radburn's veins. But then he glanced at Adele and perceived her discomfort. *A cold fish with no courage.* He focused his gaze on the scene and wished his wife away.

~~~

Adele withdrew with her children while the throng encouraged the spectacle with taunting calls. She led them to their chambers, where attendants took their sweaty, sleepy bodies to welcoming beds.

Shouts rose through the humid evening air and into the open windows.

Adele sighed. She wanted to hate her husband, but his pitiful face rose in her mind, and weariness took possession of her. She ambled to her room and climbed into bed, grateful to be alone.

~~~

Melchior observed his daughter's stoic wretchedness as she departed the courtyard, and he remembered the hard and round stone in the palm of his hand. He had sinned, and he should repent. He'd even imagined kneeling before Father Caedmon and relieving himself of his guilt, but he always hesitated. His mother had warned him that to confess a sin you were not truly sorry for would be sacrilege. He could not help but wonder would he, if given the chance again, drop the rock or aim higher?

His tangled thoughts fled as he wended his way toward the top of the villa and the little room arranged for him on these visits. The round room felt the bite of the wind, but it had a gorgeous view. The king had smiled archly when he'd told Melchior that this room would always be made available for him, for it was what he'd always wished for—a lonely place to think deep thoughts amid the clouds.

Melchior stared at the disbursing crowd, still boisterous even after the two contestants fell unconscious on the bloody ground. He had important news to tell the king, which would hit him harder than any stone. But King Radburn disdained to know of it. Melchior decided that he would stand aside and let this stone land where it would.

Chapter Fifty

Nothing Can Stop Me

Teal stood on the bank of a bubbling brook, his peasant outfit ragged and spent, and stared at the light glinting in all directions. An image flashed into his mind: Sienna's gray face as she lay dying on their bed at home. The image spun away and another replaced it: him desperately attempting to save a man being buried under rubble during an earthquake. A montage of memories collided into a swirl of terrifying helplessness. Why did he exist? He couldn't save his wife or even a stranger. Why did he live when so many suffered and died?

A throat cleared noisily.

Teal shoved the memories away and lifted his gaze.

Sterling stood to his right. "There's news, and you'd best hear it with everyone else. We're meeting at the ship."

Once on board, Teal joined Zuri and Kelesta in staring at the holopad. A segment of the universe turned in multi-colored beauty. Lux, Crestar, Sectine, Helm, and billions of life forms lived in this vast expanse.

Kelesta peered over her shoulder at Tarragon and Nova huddled in deep conversation at the far left, where maps of the ship layout were engraved on the wall behind them.

Unease crept over Teal's spine. *What's he up to?* He focused his gaze on Nova.

She listened to Tarragon in silence, her head bowed as if weighed down.

"Teal?"

Sterling beckoned from the platform on deck. "Stand

next to me, and it'll look like we have a united front."

"Sir?" Confused, Teal headed up the incline and intercepted Cerulean coming from the shadows. He motioned to his son. "You stand by me, and we'll really have a united front."

Cerulean took up his place, a frown marring his usual placid expression.

Teal stopped before Sterling. "What's this all about?"

Sterling clapped his hands. "If everyone would gather closer—Tarragon, you and Zuri especially need to hear this."

Breaking away from his confab with Nova, Tarragon offered a grimace and joined Zuri and Kelesta before the dais. The four looked up expectantly.

Sterling smoothed down his long grey tunic. "We've heard a rumor that the Ingilium and Crestonian governments plan to destroy Earth in order to prevent the Mystery Race from obtaining planetary resources for their own."

Kelesta gasped.

Nova scowled in red-faced fury.

Alarm filled Zuri's eyes.

Tarragon grinned. "Rumors are meant to cause unease. Not to be taken seriously."

Teal felt weak. His body ached, and his spirit waned.

Cerulean moved closer, his arm touching Teal's, as if offering silent strength.

Zuri stepped forward. "What's our plan?"

Sterling gripped the railing, determination flashing in his eyes. "We're going to send a detailed report to Lux, Crestar, Sectine, and even Helm, explaining humanity's incredible potential and the traumatizing loss of resources to the entire universe if we destroy this planet."

A bright glow enveloped Cerulean, while Nova straightened, her chin held high.

Zuri clasped his wife's hand.

Tarragon, an introspective listener, tilted his head.

Sterling patted Cerulean's shoulder like a general approving a soldier moving up in rank. "I'm putting Cerulean and Nova in charge of framing the report. Nothing better than young zeal to convince old cynics that we still have something worth fighting for."

Relief washed over Teal. Earth would be saved. For the first time since he had come to this planet, he wasn't the only Luxonian invested in protecting it.

Zuri stepped forward. "We'll need proof."

Lifting her datapad high, Kelesta practically crowed, "We have the life stories of those humans who have gone before, the noble ones like Aram and Ishtar, Georgios and his friends." She glanced to the doorway. "Given time, I'm certain that even Melchior will prove his worth."

Cerulean's colors dimmed.

Teal clasped his son's shoulder. "Watch closely, and you'll get the proof you need. Humanity has long struggled against evil temptations, but noble hearts, though deeply scarred, will yet respond to a higher calling."

"Wait!" Nova turned to her parents. "Tarragon offered me a position on Crestar—to assist him in discovering how to interbreed the best of our races."

Glaring at the Crestonian, Kelesta spat her words. "How dare you!"

Zuri gripped his wife's arm. "It's not his fault. Crestonians are born scientists. It's what they do. If not Tarragon, then some other scientist would try to unlock the mystery of Nova's unique life form."

A smile curled Nova's lip. "So, I can go? You'll trust me?"

Zuri clasped his daughter's hand. "We trust you. The question is, do you trust Tarragon. After all, this your very existence he's investigating."

Kelesta shuddered. "We've paid a heavy price for our choice. And so, my dear, will you. Mixed breeds do not have long life spans."

Tarragon clasped his tentacles together meditatively, staring directly at Nova. "It is your choice. I did help your father when he suffered his little lapse a while back. Neither Ingots nor Bhuaci are as advanced as we in medical resources. Perhaps *you* can live a much longer life span. It's worth a little risk, isn't it?"

His colors glowing to unusual brilliance, Cerulean blinked away and then reappeared before the assembly below. He glowered with his fists clenched. "After we convince everyone the worth of humanity, then you can go wherever you want. But we have a duty here, first."

New strength filled Teal. He was ready for the final push. "Once you get your reports ready, I'll take them to our leaders personally." He stretched, new life filling him, and his gaze fixed on the outer universe. "I can accomplish anything, now."

Cerulean looked up, meeting his father's gaze.

Teal understood. The emphasis was on *now*.

~~~

Omega roamed free, exhilaration filling him. He watched a flock of birds flying overhead, calling to each other. He could go anywhere and do anything. He had slipped away from his mother's caretakers and now no one, not even his father and mother, knew where he had gone. Having no certain destination, he could simply wander free to explore and experience as he wished, without someone always watching him, warning him.
~~~

Loneliness pressed on him like a heavy atmosphere.

On impulse, he returned to a particularly beautiful field near Melchior's abode and looked around.

Before him loomed a strange new structure only partially built.

Oliver, Melchior's unusual and often misunderstood son, sat with his back resting against a tree, wiping sweat from his brow. A single bird hopped nearby, pecking at the grass in silent communion with all of nature.

Omega discerned an unnamed connection between the man and the structure—something Omega had never felt before. How could an inanimate building, made of stone and wood, call to a human spirit?

Staring at a place near the wood line behind Oliver, Omega snapped his fingers, and a mature apple tree suddenly appeared. A fresh breeze picked up, and grey clouds swept over the blazing sun. Two birds alighted on the apple tree. He strolled over, picked a ripe fruit, and settled down in the sweet-smelling grass.

The prospect of discovering everything he could from this remarkable man swelled his heart in happiness. *Father would be proud—I want to learn, and now, nothing can stop me.*

Chapter Fifty-One

Storm on the Horizon

Oliver leaned against the broad oak tree, the rough bark prickling his sweaty back. He had awoken before sunrise and would work until after sunset in the hot, heavy air, but joy welled up inside him as if a sweet breeze blew. He glanced at the clouds mounting in the west. A storm was brewing.

A magnificent church structure stood brilliant against the sky, set on a firm foundation. It would stand for generations to come—long after his body had sloughed off its mortal shell. Others would come to this very site and view this church, perhaps lean against this same tree and marvel at the construction of this edifice made by men they never knew but must thank, even in the awed silence of their hearts.

Father Caedmon had questioned this undertaking, not relishing a job he was unfit to complete, but Oliver matched every concern with his adamant conviction that this church was God's will.

The one-time warrior, Harold, surprised both Oliver and Father Caedmon with his genius for recruitment. He had managed to hire the majority of the laborers at a very reasonable cost, some of whom had impressive skills. While the land belonged to Melchior, the king paid for the construction, merely asking that he be kept abreast of all developments and be allowed the use of a scribe or two to help manage his records. He also requested that they train his son in the arts of reading and writing. Father Caedmon had agreed. It was God's will, after all.

"Daydreaming, are you?"

Bracing his hand over his eyes, Oliver looked up.

Martha held a tray laden with a stout mug of ale and various viands.

His stomach growled in appreciation. "I thought you'd taken the children to see Adele."

"I will, but I wanted to see you first, and make sure that you have one decent meal before I depart."

Oliver chuckled and accepted the tray. "There's enough here to feed three men."

"Not really. The fish is bony and burned on one side and the bread is dry, as you'll soon discover. Honestly, I'm doing my best to teach Gilda how to run a household, but she's not paying attention. She has her eye on a certain stonemason, a fine man as young men go, but he's as poor as they come, and I've heard he worships in the Eastern Rite. Melchior will never agree to the match. I've told her, but she won't listen. Perhaps you can have a talk with the young man. He shouldn't encourage her."

A pathetically thin dog ambled in the distance, sniffing the ground.

Oliver's joy faded. "It is hardly my place to tell her who to marry. I'd hoped it was nothing more than an innocent flirtation."

"Innocent flirtation? With a girl her age? Why, she should be married and have a babe or two by now. Melchior is not doing his duty by his daughters."

Oliver bit into the bread and frowned, quickly realizing the accuracy of his aunt's assessment. While chomping the hard crust, he gestured for his aunt to sit beside him. "Rest a bit."

Martha lowered her ample frame to the ground, groaning. "Oh, it's not as easy as you think, getting around at my age. I may not be much older than your father—we're practically the same age—but my bones feel older than those stones you're piling on top of one another."

Oliver's eyes glowed at the growing monument. "They may be old now, but they'll be reborn in the dedication of this church—a home fit for God, founded on the undeceiving earth, shaped by honest stone, and willed into existence by men who wish to serve."

Martha sniffed. "You've certainly acquired a way with words since you learned to read. My poor Roland—he could hardly put two thoughts together without getting into a tangle. That's why he liked the critters so much, simple and uncomplicated. Still, please be careful. Not all plans are as honest as they seem."

"You don't believe in our sincerity?"

"Oh, I believe in *your* sincerity, but there are others involved. The king, for instance. Does *he* care for God or for the power this offers him?"

Oliver wrenched a piece of bread from the loaf. "He cannot have any power here. He must know that."

Martha stared off toward the horizon. "Look over there." She pointed.

Oliver turned as directed.

"See? From the east, it looks like a perfectly beautiful day, but in the west"—she directed him to the black clouds mounting high—"lies a threat. If you don't keep your eyes open, you won't see it until it's too late."

Oliver picked meat from the bones. After a moment of concentration, he swallowed the last fishy morsel and tossed the mess aside. "What would you have me do?"

"Even in your joy, be aware of devious ambition. When you cut into fruit, sometimes you get a nasty surprise. What looked sound on the outside was rotten within."

Oliver tossed the remains of his meal to a hungry dog that had come in response to the smell. "And Gilda, what of her?"

"Leave her to me. I mean to teach her a valuable lesson when we visit Adele. But the young man, I leave in your hands. He can become like us or leave Gilda alone. That's his choice."

"And his poverty?"

"Poverty, like wealth, comes and goes. If he were an honest Christian, I could forgive him much. But if he keeps with heathen customs, I'll hold my ground."

Oliver nodded and then helped his aunt to her feet and picked up the tray. They both watched the clouds overtaking the blue sky. "I'm grateful for your kindness."

"What kindness? I wanted your help, and I offered you a dreadful meal in payment."

Oliver smiled. "It was well meant."

After lumbering a few steps away, Martha turned around. "Oh, I almost forgot. Melchior said that there's an important man coming to view the construction. So make sure that all your records are in order."

Oliver scratched his beard. "What man? What's his name?"

"I don't know...can't remember. He spoke so hurriedly. Melchior will talk with you tonight. In the meantime, you should make sure that every scribe and laborer has been paid and that you know where all the records are kept."

Dread twisted Oliver's gut.

She scowled. "What's wrong? I thought you were in charge of everything."

Oliver nodded as drops of rain fell on his head. "I know everything there is to know about the building of this church, but..."

"But what?"

"The king has had the use of two scribes, and I don't know what they've been doing."

"Why not ask them?"

"I did, but they said it was the king's business."

"Oh, dear Mother in Heaven."

As rain pelted them in thick drops, Oliver grabbed his

aunt's hand and began running toward home. He shouted over a roll of thunder, "Yes, I fear that the king's business may have little to do with God's business."

~~~

Bishop Clement considered himself to be a very amiable man, except when crossed. He folded his arms high across his broad chest as a heavy mace dangled at his side. His rich robes flowed over his muscular body like water over stones. He marched across Father Caedmon's simple chamber. A hard bed, a desk and stool, and a candle didn't add any warmth to the space. "You're telling me that King Radburn has *never* been baptized?"

Father Caedmon sat slump-shouldered on a stool, his childlike gaze wide and honest. "He never asked, and I don't believe in forcing a man to come to the faith."

"Who's forcing? Obviously, if he's willing to support the building of a church, he must have faith! Have you even offered?"

"Of course. I have spoken with him many times. Take my word for it; he's not in the least interested. He's more liable to toast a pagan god than to praise a priest. The man has no love for me or anything I believe in."

Bishop Clement stopped pacing and leaned in. He propped one hand on the wooden table set beside Father Caedmon, boxing him in. "He doesn't like the Catholic faith, refuses to be baptized, clings to false gods, and has no respect for you, yet he builds a church? Strange indeed."

Father Caedmon stroked his cheek. "The church is founded on stone and the grace of God, though King Radburn may not care to know of it. The real benefactor
~~~

is his wife. Adele is a Christian, the daughter of Lord Melchior."

The bishop began pacing again. "Ah, yes, Lord Melchior. Another one I have my doubts about. I've heard stories..."

Father Caedmon shook his head. "None dreadful, I'm sure. He's a mild-mannered man. King Radburn gave us permission to build on Lord Melchior's lands and offered us money to do so. What should we have done? Rejected it? A church will proclaim and expand the faith, glorifying God. Soon, we'll baptize, marry, and bury people as never before."

Discombobulated by the conflict stirring his stomach, Bishop Clement drummed his fingers together. "I see that, but still, I believe you've acted unwisely." He leaned down, dropping his voice to a husky whisper. "I've heard rumors of bloody sacrifices."

Straightening, he adjusted his mace and tried to look more affable. "I know that the Widow Brunswick chose you for her own, plucked you out of the wilderness and made you a priest, and I applaud her faith and diligence, for you have done much good, I'm sure. But this matter of building—not just a small chapel but a grand church—under the auspices of a man who doesn't even believe...well, I fear this will have disastrous consequences." His frown deepened. "Can you honestly look me in the eye and tell me that King Radburn doesn't have hidden motives?"

Father Caedmon pursed his lips and shrugged. "I don't know. But shouldn't we trust in the providence of God? A church is always a gift. The king's private plans may never come to pass. God might convert him through this good deed."

Staring out the open window, Bishop Clement snorted. "If I wasn't already a Christian, your faith would convert me. Yes, God can do what He wants, but it is *men* I'm concerned about. I want your Lord Melchior to tell me all he knows about this project and his daughter's relationship with this pagan king." He turned around and faced the old priest. "How could he allow his daughter to marry a pagan in the first place?"

"I don't think Melchior had much choice."

"He was the father. He could have said *no*. Martyrs have died for less cause."

With a deep sigh, Father Caedmon struggled to rise. "The king was adamant, and the woman had a broken heart. It was a bad combination. And I'm afraid martyrdom didn't appeal to anyone."

Bishop Clement strode across the room and towered over the frail priest. "Why did *you* allow it?"

Father Caedmon lifted his hands in surrender. "Perhaps I was a fool—an exhausted fool. But I believed, and still believe, that God will make good wine out of bad water."

Bishop Clement fingered his mace. "I've been a priest for twenty years and a bishop for eleven. I have seen great miracles and greater tragedies, and always, I'm shaken by the power of God. And men's blindness."

"But God can cure blindness."

"You have to want to be cured."

The old priest's eyes softened with a look of gentle admonishment. "Have you despaired, Bishop?"

Bishop Clement clapped the man on the shoulder, nearly tumbling him forward. "God rules the universe, and there is much I don't see." He steadied the feeble soul and grinned. "I won't be too hard on your Lord Melchior or his daughter, but from King Radburn, I will demand an accurate accounting. I will have no Judas building my church."

Father Caedmon gripped the hem of the bishop's sleeve, a plea in his eye. "Speak to Melchior's son first."

Bishop Clement recoiled, disgust rising. “The one that ran away with his sister?”

“You have been listening to gossip.”

“It’s not true, then?”

“Truth is a tricky matter in this family, but that’s not the one I mean. I’m speaking of Oliver. He has learned to read and write, and I believe he’ll make a holy priest. He oversees the building of the church.”

Appeased by this good news, Bishop Clement’s nerves settled. “Fine. Where is he?”

Father Caedmon stepped forward. “I’ll get him, but remember—Lord Melchior is his father, and the queen is his sister. He loves them both.”

The bishop jabbed his finger in the air. “If he’s to become a priest, he must love God first.

Father Caedmon sighed and left his chamber.

In wonderment, Bishop Clement’s heart went with him.

~~~

Martha smiled at her happy-go-lucky niece, though an uneasy feeling niggled at her insides.

Gilda laughed as she sat on the grass in an open field in front of the king’s castle and threw a twine ball to her niece Kimberly.

The child stood with her hands at her sides, uncomprehending the game.

Her twin, Katie, ran forward and snatched the ball.

In admonishment, Gilda scooted forward. “Katie! That was meant for your sister! Now keep to your place. You’re always jumping in front.”

The toddler grinned and threw the ball, which went flipping over her shoulder.

Gilda’s laugh reverberated across the open field.

Martha sat on a dry patch of grass next to Adele, who
~~~

had a somber, far-away look in her eyes.

King Radburn hobbled closer with a servant at his elbow.

The sun shone clear and blue, and the air hung still and warm. The evening promised delights, for the king had planned a fine meal with nobles from adjoining estates in attendance. He had made a special point of mentioning this when Martha and Gilda first arrived.

Katie retrieved the ball and threw it, but this time she used all her strength and better aim, and it nearly reached her aunt.

Gilda laughed again and snatched up her niece in a smothering embrace.

King Radburn glared down at Adele's head. "Are you still aloof, angry at my just decision?"

Adele's jaws clenched, and though she said nothing in words, anger emanated from her.

The king's face flushed. "This interfering priest or bishop will leave today!"

Gilda crept nearer to Martha.

Holding her breath, Martha studied her hands.

Adele stood and adjusted her dress and her expression into amiable lines. "He simply asked to see the records. That's not unreasonable."

King Radburn stabbed the ground with his cane. "He questioned my private affairs! When I refused to discuss them, he ordered that all construction be stopped!" Shaking his staff in the air, he swore, "By the gods! Who does he think he is, coming here and telling me what I can do! If I want to build a church, I'll build a church. If I want to build ten thousand churches, I'll build them. It's my business, not his. He has no authority here!"

Gilda swung a frightened Kimberly into her arms and stepped closer to Adele.

Adele clenched her hands at her sides. "But he does!

He has the authority to say if a church is to be built here or anywhere. As bishop, he bears the responsibility of ensuring that no false churches are built under his watch."

King Radburn sneered. "*False* churches! The stone is real enough. It'll outlast the ages!"

Adele closed her eyes. "The bishop must be certain that the church is under the guidance of holy men—men who will preserve the teachings and laws of the Church."

King Radburn glared at his wife and raised his staff.

Alarmed, Martha jumped to her feet.

Throwing a glare at Martha, King Radburn turned and called for his man.

The servant hurried over and aided the hobbling king back to the castle.

Adele heaved a shaking sigh.

Gilda pressed her sister's shoulder. "I've never seen him like that before. Oh, Adele, you should be more careful! He is the king."

Adele stared, blinking, all color gone from her face. "I told the truth, and if that isn't good enough for a king, then I don't know who else will have it." She took Kimberly from Gilda's arms and clasped Katie's small hand. Following the path her husband had taken, she crossed the field toward home.

Left alone with Gilda, Martha sighed. "Being the king's wife isn't as charming as one might think."

Gilda frowned. "I suppose not, but then Adele doesn't know how to make the most of the situation. Why, this place is divine, angry king or no. I could live here as a servant and be happy."

Martha's mouth twitched as she started across the field, following Adele's path. "That's because you rarely serve. Don't misunderstand me, child. I love your kind heart, but you're a dreamer. Adele has made the best of her lot, but her lot includes an angry king."

Stepping beside her aunt, Gilda's eyes sparkled mischievously. "If *she* doesn't want him, there are others who could make him happy."

Furious at such a scandalous thought, Martha flashed a scow at her niece. "Put such thoughts out of your head! You're raised to become the wife of a good Christian man, and that's what you'll be!"

In playful teasing, Gilda took her aunt's arm. "You're ferocious today, aunt! Have I ever told you the story about the Egyptian princess? It is a glorious tale—so romantic! I know it from beginning to end."

In growing despondency, Martha marched to the king's castle, her niece jabbering at her side. A million cares crowded her mind, and grief filled her heart.

~~~

Richard wiped his lips with the back of his hand and pushed his half-eaten meal off to the side. After taking a long draught of ale, he rested his elbows on the wooden table set in his quiet abode.

He had taken his brother from Melchior's home to his own estate the year that Adele married, and he rarely returned to visit. He knew that the king had been injured and that Adele had three children now. He knew everything there was to know about her, though he learned everything through second-, third-, and occasionally even fourth-hand reports. He lived his life much as before but with little pleasure or pain, for he never seemed to feel much of anything.

After a year, Gerard requested to build his own home. Permission was duly granted and materials supplied. With his own hands and little assistance, he fashioned a crude but accommodating hut. Once settled in, Gerard seemed content like never before.
~~~

A thickset middle-aged servant shuffled his feet and coughed.

Richard shook himself free of his reverie and looked up. "Yes, what do you want?"

"Begging your pardon, lord, but I have news I thought you'd like to hear."

Richard sighed. He cared little for the news. "What is it?"

"Your niece and nephew have been seen in town north of here. It's said they're visiting the Widow Brunswick."

Richard straightened and his chest constricted. "Corliss? Wilfred? They're back? Have you told my brother?"

The servant shook his head. "No, my Lord. I thought you'd be the better man to tell. I don't know for sure...it's just a rumor. I haven't seen them with my own eyes. Perhaps it's a mistake. I'd hate to be telling an untruth, but I thought you'd want to know."

Richard nodded, stroking his short beard.

The man's eyes shifted in discomfort.

"You've done well, Brunk. Don't feel bad. It is good news at best and no news at worst. Is there anything else? Something you haven't told me?"

"Well, perhaps there is a little thing. Rumor says that Corliss is married to a fine, well-dressed sort. A foreign potentate of some kind—a rich man by all accounts, who has innumerable servants at his beck and call. They even say he owns a country of his own and has a harem."

Richard's sober expression softened as he grinned mischievously at the man before him. "A fantastic story, indeed. I must find out the truth of it and see this wonder for myself."

Brunk frowned in doubt as he gazed at his master's face, though a slow smile spread across his features.

Richard peered at the man, perplexed, then the light

dawned. "Oh, Brunk, by any chance, would you happen to know a couple of men who'd be willing to come along with me?"

"By chance, my brother and I are free at the moment—we'd be happy to accommodate you."

Richard rose. "In that case, I charge you with getting things ready so that we can leave in the morning."

Brunk bowed and turned away.

Richard called after him. "But don't mention this to my brother. I'll explain things—later."

"Yes, sir." The servant departed.

Richard picked up his ale, took a long, slow drink, and tried not to imagine his brother's face when he heard the news.

Chapter Fifty-Two

The Prodigal Son

Melchior stared at the reflection in the wavy glass. Deep lines marred the landscape of his features. A permanent scowl marked his forehead, and his mouth turned decidedly down. The summer heat suffocated him as sweat dribbled under his arms and down his legs. He was thinner than he had ever been, and he often had to stop and catch his breath.

He grabbed his vellum roll off the shelf and unrolled it slowly. Little free space remained on it, but he had two others folded away in a little box that Oliver had made for him.

A familiar voice called.

Melchior answered, "Yes, Oliver, I'm here."

When—in retaliation against the king's refusal to allow the bishop full access to his records—Bishop Clement ordered a halt to the building of the church, Oliver returned home to his routine chores and studies. He had struggled with the bishop's decision, but after a time, he decided that the bishop was right. The bishop's responsibility to God must rule the king's thirst for power. Still, grief darkened his son's days, and Melchior grieved with him.

Melchior glanced up at the approach of footsteps and attempted a smile.

Oliver crossed the upper room and knelt at his father's knee, bowing his head. "Father Caedmon is very ill. He says it's time, but he has one last request: he wants me to be ordained a priest." Oliver looked up at his father's face. "He wants me to ask the bishop if I can go to Rome—to study. But I'd need money, and King Radburn refuses to help." Oliver sighed. "Father, what should I do?"

Tears welled in Melchior's eyes, the bitter sting of so many losses—so many hopes dashed. He wiped his eyes and counterfeited strength he did not have. "You'll go to Rome if that's what you want. I'll not see another child's life destroyed."

"But the money. King Radburn says—"

"Never mind what he says! I've been forced to listen to that man long enough. Surely God doesn't want all our hopes thwarted; surely, He wants a holy priest. If He does, He'll send the means!"

Someone bellowed from the bottom of the stairs.

Martha's strained voice was on the verge of hysterics. "Melchior! Melchior, come here. There is news. You must come! We have a surprise. Such a surprise!"

Melchior's and Oliver's eyes locked in agreement before Melchior broke away. "Coming, sister. For Heaven's sake, hold yourself together! You sound like you're about to fly apart at the seams!"

Oliver trotted down the steps.

Melchior creaked after him.

With a flushed face and her hair tied in a messy bun, Martha entered the hall wringing her hands. A small entourage followed her.

We have guests? Melchior glanced at his stained tunic hanging all asunder and at his bare feet. *Blast that Martha! She screams as if the house is on fire and then waits to see what I stumble into.*

A mob of foreign kings gathered in his hall. Several tall, well-dressed and well-*groomed* individuals stood before him, apparently awaiting an introduction.

Melchior licked his dry lips and blinked in stupefaction.

Suddenly, little Martha ran forward and, with a cry,

launched herself into the arms of one of the kings.

Dizziness enveloped Melchior.

The foreigner grinned, hugged the child, and swung her around in an exceedingly friendly embrace, then he put her down. He strode over, smiling from ear to ear, and reached out. The king—or was he a prince?—took Melchior's hand, leaned in, and kissed him on the cheek.

Melchior stared at the man's eyes. He knew that brown-eyed gaze—that glint. Sudden weakness in his legs made him stumble, but the man held his hand, his grip steady. Melchior's mouth dropped open.

"Father, don't you know me?"

"Wilfred? By all that's holy, boy, you've surprised me. I wasn't expecting—I didn't know—"

A familiar voice called from the back of the crowd. "He wanted to surprise you—and by Heaven above—I think he's accomplished that indeed."

"Richard?"

Richard ambled closer. "Yes. I received word that Wilfred had returned...or at least a man bearing the same name. See, he's a man of wealth and importance now. Let me introduce you if I may."

Richard gestured toward a man six feet tall and muscled, with a neat black beard and thick wavy hair. His bearing and demeanor spoke of high culture and excellent breeding.

Nearly unhinged by the shock of it all, Melchior sucked in his breath.

"Prince Omar, Lord Melchior." Richard offered a courteous bow.

Omar nodded graciously as his gaze roamed over Melchior.

His insides quivering in embarrassment at his disheveled state, Melchior braced himself as well as he could.

Omar's composure remained perfect. "I am humbled by your kindness."

Still clutching Wilfred's arm, Melchior blustered into a hearty speech. "Thank you for bringing Wilfred home. I'd thought I lost him forever."

Omar smiled and shook his head. "I did not bring him home. Rather, you could say, he rescued me from a fate worse than death."

Benumbed by surprise, Melchior gestured toward the main hall in his most polite manner. "I must hear everything. Please, come and sit by the fire. My sister, Martha..." *Oh, Lord, where is she now?* "Martha, where are you?"

With her hair bound in a neat bun atop her head and a fresh apron tied over her dress, Martha bustled forward.

"Yes, here she is. My sister will gladly provide refreshments, and my son, Oliver...Oliver?"

Gilda called out, "He is seeing to the horses. Shall I get him?"

Melchior shook his head. "No. He's doing his duty." He looked to his guests. "I'm embarrassed. I wish I had known—I would've made proper arrangements."

Omar strode into the hall, his astute expression relaxing into a benign smile. "Don't be distressed. I've seen worse." He turned before the large central fireplace and gestured with an open hand. "Wilfred took me on a tour of your countryside. I especially enjoyed the old woman—the widow. What was her name?"

Wilfred cleared his throat. "The Widow Brunswick."

"Yes, Brunswick. Very amusing. She said kind things about you, Lord Melchior. I was sure I would enjoy your company. Don't worry about my men. They can go anywhere."

Oliver ambled into the room, sweaty and with straw clinging to his clothes.

Melchior nearly fainted with relief. "Oliver, Wilfred has come, and he's brought guests. Can you see about suitable accommodations?"

Scowling, Oliver peered over the assembly until his eyes locked on Wilfred. He marched up to him, drew his fist back, and punched him in the jaw.

Wilfred stumbled backward and fell, sprawling on the ground.

Oliver towered over the fallen man. "That's for Corliss! Where is she now? I'd like to know!"

Wilfred clambered back to his feet, his eyes blazing, and rubbed his jaw. "Corliss is fine. She has what she's always dreamed of."

"You took her off to where no man could care for her properly. And now you come back dressed up like—"

Omar's deep voice broke through Oliver's tirade as he gripped the man's shoulder. "I'll forgive you for one reason only—you believed you were defending my wife's honor. But if you ever strike my brother again, I'll personally have your head struck from your shoulders."

Silence reigned. The whole assembly froze.

Melchior was certain he had lost his mind.

~~~

Melchior sat hunched by his window, bathed in the glow of a full moon, and sucked in a deep breath of refreshing air. He chuckled. He would never forget the look on Wilfred's face when Oliver had struck him. Nor would he forget Oliver's face when Omar had threatened him.

Corliss had found her man all right. Not a king, perhaps, but a king's son and a very wealthy, handsome,
~~~

and exotic one at that. Apparently, Wilfred had had the luck to meet the prince, the intelligence to introduce his sister, and the charm to pass himself off as an honorable man. As a seventh son, Prince Omar had been languishing in obscurity. Marriage to a lord's daughter offered an opportunity to escape and explore the larger world.

Melchior sighed. The thought of escape reminded him of the wisp of a dream. Or was it a nightmare?

When they had settled down with large mugs of ale, he learned that Corliss presently resided with the Widow Brunswick. She had told her husband that she had no desire to return home and, being with child, she was too delicate to be wandering over rough terrain. Eventually, she planned to visit the king and see Adele.

Prince Omar had been happy to accommodate her wishes.

A tap on the door broke the thread of Melchior's thoughts. He closed his exhausted eyes. For the first time in his life, he was weary of intelligent conversation. The prince had recited wonderful stories, described exotic geography, spoke in four languages, and could recite poetry better than any man Melchior had ever heard. They had a rousing conversation over a large and delicious meal, thanks to Martha's ingenuity. And they drank copious amounts of well-brewed ale, thanks to Oliver's husbandry. Melchior yawned. Only the stars maintained their brilliant enthusiasm.

Oliver poked his head in through the doorway. "I know it's late, but I thought you'd like to know, Father Caedmon is near his time. If you wish to take leave of him, you must come now."

Melchior groaned. "I'll be there. Give me a moment to get into proper clothing."

Oliver nodded and retreated.

Melchior rubbed his eyes, trying to rouse his soul to face fresh grief.

Chapter Fifty-Three

The Gift of Kings

Melchior laid Father Caedmon to rest in proper ceremony with all the blessings of the Church. The modest cairn in the open glen spoke eloquently of mysteries beyond the reach of men. Before the old priest died, he commissioned Oliver to carry on his work spreading the word of God to all people. He placed his hands on Oliver's head and invoked the blessings of God, calling him no longer merely Oliver but Oliver-Gideon, matching his name to the heroic mission he must endure.

Oliver-Gideon knelt by the old priest's cairn and wept.

As the noonday sun shone too brightly for comfort, Melchior stood by his son and wondered if anyone would weep for him when his turn came.

The next day, Melchior rode into the distant fields hoping to blow the cobwebs of despair from his mind. During the ride, his horse reared up in fright and threw him to the ground. Though only bruised in body, his soul felt broken. He returned to his room and collapsed on his bed in a defeated heap.

Later that day, pangs of hunger drew him into the kitchen. He slid onto the bench and bowed his head.

A red-faced servant carried in a hot bowl of stew and sniffled.

Annoyed, Melchior rounded on her. "What ails you so, woman?"

"Adele's loss grieves me, sir."

Dread filling him, Melchior snapped his next question, "What loss?"

"Her fourth child—such a beautiful babe it was, they

say. ’Tis a miserable-hard cross, sir.” She sniffled again.

Grief threatened to overthrow Melchior’s mind. He dismissed the servant and called into the kitchen, “Martha, come bring your meal here and eat with me.”

Martha wagged her head and wiped her hands on a towel as she entered the hall. “Only for a moment. I’m behind in my work. Oliver insists on being called Oliver-Gideon, and Gilda is playing the fool with a heathen. It’s too much for my poor distracted mind.”

Melchior stifled a groan.

Martha ticked her concerns off on her fingers. “Wilfred will return with that foreign prince needing a hot supper and proper beds. I must get things together, food, bedding, a gift or two. God knows how to treat a one-time nephew who has risen to such strange heights.”

Jerking to his feet, despair squeezed Melchior’s heart. “I must go, Martha.” He kissed his sister on the top of her head and hobbled to the door.

Martha frowned. “I didn’t mean I couldn’t still talk with you—”

Melchior left the hall and stumped across the short grass. When he entered the dimly lit barn, the smell of sweaty animals, old hay, and the ripe odor of manure assaulted the nose. He stopped at the horse that had thrown him earlier and patted its nose, wondering at its meekness. A gnawing ache of confusion and discontent chewed his insides.

Melchior found a long, thick rope and, standing beneath the main arc, attempted to toss it over the beam. His throw fell short. He tried again, his shoulder aching, but the rope landed at his feet. “Oh, hell’s bells!”

“Father? What are you doing?” Oliver-Gideon strode into the barn, a smile playing on his lips. “You need help?”

Melchior rubbed his jaw. “Well, yes. I’m trying to

swing this rope over that beam, you see. I can't quite..."

Oliver-Gideon took the rope and swung it over the beam exactly as Melchior had wanted it.

Melchior grabbed the two ends and looked away, his resolve cracking. "Thank you—that's all. You can go about your business."

His son nodded and stepped over to the quiet horse. "I heard that Martha threw you."

"That she did. Most contrary creature I've ever known. You should've named her Beelzebub."

Oliver-Gideon stroked the animal's muzzle. "I named her after Aunt Martha. Don't you remember? You said she was a lamb most often but a fury when roused."

"I'd forgotten." Melchior's breath came in a ragged gasp. "If only she had broken my neck."

Oliver-Gideon stepped back to his father, his eyes dark with brooding concern. "What?"

Melchior formed a loop on one end of the rope. "You couldn't understand." Tears blurred his vision. "Go on, leave me awhile."

Oliver-Gideon peered at the rope and then at his father. With his lips pressed tightly together, he strode to the wall and plucked a knife from a hook. Then he reached up and cut the rope, leaving a small piece dangling. Wrapping the rest of the rope around his arm, he took a quick survey of the nearly bare room. He collected the knives and charged past his father to the door. "I am not going to ask because I don't want to hear the answer, but if you've ever loved me, father, you will return to the house, eat a good meal, and then take a long rest. You're overtired." Oliver-Gideon strode away.

Weak in mind and body, Melchior bowed his head, and tears slipped down his cheeks.

As clouds settled over the faint moon, covering the world in darkness, Melchior sat at the table with a bowl of hot venison stew steaming before him. He took a tentative sip and burned his lip.

Oliver-Gideon hurried into the hall, his arms swinging at his side and a smile lighting up his face. “Father! Good news!”

Exhausted, Melchior pursed his lips. *No news is good news.* The burn numbed his tongue.

Oliver-Gideon plopped down next to his father. He peered at the steam rising from the bowl and grinned. Taking the bowl in hand, he blew away the steam. Then he placed the bowl before his father with a flourish. “You’re right. God takes care of everything.”

“Not always.”

“Well, this time. Wilfred told the prince about the church, and guess what? You can’t imagine.”

“Probably not.”

“The prince has offered to support the cost of our building. He even gave me money to show his sincerity.” Oliver-Gideon drew out a bag and poured heavy gold coins onto the table. “Prince Omar believes that the Church must be free to serve God without a king’s influence. He’s going to persuade his father to visit too.”

Melchior swallowed as he envisioned an entourage of foreign kings arriving at his abode. “Father Caedmon named you rightly. You’re a warrior meant to spread the word of God, but with a pen, not a sword.” Melchior’s frown returned. “What about Rome?”

Oliver-Gideon’s eyes glowed with eagerness. “I don’t need to leave home. With good scholars, we can teach here. Men will come from all over the world to see what we have written down, what we have preserved, what we have remembered for the glory of God.”

Images of ruins, mud-caked roads, and ignorant men rose in Melchior’s mind.

Oliver-Gideon grasped his father’s cold hand. “It’s a

miracle! And through the help of a foreign king!"

The long-familiar ache in his middle warred with his son's gladness, confusing Melchior. "And this makes you happy?"

Oliver-Gideon chuckled. "Your father named you *Melchior* after a foreign king who served God through a gift of gold. This time it will be a king's son, by a king's power nonetheless, who serves God through such a gift." Oliver-Gideon clapped his hands. "God had a wonderful sense of humor!"

Melchior sat motionless, his father's gentle face rising like an apparition.

"Never give up, my son, for God is never outdone in generosity, and His strength reaches to men through men. God never abandons His own."

Pushing his stew to the side, Melchior looked at his happy son through tear-filled eyes. "Is there a priest available for Confession, you think?"

Oliver-Gideon's smile sobered into gentle understanding. "There is."

"You'll bring him to me?"

"At the morning's first light."

Melchior wiped his tears away, nodded, and patted his son's shoulder as he rose from the table. "Good."

Oliver-Gideon choked out two words, "Good God."

With new life filling his weary body, Melchior agreed.

Chapter Fifty-Four

Chaste Passion

Adele stood in the central hall of her husband's castle, watching a strong and handsome figure stride through the entryway. She shivered.

Once within touching distance, Richard stopped, bowed low, and gazed at her warmly, a smile playing on his lips.

Adele gathered her courage and met his gaze. "It's good to see you, Richard. Your niece is staying nearby."

Richard's voice rumbled in a husky undertone. "Yes, I know. That's why I've come. And to see you, of course."

As her hand flew to her blushing cheek, Adele glanced at her son standing in the doorway. "James? Come and greet a friend of mine."

James trotted forward and bowed stiffly. At seven, he seemed older than most boys his age. He stared at Richard, and then comprehension dawned in his eyes. "Mama told me about you. You're a great warrior."

Richard's grin turned sheepish. He leaned in, whispering conspiratorially, "Your mother exaggerates. I'm no warrior. I've merely survived to fight another day."

Fingering the small dagger at his side, James' eyes glinted. "Then you've done more than some."

Richard's gaze flicked toward Adele.

With a quick pat on his shoulder, Adele instructed James. "Find your sisters, now. I'm sure Master Richard would like to see them as well."

"Father, too?"

Adele's exuberance cooled. "Of course. Tell him we have a visitor."

Richard's gaze followed the boy as he strutted out of the hall. "He's smart, that one. I wonder what he'll be when he grows up."

Her stomach clenching at the thought, Adele paced across the wide room. "He'll be a king—whether he likes it or not."

Richard grabbed Adele's hand and stopped her progress. "Surely, with you as his mother, that cannot be a bad thing."

Adele gazed at the strong, brown hand holding hers and then stared into Richard's eyes. Yearning seared through her.

With regret in his eyes, Richard released her hand.

They paced toward the cavernous fireplace, where a well-worn table that stretched half the length of the room stood in readiness. They paced toward the great fireplace on the far wall, past rows of tables that seated a dozen each, to the dais on an adjacent wall. Two thrones sat upon its solid surface Made from oak and polished to a sheen, the larger throne was ornamented with carvings of bears' and boars' heads. Furs lay across it, and a tapestry hung on the wall behind, depicting a massive stag rearing back, encircled by fierce warriors.

Richard gazed upon the embroidered scene and sighed. He turned to Adele.

She stood next to him, also gazing at the tapestry. "It's vile, but the king insists that it reveals something we must never forget."

Richard waited, his hand next to hers, nearly touching.

Adele sighed. "We're either the hunters or the hunted."

Bowing his head, Richard turned from the tapestry. "You shouldn't have told your son that I'm a warrior."

After stepping onto the dais, Adele drifted to the

smaller throne, also beautiful but less ornate. She pulled the furs aside and sat, perching on the edge. "But you are. A warrior of justice and truth." She surveyed the large, empty hall. "Unlike some."

Richard waited, his eyebrows arched in a silent question.

Adele gestured to the table and bench by the fireplace. "Rest yourself, and tell me the news. How is Gerard?"

Richard leaned against the table's edge, crossed his arms, and snorted. "My brother is alive and happier than he's ever been."

Astonished and relieved at the turn of the conversation, Adele quirked her lips. "You're telling tales."

"But it's true! I know the king thought he was sending his enemy off to a miserable existence, but it's not so. Gerard has found peace in a quiet life. If only I could do the same." Richard stepped onto the dais, his eyes beseeching. "I've thought of you so often."

Adele turned her face away. "Don't!"

Richard gripped the arm of her chair and leaned in. "Adele, you're a bird meant to fly. Your heart longs not for what men are but for what they ought to be."

Squeezing her eyes shut, Adele's whole body trembled. "You see what is not meant for you." She opened her eyes, shot him a disapproving glare, and jumped to her feet, shoving him aside. "I'm glad your brother has found happiness, though I do not know how he did it." She descended from the dais.

Richard's bitter laugh followed her across the room. "He stopped caring. He's taken up carving, and now he's content."

Striding purposefully toward the door, she muttered her secret thoughts. "I envy him."

Richard ran after her. "Do you—really? What about your son and your daughters? Could you ever leave them?"

Adele stopped in the open doorway and gripped the doorpost. "When I feel like I am bleeding to death inside, I might." She turned and looked back at Richard. "But if I heard their voices calling, I would turn back." She wandered into the open courtyard.

The bright sun glared down on the short grass, and guards stood at their posts along pebbled paths.

Richard followed close on her heels, his voice cold. "You are not the woman I knew."

"How could I be?" Adele stopped and surveyed Richard's muscular frame, his brawny legs, strong arms, weathered skin, rough face, and yearning eyes. She shook her head in dismissal then strode into the open field.

Richard matched her pace. After a long silence, he inhaled a long breath and tilted his head to catch her gaze. "I still care for my queen. Is that wrong?"

A flicker of movement out of the corner of her eye sent a chill down her spine and turned her gaze. Her husband approached with James at his side. She stared at Richard, her voice softening. "Don't chain your heart to a stone."

Richard spoke low. "Just promise me, don't *you* turn to stone." Before she could react, he took her arm and led her boldly to her husband.

King Radburn offered a stiff nod to Richard and took his wife's hand. He pursed his lips as he stared from one to the other. "Richard, it has been a long time. Is your brother still among the living, or has he been released from his life of woe?"

His smile clearly forced, Richard met the King's hard stare. "As I was just telling Adele, Gerard is the happiest man I know. He's taken up carving and fashions all sorts of things. Imagine my surprise."

Adele stepped to her son and wrapped her arm around his broad shoulders.

With a snort, King Radburn turned his back on Richard

and hobbled toward the gate. “I’ll send him a log or two. That should amuse him.” He tugged at his cloak, wrapping it tightly about his thin shoulders. “It’s drafty out here. I’ll retire to my chamber, and you will tell me the news. I’ve heard about the visiting prince. Quite a showman, I hear. I suppose Corliss wishes to see Adele.”

Lending the king his arm, Richard ambled to the king’s private quarters.

Adele dropped behind.

Nudging her playfully, James whispered, “I’m glad you have a friend.”

Adele squeezed her son’s hand as she gazed at Richard’s back. “Me too.”

—A Week Later—

Adele shoved open her bedroom door and braced herself.

Corliss twisted a long strand of brown hair around her finger as she waddled into Adele’s room, her eyes roving. “It’s so simple; it’s almost barren.”

Adele closed her eyes to a memory as her hand smoothed over her flat belly. The pain and blood had shocked her. But it was the loss of her baby that nearly killed her.

When Richard had stood near, she felt young. Whenever her husband hobbled to her side, she felt ancient. Now, as a pregnant Corliss lumbered into her room, she felt insignificant.

She swallowed a sour taste. “I’m glad you’re able to visit. Compared to what the prince can offer, this must seem...” Her words dangled like a worm on a hook.

Apparently, Corliss decided to be nice. “Don’t be ridiculous! I’ve always admired the king’s villa. It’s certainly the best this land has to offer." She turned, her eyes shining brightly and clapped her hands in an ecstasy of glorious memories. "Adele, you'd be amazed—the palaces and monuments, the ancient ruins and the temples I've seen." She licked her lips as she leaned against Adele's bed. "But it's good to return home and enjoy the simplicity of my native soil."

Adele bit her lip. She gestured toward the bed covered with a thick blanket. "Please, you must be exhausted. Make yourself comfortable."

Corliss gratefully stretched out on the bed and relaxed against a mountain of pillows.

Dropping onto a chair in the corner, Adele rested her chin on her hand. "Speaking of native, have you seen your father recently?"

Corliss' eyes narrowed as she lifted her head to look at Adele.

Adele motioned toward the window. "He lives on Richard's land."

Corliss struggled into a sitting position and fiddled with the objects on Adele's bedside table. She picked up a little book. "What's this?" Her brows puckered. "Can you read?"

Adele stiffened. "Not very much. But my brother—you remember Oliver? He's become a scribe and will be a fine priest someday. He made that, and when he visits, he reads it to me."

Corliss leafed through the pages absently, her blank gaze traveling across the beautiful lettering. She dangled the book by the back cover.

Adele's jaws ached as she held back a scream.

Corliss swung the dangling book between two fingers. "I didn't think the boy had it in him to learn anything beyond sheepherding and woodcutting."

Rising quickly, Adele snatched the book away. "He's a

humble man, been put in charge of my father's estate and the building of a new church. As a matter of fact, your husband—"

Glee reanimated Corliss' eyes. "Oh, yes, I find it rather amusing that my husband can afford to do such things." She yawned expansively. "I'm glad we're able to help you." Her brows furrowed in mock severity. "But I heard an odd rumor that your king doesn't like priests or churches."

Adele shoved her precious gift into a drawer and strode to the window. As the sun touched the horizon, glorious rays swept across the landscape.

"He's a benevolent king, but the matter of church relations does have its difficulties. It's a topic best left untouched."

Her eyes drooping, Corliss nodded like a sleepy puppy. "Of course. Whatever you say. I must get a little rest now, or I'll never survive the first course."

Adele's eyes lingered over the landscape a moment before she hurried across the room and, with a smile, pointed to the door. "One of the servants will take you to your room where you can get a proper rest."

After struggling to her feet, Corliss nodded in courtly fashion. "Thank you. It's true, carrying a baby is weary work, but an experience I've come to love." She stopped on the threshold. "Where is my father, exactly?"

"On the edge of your uncle's land. Richard is our mutual neighbor now."

"He'll show me the way, then."

Adele nodded. "I'm certain he will."

Corliss rubbed her expansive belly. "I fear my father will be a pitiful sight, but Omar says it's my duty. He wants to come with me, but I insisted on going alone."

Adele's hands clenched as she remembered Lord Gerard's bloody face. She stifled a retort and simply said,

"He is your father."

"By all accounts, the man is quite mad. He hardly deserves mercy."

"He's always loved you."

Corliss' gaze bore into Adele. "You hated him." Her lips curled. "But then you love your enemies, I suppose." She arched an eyebrow. "Your marriage certainly proves your ability on that score."

Fury fixed a cold smile in place, and Adele called for a servant.

Corliss waddled forth.

Adele returned to her room and fell back onto her bed. Her hand caressed her flat stomach. Closing her eyes, she grabbed a pillow and muffled her sobs.

At suppertime, Adele waited by the door to the main hall a moment.

Corliss swept into the hall looking fresher and more vibrant than she had when she first arrived. Her red velvet tunic and embroidered blue cape set her apart from the usual guests, who wore courser clothing in earthen colors.

King Radburn stared, struck dumb and openly admired her.

Richard stood in attendance at the table.

Adele reviewed the scene and strolled to the lavishly appointed table.

Once seated, the servants offered the viands in perfect silence.

Adele fretted as she wrung her hands in her lap. *Someone must speak.*

Corliss took the initiative. "My dear uncle, would you be so kind as to take me to my father's abode tomorrow?"

Richard nodded in gentlemanly assent. "Certainly. Your brother Wilfred is arriving early for that same purpose. But you must remember, your father is not the man he was."

The king snorted. "Who is?" His chuckle died in his throat as he surveyed Richard's perfect composure. Then he scowled.

Corliss ripped a hunk of bread in two and pointed to a large slice of pheasant and then chunks of cheese, which a servant gracefully placed on her plate. Wiping her hands on the tablecloth, she glanced around, as the others accepted bread, meat, fruit, and cheese. She turned to the king and practically purred, "King Radburn, have you heard of my husband's latest venture?"

The king looked up, his eyebrows raised and an expectant smile quivering on his lips.

"He's going to build a church."

Adele could have killed the woman.

But just then, Richard choked, coughing and hacking so loudly it turned everyone's attention, and once again, he saved her sanity.

~~~

Corliss grinned all the way to her father's abode, remembering the shocked expressions on every face when she had mentioned the church. The king's face had reddened, Richard had choked, and Adele had closed her eyes.

Once he could talk again, Richard had valiantly ventured into the breach and regaled them with the tale of how Father Caedmon had blessed Oliver before he died, calling him Oliver-Gideon and charging him with the fulfillment of their dream—the building of the church. With Omar's support, Oliver-Gideon had begun work on a new, bigger, and better plan than anything he had dreamed of before.
~~~

The king had dismissed Richard's tale with a disdainful wave and insisted on seeing his children.

The three darlings soon made their appearance and pleased everyone. It was a noted fact: Adele's children were adorable.

Corliss' grin faded slightly as she returned to her present mission.

As they crossed into Richard's land, Richard slowed his horse and gestured in the direction of Gerard's shabby abode. "I sent word that we'd be coming. I hope that he's made himself presentable." Richard squinted as he peered across the landscape, leaning forward in his saddle.

Another entourage appeared to be moving toward them.

Richard scratched his jaw.

All happiness fled as Corliss' eyes narrowed. An ugly suspicion wiggled up from her middle. Her husband and her brother had disobeyed her.

Richard turned in his saddle. "I thought your husband wasn't coming?"

Corliss snapped, "He wasn't. He certainly knew my feelings on the matter—I made them clear enough!"

Richard and Corliss waited as the procession wound itself toward them.

When Wilfred arrived, he jumped in to explain, "Your husband insisted. It'd be a breach of honor to miss this opportunity to meet your father. So—"

With a forced flash of a smile, Corliss turned her horse aside and followed Richard.

In a few moments, they arrived at a thatched hut with wood walls plastered with waddle.

Corliss, aided by her husband, lumbered off her mount and followed Wilfred and Richard through the doorway.

Richard marched tentatively ahead. "Gerard? I've brought guests. Your son and daughter wish to see you."

The hut reeked of smoke, sweat, and old meat. A dark but ample fireplace adorned one wall of the structure, with a dirty pot dangling from a tripod over a heap of dead ashes. A table with a single bench leaned against another wall, and two unadorned chairs did duty in front of the fireplace. A narrow doorway led aside, while off to the right, well stocked pantry shelves hung in attendance. A dingy cloak dangled from a pair of pegs, and a variety of herbs and onions swayed from the rafters. A dirty, black pot sat on a tripod over a heap of dead ashes.

Shuffling steps across the floor announced Gerard's presence.

Corliss stifled a gasp.

Wilfred's eyes widened.

Only Richard and Omar maintained their composure.

Gerard stood before them, a gaunt figure in a stained shirt and torn leggings. His toes wiggled free in the dust. When he saw his guests, he shrank back.

Richard hurried forward. "I sent word that I was bringing your son and daughter"—he glanced over his shoulder at Omar—"and her husband has come as well. Here, let me introduce you." Richard guided his brother forward, though he resisted on stiff legs.

Gerard stared at Corliss for a long moment. Then, as comprehension filled his eyes, he nodded in understanding. "You look like your mother." He next turned and glared at his son. "You weren't mine, not really, no matter what that old hag said. Never needed a son." He rubbed his filthy hand across his face and turned toward Omar. His eyes widened as he considered his guest from head to toe. "Yes, you are about what I'd expect." His eyes flicked toward his daughter. "Made out well, didn't you? No help from me, though." Gerard motioned toward the two chairs with a sneer. "Sit down. Make yourselves comfortable."

Once Corliss and Omar were settled, Gerard scampered to the pantry.

With a cough, Richard tried to stall his brother. "We can't stay, brother. Omar has duties he must attend to, and Corliss is expected back at the king's villa soon."

With his back to them, Gerard lifted a long sack from a hook and began to bang objects on the shelf about, moving, lifting, and tossing things into the sack, mumbling under his breath.

Richard glanced at the prince, who watched in wide-eyed silence.

Corliss slouched in her chairs and rubbed her extended tummy. Dizziness engulfed her. She glanced at her husband.

After several long, strained moments, Gerard turned with the cloth sack bulging with an assortment of provisions. A stag hoof poked out from the top. He grinned mischievously as he handed the bag to Prince Omar and bowed formally. "You can't leave just yet. I must provide for my guests, and, besides, I haven't given my permission."

Richard bit his lip while his eyes strayed to the rafters.

Wilfred glared a silent question at Corliss.

Corliss dipped her head, her gaze falling to the filthy floor. *Oh, please, Lord, save me. Omar will hate me after this!*

Omar pinched the edge of the dirty bag, frowning.

In desperation, Corliss pleaded, "Father, we don't expect you to provide anything." Only exhaustion and decorum kept her glued to her seat.

Wilfred's strained voice piped up. "We just came to see you, Father, and to offer assistance if you should need it. Richard says that—"

Gerard's bellowed laugh sent crows into fits of cawing. "Don't believe everything that man tells you. As for provisions, I must give something! I am the bride's father, and even though she went off without informing me and married without my consent, I'll still see things done properly. I may have lost my lands, my fortune, and nearly my life, but I still have my honor."

He jabbed the heavy bag in Omar's hands. "You ought to pay me a bride price, but something is due on my end, so take it and be glad." Gerard clapped his hands in dismissal and retreated to the other room.

Omar stood, too stunned to react with propriety.

No one moved.

After a thoughtful moment, Omar called for one of his men. When the servant appeared, he gestured for him to take the bag. "And bring my box from my saddlebag."

The servant bowed and retreated.

Suddenly, Gerard reappeared with a tray laden with mismatched mugs and a large flask. "This will cheer us up. Melchior sent this over last year—called it an Easter offering, whatever that means, but I call it a kind gift. It shall serve us well now."

He set the tray on the table, poured the mead, and passed around the drinks, ignoring Corliss.

Omar took a tentative sip, while Wilfred, Richard, and Gerard took hearty swigs.

After wiping his mouth with the back of his hand, Gerard stared down at Corliss' hunched form and pointed to her expansive belly. "Another generation, I see. All the more reason to celebrate." He crouched down at his daughter's side and cocked his eye at her. "You'll find out—when your child plays on thin ice, *your* feet will freeze."

Omar grinned, and Wilfred stifled a laugh.

The servant appeared on the threshold carrying an ornate box in both hands.

Omar strode forward, took it from him, and presented

it with a bow to Gerard.

Gerard accepted it with a return bow, set it aside, and grinned mischievously as he lifted his cup. “To beautiful daughters and wealthy sons.” He finished his drink in another gulp. Pouring everyone another round, he inched closer to Omar. “Don’t you have something you’d like to ask?”

Omar’s blank expression showed his confusion.

Gerard jutted his chin in Corliss’ direction, his eyebrows dancing.

Omar’s face cleared. “Permission to marry your daughter?”

“Granted!” Gerard gulped his second drink as quickly as the first and gleefully clapped his son-in-law on the shoulder.

For the second time in her life, Corliss felt frozen in place, yet with overwhelming gratitude, she rose to the occasion.

Chapter Fifty-Five

Some Comfort at the End

—The Outer Universe—

Teal raced between planets to get all the signatures he needed for an inter-alien agreement to secure Earth's protection. He started on Lux before the Supreme Council, the twelve most illustrious representatives of his home-world, as a witness to the truth and proclaimed what Cerulean and Nova had eloquently outlined. Though Sterling met him at the door and guided his steps to the platform, Teal had stood alone before their judgmental stares. The memory of his son's trust-filled eyes strengthened his wavering voice.

"We are one of many races inhabiting this part of the universe, but we have always considered ourselves above the self-obsession of the Ingots, the scientific narrow-mindedness of the Crestonians, the fragile child-state of the Bhuaci, and new-world barbarism of humanity. We alone, beings of light, support the entire expanse. This is why we sent out Guardians—to protect ourselves and our allies from threats that may yet develop. But now I stand before you, pleading with you, let us not become our own worst enemy—destroying what is good in fear of what does not exist except in our own minds."

After speaking on Lux, he traveled to the next planet and the next, using the same high-toned langue as he appealed to each race, altering the argument according to the weaknesses and strengths of his audience.

On Crestar, he spouted scientific data the Crestonians understood, cajoling them with facts and humor to value the human race's potential to serve their scientific needs in the future.

On Ingilium, marching up to the Ingot representatives, he emphasized Earth's strategic location and resources and humanity's incredibly inventive nature which would eventually teach the universe how to use the planet to its fullest potential. He charged through the last part, slamming his fists together with a whispered prayer that his words would prove true.

When on Helm, he sat beside Song, the Bhuaci leader, and her attendants in a wooded glen. Teal painted pictures of innocent beings developing at their own rate, learning from their successes as well as their failures. He appealed to Bhuaci generosity, begging for understanding, kindness, and patience. Qualities he well knew they had in abundance and prayed he could develop in himself.

—OldEarth—

Teal returned to Earth dressed as a common peasant. He stretched out in the soft grass in the shade of a giant oak and understood, finally, that his duty was done. He was utterly spent.

Through his energetic travels and speeches, enthusiasm had glowed from his very essence. He could hardly wait to return home and share his success.

As he lay quiet and still, listening to the sounds of hammers and saws and men humming and chatting as they worked on the church only a stone's throw away, realization dawned. For him, home was not on Lux, where his wife lay under a cairn; it was here on Earth, where his son now labored in love.

Good Old Earth.

His mission accomplished, he closed his eyes and,

thanking God, he rested in peace.

~~~

Cerulean argued with Nova about accepting Tarragon at his word, when suddenly panic seized him.

Inside Melchior's large barn, Nova scooped hay into the horse stalls and babbled on about accomplishing great things and how she was uniquely suited to be the intermediary between mixed breeds and Cresta scientists.

Even as Cerulean filled the water buckets with practiced skill, his attention was diverted; his father had returned to Earth, but he could not sense his presence as he should. "I must leave," he blurted to Nova.

Leaning on the pitchfork, Nova pouted, her face puckering into a childish grimace. "You can't leave now. I have to give Tarragon a definite answer. Everyone has agreed to give Earth a millennium of peace with only periodic visits, so I have to make a decision. What am I going to do with my life?"

Fear tightened Cerulean's stomach into knots. He tossed the water bucket aside. "Give your life for your parents—it's what they did for you." With that, he pelted out of the barn and into the light of a bright spring day.

On the path near the road, Sterling, dressed in a priest's long black robes, stood with Zuri, dressed as a monk, chatting in hushed tones.

Cerulean rushed up, panting. "Father is back, but something is wrong!"

With a paternal smile, Sterling patted Cerulean's dusty shoulder then wiped his hand on his robe. "On the contrary, your father did what no one else could've done: he set things right in the universe. We have an agreement that should last—"
~~~

"I must find him!"

Frowning with concern, Zuri lifted the sleeve of his tunic and checked his datapad. "You're right, Teal has returned, but—" Alarm widened his eyes. "He's near the church."

A group of men crossed paths with Nova as they entered the barn.

Nova paced closer to her friends, a concerned frown on her face.

In blind panic, Cerulean screamed, "Hurry!" He took off running.

Zuri hitched his robe out of the way and started after him.

Sterling merely huffed.

It being a beautiful day and the church nearly completed, men worked in conviviality, calling over the distance in pleasant tones.

"Got that last segment bracketed and ready, Will?"

"Aye, you can set the paving stones as soon as you like."

Cerulean's gaze traveled from the marvel of the building to the glory of the sunlight streaming through the spring green leaves. His gaze traveled to the base of the largest oak tree.

A figure lay stretched out in the shade.

He ran on, outracing Zuri and Sterling, who jogged after him, clutching their robes.

Cerulean fell on his knees at his father's side.

All color had left Teal's body. When he opened his eyes, only a pale light still shone in them.

"Father?" Cerulean's aching tears and pounding heart made further speech impossible.

With a limp hand, Teal reached up and touched his son's face. A weak smile played on his lips. "My job is done. Yours just begun."

Zuri dropped beside Cerulean, choking on a sob.

Sterling bent on one knee and placed his hand on Teal's forehead. He bowed his head. "You have done well, Teal, my ever-faithful friend. The Luxonian Supreme Council thanks you for your courage and loyalty."

Tears coursed down Cerulean's cheeks. "Father, please—"

Teal's gaze shifted to some distant point. "Your mother's come to take me the rest of the—" The light in his eyes diminished, his body wavered like water shimmering on a hot day, then the edges faded in until there was nothing left to see.

Sterling fell forward, pressing the ground with his hands as if in prayer.

Three workmen strode up. "Good day, my friends."

Cerulean glanced up.

Zuri jerked backward.

Sterling climbed to his feet.

A thickset man stepped ahead, rubbing his chin. "How you managed to get through the roots is a mystery, but if you want to start the cemetery here, there's nothing stopping you, Fathers. Though you might want to clear it with the lad in charge—Oliver-something."

The second man nodded and glanced around. "A pretty spot to be laid to be rest, for sure—in sight of the church but under the shade of this mighty patriarch."

The third man pressed Cerulean's shoulder. "We're sorry for your loss, son. Your pa, eh?" He nodded respectfully to the holy men. "Glad you're able to offer some comfort at the end." He grimaced. "The dead may not need it, but we surely do."

The three men turned and ambled back to the church.

With a puzzled expression, Zuri rubbed his face. "What're they talking about?"

Sterling pointed to a fresh mound of dirt in the exact

spot where Teal last lay, a perfect gravesite. "We can build a cairn, and it'll be our memorial here on Earth to a being who will never, in truth, leave us."

Cerulean fought to keep breathing as choking sobs rose from his chest.

Sterling wrapped an arm around his shoulder and stared in communion with Zuri. "You're not alone."

Wiping his eyes, Cerulean nodded, his gaze fixed on the mound of silent earth.

~~~

Tarragon stopped some distance away with Nova at his side. He wore a large robe and hood that covered most of his bulk and a good portion of his face. "I knew when I saw him last that he was near his end."

Nova glanced up. "How?"

"Luxonians give off different infrared sheens depending on how they're feeling. Humans, of course, can't see anything, but Cresta are able to detect all spectrums."

"Why didn't Cerulean see it?"

"He probably did but didn't know what it meant. He's very young and hasn't had much experience with death."

Nova dropped her gaze to the grass under her feet.

Turning to more important matters, Tarragon stared at the girl. "Have you decided?"

Nova lifted her head, her eyes clear as she stared at Cerulean in the distance. "I will go to Crestar and do whatever you ask so long as you do one thing for me."

Intrigued, Tarragon grinned. "And that would be?"

"Save my parents first. Find some way to give them back their intended life spans, so they can enjoy each
~~~

other's company a while longer."

"Intended life spans?" Tarragon chuckled. "My dear child, you really are naive. No one has an intended life span. We only have the moment called now. What we do with that is what matters."

Flushing, Nova stepped away and faced Melchior's distant abode, the bright sun glimmering on her dark hair. "Why do you want to know about mixed breeds then, if not to live longer?"

"The term *longer* has no meaning. A millennium is too short for some and twenty cycles too long for others. I want Crestonians to be able to travel, interact comfortably with others, experience the fullness of the universe without being limited by our clumsy, water-based physiology." He shrugged. "We might gain more respect for other races along the way—who knows?"

Nova's jaw dropped open. She cleared her throat and wrapped her arm around one of his tentacles. "Be careful, Tarragon; I might start believing you."

Shocked, Tarragon considered the possibility. *Well, what do you know...?*

~~~

Abbas stood on the pinnacle of Scafell Pike and narrowed his gaze to focus on his son, who stood almost imperceptibly on the top of the church structure near Melchior's abode.

Omega stared down at the graveside scene, a serene smile on his lips.

Abbas had heard and seen all. The closest thing to contentment he had felt in a long while filled him. The Luxonian had died a good death, and that was a difficult
~~~

achievement for any being. He prayed that it would be said of him some day.

But in the meantime…

The agreement signed by the four races was doomed to fail eventually, but it did give him time—much needed time—to allow Omega to grow up.

Melchior ambled across the short grass and stood, shoulder to shoulder with his son before the imposing church structure with its arched doorways and rounded windows where light streamed through.

Sterling stood next to Cerulean staring at an empty grave.

Abbas' heart hovered close to his son.

Chapter Fifty-Six

Harold and Terrill

Harold had discovered, to his chagrin, that he was no scribe. He did, however, have the makings of a good assistant. Bishop Clement had taken a liking to him as a well-intentioned warrior and insisted that he become one of his men. The two traveled far and wide, and only when word came that the building of the church had recommenced, did the bishop insist on returning to Melchior's abode to revisit the situation and perhaps assist in the construction. Gladness filled him as he envisioned seeing his old friends and catching up on family news.

Bishop Clement found a crowded inn on the edge of a town not far from Melchior's estate and started for his room almost immediately. "I'd rather approach the situation in the light of a new day, so I'll go on to bed and get a much-needed rest. I'd advise you to do the same."

Hungrier than he was sleepy, Harold waited till the man had closed his door, then returned to the main room and ordered a large bowl of stew and a stout ale. He plunked down on a chair, ready to relax away the quiet evening.

The sound of footsteps caught his attention.

Terrill sauntered through the doorway.

The two men appraised each other but said nothing.

A serving girl set a mug before Harold and then waited upon the newcomer.

After ordering bread, cheese and ale, Terrill strode over to Harold and stood there hesitant, wringing his cap in his hands, hesitating.

Harold nudged an empty chair with his foot and

gestured. "If you don't take a seat now, you'll be standing the whole night."

Terrill dragged the chair forward and perched on the edge.

Harold eyed him over his ale. "Are you going to tell me where you've been these last years, or shall I guess?"

Terrill's gaze followed the serving girl as she passed food to the other guests in the room. He dragged his eyes back to Harold. "I could ask you the same."

Harold grinned. "I asked first."

With a shrug, Terrill leaned forward. "I went to find my relations in the north, but they'd moved west. So I traveled west and met up with an old man, some relation of father's. He told me I should return to the old country, said I could make a fair life for myself there."

The girl placed a steaming bowl of stew on the table at Harold's right hand. He sat up. "What happened?"

Terrill shook his head then glanced up as the girl gave him his drink. He passed her a coin, which she examined before she retreated to the kitchen. Terrill sipped the thick brew slowly and wiped his mouth with his sleeve. "Nothing much. I searched for relations, but they're either dead or gone. Seems our family tree wasn't very strong."

Harold leaned back and sighed. He took a swig of his ale, letting the steam swirl above his stew, and eyed his foster brother. "Just the two of us, then?"

"Seems so."

"What do you do now—to get by?"

Terrill shrugged. "I work here and there." He took a long drink and settled back in his chair. "And you? What happened to that old priest you loved so much?"

Sudden irritation rose up but was quickly washed away by melancholy. "He died."

Sadness in his eyes, Terrill dropped his gaze.

The irony of the situation forced a chuckle from

Harold. "Don't pretend grief you don't feel. I know what you thought of him and his kind."

Terrill shrugged. "Your priest wasn't so bad."

After taking a tentative sip of his stew, Harold cocked his head, staring. "How do you mean?"

"Well, before I left, your priest—can't remember his name—came to me and put a wee bag in my hand, saying, 'You might need a little something to get by.'" Gripping his mug with both hands like a child needing steady comfort, Terrill drank deep. He wiped his dripping chin. "The coins were worth a pretty amount."

Tears welled in Harold's eyes, his heart aching. "He was a kind man."

Terrill swallowed. "That he was." He straightened. "When I returned, I stopped to see Nolan. He had a plan to regain his lost lands, but when his plans sounded like thieving, I refused. So, you see, I'm not quite the man I was. Not like *you,* of course."

"What's Nolan doing now?"

Terrill shrugged. "He gets by. Still angry at Lord Melchior for allowing his daughter to marry the king, but he has no definite plans."

Harold's eyes glinted. "I work for the bishop, and I happen to know that he'd like to meet Nolan. If you could arrange such a meeting—"

Terrill laughed outright. "An old bishop up against Nolan?"

Harold cocked his head. "You've never met Bishop Clement." He chuckled as he sipped his ale, and then he glanced at Terrill with a grin. "It'll be Nolan who ends up singing a new tune; see if I'm right."

The girl returned with a loaded tray. She laid out Terrill's food, refilled their mugs, and retreated.

Terrill stretched his feet toward the fire. "You always liked to predict the future. Who do you see taking charge?"

Harold tore off a piece of bread. "No predictions. I'm quite content to live in the present. Far as I'm concerned, God's in charge."

Chapter Fifty-Seven

Universal Happiness

King Radburn awoke to the terror flickering around him and screamed, "Fire! Wake up! Get out! Fire!"

Flames licked at the walls, sending billows of heavy smoke into the air.

Smoke stung his eyes as he directed his hobbling steps to his wife and children. A heavy door stood as a barrier, stuck fast. "Oh, God!" A sob swelled in his throat, but fury and the intense heat spurred him on. He threw his frail body against the wood and then fell forward as the door was opened from the inside.

Adele's disheveled hair, wide eyes, and open mouth proclaimed her terror.

Undaunted, the king screamed again, "Get the children. Hurry! Help me!"

Adele retreated into the chamber, directing her servants in high-pitched panic.

Servants ran into an adjoining chamber, and one scooped up a whimpering little girl while the other scooped up her twin.

Adele ran to her son's bed and threw back his covers. She shook his sleeping form roughly, calling for him to rise.

Startled, James' eyes snapped open, and he jumped to his feet. "What's wrong? Why are we getting up?" His gaze darted around the room partially obscured by smoke.

Adele shoved her son in front of her, yelling to the servants, "Get them outside. I'll meet you by the stream. Take them—hurry! I must get Corliss and the others."

The servants carrying the girls bumped into each other, as if not sure which way to go.

"Hurry," King Radburn shouted, pointing toward the hallway that led away from the fire.

Adele shoved James in the king's direction. "Take him. I'll see that everyone else is out. Is Corliss awake?"

A loud bang, as if a piece of timber crashed to the floor, sent smoke billowing in all directions.

King Radburn waved her on frantically. "It's no use. The fire is spreading too quickly. Corliss is on the furthest side."

Adele clutched her throat. "I can't leave her!"

The king snatched at her arm, but she pulled away. "Take James!" she shrieked, struggling to pull her arm free of his grip. "Hurry!"

In a rage, he cursed and held on tighter, "Damn it, woman! You'll risk your life for *hers*?" With that, he shoved James at Adele. "I'm the king; I'll go!"

Hands on his face, James cried out, "My eyes! They're stinging! I can't see!"

With a sob, Adele grabbed her son and raced to the steps.

King Radburn faced the flames and limped faster than he would have believed possible on any other day.

~~~

Adele blinked her eyes open and found that she was in a strange room. Only one tapestry depicting a deer grazing in the forest and a simple woolen rug adorned the space. She sat up, frowning.

Richard, sitting beside her bed, straightened and offered a wavering smile. "Thank God."
~~~

Her face tight and painfully sore, tears flooded Adele's eyes.

Richard reached for her hand. "I'm here."

She surveyed the room, her heart pounding in fresh fear. "Where—?"

"In my chamber. Your children are resting with your servants. Everyone is accounted for."

"And the king?"

Richard bowed his head and blinked back tears. "He's alive—but barely. His feet were badly burned. But he did a noble thing in saving Corliss. She's safe. Her husband has taken her away."

Richard rose and paced across the room. "The prince offered your husband a handsome reward for his selfless deed, but the king was too delirious with pain to respond. He just waved him away." Richard returned to Adele's bedside. "If nothing else, we must all think better of him after this. It was a heroic act."

Adele nodded and then stared out the window at a sunrise she didn't understand.

~~~

Melchior stood on the top step, hidden in shadows with a scroll clutched in his hand, and took in the idyllic scene below. *Hills and valleys, my life. And what's the point of it all, Lord?*

Adele sat on a comfortable chair beside an end table in the shadowed hall, the evening light tinting the windows gold and red. After several treatments with heavy salves, she could now smile without grimacing. She lifted her embroidery closer to the candlelight and applied her needle, as her children constructed block castles on the
~~~

floor at her feet.

Oliver-Gideon and Omar sat at a long table, their heads bent over plans for the new church.

Martha bustled about, freshening the saltcellars, her hands tapping her thigh as she undoubtedly took note of anything the servants had not attended to properly.

Adele yawned.

Martha glanced over, a concerned frown etching her face. “About time you were in bed, don’t you think?”

Adele nodded. “Yes, it’s getting late. I get tired so easily these days.”

Strolling closer, Martha called for a servant to take the children. Then she faced her niece. “No wonder. Such a miracle, after that dreadful affair. But God is merciful. You’ve a new babe to think about now.”

Adele tucked the embroidery aside and rubbed her belly, a soft smile playing on her lips. “You’re right. Where are the others?”

Martha wiped her hands on a dishcloth. “Gilda and Martha have already turned in.” She cleared her throat. “There’s a young man coming tomorrow who would like to speak to your father.”

Adele’s smile faded. “Gilda seems glad enough.”

Martha snorted. “Marriage will suit her.”

With a loud sigh, Adele rose laboriously to her feet. “And how is—”

“He’s asleep. He’ll be all right...well, as *all right* as that man can ever be. Never walk again, of course, never do a lot of things again, but he’s alive. He should be grateful.”

Adele’s gaze turned to the flickering flames in the fireplace, her voice dropping to a husky whisper. “He asked Richard to be regent.”

Martha’s hands flew to her hips, astonishment flashing across her face. “Richard?”

“Says he’s the only man he trusts.”

Martha smothered her reaction with busy fingers as she gave the table one more swipe. "I shouldn't be surprised by anything that man does." She cocked one eyebrow at her niece. "And how does the arrangement suit you?"

Adele passed her hand over her swelling tummy. "Richard is a good man. I trust him too." She turned to follow her children to bed. "I'm tired. Where's father?"

"Upstairs, as usual. Let me call him." Martha started toward the steps, bellowing her familiar call, "Melchior! Come down, Brother!"

Melchior creaked down the steps with his scroll in hand. "Stop your screeching, woman; I was coming anyway." As he reached the last step, he met Adele. "You can't go to bed yet. It's much too early."

A brief flicker of amusement lightened Adele's features. "You've been writing again, haven't you, father?"

Melchior grinned. "Not writing. Just remembering. Or trying to."

Adele kissed her father's cheek. Nodding goodnight to Martha and with a quick glance at Oliver-Gideon and Omar in deep discussion, she turned and wandered up the steps.

Melchior shuffled over and took the chair by the fire.

Her arms akimbo, Martha peered at him. "You should be in bed as well."

Melchior waved her away. "I'm not a babe who needs looking after."

Martha turned to the kitchen with a sigh.

"Is he in any pain?" Melchior stared at the flames flickering before his eyes.

Martha stopped and met his eyes with a steady gaze. "I've given him something to help during the hard spells—for whatever time he has left." She crossed herself, and her face cleared of doubt. "But he's sleeping now, sensible fellow." She patted a long, drawn-out yawn. "I'll follow his good example." She gestured to the two men at the table. "Those two could talk the birds out of their nests if they had a mind to." She kissed Melchior on the top of his head. "Good night, brother. Don't stay up too late, or I shall have to tell Adele in the morning."

A glimmer of joy lightened Melchior's heart as he watched her gentle form lumber from the room.

In a moment, Omar stood, stretched, and announced that he must leave. "I'm starting my journey before the break of day."

Oliver-Gideon patted the larger man on the arm. "But we'll see you again soon?"

Omar grinned. "You have my word."

After seeing Omar to the gate, Oliver-Gideon returned.

Melchior still sat comfortably before the fire with the scroll unrolled across his lap.

Oliver-Gideon sauntered over, crouched down, and tapped the scroll. "What's this, father?"

Melchior lifted the edge and shook it lightly. "An old memory. It seemed a promise then, but now..." He shrugged.

Oliver-Gideon reached for the vellum.

Melchior let him take it. "I once dreamed that I knew something important."

Oliver-Gideon stood by the firelight, reading aloud, *"And he showed me a river of water of life..."*

Melchior's head bowed at the familiar words. But as Oliver-Gideon's strong, clear voice continued, his head rose and his eyes stared, a shiver of amazement filling him.

"Clear as crystal, proceeding from the throne of God and the lamb."

Melchior could barely speak. "You know the words?"

Oliver-Gideon pulled a chair close by his father.

"They're from the Apocalypse. They speak of the promise after the time of trial. Father Caedmon used to say that the Bible is really one story repeated in many different ways." Oliver-Gideon gazed off and recited the verses in a melodious voice.

"Then he showed me the river of the water of life, bright as crystal, flowing from the throne of God and of the lamb through the middle of the street of the city; also, on either side of the River, the tree of life, with its twelve kinds of fruit....

There shall no more be anything accursed, but the throne of God and of the Lamb shall be in it, and his servants shall worship him, they shall see his face...." From Revelation, chapter 22, one through six, I believe.

Melchior leaned forward, straining to see in the dim light. "But what does it mean? I've never understood, except when I dreamed the words."

The firelight gently played on Oliver-Gideon's smile. "That's how you'd have to approach God, like in a dream, for the real world can't understand His meaning. But God knows how we are, how we fail and—"

Melchior snorted. "You say *we*, but it isn't true. Some people fail, some people never had a chance, and some people, like you, live honest, decent lives."

Oliver-Gideon turned away, shadows playing across his clenched jaw. "You don't know me as well as you think you do." He peered at the flames, his arms limp at his sides. "I never understood people because I didn't want to. It was easier to let others decide things for me. But there came a day... I never told you, Father, but I loved Corliss even though I hated what she did to Wilfred, and I hated him for the part he played in that awful affair with Lady Nadine. I believed Wilfred deserved the trouble he got. I rejoiced when I learned he was not really my brother and that he was *her* brother, for then there could never be anything between them."

Oliver-Gideon's glance darted off his father. "You see, I'm not as noble as you've believed. When I learned about Selby, my heart was torn. No man can rightly judge—that's why there must be a God. Father Caedmon taught me to look deeper. He gave me the courage to go on—for I realized that only God could truly make me a better man." He knelt at his father's side. "That's why I want to build this church, to honor God, who can rebuild a man's soul."

Melchior murmured as he stared into the flames. *"A river... of water... of life... proceeding from the throne of God...and from the lamb."*

Chapter Fifty-Eight

Dedication

—One Year Later—

Adele marveled at the sight of incense smoke swirling into the air of her beautiful new home, completed now by the assembly of all those she loved best on Earth.

King Radburn squinted at Richard, who towered strong and tall next to Adele, while James stood erect and proud on her other side. Her daughters played innocently about Richard's perfect legs. Gilda held her youngest son, Sebastian. Gilda's new husband, Frederick, a swarthy fellow who looked as if he chewed bricks for breakfast, cheerfully exuded manly strength and health.

The castle's stone foundation glowed as the morning light streamed in through the perfectly shaped windows. Fresh wood scent mingled with the incense, which rose high into the rafters. The congregation bowed their heads during the last blessing.

"*In nomine Patris et Filii et Spiritus Sancti.* Amen." Bishop Clement raised his staff and processed out of the castle with his retinue of servers in attendance.

Adele smiled as she strolled at her husband's side down the aisle hall, while two well-trained servants carried his litter. "It was a beautiful dedication. We'll be very happy here."

King Radburn leaned back on pillows and smiled as graciously as his burned face allowed. "It will be pleasant enough. Though it's rather large for a man who will never walk again."

Richard carried Kimberly on the opposite side, while

James and the other members of the household marched behind the litter. "You'll be safe, and the children will have room to grow. James and Sebastian will serve you well."

King Radburn's eyes strayed upwards. "Not all brothers are friends." A grim smile tugged his lips.

Calmly, Richard stared ahead. "But some are."

They processed into the courtyard brilliant with sunshine, and Adele received baby Sebastian from her sister. She turned to her husband. "You have sired noble children, you have a new home, and your men are ever at your service. You're a lucky king."

"Just not a lucky man."

Adele glanced at Richard and shook her head.

Gilda hurried up and tugged her sister's arm. "When are we leaving for the church dedication? Lord in Heaven, two services in one day, and Sebastian smiles as if he were going to a festival! I never imagined he'd become such an ardent Christian!"

Adele smiled. "There's plenty of time." She surveyed the crowd. "Could you lead the children over? I'll be there soon."

Gilda nodded. "Just remember, the feast begins at sundown. I, for one, am already famished."

Adele nudged her sister forward. "Go then and tell the bishop we are coming. I'm sure he has a busy schedule."

Fluttering like a kite in a strong breeze, Gilda gathered her husband, assorted children, and their attendants.

King Radburn motioned to his servants. "Take me back inside." He met Adele's gaze. "I'm chilled, and the light hurts my eyes. Besides, I have serious matters to attend to." As his servants turned his litter, the king called out, "Richard?"

Richard hastened forward. "Yes?"

The servants held the litter motionless.

"Will you go with them—or with me?"

Richard's gaze darted to Adele. "I'm always at your service if you need me."

The king snapped, "I hardly need you, but we have better things to do than attend every ceremonial function in the land. I want to make plans for a new blacksmith shop. Since we have a new villa, it makes sense that we have better weapons with which to defend it." He stared at Richard. "A man is never done defending his own."

Richard nodded in acceptance. "So true."

The king waved his men to continue.

Offering a courtly bow, Richard met Adele's gaze, pressed her hand, and then followed the king.

Adele watched until he disappeared beyond the gates. She turned and joined Gilda and her husband, who clasped hands like the young lovers they were. Her children played, birds frolicked in wild abandon, and attendants bustled about. She hugged herself and followed the throng to church.

~~~

Melchior stood outside the ornate church doors watching the sun set as he waited for his son. Pink clouds turning red, purple, lilac, and blue dazzled his eyes.

Oliver-Gideon, now changed out of his Mass vestments and wearing a simple priest's robe, proceeded to chase his nieces and nephew across the open field.

The Mass had lasted well over two hours, and its power lingered. Though the church was not complete, they had finished the first stage. It stood dominating the landscape, a stately rectangular structure made of cream-colored stone, with a high-peaked roof and a tall cross in the
~~~

center. Later, formal wings would be added, along with separate buildings for the scribes and even a library.

Melchior feasted his eyes upon the structure. Bishop Clement had gained hefty support from Nolan and other landowners, and with this newfound security, he promised to send prominent scholars in due time. Oliver-Gideon was as happy as a man could be this side of Heaven. Finally, he could follow his heart's passion.

Adele, carrying her baby in one arm, rested her hand on James' shoulder as they strolled across the peaceful land. James tickled the baby's cheek, and they all laughed.

Once Melchior and Oliver-Gideon returned to home and hearth, Martha ruled over the evening feast, harassing the servants nearly to death about every detail, for no man, woman, or child would go hungry while she had breath in her body.

Melchior stood by the blazing fire with a cup of mead in his hand.

His eldest son stepped to his side. "It's time for the feast. Are you ready, father?"

Outside the window, birds sang in contented joy. *Clear as crystal, proceeding from the throne of God and the lamb.*

Melchior agreed, "Yes, by God, I am."

Chapter Fifty-Nine

Welcome Home

—Crestar—

Tarragon entered the shiny new laboratory and knew he was home. An attendant hustled forward with a tray laden with dissecting tools. She stood at attention by a table where a bulky form lay covered by a thin sheet.

Oozing authoritative confidence, Tarragon strode forward and stopped at the head of the table. He peeked under the sheet and then glanced at the attendant. He nodded to the rolling table. "Put the instruments there, please."

The attendant obeyed with alacrity then turned her full attention to Tarragon. "I read your work on mixed-breeds. Quite informative."

"Thank you. But that was just the beginning." He sighed, faced the table, and swiftly uncovered the top half of the Cresta corpse. His pulse raced as he contemplated the remains before him. A rather thin specimen, reminding him of his first tutor, an angular being, practically emaciated for a Cresta. But a gentle spirit. Could've taught an insect patience. "They are sure it was murder?"

Only the attendant's eyes moved, the bulbous orbs rolling to Tarragon, widening in surprise. "That's what they suspect. And that's why they wanted you to look into the matter. You have such a discerning eye."

The image of Cerulean rose in Tarragon's mind. The Luxonian boy wasn't nearly as physiologically interesting as Nova, but his position as the only approved member of the four races to observe humanity for the next millennium put him in a very discerning position indeed. "Hand me the scalpel."

The attendant complied. "You will investigate the case, then?"

Tarragon nodded and made the first incision. "Much of life is discovering who is innocent and who is guilty—and our own part to play." Then he cut deeper.

—Helm—

Zuri, his breath white in the frosty air, carried steaming drinks across the leaf-strewn ground and stepped into an octogen gazebo. Autumn woods surrounded the simple structure, a scene of bucolic beauty.

Song rested on a cushioned lounge chair but sat up as he drew near, her gaze as steady as her hands.

Zuri handed her drink over and carefully sat on a straight-back chair next to the Bhuaci spiritual leader.

Song took a sip.

Zuri followed her example, savoring the nutmeg and cinnamon spice. Warmth invaded the frozen places inside his heart. "Where did you get this? Is it native to Helm, too?"

Song smiled, a gentle glow on her face, though her somber eyes spoke of understanding too fragile for mirth. "No. I bought it from a trader in Earth goods. I thought you'd like a familiar taste of home even as you settle in here."

A crooked grin eked its way from inside Zuri. "Home should be Ingilium. But you are right, as usual. Home is not a place but a meaning—the very purpose of our existence. To be at home within ourselves."

A bow of acknowledgment and Song placed her mug on the railing. She stood and strolled to the opposite side, facing a large body of water—a cold ocean lapping against an icy shore. The sun hung low in the sky, and two pale moons ascended. "You are more Bhuaci than Ingot."

Irony played with Zuri, and he chuckled. "Perhaps I was switched at birth, and all along, I have been Bhuaci. We just didn't know my true nature."

"Your wife and daughter are your true identity, Zuri. You are very much whom you love, as every human you ever valued eventually learned."

Zuri nodded. "That's why we can't go back to Ingilium. They are still trapped inside their technology. Humanity has taught me so much, but now I can't live there. Never again to return? It's unbelievable. I am a divided soul."

Song faced him, her eyes brimming with compassion. "The moment we really love anyone, we become more than ourselves." She turned back to the thatched cottage he had come from. "Let's go and be with Kelesta and Nova and many others whom you will learn to value. For we must make the most of each day we are given—to whatever end."

Zuri took his friend's hand and followed his heart.

—The Outer Universe—

Abbas lay back on the soft grass, with one hand pillowing his head and one arm around his wife. Peering through the dark night, he stared at the brilliant stars glinting overhead.

His wife sighed. "He's safe out there? You're sure?"

Abbas swept his gaze across the multitudes of universes. "That he is out there, I am certain. That he is safe, is impossible to tell. So much depends on his choices, and you know how he is."

"Why can't you go get him?"

"Because he's old enough to decide. He must learn for himself now."

"But we're his parents. I'm his mother. I love him."

"You can love him from here."

"But what if he gets hurt?"

"He'll learn something new."

"What if he hurts others?"

"Others will learn something new."

"You make it sound easy!" She huffed and crossed her arms.

Taking his hand from under his head, Abbas pulled her into a tighter embrace. "It's never easy."

"So, what do we do now?"

"We watch and learn what kind of being we created."

"Will he ever understand how hard it is for us? Will he care about *us*?"

Abbas paused. "He already cares. But there are some things he can't understand until the time is right."

"When will that be?"

Abbas smiled. "When he sends his child out into the world—then he will understand."

—OldEarth—

Cerulean felt Sterling's hand press his shoulder as they looked for the last time on Melchior's abode.

Sterling spoke with solemn authority. "You understand, only periodic visits and only you—no one else? I will pass the approved reports to the others so each race can keep track of humanity's development. But only

Lux has the neutrality to see that the human race can grow unmolested for generations to come." He patted Cerulean's shoulder. "In the meantime, we'll take care of both Lux and Earth." He pointed to the sky. "You can't see it now—but there's a lifetime of experiences awaiting you, Cerulean. What will happen next—who knows?"

Cerulean swept his gaze from Melchior's abode to the church and out to the universe. He smiled in acceptance. *God knows.*

~~~

Teal knew his time on Earth was done, but as his spirit hovered above the crowd, he saw what mattered to him most: Cerulean stood with Sterling on Earth, Zuri conversed with Song, while Kelesta held Nova in a mother's embrace on Helm. Tarragon stood at a dissecting table in his laboratory, teaching his assistant. Melchior and his family celebrated a new way of life in the great hall.

Grieved at this parting, Teal turned his gaze, and unbounded joy filled his being at the sight of a welcoming crowd.

His wife, Ark, his parents, and all those he had loved waited with open arms. A part of his heart constricted at the thought of those left behind.

Then suddenly, the crowd parted, and there, welcomed into the assembly, were all the men and women from ages past—Aram, Namah, Eoban, Onias, Barak, Pele, Ishtar, Amin, Tobia, Gizah, Lud, Obed, Enosh, Kenan, Eva, Seth, Leah, Accad, Georgios, Alexios, Rueben, Seanan, Brighid, Ian, Earan, Liam…and so many others.

They smiled, for now, they could see *him* truly. He was
~~~

no longer hidden from their sight, and—by some unknown grace—they knew him as their friend.

Finally, and at last, his family welcomed him home.

About the Author

A. K. Frailey, an author of a historical sci-fi and science fiction series, short story collections, inspirational non-fiction books, a children's book, and a poetry collection, has been writing for over ten years and has published 17 books.

Her novels expand from the OldEarth world to the Newearth universe-where deception rules but truth prevails. Her nonfiction work focuses on the intersection of motherhood, widowhood, practicing gratitude, and rediscovering joy.

As a teacher with a degree in Elementary Education, she has taught in Milwaukee, Chicago, L. A., and WoodRiver, and was a teacher trainer in the Philippines for Peace Corps. She earned a Masters of Fine Arts Degree in Creative Writing for Entertainment from Full Sail University.

Ann homeschooled all eight of her children. She manages her rural homestead with her kids and their numerous critters. In her spare time, she serves as an election judge, a literacy tutor, and secretary/treasurer of her small town's cemetery.

www.ingramcontent.com/pod-product-compliance
Lightning Source LLC
Chambersburg PA
CBHW070612310726
48982CB00001B/55

9798987404706